I0746124

MARY CRAWFORD

Joy AND Tiers

HIDDEN BEAUTY BOOK 3

COPYRIGHT

All rights reserved. No portion of this book may be reproduced in any form or by any electronic or mechanical means including information storage and retrieval systems – except in the case of brief quotations in articles or reviews – without permission in writing from its publisher, Mary Crawford. Copyright protection extends to all excerpts and previews by this author included in this book.

This novel is a work of fiction. Names, characters, businesses, places, events and incidents are either the products of the author's imagination or used in a fictitious manner. Any resemblance to actual persons, living or dead, or actual events is purely coincidental.

All brand names and product names used in this book are trademarks, registered trademarks, or trade names of their respective holders. I'm not associated with any product or vendor in this book.

Published August 5, 2015 by Diversity Ink

ISBN-13: 978-1-945637-41-4

Covers by Covers Unbound

HIDDEN BEAUTY SERIES

Until the Stars Fall from the Sky

So the Heart Can Dance

Joy and Tiers

Love Naturally

Love Seasoned

Love Claimed

If You Knew Me (and other silent musings)
(novella)

Jude's Song

The Price of Freedom (novella)

Paths Not Taken

Dreams Change (novella)

Heart Wish

Tempting Fate

The Letter

The Power of Will

Hidden Hearts Series

Identity of the Heart

Sheltered Hearts

Hearts of Jade

Port in the Storm (novella)

Love is More Than Skin Deep

Tough

Rectify

Pieces (a crossover novel)

Hearts Set Free

Freedom (a crossover novel)

The Long Road to Love (novella)

Love and Injustice (Protection Unit)

Out of Thin Air (Protection Unit)

Soul Scars (Protection Unit)

OTHER WORKS:

The Power of Dictation

Use Your Voice

Vision of the Heart

#AmWriting: A Collection of Letters to Benefit The Wayne Foundation

DEDICATION

To all of the men and women who serve: There simply aren't enough words in any language to say enough thanks for what you do.

To the families who hold their whole world together while they're away, you give the term heroic a whole new meaning.

CHAPTER ONE

TYLER

IT'S HARD ENOUGH TO work in this shoebox-sized food truck while slamming my head on the ceiling every ten seconds, but right now I've got an overly helpful witness dogging my steps like a bloodhound. "Gidget, you have to let me do my job here. Do you go out of your way to annoy everybody or is it just me?" I glare at her, trying to get her to back away from the broken glass. True to form, she's entirely fearless and crazy bossy. It's always more difficult to be out on calls involving people you know, especially when they are pretty little spitfires who make your blood boil — and not necessarily in completely negative ways.

Heather holds up her hands in a timeout gesture. "Hold your horses, Cowboy! This may seem like a bunch of worthless junk strewn all over the counter to you. It took me a week to make all those flowers by hand for a wedding this weekend. I'd like to save as many of them as possible before you go in there with those overgrown tennis rackets you call hands and smash everything to smithereens."

"Do you mind if I go ahead and take some pictures here? The evidence team is tied up doing a huge drug bust." I pull my camera out of my gear bag.

"Fine, knock yourself out. Not that it'll do a lot of good. We did all this last time, and all it did was make my insurance rates go up. The punks messed up my truck and got away scot-free. This sucks rotten moose-balls," Heather laments.

I smile at her colorful use of language. "Hey now, Gidget, are you casting aspersions on the county's finest?" I ask, tossing the question over my shoulder to keep the mood light.

"Lord knows someone has to. Otherwise that head of yours would get so huge that your ratty ole' cowboy hat wouldn't even fit on it."

Heather grabs a broom and a garbage bag from a small cubbyhole behind the driver's seat. She's about to start sweeping up the glass when a glint of metal catches my eye.

"Stop!" I reflexively bellow.

Heather freezes mid-stride, her face set in a thunderous frown. She raises her eyebrow at me as if she's daring me to continue. Under any other circumstances, this little power game would have been fun to explore, but this is no game. It's now a matter of life and death. The time for fun and games is over.

"I think you forgot to say Simon Says," Heather responds sardonically.

"Heather, I wish this was a game, but it has just

entered the world of deadly serious. So, I'm going to need you to play the most serious game of Simon Says you've ever played. Can you do that?"

A myriad of emotions crosses her face. Fear, shock, anger, and curiosity flit across in rapid secession. I have to suppress a grin of my own when I consider how terrible she would be at poker. Scratch that — she wouldn't need skills to clean up at poker, she could just bat those beautiful baby blue eyes and show off her pin-up figure and men would be falling at her feet.

"I have a hunch I should be concerned that you actually bothered to use my real name."

"Well, it is true that I have to talk to you about serious things, but I can call you Gidget if you'd prefer."

She blushes. "Heather works just fine, thank you."

"I told you to stop because I found two bullet casings on the floor next to where you work," I explain. This part of my job is never pleasant. I hate shattering someone's formerly safe, orderly, sane world, by turning it upside down and telling them their world has become a living nightmare.

Heather's eyes are wide. "Next to me? Why would they shoot my food truck?"

Oh crap! I don't want to answer that question. I fail to mask my expression quickly enough and she reads the answer in my eyes.

She sways a little in her impossibly high heels as her face blanches to a frighteningly light shade of white.

Instinctively, I reach out to steady her, placing my hands around her waist. "Easy, I've got you. I'll keep you safe," I murmur to soothe her trembling body as she wheezes to catch her breath in my arms.

Apparently, something I said must have rubbed Heather the wrong way again because she draws herself up to her full height and spins in my arms. "Really, Superman? I suppose you've got special kryptonite in there that helps you dodge bullets? Because the last time I checked, bullets are bad for your health too. So, how do you intend to dodge bullets and come out unscathed when the rest of us can't? What makes you so special?"

The question takes me by surprise. It's something I've thought about a lot over the past two years. In fact, it pretty much torments me. I didn't expect to hear it from her. "I guess when it comes down to it, nothing. Nothing but a lucky streak makes me special," I practically spit the words out because they have such a bitter taste.

Heather looks a little shocked at the venom in my voice. "Whoa, Cowboy, it sounds like there's a story there, and I might even want to hear it someday. However, don't we have bigger fish to fry here?" She points to the shell casings she has now spotted on the floor. I notice her voice is a little shaky.

She's right; we do have bigger fish to fry than ghosts from my past. I kick myself for my lapse in concentration. I never used to lose focus this easily. I need to get her out of here because I don't even know if the shooter is still at large.

"Heather, why don't you come sit in my squad car? It's warmer in there, and it provides a little more protection. We don't know when these bullets were fired or who fired them. It could just be some kids doing target practice, or it could be something much more serious. Either way, I'd feel better if you were out of the line of fire."

"Do you think there'll be more shots fired? What am I going to do? I have a wedding cake to finish!"

I'm trying not to make light of her predicament, but in the grand scheme of things, it seems inconsequential. "Can't they find somebody else to make their cake?" I ask what I think is a relatively reasonable question.

"Who do you think I am? McDonald's? I'm an artist!" Heather yells, her eyes sparkling with rage. "People come to me for my skills with food. You can't get what I make just anywhere. Obviously, you've never been married; otherwise you'd know you have to book this stuff months and months in advance. People design their cakes with their cake artists. Artists like me spend days, weeks and sometimes months making flowers and other decorations for cakes; it's not something you slap together in the drive through." Heather points to a schedule on the wall which shows she is indeed booked out for at least the next year.

"I guess, I never really thought about it —"

"Exactly!" Heather interrupts. "Geez, Tyler, way to respect my career and all that. I could understand remarks like that if you'd never eaten my food. But since you have, I'll take it as the complete dis you meant it to be." Sarcasm drips from every syllable.

Sometimes I'm slower than a rodeo clown who has been kicked in the head far too many times. I know Gidget is a superb cook. Her passion for cooking is one of the first things I noticed about her. I didn't mean any disrespect, but sometimes my brain doesn't work quite as fast as my mouth. I'm not sure how to explain all my mental stumbles to her without getting into my whole life story, which she doesn't need to know in the next five minutes. Darn it! How do I get myself into these fixes?

"I'm sorry, Gidget, I didn't mean to hurt your feelings. I'm trying to be helpful and take some of the pressure off of you because I know all of this is stressful. I thought maybe all of you bakeries trade jobs if you have emergencies or something."

"It may work that way for the big guys, but it doesn't work that way for me. Food trucks may be the up-and-coming thing, but people still don't see them as truly respectable places to get quality food — especially high-end things like wedding cakes. I have to fight to get every customer. Even if it weren't a despicable business practice to dump a bride at the last minute, I couldn't afford to lose her as a customer. I need each one, and I need the word-of-mouth every satisfied customer brings."

I look around the cramped food truck. "Do you bake wedding cakes in here?"

Heather smirks. "Now, that would be quite the talent, wouldn't it? No. I rent a commercial kitchen when I need to bake a large cake. But I do most of my sugar work in the truck. Can you please do your best to protect as many of these leaves and petals as you can? I'd rather you didn't get fingerprint dust all over them. It took days for me to make. I'm not sure I'll have time for new ones to dry."

"Heather, I won't make any promises. I can't

compromise the scene to save your flowers. I won't destroy anything I don't have to. However, now that we found bullet casings, I will have to bring the full forensic evidence team in to go over your truck. I have a forensic background because I've worked as an MP, but you want more than just my basic background on this, trust me. We want to catch this guy."

"Okay, I get that. But, can't I at least stay and watch? If I did, I would be able to tell you if you're about to destroy something really important. I don't think you understand the deadline I'm on here. It's not like my client can just postpone her whole wedding because I'm running a little late on her cake. I'll be as quiet as a church mouse."

I have to let out a breath of exasperation. Generally speaking, I'm a pretty laid back guy. Six years in the military and two years as a reserve officer with the Sheriff's office has taught me to roll with the punches. But, for reasons I haven't figured out, Gidget always finds a way to get under my skin like a burr under a horse's saddle. She's a beautiful little spitfire who has no idea the effect she has on me. She's got enough sass in her to fill two people, but she also has the kindest heart I've ever seen. We had one of the most clichéd meetings ever since she is the best friend of my best friend's wife. Regrettably, she seems far less impressed with me than I am with her. I'm working on that. But my progress has been painfully slow. Most days, it seems she can't stand to be in the same zip code as me. This little fiasco certainly isn't going to help matters.

Unfortunately, I'm not here to be her friend. I have a job to do. So I have to literally and figuratively put my

Sheriff's hat on. "I'm sorry, Miss LaBianca. I'll have to evacuate you from the premises for your safety. Additionally, we have to sweep this location for evidence. All efforts will be taken to disturb as little of your personal effects as possible," I state in my best detached police-academy-trained voice.

Much to my surprise, Heather reels back as if I've physically slapped her. All the animation in her face suddenly disappears, and an eerie formalness settles over her as she primly replies, "Yes sir, Officer Colton. Just let me grab my purse and car keys, or are those considered evidence as well?"

"I don't know. Were they in your food truck at the time the vandalism occurred?" I ask, pulling my notepad out to write down her statement.

"No, I had those with me. I went to the craft store to get more floral wire. When I came back, the truck was like this. I don't even know who knew I had the truck in the area. I parked here to help out because Mindy has a few days off from school. Yet, this is the second time it's been vandalized in this location. Maybe somebody doesn't want me to work in this area," she responds with a defeated sigh. It breaks my heart to see her this way.

If you were to look up the word optimist in the dictionary, Heather's picture would be prominently plastered there. She is a glass half full kind of gal. Wait, I take that back. She's a great cheerleader for everyone else. When it comes to promoting her strengths, she's far more critical. I've tried to toss her a few compliments over the last few months, and she's either rejected them outright or deflected them with a joke she's usually made herself the butt of.

"Well, if you brought them in, then they aren't considered part of the crime scene. Can you show me where you walked and what you touched before you noticed something was amiss?"

"Oh for Pete's sake, Ty! I'm not an idiot," she says as she rolls her eyes and blows a curl out of her eye. It's the first time I haven't seen her dressed to the nines. She's wearing a retro bowling shirt that has 'Earl' emblazoned on the breast pocket and she's wearing a pair of well-worn Levis with a patch made from a bandanna on the butt. Her hair is tied back with a matching one. It all works except her high heels. Those, I don't understand at all. Why do women do that to themselves? Sure, they're sexy sometimes — but does an arts-and-craft session on a Sunday morning call for risking a sprained ankle?

Heather catches me scoping out her choice in footwear. "What? Jeff's demon dog, Lucky, ate my tennis shoes. It's not like I had a lot of choice this morning."

I chuckle. "I feel your pain. When I house sat for Jeff and Kiera, Lucky got my favorite pair of boots. I think the real reason he flunked out of bomb detection school doesn't have anything to do with his alleged hearing issues. I think it's his appetite for contraband."

Heather flashes me a small smile. "I think they fudged his service record so he'd get adopted right away. He's like a serial shoe killer. Speaking of killers … like I told you, I am not an idiot. I watch enough *Forensic Files* and *The First 48* to know I'm not supposed to touch anything. The second I noticed something was awry, I went out to my car and called 911. Voilà, here you are interrogating me like I'm some criminal."

Wearily, I scrub my hand over my face. "Look, Gidget, I mean, Ms. LaBianca, this isn't personal. For us to catch this person, I have to do things by the book, even if it means inconveniencing you. I know you're not an idiot, I never meant to suggest you were. Still, I have to document what happened, for the file. Little things like whether or not your purse was present can make a big difference in how the scene is processed. If you were sitting in your truck when shots were fired at it, we would be having a whole different conversation. I'm simply trying to protect you."

Heather meets me toe to toe and verbally pushes back, "Maybe I can take care of myself, and I don't need you to protect me!"

"All evidence to the contrary, Darlin'. Now, are you going to do what I asked you to do — like half an hour ago — and go sit in my squad car, or do I have to arrest you?" I ask, with a little tilt of my hat.

Once again, Heather's spine straightens out as if a rod has just been placed through it, and her speech becomes clipped and frosty as she asks, "Fine, no need to be pushy. But would it be okay with you if I take some supplies from the cupboards?"

I ponder her suggestion for a moment and then shrug. "I don't see why not. Let me make a log of what you're going to take just to be sure."

Heather rolls her eyes at me again as she comments under her breath, "How nice of you to give me access to things I already own. There's your crime-fighting dollars at work, America."

"Hey now! That was a low blow. I don't tell you how to do your job, please don't tell me how to do mine."

"Well, Cowboy, I don't like big strong men telling me what to do, and I don't like being treated like I'm an idiot."

"For the record, I wasn't treating you like you're an idiot. Nothing could be further from the truth," I reply, my voice rough with emotion. This conversation is hitting more hot buttons than she could ever imagine. However, I can't take the time to explain them to her right now. Right now, she needs to get the hell out of here. For all I know, there is still a shooter at large. She needs to get her pretty little butt out of the picture. "I'm sorry I don't have time for a long, drawn-out debate over this, but I'll say it once again. Heather, please —for your safety — get into my car so I don't have to worry about you. If I have to worry about you, I'm not watching my own back, and it makes it more dangerous for me."

"Why didn't you just tell me that in the beginning? I don't want to do anything to put you at risk." She silently picks up her purse, and her keys. She regally walks over to my squad car and gracefully climbs inside as if it's something she does every day.

I shake my head in disbelief. That's classic Heather. She'll balk at anything designed for her well-being, but if it's benefiting someone else, she's on it faster than ticks on a wet dog. I radio the call into headquarters and go to the trunk of my car to get my thermos.

"You want coffee? It's cold out here," I offer, handing her the metal lid from the thermos.

She nods. "Thank you, that's sweet of you."

She takes a tentative sip and wrinkles her nose at the bitter taste. "I take it back. What is this? A new interrogation technique? Who taught you to make coffee? Just a small chef's secret … you shouldn't be able to chew your coffee. The next time we're together, I'll teach you to make a decent cup."

"Wow! Way to be grateful —" I tease, but then I take a sip of my coffee, and I have to admit that she's got a point. It's beyond terrible. "I'll have you know, Uncle Sam taught me to make coffee. You can blame it all on him. The swill doesn't have to be good; it just has to keep you awake and alert. I guess I never got out of the habit of making it that way. You don't have to drink it if you don't want to."

Heather takes another sip. "It's not so bad after you know what to expect. I'll need the extra caffeine anyway. It's going to be a long night for me. I have a hunch I'll be making flowers — lots and lots of flowers. After drinking this … um … coffee, I'll be up for three days straight. It's a win-win for everybody." Heather shoots me her trademark smile, complete with dimples.

Before I can say anything else, the evidence van pulls up into the driveway. I'm relieved when I see who the technicians are. Javier is one of the best guys we've got on latent fingerprints and ballistics, and he takes some of the clearest pictures in the business. If this ever goes to court, the evidence will be rock solid.

As the forensic team walks up to the house, I hear Javier call out to Heather, "Hey Miss H. How are things in your world?"

For some reason, his casual familiarity with Heather

raises my hackles. He's already got the perfect family at home. What more does he want? But then I remember back to the day we all met. It was an unforgettable day to be sure. There was a big verbal dust-up with Jeff's soon-to-be ex-stepfather.

No one got hurt, but I did assist in the arrest that would ultimately lead to the unraveling of Jeff's family life, as he knew it. Surprisingly, Jeff seems totally okay with the outcome. Though, it was plenty dramatic. It completely slipped my mind that Javier had also been there.

Heather's eyes light up when she sees Javier. "Javier!" She exclaims. "I haven't seen you since move in day. Mindy loves her new computer, by the way, in case Kiera somehow forgot to tell you. Thank you so much for such a thoughtful gift. Mindy's been researching things left and right."

Javier's face lights up like a Christmas tree. "Good! I'm so glad somebody could use my daughter's old computer equipment. Otherwise, it would've still been in the corner of our storage unit. What are we doing out here today?" Javier asks looking around.

Before I can launch into my clinical explanation of what happened, Heather thrusts random pieces of paper into his hand.

"What's this, Miss Heather?" Javier asks.

"It's just some notes I took throughout the day as all this was happening," Heather explains, with a small shrug.

"You've been taking real-time notes, and this is the first time you've bothered to mention them?"

Overwhelming fatigue suddenly seeps into my bones.

"Well, yes. You never bothered to ask because you were too busy assuming I'm the world's biggest bimbo. I figured the small details might be important, so I wrote them down as soon as I noticed the break-in."

Something about the way she matter-of-factly describes the way I dismissed her opinion tells me it happens to her often. I want to kick myself in the head for being so stupid.

"You're right. I should have asked you what you did next instead of assuming," I admit, as I dig around in my gear bag for evidence markers. Suddenly, today is feeling like the world's longest day. I really wish someone else would have caught this call — it would have been a whole heckuva lot less complicated.

"Look, Cowboy, there's something about us that seems to react like oil and water. I'm not usually such a witch, either. Of course, I know it's your job to tell me what to do because you are a police officer. Normally, I wouldn't even give it a second thought. But somehow, coming from you, it feels like criticism. I don't even know what to make of that. It makes me sound like I belong in the loony bin."

I feel a strange sense of relief. At least I'm not the only one that feels completely off balance when she's around. It's strange. I feel like I've had a bizarre personality transplant. One that makes me regress to my inner third-grader. I'm tempted to metaphorically pull her pigtails and throw earthworms at her to show her I like her. Not a positive development when you're almost thirty.

"Now that the evidence team is here, why don't I take you down to the station where it's warmer? I can take your formal statement there. It will be faster, and I can even stop by Starbucks on the way so you won't have to drink that tar I call coffee," I suggest.

"There's no way I can get back in there and show them how to handle the flowers?" Heather pleads.

Well, I have to hand it to her, the lady is persistent. I softly chuckle. "No, Gidget, I'm sorry I can't let you do that. Javier is extremely careful in his work. He'll take excellent care of your babies. I promise."

Heather dramatically sighs. "I sort of figured that would be your answer. But it was worth a shot in case you were feeling more charitable. I guess I'll just have to trust Javier. But it's okay to take this bucket of gum paste and my tools, right because they were in the cupboard?"

Now, it's my turn to sigh under my breath. "Yes, I've already logged that stuff out for you, so you may take it," I advise.

"Thank you very much, Officer Colton. I appreciate your help with this matter," Heather replies primly, but there's a sparkle in her eyes that wasn't there the last time she addressed me by my last name.

"Now, is that a yes or no to my offer of decent coffee, Miss LaBianca?" I tease as I pull the seatbelt over her and latch it.

"Here I was giving you all this credit for being a smart guy, Cowboy. Don't ruin the illusion. What do you think?" Heather raises a questioning eyebrow.

After Heather completes her statement and I hand her case off to the local detectives, I go for broke. I have this little theory that she doesn't hate me, any more than I hate her. We seem to have a special talent for pushing each other's buttons. Under the right circumstances, it could be scorching hot. I just have to figure out what those circumstances are. So far, the closest I've ever come to making Heather happy was at Jeff and Kiera's wedding reception.

The wedding was something straight out of a fairytale. I felt like I had been cast as the lead in some romantic comedy. Usually, I'm the guy who keeps the barstool warm all night, and the barkeep well stocked with tips. Because I'm a big guy, I tend to get drawn into fights which aren't even mine. But I'm nearly always the one to stop them. I suppose it's why I ended up as an MP until I switched my MOS to logistics. Not too long after I graduated from high school, I went to college on a football scholarship. But, I was young, dumb and thought I was invincible. When my grades slipped because I spent too much time being the big man on campus and not enough time studying, I lost my scholarship and joining the Army was plan B.

I had a girlfriend back then, but she was only interested in being my groupie if I was a jock. She wasn't interested in a soldier. She said she would stick by me through thick and thin, but her promise didn't last much beyond Basic Training and Advanced Individual Training, better known as AIT. My college buddy Galen, who still played running back, was more her speed. The whole situation was a mind-bender and a half. I carried her engagement ring in my pocket for two years before I finally sold it at a pawn shop and got myself a sweet little motorcycle. I ended up having to leave my bike in the Iraqi desert, but that's a whole other story.

Unlike what's-her-name, Heather is incredibly loyal to her friends and family. She takes no crap from anybody. If you tick her off, you'll know about it — usually in some pretty creative language. She uses very unique colloquialisms, and she has a vividly funny story for any situation you could ever run across. I swear, that woman never forgets anyone she's encountered anywhere, anytime or anyplace. Her comedic timing is brilliant. If she were not such a phenomenal cook, she could give stand-up comedy a run. If comedy isn't her thing, she could have a career in fashion design. I've never seen a woman pull off as many looks as she does and always look impeccably polished. The first time I met her, she looked like she had just walked off the pages of a vintage copy of Life Magazine, and as much as she looks like a vintage pinup girl like Betty Grable or Veronica Lake, there is an innate wholesomeness about her. Heather's refreshing lack of guile and diminutive size compared to me, earned her the nickname Gidget. As an added bonus, it seems to annoy her and bring out her sassy side.

In truth, I've been thinking about asking Heather out for months. I've just never worked up the nerve to do it. There's been so much darkness in my world lately, it would be unfair to bring someone like Heather into it. She's irresistible to me. I don't know if Jeff and Kiera are playing matchmaker, or if it's just coincidental. Still, every time I turn around, Heather seems to be there, dancing around under my nose like forbidden Christmas candy.

This time, I'm going to do something about it. I want to answer at least the fundamental question of what happens when we're in a room together for more than a few minutes alone. It'll go very well, or it will be an unmitigated disaster. But first things first, I have to get her to agree to go some place with me without threatening to arrest her first. I think this time I'll shoot for someplace casual.

After I've finished my formal interview, I grab a bottle of water from the refrigerator in the break room and walk to the bench where she is sitting in the reception area. As I hand her the bottle, I casually ask, "Are you hungry? I feel like pizza tonight. I know this great Italian place where they toss the dough by hand. I'll even let you pick the toppings."

"Ouch, you sure know how to find a girl's weakness. I'm starving, and pizza is absolutely my favorite food. Unfortunately, I need pizza like I need another hole in my head," Heather says wistfully.

I flop down beside her on the outdated vinyl bench. Turning toward her, I shake my head in disbelief. "Gidget, I know we've had this conversation before. But could you please explain it to me again? Why would someone as bright and pretty as you are, deny yourself something you clearly love when you freely admit that you're hungry? It just doesn't make any sense."

"Tyler, don't tell me you haven't noticed that Tara is about the size of half a toothpick and Kiera isn't much bigger," Heather points out.

"So? Kiera has red hair, and you have blond hair. Tara is about eleven feet tall, and you're not. What's your point? I don't know how many ways I have to tell you I think you are knockout gorgeous. You are pin-up worthy all on your own. Don't you realize women everywhere are having surgery to have bodies like yours?"

Heather laughs out loud. "I think you have me confused with someone else. Either that or my clothes hide a lot more than I thought. I have a lot more in common with a Weight Watchers 'before' poster than a pin-up girl."

I have to will myself to relax. This woman doesn't need anyone to beat her up. She does a fine job of it herself and it totally pisses me off. I just want to magically show her how she looks through my eyes. Maybe that would shut her up. So, I try again.

"Gidget, do I look like a man who doesn't know what I like?" I ask, not bothering to disguise the frustration in my voice. Man, this woman can frustrate me faster than a kitten with a ball of yarn.

Heather smirks and tilts her head sideways, inspecting me. "No, I'd say you're the type of man who pretty much has it all figured out."

"Well, I'm not sure I'd go that far. But I know I like what I see. Are you saying I don't know what I'm talking about, or are you calling me a liar?"

"No, I don't mean it like that. It's just that you and I view the situation very differently. When I look at myself in the mirror, I hear every fat joke my family has ever told at my expense. I also hear every PE teacher and trainer's voice in my head. They would say, 'Heather is a pleasant girl; however, she might have more friends if she were thinner.' Even the voices of well-meaning strangers echo in my head. 'You're so pretty, honey. If you would just lose weight, you could catch yourself a real handsome man. I try not to let it affect me. But after a while, it wears you down and changes who you are on the inside."

"It doesn't help that I'm often surrounded by perfectly skinny friends and family. I feel like I'm part of that Sesame Street game —'One of these things is not like the others'. I'm always the thing that's not like the others. Most of the time, I ignore it and let it roll off my back, but sometimes it gets to me. Being asked out by a cute guy is one of those unavoidable triggers for me. I wonder whether you want to go out with me because you like me or because dating a fat girl is such a novel experience, you want to check it off your bucket list."

I cringe at the idea that she considers herself a fat girl. "Have I ever given you any reason to believe I don't find you totally, off-the-charts-attractive?" I lay it all on the line. "In fact, I think that you're so hot, for lack of a better term, I was having a hard time concentrating on my job today in what could've been a life-and-death situation. I spend a lot of time thinking about you, and I can tell you that not a single, solitary moment of that time is spent thinking about whether or not you eat too much pizza."

Heather blushes a pretty shade of pink. "Really? You think about me even when I'm not around?"

"Yes, and I don't waste a single second of that time wishing you could fit into smaller jeans, that you would eat more salad, or any other related nonsense."

"Do I even want to know what you wish for?" Heather asks, a dubious expression on her face.

"Probably not," I answer, after a long beat of silence. "Even if you asked, there are certain things a gentleman really shouldn't share."

Unbidden, some of the dreams I've been having over the past few months flood my brain. None of them are exactly tame. If the mere thought of her makes me react this way, I'm going to combust if and when I get to touch her.

"Heather, I'll ask you one more time. What are you really craving? Not what you think you should be eating. Not what society thinks is socially correct for you to eat. Not even what your parents would wish you were going after. What are you, Heather Lydia LaBianca, hungry for?"

"Honestly, I would love a deep dish sausage and pepper pizza topped off with a root beer float," Heather admits, the words spilling out in one large breath.

"Sounds good. How do you feel about Hawaiian pizza?" I answer.

"I can take it or leave it. The only thing I'm not a big fan of is barbecue pizza. Barbecue sauce on pizza doesn't make any sense. Make it a traditional red sauce or traditional white sauce — anything else is pizza sacrilege."

"What about pesto?" I tease.

"Darn it. You got me there. I like pesto sauce on my pizza, especially if there are artichoke hearts involved."

"I don't know about that combo. Might be too much green stuff for me. Whatever happened to good old pepperoni?"

"Pepperoni doesn't have enough green stuff for me," Heather challenges. "You're asking for a stroke before you turn thirty if you eat it very often."

"Well, I doubt any pizza can be called health-food, but I suppose vegetables would help the cause. I guess I like pepperoni because it reminds me of my childhood," I explain. "Every time we had an accomplishment at school or in church, we always went out for pizza to celebrate. So, I always associate pizza with happy times. If I'm having a bad day, I'll opt for pizza as a way to focus on the good things in life. I know it's corny. When you're a soldier stationed overseas, you spend a lot of time reliving all the sentimental parts of your life and wishing you could re-create them."

Heather holds up her palms. "Okay, okay, I surrender. Who can hold firm in the face of great pizza and an emotional story like that? I've got no choice. I have to cave. At least, that's what I'll tell myself when I step on the scale in the morning."

"Remember what I said about scale stepping? I like you just as you are. If I wanted to date a twig, I would. But I don't. I want to date *you*. In case you haven't noticed over the past few months, I fancy you."

"Well, you could've fooled me. I was pretty much sure you hate my guts. In fact, I wasn't even sure you cared enough about me to learn my name."

Chapter Two

Heather

"What do you mean, you don't like pasta? Everybody likes pasta!" I exclaim. I can't even wrap my head around the concept. I have pasta water running through my blood. "You don't like any pasta? No Fettuccine Alfredo with tons of garlic, or spaghetti with meatballs? Not even the Kraft macaroni and cheese with the weird yellowy-orangey-powdered cheese that isn't really cheese?" I'm incredulous at the idea of someone excluding an entire food group I consider essential to daily living.

Tyler leans back in the wrought-iron chair and stretches out his long, lanky legs in front of him. "Nope. Sorry, I just can't do it. That stuff is just downright nasty. Library paste comes to mind."

"Library paste? Goodness gracious, Ty! I'm wondering about the caliber of cooks in your life. First, we had the issue with the coffee, and it's becoming abundantly clear you've never had decent pasta. Properly cooked pasta could never, ever be confused with library paste."

"Whatever you say, Gidget. I guess I'll just have to take your word for it. I'm a grown up now, and I don't have to eat stuff I don't like."

I can't disguise my giggle. "Real mature approach there, Cowboy. Are you running late for recess or something?"

"What?" He shrugs defensively. "I'm a grown man. If I haven't earned the right to eat what I want after serving two tours in Iraq and one in Afghanistan, I don't know when I'll ever be able to."

"Okay. You have a point. But what if I told you I can make you pasta you'll love? In fact, I'll bet it becomes one of your favorite dishes."

"Oh, Gidget, you don't know this about me, but you just said a couple of dangerous words. I never turn down a bet." Ty challenges with a wicked gleam in his eyes as he rubs his hands together with absolute glee.

I suppose I should be nervous right about now, but Tyler doesn't know me very well either. Competition is a huge deal in my family.

It may be my hunger, the stress of the day, or the fact that I've been drooling over this sexy lawman for several months; but I throw caution to the wind. "Hmm, that's interesting because I'm not the kind of lady who backs away from a wager either. Might be fun," I quip with far more bravado than I have. "What are the stakes?"

Tyler examines me for a moment and tips his hat down over his forehead. "Gidget, I'm not sure I know you well enough to assign the appropriate wager. I want to make sure that when you lose, you know you're paying a penalty. Otherwise, it's no fun to play the game. So let's do a wager with stakes to be named at a later date."

"See, I find it interesting that you think I'll lose. That's a fascinating approach. You don't know me very well if you think I'm going to surrender easily. I don't enter competitions I don't plan to win. Therefore, after I fix you the best meal you've ever eaten, you're also going to be eating some crow, and I'll be collecting an appropriate marker. You might be surprised at how creative I can be," I retort boldly.

"You know, I'm finding this conversation to be very enlightening. I always wondered if we would find common ground if we ended up in the same room together. It seems like we might have done just that. If we choose our wagers wisely, this could be good clean fun — unless you don't want it to be," Ty gives an exaggerated wink. Although his offer is made in a teasing tone, something tells me, given the right circumstances, he might just be dead serious.

"Consider me forewarned, Cowboy. Although, I'll choose my reward carefully because I wouldn't want you to get too —"

I pause for a second before adding, "cocky."

"'Cocky'? Me? Never! As I recall, you're the one who promised me the best meal I've ever eaten. If anyone is cocky in this situation, I would think the word cocky applies to you."

I brush my fingertips across the front of my bowling shirt as if I'm buffing my nails. "Nah, it's only cockiness if I can't deliver. I'm not bragging, I'm merely stating facts. You'll see."

Ty just grins like a Cheshire cat. "I think I should

probably tell you that unless I was ordered to eat it by my drill sergeant, I have had no form of pasta since I was about seven. There's a great deal of ingrained stubbornness involved. This is not a faddish vegan diet choice we're talking about here. At this point, you can pretty much consider it a part of my personality."

"Oh, I see. You think I can't rise to the challenge." I respond as I poke him in his well-defined chest. "Well, prepare yourself to be shocked. I might even find a sophisticated palate under all those baloney sandwiches, microwaved hot wings, and pork rinds. What would you do if I did?"

Ty chuckles as he shakes his head, "Can't be done with pasta, Darlin'. I'd faint first."

"Well then, I should probably brush up on my first aid skills," I tease. "Because your diet is about to undergo a major overhaul. You might even find you — gasp — like real food. Wouldn't that be a novel concept?"

"Well, I'll put this conversation in the win column for me. It shows you pay uber-close attention to what I eat, so at least I'm on your radar."

"Don't flatter yourself too much, Cowboy. It's an occupational hazard. Food is my job."

"Not to disparage the food truck or anything, but I have had your food before and — believe it or not — my little aversion to pasta aside, I enjoyed most of it. I don't think you'll convert me to hummus any time soon. I have a texture thing with garbanzo beans. You are far too talented to slave away in a space that's only four by six feet. I have to wonder why you do it."

"How long do you have?" I grimace.

"Take as long as you need. I just came off my third twelve-hour shift in a row. I've had my pizza and caffeine. I'm all yours for the foreseeable future," Ty assures me as he grabs his large glass of Coke and moves over to a well-worn leather couch in the quietest corner of the restaurant. He motions for me to sit beside him.

Suddenly, all I want to do is curl up beside him and tell him the whole sordid story, but that's not the way I operate now, thanks to lessons learned the hard way. There was a time in my life when I would have freely shared every last detail, but not lately.

"I'm sure you could find a thousand more interesting things to do with your time than listen to my sad, pathetic tale of woe."

"I wouldn't have offered if I weren't interested," Tyler insists. "Come on. Take a load off those feet and tell me what's going on."

It may be the compassion in his eyes, my overall fatigue level, or simply a chance to share my story with someone who seems to care, but I can't turn down his invitation.

The relief must be clear on my face because Tyler's body language changes as he watches me cross the room. He immediately stands and, without a word, he opens his arms and gathers me in a warm, comforting hug. It's all I can do to fight back my tears. Tears I didn't even know I needed to shed. Abruptly, I remember why it feels so nostalgic. It's been a full decade and a half since I had a hug quite like that. In a strange twist of fate, the man who I thought I could have nothing in common with wears the same cologne as my favorite Nonnino and even tucks me under his chin the same way. I shouldn't make assumptions about people without knowing them. Ty may be less like my dad and his cronies and more like my grandfather.

As I blink back my tears, I realize Tyler is whispering something under his breath. I struggle against the blanket of the past so I can concentrate on what he's saying. "Hush Darlin', there can't be anything so bad, it won't be better if you spread the load."

The sweet sentiment under his rough voice is enough to make me come close to losing it again. I take a deep breath and swallow hard.

"Well, this isn't easy for me. I suppose you probably already think I'm a big bimbo, and this is only going to confirm your suspicions. Well, yours and everyone else's," I confess.

Ty puts his hand up to stop me. "Gidget, you have me all wrong. I never said I thought you were a bimbo. In fact, it's is pretty much the opposite. I admire people who can be artists. I think some of the smartest people on the planet are artists."

"Anyway," I continue before I lose my nerve. "I'm never sure where to start this story. I'm not sure where it all begins. It might've started when I was a little girl trying to compete with my athletic superstar big brother and model-perfect little sister. I never fit in with my stereotypical upper crust suburban Italian family. No one knew what to do with me — except my grandparents. My dad was grooming me to be his next administrative assistant because, in his opinion, girls couldn't be responsible CPAs. He wanted my brother and me to run his business for him eventually. However, my Nonna could see I had the heart of an artist and the palate of a cook from an early age. She allowed me to bake at her knee almost from the time I could walk. I owe my career to her. Anything I know in the kitchen today had its start in what I learned from her. My grandpa, or Nonnino, was my biggest cheerleader. He was brave enough to try every dish I ever made. Let me tell you, some of those early dishes were very, very scary. Yet, he never seemed fazed."

"That sounds great, it sounds like your family supported your dreams."

"Sadly, that's where it gets dicey. Part of my family supported my dreams; I always seem to be a disappointment to the rest of my family. I felt stuck in the middle. It never seemed to matter what I chose to do; I was always disappointing somebody. I guess that's how I became fantastic at trying to please everybody. I don't want people to be upset with me. I pretend to be happy when I'm not. I pretend not to be hurt when I am. I'm often nicer to people than I should be because I'm afraid they might be disappointed in me. The craziest thing of all is that I expect more of myself than others ever think of asking of me."

Tyler puts his arm around my shoulder and gives me a gentle squeeze. "Ah, Gidget, don't be so hard on yourself. Being a nice person is a good thing. It's what sets us apart from the barbarians and the witches of the world. At some point, all the good you put out in the world will come back to you."

"I wish it were that easy. Unfortunately, not everybody lives by that code. I had somebody totally take advantage of my generosity and essentially rob me blind. In the process, he destroyed my trust in people — specifically in men — and seriously damaged my relationship with my father. My dad doesn't believe I can be trusted to make smart decisions about anything anymore. It doesn't seem to matter to him that before I decided to change my major to culinary arts, I was a business major with a solid grounding in accounting. One serious mistake made all of it count for nothing. I feel like such a fool."

"Well, I haven't known you for years, but I have known you for several months, and I know you are bright, intuitive, and you're nobody's fool. Everybody makes mistakes. Your parents have probably made more than a few of them as well. It's not fair for them to be judging you so harshly."

I'm dumbfounded by his quick defense of me. If I were to guess based on our previous interactions, I would've told you Tyler Colton could barely stand the sight of me and thought I was one of the biggest flakes on the planet. This apparent about-face is a stunning development.

"Wow, at the risk of sounding like Sally Field, I think you like me. You really, really like me," I stammer.

"I think I've mentioned it a couple times today, at least," Ty replies. "For the life of me, I can't figure out why it's so hard for you to take a compliment."

"Maybe it's because I don't know what I've done to deserve one," I answer with more honesty than I intend.

"Whoever told you that you have to earn compliments? I was always taught compliments are like gifts with no expectation of anything in return. It's like finding an extra dollar in your pocket you didn't expect. A complement is something you give someone to brighten their day. They don't have to do anything special to earn it or deserve it — it's just there."

"But—" I start to argue.

Tyler softly presses the tip of his finger against my bottom lip to silence me. "But, if you want to look at it from your frame of mind, I can think of many things you do to deserve compliments. You are friendly to everyone from the person who delivers your newspaper to the meter maid who gives you a ticket. In my opinion, being nice to someone who just slapped you with the fine is going above and beyond the call of duty."

"It's a hard job and nobody likes them. They aren't like teachers or nurses."

Ty chuckles. "See? You're good to the core. Definitely compliment worthy. You cook with a passion for every meal. Even something as simple as grilled cheese sandwiches or peanut butter and jelly are special gourmet treats when you make them. I confess I come over at mealtime just so I can see what you make from the leftovers in Jeff and Kiera's fridge. I know you stop and talk to Harry, the homeless veteran who lives behind the carwash. Not only do you stop and talk to him on a regular basis, you often bring him food. Not just a little food either, but enough to feed several of his friends. Many people in your situation with a restaurant would look at that as an opportunity for free publicity, but you don't," he continues.

"Tyler, every decent human being would do the

same. It's nothing special. It doesn't even deserve a compliment. I would feel guilty if I didn't do that stuff." I shrug my shoulders defensively. This is the kind of argument I get into with my dad all the time. My dad thinks charitable agencies should do this type of stuff and that I should just mind my own business, which is why I never tell anybody what I do. I am shocked that Tyler, who barely knows me, has taken the time to notice what I do in my spare time.

"You'd be surprised, there are some pretty cold hearted people out there. Unfortunately, I seem to specialize in dating most of them," Ty jests. I am familiar with the strategy of hiding a bit of truth in your jokes so that the truth doesn't sting quite so much.

"I'm sensing you have your own 'not so happily ever after story' to share. The offer is reciprocal you know, I have big shoulders too."

Tyler runs his hand through his short-cropped hair as if it's a sensory memory.

He shrugs his shoulders and loosens the muscles in his neck. "To be honest, I would just as soon forget about that time in my life, but if it would help you understand me better or build our friendship, I'll trot out the grisly details for you. Put simply, I trusted someone to be there for me. She wasn't — even though she promised she would be. Period. End of sentence," he explains curtly. Though now that he's started, the story continues to burst from his lips like water through a broken levy.

"She had a lot of flimsy excuses as to why her behavior was okay, but it still sucked. My best friend's behavior sucked too. But, then he went and got leukemia so, I couldn't even be mad at him anymore. I just had to be mad at God and my ex-girlfriend. Well, them and terrorists, insurgents and other random bad people I got to shoot at until they blew up my people and tried to blow up me. Then, my life got craptastic. But, that's a topic for a whole other day or maybe even a whole other year, but we don't need to talk about it today," he sighs as his monolog trails off.

"See, I knew my problems were petty and stupid compared to real problems."

Ty puts his hands on my shoulders. "May I remind you that you were shot at today. I believe it gives you a little bit of leeway. In fact, I think that qualifies as a very real problem."

"Speaking of things I'd rather not remember —" I roll my eyes. "Really, Cowboy did you have to go there? I was doing a pretty good job of forgetting why we were stuffing our faces with pizza." I sigh heavily. "By the way, I'm not giving you a free pass on telling me the rest of your story. You don't need to tell me everything, but I think you left out some key details that it would be helpful for me to understand. Fortunately for you, I'm on a deadline today, and I wasted far too much time telling you my sob story. I need to get back to work on my cake order. I got a text from Kiera, and she said I could use their kitchen. They'll board the shoe thief with their friend the veterinarian so I can work on the flowers," I explain.

"I guess that means I get a rain check?"

"Yes, it would stand to reason," I reply uncertain about the strange direction of the conversation.

Suddenly, Ty flashes a huge grin as he announces loud enough for everyone else in the restaurant to hear, "Why yes Ms. LaBianca, I would be more than happy to go on a date with you. I very much enjoyed this date, a follow-up date would be lovely. Thank you for asking."

Abruptly, all the noisy background clatter and conversation in the quaint little Italian bistro seems to vanish. Everyone is waiting to see what I'll say. It isn't often that someone can throw me off my game, but Tyler seems to have uncanny aim. I guess it's time to put on my game face. I summon my inner Lauren Bacall and look up at him through my eyelashes. After one long blink, I sassily retort, "Well, someone had to step up to the plate and do the asking because I've been waiting for months for an invitation and nothing happened. So, I figured I'd show some initiative." I turn to the people watching with rapt attention and slip them a small wink when Tyler isn't looking.

Tyler chokes back a chortle of laughter. "Well played ma'am. I should've known better than to go up against the master of verbal play."

As I stand and give a mock curtsy, It's one of the things that makes things so interesting with Tyler. He isn't afraid to challenge me or listen to my ideas. We always have a great spirited conversation, no matter what the topic — even if it's about scheduling our next date. It's a refreshing change when I'm used to my opinion not counting for much.

◆

"Dad, it's not a big deal. I wasn't even in the food truck

when it happened. No, we don't know who did it. It's probably just some neighborhood kids playing around. Tyler's got it all under control. I'm sure he'll figure it out."

I have to pull the phone away from my ear to be able to deal with my dad's response. Although, I don't know his exact words, the gist is clear. "Oh for Pete's sake, Dad! I'm not sleeping with the man. I went out for pizza with him. He's the friend of a friend and happens to be the officer that responded to the break-in. I think I can control myself long enough not to ravish him in the middle of a restaurant," I reply with an eye roll, even though my dad can't see it through the phone.

I listen as my dad berates me some more, and I try again to defend myself as we have the same conversation we've had every year for the past four years. "No, dad you're right. I have terrible taste in men, and I've been known to make stupid mistakes. However, the break-in was not my fault. I parked the truck in a well-lit area, and it was secure when I left it."

As the tongue-lashing continues, I wonder why I even bother to engage in these conversations. I sigh as I try to defend myself, "Yes, the security system was set. No, I will not come home and marry your partner's nephew just because it's the sensible thing to do. I'm sure he's a nice guy, but I'm not interested in being married to a golf pro. Listen, dad, I need to go, I have a wedding cake to make."

I hang up the phone feeling exhausted. I cringe whenever I hear the ring tone associated with my dad. I wish I didn't feel that way, but sadly I do.

I tuck my phone into my jacket pocket and try to

put the conversation behind me as I unpack the supplies and put them on Kiera's kitchen counter.

Mindy comes bounding up — because like me — she never approaches anything slowly. "Whoa, Mindy! Remember what I told you about running in the kitchen? It's never a safe practice for any chef," I caution.

Mindy's face scrunches up with confusion, "I thought the rule was only if I was carrying knives," she replies.

"Nope, it's pretty much true always. If I had had a pan of hot sugar, you could've been in real danger," I explain.

"Okay, if I'm careful, can I help you?" asks Mindy hopefully.

"I brought you some cake scraps so you can make cake balls and if you want to, you can play with the gum paste scraps because I am making flowers."

"That's rad!" Mindy bounces from one foot to the other.

"First, you have to go wash your hands. It's always the first rule of safety. Are your mom and dad here?"

"Sure, Dad's down in the basement with Tyler," Mindy answers as she runs toward the bathroom.

"Tyler's here?" I practically shriek.

"Well, Duh! He came over to watch the NASCAR race with Papa," Mindy clarifies as if she's talking to a simpleton. "What's wrong Miss Heather? Mr. Tyler is so nice. He gives me piggyback rides, and he's going to teach me how to ride his horse."

"Nothing's wrong Mindy Mouse," I say quickly,

trying to cover my earlier overreaction. "I didn't expect him to be here."

"Then how come you're all red like a stop sign?" asks Mindy as she plays with the ribbons on her ponytails. "Hey, did you know Uncle Ty is a real cowboy? He has a ranch-n-everything. The barn is even red just like in the movies."

"That sounds neat. Weren't you planning to learn to ride a horse so you can ride at Justice Gardner's ranch?"

Mindy nods as she exclaims, "Uh-huh, Uncle Tyler said he would teach me when we have school vacation if the fields aren't too muddy. I'm so excited. The Judge-man said I was a very good horseman. I thought it was funny because I'm a girl."

"Well, you're braver than me. I'm too scared to ride a horse."

"No, way!" Mindy's mouth gapes. "How can you be a grown up and not ride horses? I thought everybody rode ponies when they were little."

"Nope, I was too big of a chicken. I was afraid they were going to step on me. I never even tried. I wish I had been braver when I was little. Now, I feel stupid for wimping out."

Just then, Tyler emerges from the basement. It's clear from his expression he's overheard our conversation. He is studying my body language as he asks me, "Would you mind coming out to my ranch so I can show you my babies. They're so gentle they wouldn't hurt a fly. Literally. In fact, I think Fannie Farmer is harboring a family of fugitive flies in her mane."

I giggle, and Ty gives me an odd look. "I'm sorry, but the name of your horse is funny in light of our conversation this afternoon. I don't know if you realize this, but your horse is named after a vintage cookbook. I find that ironic, especially since your favorite food is microwavable pizza."

"If you think that's funny you'll get a kick out of the fact that I have two other horses named Julia and Jacques."

"You're kidding me! Please tell me it's not coincidental and that you get the cultural reference behind their names."

"Gidget, I didn't say I was never exposed to cooking. My mom is a huge fan of Public Television. I think you're reading far too much into my dislike of noodles. My transition from dorm food to the Army's finest cuisine didn't do much to develop a sophisticated palate either. But, it doesn't mean I'm a total idiot. In fact, my mom would be pleased as punch to meet you. She always wanted to go to culinary school."

"What does your mom do now?" I ask, realizing that I've never seen her at any of Jeff and Kiera's family events.

"My mom is a retired third-grade teacher and my dad owns a local hardware store back in my hometown in Oklahoma."

"You're from Oklahoma? I knew you had an accent, but I didn't realize that's where you're from."

"I've been from so many places recently, sometimes it's hard for me to remember. What? You don't think I have an authentic Ory-gun accent?"

"I'm probably not the person to ask about that since I grew up around Harvard Yard and spent my summers in North Carolina and Texas. My dialect is so confused it doesn't know if it's coming or going," I tease.

"Speaking of places to visit, I would like you to come see my ranch, remember? You never answered my question." Ty pins me with a direct gaze. I look into his eyes that are so sexy, and I almost forget what my objections are.

"I was hoping you would miss that artful little dodge," I confess "If I come see you, do I have to touch the horses?"

Tyler chuckles. "No, Heather, I wouldn't make you do anything you don't want to do. I promise. We'll just have a nice visit. Maybe you can even Skype with my mom and say hi. That way you can hear what a real Oklahoman accent sounds like."

"Okay, that doesn't sound too dangerous," I remark.

"Well, Gidget, I suppose the level of danger is entirely up to you."

Chapter Three

Tyler

I can't believe I cut myself shaving today. I haven't done that since I was a kid. I guess it goes to show how nervous I am — which is weird because this isn't even my first date with Heather. If you count the time I spent helping her with the wedding cake, it's almost like our third or fourth date. The whole food truck fiasco turned out to be a positive experience for me because it's given me an excuse to hang out with Gidget. Although, it feels odd to call her that now because I can see her fashionable clothes are more of a defense mechanism than a reflection of who she is.

The lot where her food truck was parked turns out to be the center of a turf dispute in a gang war between drug factions. They had actually been shooting at each other from inside her truck like some sick kids game using her humble little business as their home base. The narcotics task force in Salem made an arrest. Hopefully, that nightmare will soon be over. Unfortunately, because of the complexity of the case, her food truck has been tied up as evidence far longer than any of us expected. There was a fire in the commercial kitchen she rents, which complicates matters. She got permission from her client to use my kitchen at the ranch to make the cake since the facility was once used as a bed-and-breakfast.

This process has been entertaining and educational for me. At first, she didn't want me to help her. She was shocked to learn that I have a food handler's card. I'm so grateful for the time I spend with the Explorers program, which requires me to have one. She and I spent a very adventurous evening baking cake under Kiera's watchful eye. Kiera wasn't able to help as much as she typically does since my kitchen isn't set up for her wheelchair, but she was very helpful in giving me step-by-step instructions. Even Heather said I make an excellent sous chef. I also showed off my woodworking skills when I built the structure for the cake. The cake design was very abstract, with lots of odd angles that needed to be supported so the cake would not collapse on itself. I've seen cakes like that on television, but I had no idea they required internal supports. It was fascinating. I think the most entertaining part was making all the flowers. It was tedious in a way, but also a lot like playing with Play-Doh. Heather was sweet and didn't tell me my stuff looked like a first-grader made it, so I guess I did fine. Heather told me the bride emailed her and told her she was thrilled.

Heather was here a couple weeks ago when we did the cake, but she didn't go anywhere near the barn. So, I'm trying to figure out a way I can introduce her to the barn without it overwhelming her. At first, I thought she was embellishing her fear of horses for dramatic effect to entertain Mindy. I quickly found out the truth. Even talking about them makes her nervous. It seems so opposite to her typical personality. In many ways, she's the type of person who takes on any challenge with absolute fearlessness. I can't even begin to fathom being afraid of horses. Being raised in Oklahoma, I was around horses before I could sit up on my own. I had Julia and Jacques shipped from Oklahoma after I returned from Iraq. I adopted Fannie Farmer from the Humane Society, and I can't imagine my little herd without her. She was a senior horse they considered un-adoptable because someone had allowed her hoof infection to become so advanced. Fortunately, with a little tender loving care, she healed right up, and she's my most gentle horse now.

I've decided that we're going to play some traditional yard games in the field outside of the barn. I know Heather has a competitive streak a mile wide; I figure if she's playing a game, she may not notice how close the horses are to us. I thought we might play a rousing game of lawn bowling and croquet. Heather likes retro things, so I thought she might get a kick out of it. I hunted long and hard on eBay for an intact, authentic lawn bowling set.

I examine the food I picked up from the nearby specialty deli and hope it meets her expectations. She's a phenomenal cook, but I know very little about her personal tastes in food. She is reluctant to eat in front of other people, so I don't get a chance to check out her preferences much. I checked with Mindy, my secret source of information on all things Heather, but Mindy didn't seem to know much either, except to say chocolate bars are always a good choice.

At noon exactly, the doorbell rings and I'm

presented with the gift that is Heather. Today, she's exquisitely wrapped in a traditional red and white gingham shirt and overalls, with red Converse shoes. She even has little cowboy boot charms on the end of her shoelaces, and it's hard to miss the fact that she's brought one of her famous pies along. I grin because her pies are legendary. In fact, Jeff and Kiera credit a peach pie, which she helped make, with bringing them back together after a disagreement.

When I take the pie from her, I notice she's done some incredibly intricate latticework and placed a cool design around the crust. "This looks like a piece of art!" I exclaim. "Are you sure you want us to eat this?"

"Sure, why wouldn't I? It's only apple pie. I usually make apple cranberry, but I thought you might like a more traditional pie."

"Heather, our bet is only about pasta. You can make anything you want to. I like cranberries, but regular apple pie is amazing too. I'm not picky. I'm just happy to eat something that's not in a box or from a takeout menu."

Heather wilts a little. "Darn it, I knew I should've gone with the cranberries."

"Gidget, honey, I'm blown away you brought me anything at all. I don't care if it's got cranberries, apples, pumpkins or lemons. I'm gonna love it because you made it for me," I insist.

"I get weird about this stuff, I guess. I want everything to be perfect," she admits with a shy grin. "I drive Tara and Kiera crazy, always trying to fix recipes."

"I can understand where you're coming from. In my spare time while I was stationed overseas, I started making small jewelry boxes and clocks out of wood and antlers. I wanted to do it right, so I studied hundreds of woodworking sites online when I had access to computers in the barracks, and I downloaded books on it to my Kindle. I took a long time to get up the courage to show anyone anything I had made. Even after people started telling me they loved my stuff, I wondered if they were just telling me that because I was their commanding officer or their friend, or if really they liked it. I've been doing them for several years, and I even have a website now, but there are still days when I wonder if I am any good at it."

"I know what you mean about the boundary between friends and constructive criticism. Fortunately for me, the Girlfriend Posse knows they can tell me anything without hurting my feelings. My family is a whole other story, of course. Can I see something you've made? I promise just to look and not say anything."

"Since when have we ever kept our opinions to ourselves?" I tease. "If we did, it would fundamentally alter the nature of our relationship. I like our relationship the way it is, so feel free to give me a butt-kicking if I need one. Consider this a people-pleasing-free-zone."

Heather gives me a slightly menacing grin, "Just remember you said that. Someday, you may be sorry you ever uttered those words. I often have strong opinions, and I don't always share them. My grandma taught me to be a nice Southern Belle, even if I had to bite my tongue in half to do so."

"Southern grandma? I thought your Nonna was Italian."

"I had both," Heather answers with a laugh. "Imagine how confused my childhood was. My dad was an East Coast Italian from New Jersey. He was one of the first in his family to go to college and he's Mensa smart. He got a scholarship to Harvard. Well, my mom is from North Carolina and was visiting one of her high school friends at Harvard. My dad apparently was quite a looker in his day, and my mom fell head over heels for him. Well, imagine my mother's surprise, with her very cultured, North Carolinian debutante background, when she found out that the Harvard scholar she was in love with was from the projects in New Jersey. They stayed together, but they did everything in their power to reinvent themselves as a moneyed, yuppie couple, with picture-perfect kids, and a manicured lawn. It was a mixed-up world to grow up in. I had grandparents who were very proud of their heritage, and parents who were running away from theirs as fast as they could. I didn't know where I fit into all of that. Added to all the confusion was the fact that I didn't conform to the family mold. It didn't take much to get me labeled a complete rebel."

After what I've seen in the military, the idea of Heather being in the role of the rebel is ludicrous to me, but I know family politics can be complicated. "How did you end up here in Oregon? It's a long way from Harvard Yard."

"Yes, it is. Kiera and I met when she came to Boston's Children's Hospital for an experimental treatment when she was younger. When I changed my major from business to culinary, I decided to follow her to Oregon. It took me a while to be brave enough to take the plunge as a chef. I tried more 'respectable' careers like accounting and teaching first. I finally decided I needed to follow my passion without guilt. My dad held all the purse strings, and that made it difficult. Thank heavens for Kiera and Denny. They let me move in for free and fed me. Denny treated me like a daughter."

"They're good people. Jeff found himself a keeper when he found Kiera and her family."

"I think Kiera is lucky to have found Jeff, too. How did you guys become friends?" Heather inquires.

"We met in college. He ran track, and I played football. Jeff was one of the few people who wasn't okay with my 'lifestyle choices' and tried to steer me in the right direction. I was too stupid and stubborn to listen, but Jeff was decent enough to stick around while I collected the pieces of my life and started over in the military. He was there for me again when my life blew up a second time. I didn't even need to ask him. He's just that kind of guy," I explain.

"It sounds like you've been through a lot. This time, I have all the time in the world to listen. It's my turn to have broad shoulders."

"I appreciate the offer, Gidget, but I'm not a touchy-feely kind of guy. I've had a lot of crappy stuff happen to me along the way. Some of it I deserved, and some of it I didn't," I reply vaguely, feeling regretful about my inability to trust people.

"I understand. You don't have to tell me your entire life story, I wish I knew a little of your history so I don't step on any land mines," she responds.

I raise an eyebrow. "You mean, for instance, land

mines like … talking about land mines?"

Heather turns ghostly white and puts her hand over her mouth as she gasps, "Oh my Gosh! I'm so sorry! Is that what happened to you — I mean, is that why you're not a soldier anymore?"

I gather her hands up in mine, and I notice they're cold. "Heather, take a deep breath. I was just flicking you crap. I'm fine, we can talk about it all you want. I want you to be comfortable with me. I'll be happy to answer questions about whatever you want to know. Feel free to ask."

Heather slumps down a little as she breathes out a sigh of relief "Oh, thank Gosh! I was afraid my thoughtless remark might have caused you a great deal of pain. I never want to do that."

"Sometimes, I let my smart mouth run away from me. I didn't mean to freak you out. I was only kidding. I do have some post-traumatic stress, according to the fine folks at the Veterans Administration, but I'm not so damaged that I can't talk about it in general conversation. I'm still a soldier. I serve in the National Guard now."

"Were you badly hurt?"

"I caught some shrapnel and was burned. I tore up my shoulder pretty severely and had to have a couple of surgeries to repair it, but the worst was the bell ringing I took to my head. The rehabilitation specialists say I may never fully recover from it. It's a lovely stew of confusing side effects. Sometimes I can't remember words I've known since I was in kindergarten. Other times I'll find myself crying at stupid television commercials that aren't even intended to be emotional. That's probably the most frustrating thing of all because I was never 'that guy'. Unless I was sloppy drunk, I was pretty much always in control of my emotions. Now, they can sneak up on me out of the blue. The worst thing is coping with the death of the other members of my unit. They were under my command, and I was responsible for them. They died because of decisions I made that day, and I'll have to live with that for the rest of my life. I think that changed me probably more than anything else."

"I know that you laid your life on the line as a soldier, and it's still on the line every day as a law enforcement officer. I think if I had gone through what you went through, I would be curled up in my bed like a pill bug and never want to leave it. The fact that you still go out and serve the people every day is astonishing. I respect you so much for it."

I swallow hard and shift in my chair. I fight the urge to run from her gentle, well-meaning words as they continue to rain down. They're meant to be as soothing as a summer rain, but they burn like acid. They make me flinch.

Heather's expression fills with sympathy. "I've been told by other soldiers that there's a cost of war. If you did your best, it's part of the risk they signed up for. I'm sure they don't blame you."

I hate the pity. Everyone gets the same look. In the space of a conversation, I'm suddenly half a man. If it's bad for me, I can only imagine what it's like for the driver of that convoy, Jason Fletcher. He came out of the ordeal as a double amputee. Trevor Black ended up maimed too.

"I wish it were that easy," I answer in a harsh

whisper. "You didn't see those guys when they died. I held one kid, barely old enough to shave while he drew his last breath. Another guy in my unit was two frickin' days from retirement. His daughter was going to have a baby. Their lives were lost because I trusted the wrong people. I can never take that back."

"Did you make that decision all by yourself?" Heather asks softly. "I don't think the military worked that way. Don't you decide things in duplicate and triplicate?"

"There is that. The Army specializes in redundancy. No, I didn't make the decision alone. You can't take a piss without paperwork. But that doesn't change that I was responsible for those men."

Heather scoots back her chair, walks over and gives me a gentle hug, resting her cheek against my shoulder. "I'm sorry you feel that way. It must be a terrible burden to carry. However, I know you to be a decent guy, and I'm sure you didn't put your men in harm's way on purpose. I'm sure they knew that too," she murmurs, her words muffled by the corduroy fabric of my shirt.

"Thanks so much for saying that. It's just something I need to work through." I wrap my arms around her and give her a gentle hug.

"Are you ready for lunch?" I ask, more than ready to change the topic to happier things. "The guy at the Greek Deli said I bought the best stuff on his menu. I'm eager to see if you agree."

"It looks phenomenal, and I can't wait to try it. How did you know gyros are my favorite food?" she asks, as she opens each container to examine the contents.

"Honestly, I didn't," I admit. "It was just a lucky guess."

"You should go buy a lottery ticket, because you were spot on."

<hr>

"We're going to do what?" Alarm makes Heather's voice squeak at the end of her sentences. "That's close enough for the horses to see us."

"Well, I doubt that they'll be keeping score," I grin. "You can still cheat at croquet if you want to. They won't tell on you."

"Can you get them off of me if they decide to attack?" Her eyes are wide as her panic sets in.

I smother a laugh as I try to reassure her. "Heather, I've been leading horses around since I was about four years old. There isn't a horse I can't handle. If one of them got a wild hair up their butt and decides to do something totally out of character, I can handle it. I promise."

"Really? You're not just making that up to make me feel better, right?"

This time, I chuckle. "No, Heather, I wouldn't lie to you. I'll keep you safe. Why are you so afraid of horses?" I ask, genuinely curious because Heather is typically fearless.

"Oh honey, you have no idea. I'm scared of most things that don't walk on two feet. I can handle house cats, but not so much alley cats. In that case, I'm on the fence. I was making friends with Lucky until he ate my shoes. Now, I'm beginning to reassess my decision to trust dogs."

"Lucky has a shoe fetish, I admit, but there's no reason to be afraid of him. He's a super nice dog. Look how well-behaved he is around Becca."

"I know it's not rational," Heather explains. "You're the first person I've ever told about my fear of house pets. I guess it started when I was a kid. People would tell me how nice their animal was, and how it would never bite anyone. Then it would turn around and bite me, and only me. Early on, I learned that I can't trust animals. They call me the anti-Dr. Doolittle in my house. One of my mom's favorite charities is a Greyhound rescue group, and she is very disappointed that I never help with her charity work. Have you seen those dogs? They look like walking skeletons. It's Halloween every day around them."

"I can see I'll have to teach you to use some of your moxie around animals. If you act nervous, it makes them nervous. I'd be more than happy to work with you, on your confidence. I have a sweet border collie who can serve as your personal therapy dog to help overcome your phobia. Annie loves everybody."

Heather grins nervously. "You do realize that's what everyone says just before their dog takes a big chunk out of my calf. It would stand to reason horses would be an extremely bad bet for me."

"Gidget, I understand your reluctance. But I'm totally sure I can keep you safe. My grandpa used to have a cattle ranch in Oklahoma; I used to help him train horses and herd cattle and sheep. I know I can keep my lazy riding horses well in hand."

Heather visibly relaxes "Okay, I'll let you handle it. Just to let you know — I totally scream like a girl. Mindy accuses me of trying to break her eardrums. You might want to avoid that if possible. It's not pleasant."

"I'll keep it in mind and do my best to avoid the pain. But I've got you covered. Do you want to start with croquet or lawn bowling?" I try to get her mind off the presence of my big four-legged babies.

"Lawn bowling? You mean the traditional kind?" Heather's eyes light up with excitement.

"Yep, I've got a gen-u-ine vintage old person's game here. We can pretend we're an old married couple livin' in Florida or something."

"It's funny you should say that because I learned to play it from my grandparents. We used to play every Sunday after church. My grandpa was a serious competitor. He even wrote down the score on a little pad with a small red pencil. After he passed away, my grandma found boxes of used pads where he had kept the scores for years. I don't know if he was planning for an epic rematch, or what. I have to warn you, I'm pretty good."

"Well, I haven't had the advantage of being well schooled in the proper use of lawn bowling equipment, but we spent a lot of time improvising games while serving in the desert. I played several games with rocks which strongly resemble lawn bowling, so I might just give you a run for your money."

"Oh, you're so on, Cowboy! If you win, I'll make you a batch of cookies or a pie of your choice," she offers magnanimously.

"That's a generous offer, considering you'll lose this bet. Are you sure you don't want to reconsider?" I tease, waiting to see if she'll take the bait.

"Yes, I'm sure, and when I win, you're going to have to give up something for me. Have you considered what that might be?" Heather asks, with a decided twinkle in her eye. I suspect she gave her big brother a run for his money when they were growing up, so I consider my options carefully.

"Maybe you would prefer it if I offered you an opportunity not to do something for a prize instead?" I tease.

"Well, if you ever want me anywhere near these horses, then you better play this game hard." She continues "You gave me a powerful incentive to play the most accurate game of lawn bowling ever played. I could make the Olympic team of lawn bowling just to avoid getting near your horses."

It's too bad Heather's so afraid of horses. Otherwise, I could see her as the quintessential rodeo queen, with big curly hair, audacious makeup, gaudy rhinestone shirts, skin tight Levi's, and shiny boots. She has the personality and the vivaciousness to pull it off in a heartbeat. I've watched her with Mindy and Becca. She is tender and caring. I know she'd have a wonderful affinity with animals, if only she can overcome her fears.

"Heather, are you going to give this a chance? I think I can help you with the horses if you let me. But I don't want to force you into something you don't want to do."

"I honestly don't know how I'll react. It's the closest

I've ever been to any horses, ever. I would like to say I totally trust you to keep me safe. But, to be honest, after all I've been through with men in my life, I have issues with that too. So I don't know what to tell you, other than, 'I'll try'." Heather gives a helpless shrug. "I'm sorry. I don't mean to disappoint you."

"Hey now, stop that. Remember what I said about this being a people pleasing free zone? It applies to me. You can't disappoint me just by having an opinion or a hang-up. Everybody's got hang-ups. I have a whole truckload of them. We would need a day and half to catalog all of mine."

Heather blinks back tears. "Thanks for being so understanding; not everyone would be."

Her response baffles me. I wonder what type of relationships she's been through before to make her feel like she doesn't have the right to an opinion. Even when I was in a dark place with Stacia, we each had our points of view and voiced them loudly and often. As far as I know, Stacia was never apologetic for anything she ever did, even if she was wrong. I can't imagine my former girlfriend apologizing for making me slightly uncomfortable. She would've probably just laughed at me.

"Gidget, it's no big deal. Trust takes a long time to build, and I need to earn your trust."

"Really? Because I would totally get it if it's a problem. Don't worry, I've had lots of people tell me I'm not worth their time. You wouldn't be the first."

"If you think I'm stupid enough to let a woman like you slip through my fingers, think again." I declare as I take Heather's hand and lead her to the lawn bowling course I set up.

I don't think I've looked forward to something quite so much for a long while. Now, I just need to decide if I want to win or lose. Given our wager, it might be hard to tell the difference.

Chapter Four

Heather

"Are you sure this course is regulation?" I ask skeptically. "Everything seems very far apart."

"Well, I followed the directions and measured it off myself." Tyler surveys the course with a confused expression on his face.

It doesn't take me long to figure out what happened. All you have to do is look at Ty and then look at me. "Let me guess, you measured it off with your strides, didn't you?" I ask, confident I already know the answer.

"What's wrong with that? It's a legitimate way to measure things," he protests.

"If you're average size, perhaps. However, you border on being a giant. Your strides are about equal to one and a half of an average person's. So this course has been super-sized."

The look on his face is priceless as my explanation sinks in.

"Oh man! I was so nervous about you coming over today that I wasn't even thinking. I am a woodworker. I do have tools, and I know how to use them," he says sheepishly.

I wink at him. "Oh, I bet you've got tools. I bet you've got a really nice set of tools."

"Miss LaBianca! I'm shocked by your bawdy sense of humor," he exclaims with mock outrage.

"Who me? I was merely commenting on your chosen hobby as such a meticulous woodworker; you must have an impressive collection. My grandpa was always really proud of his Craftsman tools. Did you think I meant something else?" I ask with my tongue firmly in my cheek.

"Heather, never play poker. Your intentions are written all over your face. In fact, if you went to Vegas, I don't even think it'd be safe for you to play Go Fish," he teases.

"Geez! You sound just like my brother, Carlton. He always says I can't bluff worth beans either. I just don't get it. He can get people to believe in anything. He left my dad's business to sell insurance, and he can sell flood insurance in the middle of the desert. It's the craziest thing you've ever seen. Sadly, I couldn't sell a candy bar to a famine victim."

"Trust me, Heather I would rather have one of you than a million other girls who are good at subterfuge. Being good at telling lies is fine as a party game, but it's lethal for a relationship. I'd rather have someone like you any day of the week." Ty seems lost in his memories.

"That's good because I can't even lie to the meter

reader. Everybody laughs at me." I try to lighten the mood a little.

It works. Tyler grins at me. "I can so see you confessing your sins to parking enforcement. I can also see you feeding everyone's meter. Did you know technically, we're supposed to issue citations for that? Those are the days I suddenly become very nearsighted. Why would I give a ticket to somebody who's trying to do something nice for somebody else? It's just crazy to me. I don't want to waste my time doing paperwork to punish nice people. Can you imagine me having to go to testify against someone in court who was plugging the meter for somebody else?"

"No, that's just stupid. Are we ever going to play this game? Because I'm ready to kick your butt. Although, you should give me a head start because it will take me twice as long to complete the course as it takes you."

"Yes, I'm ready. I've been ready for hours. I know it sounds dumb. But I've been looking forward to this," he concedes with a half shrug.

"Me too. Lawn bowling is surprisingly fun and competitive. My grandparents never made the game any easier for me because I was a kid; so I'm used to nail-biting competition. As long as my wrists and shoulders hold out, we've got ourselves a game."

I grab one of the balls for the field shot and proceed to tell Ty a bit about my journey from an introverted kid to being thrust in front of a microphone. I had forgotten how much fun it is just to shoot the breeze while whacking things with a stick.

"That's right I remember Kiera telling me you spent

an awful lot of time on stage as a kid," he remarks.

"Unfortunately, I did spend some time on the pageant circuit because my mom thought it would make me fit in better with her peers and encourage me to be less shy. I guess, it did work to a certain extent. I learned to be a great pretender and a people pleaser so that people didn't know I was actually more shy than outgoing."

"Gidget, I think this is one of those situations where you and I see it differently. I think all that practice made it easier for you to talk to people, especially virtual strangers. In a crowd, you are the most gregarious person there whether you know it or not. You always engage in friendly conversation with everyone around you like you're totally fearless."

"That's so sweet. I'm glad you see me in such a positive light. Though, I think you'll find the real me a little less bubble-gum pink than you imagined. I am quite sarcastic and snarky on occasion. Some folks find me downright annoying."

"I've faced down terrorists, I think I can handle a little snark," he parries with a wink.

"You may want to rethink your opinion after you've seen me before I've had my coffee."

Tyler pulls his cowboy hat off and wipes his forehead with his forearm. I don't blame him. What started out as a comfortable day has become a real scorcher. I peel off my gingham over-shirt, glad I decided to wear a cute little tank underneath.

The expression on Tyler's face is priceless when he notices what I'm doing.

He studies me quietly for a moment before he whistles low between his teeth. "Da-y-um Girl!" he exclaims admiringly, stretching the simple phrase into several syllables. "I thought Aidan had some pretty impressive ink. Why haven't I seen that before?"

I shrug and look down toward the ground before I answer, "I don't know. For a long time, I didn't show it to anyone. I did it for me. Whenever I exposed my arms, I covered it with makeup. It got to be a habit, I guess."

Tyler's eyes narrow as he scrutinizes me. "If that's not a load of horse feathers, it should be," he announces.

"What?" I ask, shocked at the vehemence in his voice. "What does that even mean?"

"Obviously, there's more to your tattoo than just some stars and hearts most people have done when they turn eighteen so they can check it off their bucket list. I'm new to the world of tattoos myself, but I know that represents days' worth of work. So, you don't put yourself through that kind of torture unless there's a story behind it. So, if you were brave enough to endure it, why hide it?"

Once again, his instinctive level of insight into what makes me tick surprises me. Most people are content to accept the wisecracking, bubblegum chewing, fashionista character I've created and don't even try to find out who I am underneath my façade. Tyler already seems to realize there is more to me than what I project. It's a little terrifying.

"I'm not sure there's an entirely logical explanation for my actions," I respond with a self-deprecating laugh. "Are you sure you want to hear this? It's a long, drawn out story."

Tyler nods as he grins. "Aren't those the best kind?"

"Don't say I didn't warn you," I caution.

"Quit stalling, I want to hear this. It's a work of art. So, tell me your story. You're not ashamed of it, are you?" he asks as almost an afterthought, with a look of confusion on his face.

"Oh, Geez no! At least not in the way you think. The decision to get a tattoo was personal for me. I didn't care if another person ever saw it, especially, my parents, because they despise tattoos and made their feelings widely known. I started covering it so I would have one less thing to fight about."

Tyler reaches out and traces the intricate design with his fingertip. "The level of detail in this is downright phenomenal."

"Thanks, I agonized over the design forever before it finally came together."

"You drew this yourself?"

I let out a chortle of laughter as I respond, "You don't know me well enough to know how funny that is. But, I leave the serious drawings to Tara. I'm limited to stick figures and cake sketches. In this case, there was an intern in my dad's office who specialized in Asian art. He and Tara worked on it together via email until it was just right. I thought we were going to drive each other crazy before it was all said and done."

"It must've taken a while," Tyler observes sympathetically.

I sigh as I remember, "Yes, it did. That was a long

year for lots of reasons. I worked on rebuilding my life at the same time I got the tattoo. I think I kept it covered because it felt like it was my secret map to escape what had become a life which wasn't mine."

"What do you mean?" He waits for me to explain.

"Well, I got a new piece of the design as an inspiration to take the next step of my journey. For example, the koi represents personal strength and overcoming adversity. So, when I faced having to press theft charges against the man I thought would marry me," she explains. "Looking at the tattoo reminded me that my identity was not his and even though he made me feel helpless, I really wasn't. The koi also represents determination, courage and desire for success so in a way this gave me the strength to apply to culinary school."

I point to the delicate blossom that's interwoven into my piece. As I describe it, Tyler reaches out and lightly follows my words with his fingertips. The effect is mesmerizing; the tattoo feels like a living thing on my warm skin.

"The next portion I added was the lotus flower. The Lotus is a metaphor — it represents elevating myself. The lotus is born at the bottom of a muddy pond. The plant pushes its stalk up through the mud and murky water to the surface where a beautiful blossom eventually grows. I felt like this was the process I was going through by defying everything my family wanted me to do and striking out on my own to go to culinary school. They were throwing all sorts of mud in my direction, metaphorically and otherwise. It had gotten downright nasty in the LaBianca household before I left. Sadly, things have never been the same."

Ty reaches up and wipes away a tear which has gathered on my lashes.

"I'm sorry it was so rough. What happened when they found out?" he asks as he places his hands on my waist as if they had every right to be there.

"My parents weren't happy, but I kept adding with each milestone. I added the last piece after I graduated from culinary school. The waves represent movement, strength, fluidity, and life. Mine is open—symbolizing the expanding of the soul and spiritual awakening. The wind represents change because I never want to feel as stuck as I did after I found out I was betrayed by the person who supposedly loved me. I was strong enough to branch out on my own and get a degree in culinary arts so I'll never be that reliant on another person again."

Tyler gently kisses my forehead. "See? I told you. Horse-feathers. Someone as smart and beautiful as you wouldn't randomly scribble on your skin without a great story behind it."

"I guess I never thought it would mean anything to anybody except me," I explain.

"Well, I find it, and everything else about you, compelling."

I back away and give him a saucy wink as I comment, "If I didn't know better, I'd say you were trying to distract me from this game of lawn bowling."

Tyler grins at me. "I have absolutely no idea what you mean. Wasn't I winning?"

Chapter Five

Tyler

Heather wasn't kidding when she said she's competitive. I have competed with former Olympic athletes who aren't as cutthroat. I briefly toyed with the idea of just letting her win the bet so she could name the stakes. However, it becomes clear about ten minutes into the game there's going to be no "lettin'" going on here. She is beating the pants off me fair and square. She's such a good player, my competitive juices are going crazy, I feel like I'm back on the football field facing down a linebacker. It's been a long time since I've competed just for fun. It's exhilarating to be playing for silly stakes like pastries. I wonder what price she would exact from me if I cheated? I think just for fun, I'll encourage her to make my punishment pretty harsh just to see what she might have in mind.

I'm feeling pleased with my creative plan when all of a sudden she tosses one of the beanbags from the children's game in the lawn bowling set at my head. "Earth to Tyler Joseph Colton, is anybody home? I've been trying to get your attention. You were not only a million miles away; you were in another solar system," Heather comments with a bemused grin.

It takes a second to bring my brain back into real-life focus before I can answer her, "Honestly, Gidget. I was thinking about how to lose graciously. You're kicking my butt. I seriously thought I would have the advantage here because I played so many games with rocks and sticks and other found objects in the desert." I walk over to give her a polite high five. "I figure there were few people on the planet who can match my skills honestly. But it looks like you might be up to the task. Just how much of this do you play again?" I ask facetiously.

"Well, my grandfather was retired and he didn't have much else to do during the summers except entertain me and play senior citizen games. Therefore, I'm an expert at lawn bowling, croquet, and shuffleboard."

"You deserve to be admired. You whipped my butt like whipped cream."

"Okay, I won't gloat," Heather says good-naturedly. "But, I did try to warn you. I'll go easy on you. My punishment — or reward as the case may be, is that I want you to cook me dinner for a change because I always make the meals for everyone else."

"It may indeed be a punishment. You have no idea whether you may be eating Lucky Charms for dinner, or I might have a hankering for pop tarts and chili dogs all in the same meal," I tease.

Heather wrinkles her nose at me. "Well, that's just a risk I'll have to take. I trust that your mama taught you better. No fan of Julia Child would raise her boy to serve pop tarts and chili dogs in the same meal. So, I'm guessing you're just pulling my leg. But, if you're not, I'll just have to be adventurous. Either way it will stretch my culinary horizons."

"When I want to be, I can be a decent cook. I just tend to be lazy when I'm cooking for just myself. Pizza and microwave meals are easy when I have nobody to impress, but me. I work some pretty crazy shifts with the Sheriff's Department so I rely on easy. Tell me, my lady, what would you like to eat?"

"Oh no, that's where the dare comes in. You have to guess. I only have to show up with my appetite and my table manners.".

"Oh wow! You are brave. Perhaps I should take advantage of your bravery and see how far it goes."

"Umm Ty — did you forget that I've gone to culinary school? I doubt there's anything you can fix that would scare me. I've pretty much eaten it all. The good, the bad, the ugly and the totally unmentionable I'd rather not talk about," Heather's body convulses in a full body shudder.

I have to laugh at her antics. As I think about it, I suspect she had to eat some pretty nasty food at culinary school. Not all students are created equal, and someone has to eat the food of the people who didn't do so well. Heather strikes me as the type of person who would eat everyone's food and try to say something nice about it regardless of how terrible it was.

"What was your favorite course in culinary school?" I ask with studied nonchalance.

Heather chuckles. "Nice try Cowboy. Apparently, you don't need fishing poles and worms to go fishing. Okay, I'll give you a couple of hints. Although you probably could have guessed. Pastries were clearly my favorite. I also liked working with savory food on the grill. I can make a cut of flank steak do things that would make you cry."

"It sounds like a plan to me. Let's settle the great pasta debate first, so I know what I'm up against. Then we'll even the score up with dinner here," I offer. "Are you ready to go take a walk around the ranch?"

"Do we have to? I feel perfectly safe in this one spot," Heather replies as she looks around anxiously. It's then she spots Fannie Farmer munching on some fortified alfalfa I've placed in a special feeding trough outside of her barn door. For fun and whimsy, I placed a straw hat on her head to help keep the flies off. It also gives her a very cartoonish appearance and makes her look extremely non-threatening—as if she ever could look threatening.

"Aww look! Isn't that the cutest thing you've ever seen? She looks like she just came from a Beatrice Potter book or just escaped from the one-hundred-acre woods and is going to run into Winnie the Pooh any second. I half expect Piglet and Roo to come bounding around the corner. How do you get her to leave the hat on?"

I shrug. "I don't know. It fits around her ears. I suspect she finds it less annoying than the flies, so she would rather just leave it there. Or, perhaps she knows she looks fetching, and she feels especially beautiful and likes to wear it."

"Oh, I agree she does look beautiful. But how does she know she looks beautiful? Did the other horses tell her she looks pretty? Are they jealous of her amazing fashion choices?" Heather asks her eyes twinkling with amusement.

"You know, I never really thought about it. But, I do know it's way too soon after lunch to be delving into matters this philosophical. Would you like to go ask her?" I suggest.

In what I know is a huge show of bravery for her, Heather nods slowly as she lets out a deep breath. "Yes, I think I would. She doesn't look as scary as I thought she would. In fact, she looks rather sweet. She hasn't eaten any small children recently has she?" Heather asks with wide eyes.

I am tempted to guffaw with laughter, but I'm not sure she's not asking a serious question. So, I shake my head solemnly and reply, "No, not recently. She usually restricts her diet to horse feed, hay and a few treats like sugar cubes, carrots, and apples."

"So, you're telling me she's not that much different from me. She's a little oversized and has a huge sweet tooth?"

I can't stop myself. I glower at Heather. "No, she's not just like you. You are not oversized. In my eyes, you are just right. But, you are correct, she does have a sweet tooth which rivals a five-year-old's. Just keep sugar cubes in your pocket and you'll become fast friends."

"I don't know if I'm brave enough to try. Do you think she will bite me? What if I get scared? Do you think I should try? Am I thinking about it too much? What if I chicken out? Are horses like dogs? What do you think I should do?" she spews in a stream of consciousness.

"Heather, I can't answer all of that for you. Only you know if you can find it in yourself to be brave enough to do it. I know Fannie is the sweetest horse I've ever come across. I'll be right here, just do what you feel comfortable with," I reply as I hold out my hand and offer to escort her over to the barn.

As she places her hand in mine, I notice it's trembling slightly, and she is breathing rapidly. I stop and turn her toward me. "You understand you don't have to do this for me, right? If you are uncomfortable with this, please don't push it."

Heather gives me a small, tight smile. "No, Ty, I'm not doing this for you; I'm doing this for me. It's important for me to get to the bottom of my fears and overcome them."

I gather her gently into a hug. "I totally understand that, and I'm here for you any way you need me. So, let's go introduce you to Fannie. She always needs a new friend."

"Okay, let's go do this thing before I lose my nerve," Heather declares in a rush of words.

"That's my Gidget. Totally fearless. I'm so proud of you." I lead her into the barn area.

Fannie nickers and blows her breath out excitedly when she sees me. The noise scares Heather, and she jumps.

"Heather, it's fine, babe. Miss Fannie's just telling us she is happy we're here, that's all."

"That was her hello? She wasn't just licking her jowls in anticipation of a good meal?"

"Gidget, human beings are not on a horse's diet. There is absolutely no danger you're going to get eaten for her dinner. Trust me, she'll be far more interested in the sugar cubes in my pocket than your flesh."

Scrunching her eyes together like a little kid, Heather holds her arms out for me to lead her to the barn. I shrug as I comply, forgetting she is unable to see my response. "Okay, here we go. Watch your step." I guide her between the buildings on the way to the barn. As the odor of the hay becomes stronger, her breathing becomes shallow. "Heather, you have to take a deep breath or you'll faint. It's okay, I've got you covered. Nothing bad will happen to you. Do you trust me?"

Abruptly, Heather looks up at me as if recognizing me for the first time in several minutes. I can see her giving herself a mental shake.

"I can do this, right?" Heather whispers half to herself as she creeps closer to Fannie.

At last, Fannie notices the newcomer and swings her head around to greet Heather. Heather practically jumps out of her skin at the sudden motion. When she jumped, Fannie startled. This causes a rather comical chain reaction of jumping and jerking. To stop what could be a huge comedy of errors, I pull a sugar cube out of my pocket and offer it to Fannie. As I suspected, it distracted Fannie right away.

Heather watches in total astonishment as Fannie gently licks the sugar cube off of the palm of my hand.

"Look at that! She totally loves it. Look at the size

of her teeth. Aren't you afraid she'll bite you?"

"Nah, see how I have my fingers flat? That's so she doesn't catch my fingers with her teeth. She's not interested in my fingers she just wants the sugar. She knows if she gets aggressive, I stop giving her sugar; so she stays gentle. Would you like to try?"

Heather shakes her head. "I don't think so. Can I watch you again?" She wipes sweat off the palm of her hands on the back of her overalls.

"Sure, I can give Fannie a couple more. But, I need to spread the love a little and give some to Jacques and Julia."

"Really? I don't see them anywhere."

That's because they're in the field behind the barn," I respond. "But if they see me handing out sugar cubes, they'll come strolling back in a hurry."

"You mean they might come charging toward us?" Fear rings clear in her voice.

I put my arm around her waist and pull her close. "No, I didn't mean to panic you. I simply meant that they'd come loping into the barn and try to stick their nose into my pocket so they can get my sugar cubes. They probably won't even notice you exist until all the sugar cubes are gone, and even then they will only notice you to the extent that you can scratch their itchy spots. They are just big spoiled babies. Think overgrown couch potatoes." I grin as I look down at her.

"If you say so, they're mighty big to be couch potatoes. When I think of a couch potato, I think a medium-sized Basset hound, not a huge horse," Heather argues.

"Trust me. They are very low-key. The Humane Society thought maybe they were ridden as ponies in a circus act for kids. They give new meaning to the word mellow," I respond.

Just then, Fannie nudges Heather in the hip, and I chuckle. "It looks like she thinks it's your turn to give out the sugar cubes."

Heather's eyebrows climb to her hairline. She looks shocked at the intrusion. "Do you think she likes me? Do you think I can give her one?" Her eyes are wide with wonder.

I try not to chuckle at Heather's childlike expressions; she looks a lot like the kindergartners we invite to the ranch on their school field trips. "Sure, knock yourself out," I encourage as I hand her a couple of sugar cubes. I demonstrate the proper way to hold out her hand palm side up with the hand as flat and compact as possible.

I feel her hand tremble as I drop the sugar cube into the center of her palm. Her breaths are so shallow that her lips are turning blue. "Ty, I'm scared. Will you do it with me? I can't believe I'm this much of a chicken. You must think I'm nuts," Heather murmurs under her breath.

"No, I don't think you're crazy. I think you're scared of something you haven't encountered before. In my book, that makes you cautious, not crazy. Where I come from, cautious keeps you alive and that's a good thing. I'd be happy to help you. I'm going to put my hands under yours to keep yours steady, okay? But, you need to take some deeper breaths."

"I guess I'm as ready as I'll ever be," Heather states as she places her trembling hands over the top of mine, palm sides up. Fannie's ears twitch with interest and her nose immediately moves to the center of Heather's hand.

A look of stark terror crosses Heather's face as Fannie's large head comes closer and closer. As soon as the horse's lips touch her hand, a peal of laughter comes bubbling from Heather, uncontrollably erupting. I give Heather a questioning look.

"I didn't expect it to tickle. She's got stray whiskers on her mouth, and they're poking me."

"They do that. It's completely normal."

"I guess I was scared for nothing because she was as gentle as a baby kitten. Do you have any more sugar? I'd like to try it again. This time I want to do it by myself," Heather announces with more confidence.

"Sure thing, Gidget. I knew you'd be a natural. Fannie has taken a shine to you. I should be jealous. I bet you guys will be best friends. I'll be the odd man out. I'm going to have to teach Mindy how to ride so I've got someone to hang out with."

Heather smirks. "Somehow, I don't think she's going to have a problem with that. She already told me she has you booked for the entire Christmas break. "

"Oh, she does, does she? It's nice of her to keep me up-to-date on our social calendar," I say with a chuckle. "Although, I never regret any time I spend with her. She's a pistol. She brightens anyone's day."

Heather grins. "I totally agree with you. That little girl is a total work of wonder isn't she? She has every right to hate the world and everything in it, but she doesn't. Whenever I am feeling down and grumpy, I invite Mindy over for a play date and my problems seem a little less insurmountable."

I hand Heather a couple more sugar cubes. "Are you ready for this? Remember, palm flat, fingers tucked."

She turns to Fannie. "Hi there, pretty lady. Do you want a treat? I understand you have a penchant for junk food just like me. You and I should get along just fine." She holds out her hand to allow Fannie to take the sweet treat. Ever so gently, Fannie removes the treat from her hand making soft snuffling noises. Suddenly, Fannie lays her muzzle against Heather's shoulder and leans in. At first, Heather jumps in surprise. Then, she seems to collect herself and gives a wry chuckle. "Well, you're welcome. I like you too."

I can see that there are tears in the corners of Heather's eyes as she looks up at me And whispers, "Can you believe I just did that? I think she likes me."

"I think you'll be riding in no time. But, we'll tackle that another day. For now, there are chocolate lava cakes just waiting for us."

"Hmm, Cowboy — for a guy who doesn't know me. You guessed pretty darn well." Heather walks away with a sassy grin.

———— • ————

Tonight's the big night. I have to put up or shut up. As I'm driving over to Heather's house, I'm still not sure how I'm going to approach this. I really don't like pasta. It's not just something I made up to irritate her. I think it's a texture thing for me. Overall, my mom is a good cook. She tried to buck the stereotype of the Midwestern housewife of only cooking meat and potatoes. So, we didn't always have the typical fare of meatloaf and mashed potatoes or pot roast with peas. Despite that, pasta is the one thing I could never quite stomach. My college buddies thought it was funny I didn't like Top Ramen noodles. When you're in college, that's almost considered sacrilege.

I'm so discombobulated by today's activities; I wasn't even sure how to dress. I finally decide to wear my favorite 501 Levi's and a well-worn denim western wear cowboy shirt. I know I look like a walking stereotype, but I figure if anyone can appreciate that, it's probably Heather. As she opens her front door, I feel instant relief. Heather looks like something out of a 1950s ad campaign for Good Housekeeping magazine complete with red lipstick, apron and patent leather pumps. She looks like an incredibly sexy housewife. I'd like to kiss off her lipstick, but I doubt she'd appreciate that. So, I settle for handing her the bouquet of Gerber daisies Jeff's mom Gwendolyn made up for me. They have a brightly colored bow around them that matches Heather's dress. I wonder if Gwendolyn had inside information about tonight's plans.

"Wow! You look different!" Heather exclaims as she opens the door. "I was getting used to the beard. I don't think I've met a guy who changes their look as often as you do." She reaches up and runs her hand along my now smooth jaw. I'm taken off guard by the brief contact.

I have to shut my eyes for a moment and focus on

the present. I force myself to answer her unspoken question as I explain in a rough voice, "I sometimes help out on the undercover teams when they need someone to play the out-of-town-redneck-meth-head. So, I had to grow a little scruff."

When her eyes grow round with shock, and she gasps softly, I realize I may have been a bit too forthcoming. Most of my friends think I'm just a step above parking enforcement. I usually just share G-rated stories about rural policing that make my job sound about as dangerous as escorting little old people across the street in Mayberry. There are guys on the force that like to brag about the adrenaline-pumping hazardous parts. I'm not one of those guys. Once you've lived through hell and survived to tell the tale, you soon discover that no one cares what it's like, and the words bring back pictures you would just as soon forget.

Heather takes a deep breath and swallows hard. She reaches up and worries a lock of hair between her fingertips. Finally, she seems to settle on words. "Talk about your mixed blessings. On one hand, you wouldn't get bored at work, but then there's that whole getting shot thing to deal with."

Startled, I laugh out loud. Of all the things I thought she might say that wasn't it. "True, it's a mixed bag."

I watch as Heather shudders and then dons an engaging smile. I can almost see her giving herself a mental shake, trying to dispel the graphic images like a sheep dog shaking after a bath. She turns to me with a bright twinkle in her eye. "Ty, these are beautiful. Thank you so much. I'll just go put these in some water. How was your day?" Heather asks as she takes my coat and hangs it on a hook by her front door.

There is something so strangely normal about that simple domestic act, it almost makes me dizzy. It's been so long since someone was interested in the details of my life that I'm not prepared for the emotional impact of that question.

"Are you okay?" Heather inquires, as she studies the perplexed expression on my face.

"Yeah, it's just been a long day," I reply, trying to cover my bizarre reaction.

Heather motions me over to a big recliner chair in the middle of her living room. I'm a little surprised to see it in a woman's house, but I try not to let it show. "Would you like something to drink?" she asks as I sit down. "I can get you a beer or I've got soda or sweet tea."

"I think I'll stick to tea because there's a chance I may get called back in tonight, so I really shouldn't drink," I answer.

"Okay, tea it is. Something to snack on while we wait?" Heather offers as she turns to go back into the kitchen.

"Sure, I'm at your mercy tonight — I mean — I'm looking forward to whatever you serve me," I respond with a wink.

"You hush up now, Tyler Joseph Colton! You'll be thankful that you had this meal. You're not even going to know what you did before you met me. Your taste buds are going to weep with joy."

"Well, that's what you say. But, just so you understand the full extent of the challenge before you. I don't just mildly dislike pasta. I really, really can't stand it. It's right up there with liver and onions for me."

Heather just takes my hat off and taps me on the head. "What is it you told me about the horses? Oh yeah … 'I've got you covered.' That was it. So, that's what I'm going to tell you right now. Ty, put your feet up, sit back and relax because I've got you covered. You don't have to worry about anything tonight except having a great time. So, what are your music preferences? I guess they run toward Garth Brooks or Travis Tritt, am I right?"

"Well, I like Garth Brooks and Travis Tritt just fine. I am more of a Zac Brown Band and Keith Urban fan myself, but I'm not picky. Do you have all that music in your house?" I inquire, curious about her music taste.

"No silly, that's what Pandora's for. You can make your music taste be whatever suits you on any particular day," she answers. "I'm eclectic, so it works well for me." Heather points to her clothes and continues, "My mood can change daily, so I often change my music to match my wardrobe."

"What would you suggest to go with your wardrobe today?" I ask, studying her whimsical outfit.

"Well, that's a good question," she responds thoughtfully putting her finger to her lips as she thinks. "Do you want a country flair or not?" She disappears into the kitchen.

"I'll leave it up to you, you're the one going with the theme and you know where you're heading with dinner," I answer.

Heather yells out from inside the oven, "There are so many good choices. If you wanted country to go with my outfit, you could go with the classics, Loretta Lynn or Patsy Cline. Or if we were just going to stay true to the ambiance, we could choose anyone in the rat pack. Frank Sinatra or Sammy Davis Junior. I particularly love Nat King Cole and Lena Horne."

"Is there any reason we can't put them all in the rotation?" I suggest.

"Nope, that's a great idea," Heather replies as she brings four plates to the table. There are two different appetizers. Each decorated exquisitely. They look like they came out of some fancy food magazine.

"Heather, these look amazing!" I exclaim as I walk over to the table. I pull out her chair and wait for her to sit down. She looks a little surprised by the gesture, but gives me a grateful smile and sits down gracefully.

"Thank you so much. What a gentleman," she murmurs.

"So, what am I eating?" I examine the food in front of me with a sense of trepidation.

"Normally, I would tell you. However, given your food phobias, I think it's better you don't know. I'll tell you when we're all finished. You'll just have to go on blind faith. That was the deal, remember?" she states, but she looks a little nervous.

Darn! I thought she'd forgotten about that part. "Okay, Gidget I'm putting my life in your hands, or at least my taste buds." I pick up the first item that looks like a piece of origami art there is an orangey-red sauce beside it, so I suspect she intends it to be a dipping sauce.

So, I dunk it in and take a bite. It's fried and crunchy on the outside, and the inside has meat with an Asian flair. It's phenomenally tasty. I could eat twenty or thirty of these.

I look up and I see her looking at me expectantly. I shove the bite in my mouth like a kid hoarding the last of the Halloween candy.

"Well?" she asks, raising her eyebrow in question. "Ready to give me a score?"

"A score?" I wheeze as I practically choke. "You're kidding right?"

"Nope." Heather shakes her head sending her golden curls tumbling forward, distracting me. Geez, I'd love to run my fingers through it.

"Do you think I worked half a day for absolutely nothing? If I'm going to work this hard, I want some usable feedback on my recipes," she explains as she hands me a card with five emoticons on it. They range from tears to elation. "Please circle the one that applies to you."

Taking the card from her, I slump in my chair as relief courses through my body. I had expected the test to be much more difficult. This, I can do. I take the marker from her hand I laugh as I get a good look at it. "Sparkly bubblegum?" I ask with a snicker.

"Umm — I don't suppose you'd buy the line that it's Mindy's?" Heather stammers as she blushes.

I chuckle. "Well, I might have until you blushed as pink as the pen, but that's a dead giveaway."

"In my defense, the regular pens stink. You can't judge a girl for wanting to smell good," she pleads with the wink. "I didn't want to smell like a tar pit in the middle of a highway resurfacing project."

"Oh, I'm not arguing with you there. I think it's a beautiful pen, and it suits you perfectly. Most people would use an ordinary pen. I think it's great you choose to use an extraordinary pen for mundane things just because it makes you happy."

Heather looks confused by the conversation as if she can't decide whether I mean it as a compliment or a slight against her character. Finally, she says, "Thank you, I think."

"Yes, Gidget, I very much meant it as a compliment. I admire your free-spirit a great deal. More people should be like you," I respond as I circle the happiest emoticon on the card. "Okay, I'm ready to try the next one. If it's anything like the first one, I'm totally down with the rest of the experiment."

Heather pushes the next plate in front of me. This one has four small golden brown squares on it. It looks like there might be some grated Parmesan cheese on top. There's a little ramekin of red sauce. It smells like marinara sauce. This is a positive development because I love meatball subs. I cautiously pick one up and bite into it. Well, what a surprise! On the inside is some vegetable mixture of spinach and something else green — maybe artichokes with Parmesan and mozzarella cheese. She must be saving the pasta until the later dishes. These are also amazingly delicious. It doesn't take me long to polish off all four.

When Heather sees my expression, she pushes her plate over and says with a grin, "You're welcome to finish off mine too if you want."

I look at her with surprise. "Seriously? Are you sure? These are great!"

"I had some while I was cooking, so I'm not as hungry as you are," Heather admits.

"Okay, if you don't mind, then I don't mind if I do," I reply as I pop one into my mouth.

"I hope you're hungry. I made you an insane amount of food. I wanted you to try a wide variety of things. I hope you brought your appetite."

"Well, my mama still refers to me as a growing boy and claims I still have a hollow leg every time I go back to see her. As a matter of fact, I skipped lunch today because we were out on a call. To say I'm hungry is an understatement. So, bring it on," I say with an exaggerated gesture.

"Okay, give me about twenty minutes and I'll be out with your first course," Heather instructs. "Make yourself comfortable. You can turn on my PlayStation if you want. I've got some games. There's everything in there from Madden Football to Sims 3."

"Sweet! Is this your brother's?" I ask as I choose the Madden football game and settle into the recliner.

"Get real. My brother play video games? Nope, those are mine." Heather responds with a wink. "On another day, I'll beat your pants off. Unfortunately, I'm kind of busy today."

Looking at her with a whole new level of awe and respect, I salute her. "I don't know about that, Gidget. I've had a lot of practice playing video games."

She looks back over her shoulder at me as she walks away, "Who's to say, I haven't, Cowboy?"

Everything I learn about her is a great new surprise that's more interesting than the last. I almost can't wait to see what's next.

"I can't wait for the match up," I challenge. "Should we have a wager on that too?"

I hear Heather laugh from the kitchen as she responds, "I don't know if you can afford to bury yourself in a hole any more than you already have. You're working up a powerful debt with me. Pretty soon, you're going to be practically my love slave."

"All the more reason for me to bet." I respond.

Heather snickers from the other room. "Yeah right, like I've got men tripping all over themselves to be my love slaves. Not on this or any other planet."

"Well, it's not my fault those other guys aren't paying attention to what's right in front of them." It's too bad she's in the other room and can't see that I'm dead serious.

Heather makes a *tsking* noise. "Ty, you don't have to patronize me. I am well aware I don't look like a fashion model and most days I'm okay with it. On the other hand, I also know I'm not going to end up like Ken and Barbie either. I've built a life without all that stuff. Although, I'll admit having Kiera and Jeff around with their perfect little family has made it a little more difficult because all the things I'm going to miss are paraded in front of my face. It makes them a little harder to ignore."

"Gidget, if you knew the things going through my

mind when I think of you, you would go running. I don't want a skinny, twig of a girl who spends far too much time baking herself under a lamp and not enough time eating and being outside. If I did, I could collect those girls any day of the week because they're a dime a dozen. On the other hand, a girl like you — well, let's just say you're a rare commodity. Do you really think Jeff and Kiera really couldn't figure out how to set up their barbecue, their new computer network or the kiddie pool for Mindy?"

"I don't know. Come to think of it, it is unlike Kiera to ask for help with that kind of stuff," Heather mutters under her breath.

"I've been hanging out with them so much because I've been looking for opportunities to be around you. It's just that simple. I can't believe you didn't notice."

It grew strangely quiet for a moment, and all I could hear was the sound of a spoon hitting the side of the pot as she stirs something in the kitchen. I can't imagine what she's thinking regarding my bizarre ramblings. "To be honest, I was beginning to wonder if you have stalker-ish tendencies because you seem to be under my feet everywhere I turn."

A large guffaw of laughter escapes me as I hear her comment because it's not far from the truth. "I can see how it might look that way. I like being around you and I wasn't sure how receptive you would be to the whole dating scene after we got off to such a rough start. Speaking of that, are you interested in dating me?" I ask, immediately kicking myself for my impulsiveness.

"Holy cow, Cowboy! Way to put a girl on the spot.

I think maybe we should wait and see how dinner goes first before making any huge decisions."

"Okay, I'm good with that," I answer, suddenly feeling even more pressure to get over my aversion to pasta. As I load the video game, I take note of her high score, and I realize I was a little too hasty in my assessment of my ability to wipe the floor with her. Now, I'm even more curious about where she developed her video game prowess.

After a few minutes, Heather emerges from the kitchen. Her artfully styled hair is a little worse for the wear as it's now damp and curling at the temples. Her cheeks are rosy red, but her eyes are sparkling. She clearly enjoys this. As she sets a dish down in front of me, I see an oval-shaped ramekin full of what looks like rice. The smells coming from this dish are phenomenal. I love the smell of garlic and onions. It looks like there are also some mushrooms in this dish. I'm ambivalent about mushrooms. I don't love them, but I don't hate them either. It looks like she broiled cheese on the top. Melted cheese is almost always good.

The anticipation is killing me. It looks like this dish will be as amazing as the last two. She holds out a bite for me to try. She's so cute as she blows on it to make sure I don't burn my mouth. My stomach growls as I lean forward to take a bite. Heather giggles as she hears the obnoxiously rude noise.

"I'm so sorry! How rude of me." I murmur as I swallow the heavenly bite. I swear, my eyes practically roll in the back of my head from the amount of positive endorphins in my body. I can't believe I ever thought I didn't like this kind of food. If this is what it tastes like to eat crow, I'll eat it every single day of the week.

Heather laughs at my expression. "Like that, did you? Are you ready for the next one or do you want to wait?" she asks with a wide grin.

I dramatically sigh as I announce, "No, I don't want to wait a second longer than necessary to try any more food. I hereby pronounce you a world-class chef."

Heather curtsies as she replies in her best Elvis impersonation, "Why thank you, thank you very much. I'll be right back with your next dish."

This time when she returns, she is carrying a small casserole dish.

This is just what I feared would happen. Casseroles are the bane of my existence. I have to fight back my gag reflex. It's nothing Heather has done. In fact, the dish she brought out looks delicious. I try to focus on the fact that it smells phenomenal. It has a rich tomato sauce and lots of herbs and spices. I can see lots of melted cheese and smell garlic and onions. I'm trying very hard to push back against decades of ingrained habit.

A look of concern crosses Heather's face as she studies my reaction. "Would you like me to take it away?" she asks softly. "This was only meant to be a silly bet, not a form of torture. If it's that difficult, I'll just stop it all now." She takes a set of hot pads and picks up the offending dish and starts to carry it back to the kitchen.

I grasp her arm to stop her. "Please Gidget, stop. I need to try to do this. It's just a stupid thing I need to overcome. Let me try it. I'm sure it's delicious," I plead.

Heather looks dubious but nods as she murmurs, "Okay if you're sure. But, if you don't like it, you don't need to eat it. You won't hurt my feelings, I swear."

"Heather, you understand this is not about the quality of your cooking, right? It's all about my weird childhood hang-ups," I hasten to reassure her.

"I get that. But, if I'm any good, I should be able to cook in a way that doesn't trigger those emotional cues for you."

"Gidget, I think you're putting too much pressure on yourself. I've had these weird food issues for a long time. No one else has been able to get around them, I think it's a little unrealistic for you to expect that you'll be able to cure me in one single meal."

"Well, you know me. I'm the quintessential optimist, and I'm sure as heck going to give it a try."

"That's true, you are a natural-born-cheerleader. So, I'm going to count on your winning spirit to distract me from my gargantuan sized phobias around eating anything that resembles a casserole."

Heather giggles. "You're flipping out because you think you have to eat casserole? I know I said I wouldn't do this, but let me put your mind at ease. In no way shape or form are you eating a casserole. You are eating freshly made lasagna with handmade pasta noodles and freshly made ricotta cheese. Nothing like anything you probably grew up with and nothing like you can get out of your freezer section in the grocery store. So, if you're trying to avoid the memories of childhood casseroles, I think this is probably as far away from them as you can get."

I find my stomach growling again at the mere

description of the dish in front of me. "It sure sounds completely different from what I remember."

"Are you ready to try again? Would it help if you had some incentive?"

"I don't know, Gidget. I hadn't considered that option. What did you have in mind?"

"I think I'll leave it up to you," Heather responds. "I'm not sure I know you well enough to know what motivates you."

"I have a few ideas, but I'm not sure what you'll think of them," I reply, feeling only slightly guilty.

Heather is immediately suspicious — and rightly so. "Dare I ask what you've come up with?"

"Well, since this is going to be so difficult for me, I think I would like a kiss for every bite I take."

Heather looks a little stunned by my proposal. But, then she bursts out laughing. "Uh-huh, I can imagine you do. But, see I drive a hard bargain too. So, I want to know what's in this deal for me," she counters.

I give her a look of mock outrage and hurt. "Well, me of course. I've been told that I'm an excellent kisser. You wouldn't want to miss out on that experience. Besides that, you won't get a more honest opinion of your lasagna than mine."

Much to my shock, Heather shrugs and announces, "Sure, as long as I get to pick the placement and duration, I'm game."

I'm almost certain I didn't hear her correctly, so I try to clarify what she said, "Are you sure Gidget? I want to be a gentleman here."

"I'm sure. I don't ever take a gamble I don't feel comfortable with or a bet I don't intend to win," she clarifies. "Besides, I'm trying to help you here. You have the most to lose in this situation."

"Then, by all means consider me incentivized," I say with a grin. Before I lose my nerve, I grab a fork and take a bite. To my relief, it has none of the spongy, mealy taste I have long associated with casserole and lasagna. In fact, that overly squishy library-paste-type texture that was present in every pasta dish I remember my mom ever making is just not there. Instead, it's warm and cheesy and flavorful. Eating this is not going to be nearly as difficult as I had anticipated. Given our current wager, I'm not sure how quickly I'll clue Heather into my new state of mind. It might be fun to draw the situation out just a little while longer. A sympathetic Heather might be a little more fun to play with.

I chew my food carefully and swallow it with deliberation. I carefully take a sip of my iced tea and hold my mouth open like a five-year-old for her to inspect.

She laughs at my antics, pats me on the head and compliments me by saying, "Very good." She proceeds to reward me by kissing me chastely on the cheek.

"That wasn't what I had in mind, Darlin'," I remark, "but I guess it'll do for a start."

I pick up another fork from the table and dish up a bite for her and feed it to her. After she chews and swallows, I praise her, "Very good, Gidget."

Heather snorts with laughter. "Very clever." She presents her cheek for me to kiss. Gallantly, I place a light kiss on her beautiful cheek even though I'd like much more. Her skin is as soft as a rose petal.

Mentally, I fast-forward the game a few more steps in my head and decide that it could get interesting. Suddenly, whether I like or dislike pasta has become largely immaterial in the grand scheme of things.

Apparently deciding this is a fun game of tit-for-tat, Heather takes my fork from me and serves up another bite. As I try to maneuver it off of the fork without making a huge mess, I notice her eyes darken, and her nostrils flare. Who knew something as simple as taking a bite of food could be so sensual? Instinctively, I move toward her. Initially, she seems caught up in the same spell. But, then she blinks and backs away slightly.

Taking the tactful hint, I make a theatrical production of presenting my other cheek for her to kiss. She is seemingly grateful for the choice as she gives me an exaggerated smack leaving a large lipstick ring on my cheek, which she proceeds to dab off with the napkin leaving a perfect impression. When she turns away to get me a piece of garlic bread, I tuck the napkin away in my pocket for safekeeping.

I break off a piece of the bread and give it to her, and when her lips touch my fingers, it's quite distracting — which I suppose is the whole point of the exercise. But, it's enough to make a man wearing jeans quite uncomfortable.

"Would you like more lasagna?" I ask as I pick up her fork, preparing to give her a bite.

"Oh, no thank you," she answers. "I had more than enough to eat today. I'm stuffed. I really couldn't take another bite."

I shake my head in frustration. "Gidget, didn't we have this conversation about you having what you want to eat because you want it not because someone tells you it's the right thing to eat?"

Heather shakes her head. "Relax, Cowboy. This time it doesn't have anything to do with my body image. I'm just ridiculously full. Do you know how much I eat when I'm cooking?"

"Okay, I guess I'll climb off my high horse. I didn't think about that. Are you sure you're not just claiming you're full so I don't get to kiss you?"

Heather wrinkles her nose at me. "Yes, I'm positive. I don't welch on my bets. If it makes you feel any better, you can still kiss me as if I've taken the bites."

"Oh, Darlin' that would most definitely make me feel better." I tease. "The question is would it make you feel better?"

"I don't know. It's still a little early to tell."

"Well, I've got nowhere pressing to be. Do you?" I respond in a teasing voice.

"I'll have to see how well you do. I still reserve the right to need to wash my hair," Heather replies, flipping her gorgeous mane of hair over her shoulder.

My eyebrows raise in surprise. "Do women really use that excuse?"

"Cowboy, you never want to be in a situation to find out. Because if you've ever heard it, it's time to hit the panic button for sure."

"Really?" I ask, thinking of all the lame excuses I've heard over the years. "What about 'I have to change the oil on my bosses' car.'?"

"Possible, but also unlikely. I'd call the BS card."

"I have to give the dog a bath?" I venture, certain I already know the answer.

"Definitely a stalling technique," Heather answers with a look of pity. "What are you doing to these poor women? It seems like you've had every line in the book used against you."

I hold up my palms in a gesture of innocence. "Nothing! I swear I'm a nice guy. Maybe too nice, I don't know. I'll admit I can be sarcastic sometimes, but at my core I am just a Southern gentleman with Midwestern roots. I guess I feel out of step with a lot of people. I feel like I need an updated rule book for dating. The one I was raised with doesn't seem to cover the real world anymore."

"I think we all feel that way. Dating is a nightmare" Heather cuts up another bite for me to eat.

"That sounds like there may be a personal story there—" I reply and wait for her to fill in the rest of the story.

"Oh Lord, Cowboy, you don't have time for all of my stories that fit that scenario," Heather admits, rolling her eyes in a self-deprecating manner. "If we hang out together long enough, I'm sure you'll hear about most of them. I'm legendary in the epic-relationship-fail department. In fact, they could probably write one of those semi-tragic romantic comedies about my sad, pathetic life."

"You had me fooled. You have one of the best

attitudes about life I've ever seen," I remark.

"Don't feel bad, that's how it's supposed to sound. I've had years of practice pretending to be things I'm not. It's pretty much second nature to me. Sometimes, it's hard for even me to draw a distinction between the real Heather Lydia LaBianca and the one that was invented to make people happy." She looks at me and raises the signature eyebrow in question and waves the fork in my direction as she asks, "Bite?"

"Sure, why not?" I reply with a shrug as I open my mouth and take a large bite. "At this point, the benefits far outweigh the costs."

Heather gives a chirp of laughter as she responds, "Tyler Joseph Colton, no wonder your dating life is on the skids. Your table manners are abominable. You shouldn't be talking with your mouth full, even if it is with my food. I don't even know your mama and I know she taught you better than that."

Already envisioning a meeting between Heather and my mom, I smile. It would be a wild pairing, regardless of how you slice it. I certainly wouldn't get away with much with those two women in my life. I snicker as I respond, "Yes, she did teach me that and virtually everything else good I know in life. So, I owe you an apology for being so rude as to talk with my mouth full. I should say, 'I'm sorry, please forgive me.' — or words to that effect."

Heather gives a small sigh. "Well, I suppose I can forgive you for being a momentary brute if you can forgive me for being too much of a mother hen. Sometimes, I can sound a bit like a kindergarten teacher instead of a friend or a girlfriend."

"Oh, does this conversation officially establish that we're dating?" I ask in a teasing voice. I've never been so eager to establish a relationship with someone faster than I am with her. I'm not sure what it is about her that made me flip the 'commitment' switch, but for the first time in my life, I'm not looking for excuses to run away from it but rather for ways to make it happen.

"Tyler Colton! You give the word pushy a whole new meaning. We haven't even eaten dessert yet. I've figured out part of the reason you get so many excuses from women. It's not because you're not a nice guy, it's because you're completely overwhelming. Everything about you is big and bold. From your size and mannerisms, to your pronouncements. You might want to try taking it down a notch or two. I have a hunch you might be a little more successful if you backed off a little."

"Point taken, I suppose," I concede. "But, I'm a take-charge kind of guy by nature. I mean, look at my professional life. Choose any of them. I'm a soldier. I'm a law enforcement officer and for fun, I wrangle wild horses. I'm not exactly the shy-and-retiring type."

"Tyler, don't get me wrong. I'm not asking you to change your personality or who you are. I'm just suggesting you temper your approach. When you're on a call for the police department do you approach every situation with the same intensity?" Heather asks.

"No, of course not," I answer. "One of the things I love about my job is the fact that every situation is different."

"Well, I don't mean this as criticism, but sometimes your laser focused attention, and enthusiasm can be overwhelming. Maybe, if you took time to take a better reading of what was going on in the room, you would get a better response," Heather replies tentatively.

I consider her answer and realize she's more accurate than I'd like to admit. "Heather, I'm sorry."

"That's okay Ty," Heather says, as she lightly pats my shoulder. "Just, try to go in with a softer approach. It's all I'm saying."

"So, you're sayin' this probably isn't the time for me to collect my reward for taking my bite?" I jest.

"No!" she immediately protests, "I did not suggest forfeiting the bet, Cowboy. I still plan to win."

"Oh, is that so?" I ask, amused at the competitiveness in her voice. "Perhaps I need to step up my strategic approach."

"Mmm hmm, do whatever you feel you need to do," she offers magnanimously. "But, my skill will beat strategy every time. So, you might be thinking about your possible penalties. Because it's only a matter of time until I'm victorious."

"You'll pardon me if I don't focus on the penalties right now. I'd rather focus my energies on the positive features of the bet. Right now, that would include the fact that I earned myself the reward of kissing you," I say as I walk over and stand in front of her. She pulls her apron up over her head and takes it off in one fell swoop. When I'm a couple feet away, I reach out and cup her chin.

As I gaze into her crystal blue eyes, I murmur, "You

are simply stunning, Gidget. I think I would eat anything in your whole kitchen for the pleasure of doing this —"

It is at that point, I make the riskiest move I've made all night. I thought the scariest thing I was going to do was to eat pasta. But, this is by far the most heart-pounding thing I've done. Our relationship runs so hot and cold that it's hard for me to tell how Heather feels about me. Sometimes, I could swear that she thinks I'm her worst enemy. Other times, I think she's really into me. So, this move is going to be the ultimate litmus test. Unfortunately, it's also going to be one from which I can't gracefully retreat if it doesn't go well. It's an all-or-nothing move for me. After this, all my cards are on the table. My intentions will be very clear. It seems rather counterproductive after she's just told me I need to tone it down, but I feel like I need to make a bold statement.

Slowly, I lean in and kiss her gently on the lips. Since this is our first kiss, I try to be a gentleman and show some proper restraint. But, her reaction makes it difficult. As I kiss her, her long lashes drift shut, and she gasps lightly. When we pull apart, I can feel soft puffs of breath on my neck, and I can see her pulse beating quickly near her collar bone.

"Wow, Cowboy. You sure can make a girl swoon," Heather comments, as she catches her breath. "I can see how this could get addicting. If that's the reward, I might have to keep cooking. Are you ready for dessert?"

"That's funny" I tease, "I think I just had dessert."

Heather groans.

"No, it's true. You're sweet and completely addicting. I want more and more of you. It sounds like you have all the prerequisites of really good dessert," I comment.

"Oh you're so good. A girl could just melt." Heather concedes. "You might have a point. But, in this case, I did make dessert. I believe you'll think it's scrumptious."

"Okay cool. I like dessert in any form," I reply as I lick my lips in anticipation.

Heather leaves to go into the kitchen again. I admire the view as she walks away, gently swaying her hips.

When she returns, she is carrying a tray of artfully designed tarts. Immediately, I recognize chocolate and almonds. I breathe a sigh of relief at the familiar ingredients. I can deal with these. But, then I spot the shells. My stomach tightens I remember facing these little suckers down as a kid in my mom's version of mac-n-cheese. The memory isn't a pleasant one. I take a deep breath and try to keep my thoughts focused on the here and now. This lovely creation is not the nightmare concoction from my past. It's likely to be a delightful morsel just like everything else I have tried today. I swallow hard and reach to pick one up.

Heather reaches out to stop me as she lifts one toward my mouth, "Please allow me," she offers.

Gingerly, I take a bite. Heather swipes my bottom lip with her thumb. The unexpected contact makes me jump.

She winks and grins as she shows me the trace of brown on her thumb. "Sorry, you had a bit of cocoa powder on your mouth," she explains.

"Darlin', you can touch me anywhere, any place, any time you please," I quip.

Heather blushes and pulls her hand away. "You may need to work on your 'toning it down' skills a bit," she instructs.

"I understand what you mean. I am just choosing to disregard your instructions because they don't fit my overall objective. In this situation, I think my approach will work best," I advise.

"Oh my word, Tyler!" Heather exclaims. "I can see why you were getting the Encyclopedia of Brush-Off Lines from women. You're just choosing to be tone deaf."

"I am not," I argue defensively. "I think you need something different from me."

"It's amazing you don't get crushed under the weight of that ego you're carrying around," Heather remarks with a smirk.

I flash her my most winning smile. "Look, I'm not trying to be a jerk here. I'm a confident guy by nature. Once I set a course of action, I rarely second-guess my decision. I can admit that you proved me wrong about the pasta stuff. It's hard for a guy like me to admit that I've been wrong my whole entire life. I enjoyed the lasagna. Who would've thought you could have converted a person like me into a pasta lover?"

Abruptly, Heather breaks out into peals of laughter. When she finally stops, I raise my eyebrow in question. As soon as she catches her breath and can talk, she finally wheezes out, "Boy, have I got a surprise for you."

Trepidation fills me as I see her expression. "What

are you not telling me?"

"Cowboy, you ate pasta in every course tonight. Well, technically not every course because risotto is rice, but it's a close cousin."

To say I'm stunned is an understatement. I had an idea about some of it because I saw the pasta shells in the dessert, but she did a great job of disguising the rest of it. "Seriously?" I probe incredulously. "Even in the Asian thing-a-ma-bob?"

Heather answers with a wide grin, "Yep. That was a chicken wonton. A wonton wrapper is a form of pasta. It was brown and crispy because I fried it."

"Well, it was a total home run. It's safe to say I loved it. What about the little square things?" I ask, curious now about her method of disguising pasta into unrecognizable forms.

"Those were homemade spinach and artichoke ravioli with Gorgonzola and Parmesan cheese with a marinara dipping sauce. I deep fat fried those too. Because every good chef knows most things taste better fried."

"Without ruining any of your trade secrets, how did you make your lasagna so it wasn't all squishy and gross? That was always my biggest objection to pasta before. I couldn't get beyond the texture. But nothing you fixed me tonight had any of the sliminess I remember. That's what I find so amazing about what you did."

Heather blushes a little under the compliments. But, then she gives me a serious answer, "I think it's a combination of things. This is my craft. I work hard at it. I studied hard to learn the science behind the food. Then, there is the art of cooking which is that immeasurable part of cooking you can't quantify. It's what turns us into food artists. In the case of the lasagna, I think it's because I rolled pasta very thin, seasoned it well and I made sure it didn't overcook. Overcooked pasta tends to be mushy and lose its texture. Al dente means 'to the tooth' it's supposed to have a little body left in it when you cook it."

"You know, I'm starting to feel a little guilty for all the times I go out to eat and just scarf down my meal without even considering all the work involved. Or, even worse the times that my mom made an elaborate dinner and I blew her off to go hang out with my friends or something," I confess.

Heather runs her fingertips over my brow as she instructs, "Cowboy, don't look so sad. I felt the same way when I started culinary school. It's easy to overlook the people who work behind the scenes. I can tell you I'm a much better tipper than I was before I started this whole journey even though I'm much poorer now. My empathy factor has gone off the charts."

"What do you mean you're much poorer now?" I ask, still confused about Heather's complex background. I've tried asking Jeff about her history, but he was circumspect, telling me if I wanted to know anything, I would have to ask Heather directly. I was pretty surprised by his approach because usually he's pretty free with information if I like someone. I figured it probably has to do with the fact that Heather is one of Kiera's best friends, and Jeff didn't want to get stuck in the middle.

"Oh, it's just one of my dad's little quirks. He didn't think culinary school was worthy of the LaBianca name.

So, after I withdrew from business school, he cut me off. I've had to pursue this dream on my own. I guess in many ways, I'm grateful for this because I get to take complete ownership of everything that happens from here on out. So, if one day I get to open a restaurant or a bakery, my dad won't have any say in it." The look on her face is so profoundly sad that I'm not even sure what to say. My parents have never been well off, but they've always been supportive of whatever I wanted to do no matter how hare-brained or stupid my plans have turned out to be. They were profoundly disappointed in me when I destroyed my chance at my college scholarship by being repeatedly busted for underage drinking. But even then, I knew if the chips were down, they would be behind me. I can't imagine what it would feel like if I knew I couldn't count on my parents.

"Gidget, after what I saw tonight I have no doubt that someday you will make it huge in the food industry. I don't know if you'll have some big-name restaurant or a show on the Food Network but in some capacity you're going to be huge. I know it. I hope you believe it too." Somehow, it's become critically important to me that Heather knows I believe in her dreams.

Heather sighs as she admits, "Today was the most fun I've had cooking in a long time. No one has challenged me in a while. I like to cook for the simple joy of cooking. It's nice to be recognized for being good at what I do." Heather starts to clear the table. She seems surprised when I stand to help.

"Heather, you are more than just good, you're amazing."

"Thanks, I wish my family could recognize that I am as good at this as they are in the business world. It's just a different arena. Just because it's different doesn't mean it's inferior. I can't seem to get my father to understand. My dad thinks because it's not a nine to five job, somehow it doesn't count. As much as I hate to admit it, somewhere deep inside me, the little girl who wanted to be daddy's Little Princess still wants to get his seal of approval. So, as happy as working in this field makes me, I know I'll probably never be happy because I can't ever get my family's seal of approval. How twisted is that?" Heather worries her bottom lip until all of her lipstick is gone.

Having never met her father, it may be a little early for me to make a character assessment. But seriously, who is he to decide whether her career choice is worthy of his stamp of approval? Has he seen what some of those famous chefs make and even some of the not so famous ones? Forget that — has he even tasted the food his daughter makes? That in and of itself should be enough to convince him of her skill level.

"Well, I think you deserve a huge reward for all you accomplished today, and you did win the bet fair and square. In fact, you won it several times over. So, Gidget what have you decided to name as your prize?" I ask, waiting with great anticipation to see what she might collect from me.

Chapter Six

Heather

"Remember, I told you that even though I wasn't eating, we would play this game as if I were? I still owe you some kisses," I inform Ty as he lounges in the kitchen chair trying his best to look casual. He reminds me of Mindy when I tell her I have a surprise for her but she has to wait until later to find out what it is. The look of shock on his face is priceless.

"Umm, okay. I can handle that. But are you sure that's what you want your prize to be?" he asks, the confusion clear on his face. He almost needs a thought bubble above his head like a cartoon.

"Relax Cowboy. I won't ravish you here in my kitchen. I'm just squaring stuff up with our bet so everything is even-steven."

Ty grins at me with a lascivious grin as he challenges, "Oh, by all means feel free to ravish away."

"I don't know if I'll go quite that far, but I'd like to give you a few well-deserved kisses for all of those wonderful compliments you've been handing out like

Christmas candy. You sure know how to make a girl feel great." Now, the challenge is how to accomplish my idea. The logistics are tricky. Ty is a huge mountain of a guy. It's not as if I can just climb him to get to those amazing addictive lips, and I'm far too big to cuddle on his lap.

Ty must've noticed my look of consternation. He gives me a crooked smile and sits up straighter in his chair. He plants his feet further apart and spreads his knees making a place for me to stand. Drawing me closer to him, he murmurs, "Com're and make yourself comfortable, Darlin'. No need to strain that gorgeous neck of yours."

I step into the opening, feeling self-conscious about my size. I wonder if Ty will notice how wide my hips are compared to his muscular thighs. As this script of self-doubt is running through my head, I look over at Tyler and notice him looking at me with an expression of pure lust and desire. The intellectual side of me kicks in and tells me I should feel objectified and cheapened, but then my inner goddess tells it to shut up and bask in the inherent complement present in the sizzling look.

The intensity of his gaze makes me squirm. To be honest, I'm really not used to anyone thinking I'm particularly sexy. A few people have said I'm pretty. But, most people qualify their complement with the caveat that I would be prettier if I lost weight. So, before I lose my nerve, I carefully place a kiss directly on his lips. As far as moves go, this is bold for me. For a man with such hard edges, his lips are remarkably soft and responsive. He smells fresh, like laundry that's been hung outside to dry. He shifts his head and changes the pressure on my lips. The change is minute, but it seems to hit a pressure point for me. Unbidden, a moan escapes from me. I'm startled by the noise.

Tyler pulls away and rests his forehead against mine. He's breathing a little heavy as he murmurs, "If we can generate that much of a spark with a simple kiss. It's mind-boggling to consider the possibilities down the road."

I nod slightly, moving his head along with mine. "The idea of us together is a little daunting, isn't it?"

Tyler grins widely. The man is gorgeous close up. "Yeah, but I don't do boring, remember? Exciting is my middle name."

"Actually, your middle name is Joseph, but that's neither here nor there. You do realize there is a chance of spectacular failure, right?"

Tyler kisses the end of my nose. "Who's the pessimist now? I'm just not willing to go there. As the saying goes, 'I'm in my happy place right now.' Don't bug me. Now, you were about to tell me what your real wager is going to be. I'm looking forward to this."

I back away and put some personal space between us, but Tyler grabs my apron strings to anchor me in place.

"Hold on there. Where are you goin'? I like you just fine right where you are."

"Um, I guess I'm not going anywhere," I stammer as I blush. I remember Kiera used to complain all the time about how much she blushed when she first met Jeff and how much it annoyed her. I didn't understand what she was talking about at the time, but I'm getting a sense of it now. I don't think I've blushed as much in my whole life as I have in the few months since I've met Tyler. I feel like my body is suddenly betraying me. I don't know what's happening.

"So what was it you wanted again?" Ty prods, a curious expression on his face.

"Look, I don't even know if you can do this with your job with the Sheriff's Department and I don't want you to get in trouble over it."

"Wow, with the build up like that, I can't wait to hear what it is. Don't hold me in suspense any longer. Just spit it out," Tyler challenges.

"Okay, okay. It's really stupid. Promise not to laugh? I want you to teach me how to shoot," I reply, cringing despite my best intentions.

Tyler's eyebrows shoot to his hairline as he exclaims "A gun?"

"Yes, of course, a gun! What did you think I meant?" I sputter with a scowl on my face, placing my hands on my hips.

"I'm just curious why you think you need to be able to shoot a gun," Ty states as he studies my demeanor.

Well, his dismissive comment makes me mad, so I tell him so. "Shall we examine my life during the last two years? A couple of weeks ago, someone broke into my food truck and left behind a few souvenir bullet casings. Not to mention this was the second time this year my truck was vandalized, and I actually could've been inside. Then there was the crazy ex-father-in-law who went on a rampage at Kiera's wedding. If that weren't bad enough there are Mindy's biological parents who are child abusers and drug addicts. Who's to say they won't come after her and Becca and try to take them back? Isn't that enough craziness in my life to justify the need to be armed?"

Tyler rakes his hand through his hair in an agitated manner. "I wish it were that easy, Gidget. But, you have to get a concealed weapon permit, and there's a waiting period before you can purchase a weapon. You will probably need your own weapon because the ones I have will be too large for you."

I walk over to the freezer and get my keys out. I go over to the pantry and remove a lockbox. After I unlock it, I remove the contents and place them on the table in front of Tyler. "You mean like this?" I ask.

I wish I had a video camera to capture Tyler's reaction. I figure it's roughly equivalent to how I look when I go visit the vintage clothing store in Portland. His eyes widen, and his jaw goes slack. Ty gives a low wolf whistle as he carefully picks up my 1849 Derringer. He practically caresses it as he checks the chamber to make sure there are no bullets loaded, and he grins as he spins the cylinder. He closely examines the elaborate filigree engraving and snow white mother-of-pearl handgrips and checks the date stamp and shakes his head in disbelief.

"Do I need to give you a moment?" I ask with a teasing grin.

"I don't know, I might just need one. Do you have any idea what you have here? It's in pristine condition. Did I see you pull this out of your freezer?"

"No silly! Who would keep a gun in the freezer? I only keep the keys to the lockbox in the freezer. I don't want the bad guys to find them."

"Where did you get this? It's a museum quality piece," Tyler states.

"My grandpa gave it to me. It's been in my family for years. He said every woman should be able to defend herself. Unfortunately, he passed away before he had a chance to teach me much about shooting. I only got to go target shooting with him twice. The first time, he said he feared for his life because I couldn't hit the broadside of a barn. But, by the end of the second time, I had gotten much better and was murdering watermelons with frightening ease." I explain.

"He let you shoot this gun? This specific gun? How old were you?" he asks incredulously.

"I don't know, I guess I was about twelve," I clarify. "Why? It's not like I'm a mass murderer or anything. We were shooting at soda cans and watermelons in the middle of his field against a barrier made of hay."

"Gidget, I wasn't casting any aspersions on you. It's just that in the condition that this gun is in, it's pretty much a priceless antique. If you would've dropped it in the dirt or something, you could've done irreparable damage to it. I'm just surprised he would take that kind of risk."

I raise my eyebrow at Tyler. "Well, I was a cute kid, maybe I was overly persuasive."

Tyler's eyes sparkle with mirth. "You're still pretty cute. But, I wouldn't recommend using this gun. If I can find you a suitable replacement, would you consider using a different gun? I think I can find you a modern version of the same gun and let you enjoy the sentimental value of this one."

"Really?" I ask, excitement tinging my voice. "Does this mean you'll teach me how to shoot?"

"Of course I am," Ty answers as he gingerly places my gun back in the lockbox. "A deal is a deal. Besides, you have a valid point. If you feel threatened, you should be able to defend yourself. And if you're planning to carry a gun, you should be properly trained to use it. There is nothing scarier than someone who feels they should carry a gun but doesn't bother to get the proper training. Do me a favor, though, don't ever show Mindy you keep the keys to the lockbox in the freezer. You wouldn't believe how many gun related incidents I go on with the Sheriff's Department that involve family members. By the way, I give you points for a creative hiding space. I would have never guessed that the container didn't hold frozen orange juice."

"For the record, I'm going to state again that I'm not a bimbo. There's a reason I hide the keys and keep the gun in the lock box. I may live alone, but I'm not stupid. I know I have kids coming in and out of my house. It won't be long before Becca is as curious as Mindy."

Tyler has the grace to look chagrined. "I'm sorry. It's one of the hazards of the job. Sometimes, I forget that I'm not always on duty. If I get this way, you can always tell me to shut up and just remind me I'm not always Officer Colton. Sometimes I'm just Ty."

Tyler looks so sad and dejected, I feel like I need to do something to remind him this is a casual setting and he's not on duty right now. So, I step away from the table and back between his legs. I run my hands lightly down the sides of his face, along his angular cheekbones and capture his face between my hands. Then, I slowly kiss him. "There … does that help you remember that I'm on a date with Tyler Colton the private citizen, not Officer Colton, law enforcement officer extraordinaire," I ask when we finally surface for air.

"Holy smokes, Gidget," Ty exclaims as he shifts in his chair. "I may never forget or forget every day depending on what gets me more of that. That was incredibly sexy. I think it was dangerously hot because I completely forgot what we're talking about or why. I want more kisses like that."

The honesty of his response is a huge turn on for me. I meant the kiss to be just a comfort measure, not something more, but my body doesn't seem to be listening. I try to collect my thoughts. "Shooting lessons. We were talking about scheduling shooting lessons for me. I'd like some, please. Given all the craziness that's gone on in my life recently, I think sooner would be better than later, don't you think?"

"Probably so, Heather. But, for you to get any use out of it at the food truck, you need a concealed weapon permit," Ty replies.

"Oh, I've got one of those. I've had it for a while. I got it back when the first break-in happened. I don't like it when weirdness happens in my life. I want to be able to protect myself and especially Mindy and Becca if I'm babysitting."

Tyler looks at me with concern on his face, "Gidget, if you were so freaked out, why didn't you say something to me before? We could have taken care of this months ago," he offers.

I blush again. Darn that stupid blushing. "I guess I didn't want you to see me as some crazy hysterical female who couldn't handle my own problems. So, I didn't say anything. I wish I'd said something much sooner because I haven't been sleeping well since the first incident and since we found bullets during the second one, I have turned into a real insomniac. Every time I shut my eyes, I think about what would've happened if I had been there. Even worse, what if the girls had been visiting me? Sometimes, if it's an in-service day at school, Mindy comes and volunteers to be my cashier. She rakes in the tips better than any veteran waitress I've ever seen. But, if we had been in the truck at the time that the bullets were fired, they could have been hurt. Mindy would be heartbroken if she had to stop coming," I explain, spilling all my words in a rush. It seems like I've been holding in my feelings for months now, and it feels cathartic to let them out even for a moment. I guess I didn't realize how much I've been keeping inside.

"Gidget, we got those guys remember? I don't think they'll be bugging you anymore. You just happened to park your truck in the wrong place at the wrong time," Ty says in a calm and reassuring voice. "But, I'll be happy to take you to the gun range so you'll feel better prepared."

"I wish I had Tara's kick ass self-defense skills. Have you seen her in action? She could give Jackie Chan a run for his money. But, I can't move this big ole' body like she can."

"First of all, you're not all that big. Secondly,

comparing yourself to Tara is really not fair because Tara has had tons of classes. Does she compare her cooking to yours?"

I practically choke on a snort of laughter. "I should hope not. If it weren't for Kiera and me that girl would starve to death. Cooking is not her primary gift. She knows her way around the can opener and a box cutter, but that's about it."

"Do you judge her for that?" Ty asks, his eyebrow raised in question.

"Of course not! She didn't even have a mom to teach her how to cook. So, it would be mean as well as stupid to compare our situations."

Tyler grabs my hands and holds them between us as he states firmly, "Exactly. So, tell me, sweet Gidget. Why are you so nice to everyone else and so mean to yourself?"

His question brings me up short. He's absolutely right. I am so willing to cut everyone else a break yet shred myself to pieces for the smallest thing. I'm not exactly sure how he knows that about me. It's not really something I willingly show to the world, but he seems to have figured it out, nonetheless.

I look up at him. He's clearly still waiting for an answer. I decide to be brutally honest when usually I would deflect with silly humor. "I don't know," I whisper.

"I wish you could see the beautiful woman I see when I look at you," Ty softly kisses the top of my head. "Let me help you with these dishes. I can't imagine how many you probably have to do after cooking all that food."

Just then my phone rings. My heart sinks when I recognize my father's ringtone. It's never a fun phone call from him. What a way to put a damper on a great night.

CHAPTER SEVEN

TYLER

HEATHER'S PHONE RINGS, BREAKING the mood. Her face contorts into a sad frown when she recognizes the ringtone. She puts her index finger to her lip to indicate she needs to take the call. I take the hint and head to the kitchen.

As soon as I hear her sobbing I run around the corner as if the house is on fire and kneel at her feet. "Heather, what's wrong? Are you hurt?" I probe as I pull out my small flashlight and examines her arms and legs for injuries.

Mutely, she shakes her head as tears are streaming down her face. Heather draws in a deep breath and tries to explain. "No, it's my grandma. She d-d-died."

"Aww, Gidget, I'm so sorry. That's rough. Mine died when I was in Iraq the second time." I take my hand and lead her over to the big recliner chair. I sit down and pull her down onto my lap. I wrap her up in a huge bear hug and allow her to sob on my shoulder while I hold her tightly.

When she calms a bit, she says, "This used to be my grandfather's chair. It was the first piece of furniture my grandparents bought together back in the day. After my grandfather died, I paid to have it shipped from Texas and saved up the money to have it recovered in a style similar to the original brown leather my grandfather had in his den. I remember my grandmother telling me stories of how she used to nurse my mom in this chair. My poor grandma spent so much time trying to teach me how to embroider and cross stitch while I sat Indian style in the huge leather chair. Now, you're hugging me in this same chair, it seems as if it's my last tangible connection to my grandparents." She pauses before she mumbles into my shirt, "Do you think a brain aneurysm hurts?"

"No Darlin', she might've had a headache. But, it's a fast way to go."

Her shoulders slump with relief. "I couldn't bear it if I thought she suffered. She lived such a bright and shiny life that she would not have coped with pain well. She had a sister who had Lou Gehrig's disease and she watched her lose all function. She always told me she never wanted to live that way. I'm grateful that she passed quickly, but I'm so sad that I never got a chance to say goodbye. I kept promising her I'd have pictures taken with Mindy and the rest of the Girlfriend Posse so she could see us being silly. But, we never seemed to find the time to do it. Now, we'll never have that chance. I'm kicking myself that I didn't take the time on a Sunday afternoon to take Mindy to the mall." As she talks, a fresh round of tears overtakes her.

"It's okay. You had no idea this was going to happen." I just hold her a bit tighter and murmur words of comfort in her ear as I rock her slowly.

The shrill tone of Heather's phone breaks the oppressive silence again, but she's sobbing too hard to answer it. I look at her with a questioning gaze. She nods at me indicating her permission for me to answer her phone. She curls up into a ball and retreats into her emotional cocoon.

After a few minutes, I stroke her hair and murmur, "Gidget, babe, do you want to talk to Tara?"

She nods tearfully.

I look at her face and dig into my pocket. I pull out an old-fashioned cloth handkerchief. "Heather, come on blow Darlin'. You'll feel better," I cajole.

Heather shakes her head. "I can't do that. I'll get your handkerchief all gross."

I chuckle lightly. "Well, Gidget, that's kind of what they're for. I really don't mind. I've got a drawer full of them. I put this one in my pocket this morning. It's clean. Go ahead. I won't even watch."

True to my word, I turn my head away as she blows her nose. When she's finished, I hand her the phone.

"Hello?" she answer tentatively after she puts the phone on speaker.

"What's wrong?" Tara demands.

"I just found out my grandma died of a brain aneurysm." Saying it out loud brings a fresh round of tears.

"I'm so sorry to hear about Lydia Rose, but I'm glad you're not hurt," Tara says in a rush. "Aidan and I are in a time crunch, but I wouldn't stop pestering him until he let me check on you. I knew something wasn't right. Are you going to be okay?"

"Tara, I can't believe she's gone. We just had a Skype call with her a few weeks ago remember? Mindy did her little recital piece for her. I feel so guilty that we didn't have those stupid pictures taken," Heather laments.

"I didn't know your grandma well, but from what I did know of her, she wouldn't want you to feel guilty over something as silly as that. She would want you to celebrate all the good times you had together. She was a lot like you — you know. Fearless to take on life and always up for a new adventure. She was always supportive of her friends in her gardening and quilting clubs. Remember how she learned how to use Skype and Facebook so she could promote her friends businesses. You should be proud."

Heather smiles at the memories. "My grandma was a pistol for sure. I'm flattered you think I'm anything like her. That's the biggest compliment anyone can give me. I hope she is proud of me and I hope she's happy with grandpa now."

"I bet they're up there swing dancing by now," Tara answers. I can hear the warm smile in her voice.

"I hope so. Remember how excited Grandma was when she found out you were a dancer? She always bragged about the Arthur Murray dance classes she and my grandfather had taken when they were engaged. They used it as a socially acceptable reason to touch each other in an era when it wasn't allowed. My grandfather was so proud of himself for finding a way of getting around my grandma's dad."

"Yeah, I love that story. I have to go because Aidan and I are about to get on a plane, so I'll talk to you when you get back" Tara says as I hear the overhead speakers blaring in the background. "If you need anything, call me. You should talk to Kiera. She would want to know what's going on. Someday soon, you're going to have to let me know what's going on between you and the Cowboy."

Heather blushes bright red. "Okay, I promise. We'll have lunch when I get back from Texas. Have a nice flight."

As she pushes the end button on her phone, I study her with great interest. "Dare I ask why her question made you flush as red as a rooster comb?"

My question makes her blush even more. "Tara asked about the state of our relationship and I wasn't expecting that," Heather mumbles sheepishly.

————————————————"I was so shocked, I couldn't think of anything to say. I basically punted. I don't think we have a relationship status yet to be define. I define us as I always have — confusing. How do you define us?"

"I don't find our relationship confusing at all." It's simple. I like you."

She looks at me with a befuddled expression on her face. "What about the fact that we spend half our time arguing?"

"Gidget, it doesn't bother me if we have a few fireworks between us. They just keep things interesting. If we got along like two peas in a pod, things would surely get boring in a hurry, don't you think? If we have differences of opinion, then there are endless things to talk about and discuss," I explain with a casual shrug.

She glances at me with a dubious expression. "Okay, that might explain our conversations, but it doesn't explain why you act like you hate me sometimes."

"I'm not angry at you. I'm angry with myself for not being able to control my reaction to you. I've been trying to get my head in the right space for a relationship for a while. To be honest, I wasn't looking to find anybody. Yet, there you were looking all hot and gorgeous everywhere I turned. I was still prepared to ignore you, and I was doing a pretty good job of it. But you turned out to be as sweet as apple pie and you wore down my defenses."

"That's just weird," she mutters. "You can't control your body's reactions."

I sigh and scrub my hand down my face in frustration. "Let me try to explain. At first, it made me angry. I thought maybe Jeff and Kiera had told you my story, and you were trying to be the perfect girl to get past my walls and then just hurt me like all the others. But, then Jeff set me straight and told me they had said nothing to you and that you were just being yourself. Then, I saw how you came through for Gwendolyn and Donda in their crisis. You truly impressed me. It took a lot for me to look past my preconceptions of you, but when I did, I liked what I saw. I wanted to give us a fighting chance. I started trying to get your attention. Though, by then it was too late because you were confused and ticked off."

Heather frowns. "I guess I'm still confused. I don't know why you would think being attracted to me is a bad thing unless you don't want to be in public with me. I would understand that point of view, I guess. It wouldn't be the first time I've heard something like that."

"Just shut up with that kind of talk," I growl at her through clenched teeth. "Remember what I said about being mean to yourself? How many times do I have to tell you? You are drop-dead gorgeous. I would be honored to have you on my arm. If I am that lucky, I won't stop showing you off, so don't you worry about that. I don't know who put those ideas in your head, but you need a different frame of reference because yours is a little skewed, Gidget."

"So why all the resentment?" she probes.

"It has precious little to do with you — except the fact that you are female. Someone of your persuasion worked me over really good, and it's not an experience I want to repeat. So, you'll pardon me if I'm a little gun-shy."

"Well, not all women are like your ex," she argues defensively.

"I sure as heck hope not," I respond bitterly. "She practically ruined my life."

"I don't know about that You seem to have succeeded beautifully in spite of her. I, for one, thank her for screwing up royally — because of her stupidity I have a shot at a relationship with you."

The corner of my mouth quirks up. "Wow, Gidget! You have a talent for finding the positive side of virtually everything. I didn't think there was a positive side to be found in that situation, but you seem to have found the barest of the silver linings in the tornado that was Stacia."

"How long ago was this? I hope it wasn't too recent. I don't want to be your rebound."

I flush a dusky red this time. "Umm, I was nineteen," I mumble under my breath.

"What?" she exclaims in a shocked voice. "You mean to tell me you almost didn't ask me out over something that happened almost a decade ago?" She dissolves into giggles. "And they say women hold grudges? We've got nothing on guys like you."

"Hey! It was a big deal!" I counter defensively. "She left me for my best friend while I was stationed overseas serving my country just because he was a jock, and I was a soldier. She went after him because he had a paycheck with more zeros than mine."

"That was a terribly scummy thing to do, and I hope karma bites her in the butt one day, but it doesn't reflect on you. You honorably served your country while going above and beyond the call of duty by serving multiple tours. Obviously you are a man of great character, and she has no character to speak of. It sounds like you're better off without her."

"On my more mature days, that's how I view it. On the days I'm really angry, all I can think is I didn't deserve it. I was doing the right thing by enlisting, and she shouldn't have dumped me for making the decision. I mean I was going to ask the woman to marry me, for Pete's sake. I truly thought we would have the white picket fence like my parents had, so her betrayal completely blindsided me. Then, to have her leave me for my best friend made it cut even worse. Did I tell you they're still together with the proverbial two-point-five kids in the middle of suburbia? After he recovered from cancer, he became a hotshot orthopedic doctor somewhere. I guess she got what she wanted."

"Well, I'm here to tell you that life in upper-crust suburbia is not all it's cracked up to be. You might not know what's going on behind closed doors. It could be all sorts of screwed up in their house. If there are problems there, it may be a very well-kept secret."

"I suppose so. But, it's just so infuriating watching him have the future I was supposed to have with her," I admit.

"I don't know if you've hung out with Kiera's friend Tara much, but Tara is a big fan of God or destiny or fate directing our lives. She believes that there is an omniscient power that directs who we are and what we do. It is our responsibility to coexist with that energy force and try not to disrupt it. "

"I've only met her a couple of times, but she reminds me of some sort of Buddhist monk. She has a very calming energy about her," I roll my shoulder.

Heather grins at my description of Tara. "I know, right? It's almost as if she was someone else in a different life. Her spirit certainly doesn't match someone who looks like she could step off of the pages of Vogue. I'm not saying that this is true because I don't know yet. But hypothetically, what if God or fate meant for us to be together after all the crazy circumstances both of us have overcome? Come on, you're not the only person with a crazy ex or two in your background. So, maybe all that pain was meant to teach us lessons so we could find each other in the end."

I reach up to brush a big tangle of hair out of her face. I smile tenderly. "You know the more I think about it, the more I like your interpretation of things far better than mine."

Heather swallows hard and rubs her temples. "I wish I could be happy about us. Unfortunately, I have to figure out what to do about Grandma Lydia. For so many reasons, I am dreading the future right now. I'm just not prepared to face everything."

I open my arms and she walks into them. "I'm so sorry." I whisper against her hair. "I wish I could fix everything."

<hr>

If I have to go on one more domestic violence call where the victim bails the perpetrator out of jail, I think I might pull my hair out entirely. This is the third time this month I've been out to this particular property. The woman hasn't even gotten her cast removed from the last time her boyfriend beat the snot out of her. As I'm processing the evidence in the car, after his arrest, I come across paperwork from this morning indicating that she signed to spring him from the county jail where he was being locked up for assault and battery from their last dispute. I suspect one of these days I'll be doing a death notification to this young woman's parents and delivering her children to protective services. It's so frustrating to be entirely helpless to stop the cycle.

Some days I feel like a glorified taxi service to all the various stops within the system. It never seems to change; I shuffle people from one place to another and then I shuffle paper from one pile to another justifying how I moved the people from one place to another. It's a monotonous cycle day in and day out.

When I check my email, there's an urgent email from my commanding officer with the National Guard. My heart sinks to my feet. These are never good. Lately, the subjects of these emails have been related to the death of many of the men in my unit. Men have died on the battlefield and others on the home front from alcoholism, drug abuse, and suicide. I dread opening the email. It's been an awful day, and I'm not looking forward to whatever's inside. Yet, it's my duty to deal with whatever news is coming my way.

Just then, my commanding officer with the Sheriff's Department pokes his head into the little shoebox I'm using as an office. "Hey, Colton, you got a call from some muckity-muck at the Guard. You're supposed to call back. When I asked for a name, they said just to tell you that you're supposed to check in with your unit and you would know what he meant. He said he sent you an email and you should check it as soon as possible. I hope this message makes more sense to you. Anyway, consider yourself told," he says with a smirk as he walks off.

I've never liked that guy much. He's got himself a fancy degree from some Ivy League university, and he thinks he knows all about police work. I bet he wouldn't last two days on the streets.

Now, I'm even more worried. For my CO to both call and email. It must be something serious. I fish my thermos out of my backpack and take a big swig of lukewarm coffee to fortify myself.

As I read the email, it isn't what I expected at all. Members of our unit are being asked to volunteer for a special task force to train Iraqi security forces. I have to work hard to tamp down my rage. Train my butt. It was one of theirs who practically wiped out my unit. They were supposed to be working with us the last time. Unfortunately the bozo who tried to blow us up apparently didn't get the memo. Now they want us to go back and try again. The problem is when Uncle Sam asks you to go on a "volunteer" mission, it isn't really a polite request. It's more like a prettied up order. I know I don't have much choice but to go whether I agree with the mission or not. This basically just burns me. The higher-ups who move little pushpins around a map have never had to hold dead soldiers in their arms and explain to their parents how little Johnny's arms and legs got blown to pieces by some terrorist who was supposed to be on our side.

Speaking of parents — mine will be devastated when they find out I have to go back over and serve again. I think they thought I was done when I dropped back down to the Guard. It'll suck to tell them I'm going over one more time. My mom worries about me so much when I'm gone. I feel like I break her heart every time I write or call. On the other hand, if I don't call her she worries even more. It's the ultimate no-win situation. Or, at least it was until I met Heather. This situation might be even tougher now. Things look like they might be going somewhere between us finally, and now that's going to come to a screeching halt. I tried the "relationship in the military" thing once before, and I already know the ending to the story and it doesn't end well, so there's no point in even starting down that road. It's too damn bad. I really believe things could have been great with Gidget too. *Stupid war.*

I have to get my head on straight because I have to call my commanding officer, and he doesn't care about my personal problems, my philosophical problems with the plan or anything else. I try to think about how Heather would approach this situation as the eternal optimist. First, she would probably point out that this is an opportunity for me to see my friends I haven't seen in years. Then, she would remind me it will be a great way for me to get even with the bastards who blew up all my men. Lastly, it's a way for me to stack on some rank before I decide to retire completely. I'd like to go back to school and finish up my degree before I get too old to have a career.

So, I guess there are some positives to going back over to the hellhole if you can look at it like that. Trying to leave my brain in that frame of mind, I call my commanding officer.

"Captain Smith, this is Lieutenant Colton. I understand you called today, sir."

I listen as he commences the perfunctory small talk. I always find this part nerve-wrecking. I'm never really quite sure when to schmooze and when to get down to brass tacks

"Very good sir. Yes, sir, the weather has been wonderful. Yes, sir, the wedding was very nice. No sir, it was not my wedding. My best friend got married. My mother is fine sir, and my father is looking forward to retiring from the hardware store soon," I answer, trying not to let my impatience show. In all honesty, I wish he'd get to the important topic. I know from experience he'll share the details only when he's ready. I just have to be patient. I think this little exercise is a holdover from the days when he used to be a drill sergeant.

"How is your family, sir?" I ask just to be polite.

"It's all good, Lieutenant. It's good to be home. Although I will say I'm not thrilled Andrew is failing PE. It's a little embarrassing since people know I'm his dad. I think he does it so there's no danger he'll ever have to join the military," Captain Smith jokes.

I chuckle. "Could very well be, sir. What do you know about this upcoming mission?" I transition as smoothly as I can into the topic burning a hole in my brain.

Captain Smith snickers. "Well, Colton, I've got to hand it to you. You lasted longer than I thought you would. I thought you'd be tearing me apart limb by limb for answers the second you got on the phone. Anyway, the email was just a heads up. This isn't even an official mission yet. The policy wonks in Washington still have to fund it, and then they have to get final mission approval from the Pentagon. They're worried about a conflict with the draw-down directive. So, those of us on the ground are trying to get our ducks in a row in case we're called up at the last minute. So, just be forewarned, if this comes down the pike you could get three hours, three days, or three months' worth of notice before we need to deploy."

"Don't worry, I keep my ruck pack ready to go at all times.

"Well, shoot son, we need more like you."

"Please keep me informed about what's going on and I'll talk to you later. Have a good night."

Today, Heather has her food truck parked down in Corvallis because there's a football game at Oregon State University. I love the way her friends rally around her to help her in her business. She has gotten permission from a closed business park to take over a large portion of his parking lot. She's got her little sideshow running. Tara has a booth where she's painting faces with an airbrush. Gabriel, Jeff's nephew, is drawing cartoon characters of people while his mom is manning a little makeover booth. It still blows me away that Jeff's claim to fame is braiding hair. But, hey whatever works for him and given the state of his seemingly blissful marriage, something is clearly working for him. Kiera is holding court in a homemade puppet theater of sorts with tons of Mindy's dress-up clothes in a big steamer chest. She's helping kids change in and out of clothes and reading them Pirate and Princess stories while their parents scarf down food. Even Javier is in on the fun. He set up a bunch of big-screen TVs in the parking lot and is projecting the game from his tablet so nobody misses any football. Heather is selling food faster than she can make it. She has a line all the way around the truck. I wash my hands and step into the truck.

"Wow, I've forgotten how small this thing is with two of us in here," I comment as I almost smack my head on the ceiling.

"Piper and I work in here just fine. I think it's because you're approximately the size of the Jolly Green

Giant. Do you need something?" she asks pointedly.

"Yes, actually. You look extremely stressed. I came to see what I could do to help."

"How much experience do you have on a flat top?" she asks eyeing me skeptically.

"A fair amount, actually," I answer.

"Enough not to burn bread?" Heather raises her eyebrow.

"I think I can manage without too much difficulty," I reply. "I eat microwave pizza, but it doesn't mean it's the only thing I know how to cook. If I screw it up, I give you permission to take me off the line, Chef."

"Wow, I'm impressed! You use the right vernacular and everything," she teases.

"It's amazing what working two months at Denny's will do for you," I confess with a sly grin.

"What did you do? Get fired for your lack of taste in food?"

After a beat of awkward silence I answer, "Nope, I enlisted in the Army. After that, my taste in food went from bad to worse out of necessity."

I hear Heather mumble under her breath. I step closer so I can hear what she's saying as she is muttering to herself, "Great job, Heather — Land mines. Stupid emotional land mines. Please … try a little harder H. Maybe next time, you should just step on each one of them."

"What are you being hard on yourself about this time? Didn't we talk about this? You were going to be nicer to yourself, remember? You had no way of knowing the reason I left my job at Denny's was because I went to basic training. Why would you criticize yourself for not guessing?" I tuck a piece of her hair back under her hair net.

Heather looks up at me with wide cornflower blue eyes. "Well, I was trying not to make things awkward; but when you say it like that, it does sound stupid."

"Gidget, I appreciate you trying to be sensitive. But, I can talk about my military service. It hurts me to talk about the day of the incident, but if I didn't talk about the time I spent in the military I have to disregard nearly a decade of my life between the time I spent in active service and the time I've spent in the reserves. My mom would be bummed if she couldn't show off all those pictures of me in my uniform."

The corners of Heather's mouth tilt up in a sexy grin and her eyes sparkle. "Ooh, I bet you look sexy in your dress uniform. Heck, I bet you look sexy in any uniform. But, especially in your dress greens."

"I can only hope my mom isn't thinking about how sexy I am in my uniform when she's showing off my pictures at her bridge club." I shudder for good measure. But, I have more pressing matters. I collect myself and turn to Heather, "Speaking of the military, I need to have a quiet conversation with you one of these days soon, but not here, okay?"

"Yikes, that sounds serious. Should I be scared?" Heather asks, examining my face for clues.

"I can't tell you that you should never be scared, but for now, I think things are stable. I'll try to always give you as much warning as I can if things get dicey," I promise.

"We've got to get moving on the sandwiches, they're not going to make themselves," Heather says as her lips compress into a grim line.

"What can I do to help?" I ask as I roll up the sleeves on my shirt.

"Can you butter those hoagie rolls and toss them on the griddle top. I want them golden brown. Nothing special except butter. I'm putting them on the French dips today. I've got Reuben sandwiches, and patty melts too. You can help me set up the ingredients for those too if you want to. We need to set up some sort of assembly line. I think Javier's wife is going to come play cashier for me. That will help take off some of the pressure. She should be here anytime. Thank goodness Gwendolyn has Becca today, so we don't have to worry about her."

I'm amazed how efficiently and calmly Heather works once she settles into the groove. We seem to form a little unit between us. It's almost as if we can read each other's minds. I noticed it when we were working on the wedding cake, but it's even more apparent here as we're working under massive time pressure. We're working together like we've done it our whole lives.

By the end of the day, Heather's little food truck has raked in nearly $2,300 in five hours. She's ecstatic. After a round of high-fives and hugs for everyone involved, she stops in front of me. "I'd like to hug you too, but I probably smell like a pig that has wallowed in sewage all day. I'd rather smelly not be the lasting impression you have of me if you don't mind," she admits with a self-deprecating grin.

"Do you have any spare clothes in this thing?" I ask looking around her cramped truck.

"Of course I do! What kind of girly-girl do you take me for? But my nastiness goes beyond just dirty clothes. I have an embedded level of funk."

"What if I told you I can offer you a shower?"

"Then you would get more than just a hug," she promises.

"Consider it done. A friend of mine owns a truck stop just outside of town which has what can only be described as luxury showers. He's always trying to get me to stop by and see him. This is a perfect excuse. I've got clothes in my truck as well. We could get all spiffy and go out to dinner. How does that sound?"

Heather sighs. "That sounds heavenly. My feet are killing me. I'd like to go out to eat somewhere where I can sit down and have someone serve me for a change. Since the game is over, we might get seating."

"You have the keys to this parking lot, correct?"

Heather nods.

"How about if we break down your truck and put all the signs and stuff inside and just lock everything up. I can take you over to Nathan's place in my truck," I offer.

"Well, if you want to take your life in your hands. I stink to high heaven."

"Did you forget I worked beside you all day? I probably don't smell any better than you do. In fact, I'm certain I smell worse because I know I didn't start out smelling as good as you did. So, don't worry your gorgeous little head. After we use Nathan's super-duper luxury millionaire showers, we'll be so clean our mamas won't recognize us anyway."

Heather smirks at me, "Whatever floats your boat, Cowboy. I'll just be happy not to smell like sauerkraut."

"You mean you don't use sauerkraut as an ingredient in the special soap you make?" I tease.

"How do you know about my soap?" Heather asks, accusingly.

"You may have noticed I practically live over at Jeff and Kiera's house, and they both sing the praises of your soap. Can I tell you my buddy has never smelled better in his whole life? I hate to tell you this, but that man's feet can build up some serious funk."

Heather laughs. "Well, I'm glad I can do something to help them avoid some marital strife. Hmm. I wonder what I would put into soap and shampoo for you. How do you feel about Wintergreen?"

"Like the gum?"

Heather nods. "Yes, do you like the smell?"

"I've never really thought about it. I do like it. It reminds me of Christmas. My parents used to get me those packets of Lifesavers that look like books. I don't like the fruit-flavored ones, so my mom would get me the ones which had spearmint, peppermint and wintergreen lifesavers in them. Strangely enough, the Wintergreen ones were always my favorite. I'm not sure how you even knew since I just pulled that memory out of a deep hole."

"I don't know either. I remember you told me you like to take your horses to Eastern Oregon to ride during the wintertime. I have visions of you in the backwoods somewhere in the snow. Wintergreen is the sensory memory which came to mind when I think of you. This is the reason I don't do my soaps and shampoos on a big scale because, I need to get a sense of who the person is on the inside before I can match the fragrance to them," Heather explains.

"Wow, that sounds complicated."

"It's not really. Once I get to know somebody, it comes naturally. Would you like me to make you some soap? You don't have to use it if you don't like it."

"I doubt I will dislike it. I've already sampled several of the ones you've made, and I like them all. I'm particularly fond of the cotton candy scented one you made for Mindy. I'd be honored if you made me my personal fragrance."

Heather grins at me. "I still would've been making sandwiches if you hadn't stepped in to help. I would have been lost without you. Thank you so much. So, consider my custom-made soap and shampoo as a thank you gift for your help on the wedding cake and my food truck today."

"There was no other place I would've rather been today. It was actually kind of fun. Don't tell my macho guy friends, but I had a great time helping with the wedding cake. It was even fascinating to make the flowers. I probably shouldn't go around bragging about it, but I don't care if you know that about me."

***

"How did you even find this place?" Heather asks as she steals a bite of my prime rib.

"I know, it doesn't look like much from the outside does it?. When Jeff and I played sports in college, one of the guys on my team had a family member who owned this place. I don't know if they still own it, but it seems like they might because the food is still just as good. But, you should've seen them try to feed a whole team of college football players. It's a wonder they didn't go broke. Whenever I'm in town, I try to come back here to help repay them for their kindness."

"You know, for a rough and tough cowboy turned big bad cop, you're just a big ole' marshmallow in disguise."

"I seem to remember trying to tell you I'm a nice guy."

"Well, you're getting evidence stacking up in your corner. Your case is looking stronger and stronger."

"Does this mean you have evidence to the contrary?" I ask, in jest.

"Well, as nearly as I can tell, your biggest Achilles' heel is holding onto grudges when your life would be better if you moved on," she answers pointedly. "You also seem to have an unnaturally strong dislike for the New Orleans Saints, which I don't quite understand — but I'm sure you'll tell me all about it someday."

"Oh, if that's all, then I'm in pretty good shape."

"I definitely agree with your assessment," Heather says as she leisurely scopes me out from top to bottom. The only extra clothes I had in the truck were an old pair of Wranglers which have seen better days and are particularly thread-bare in the butt region. She's unabashedly checking me out. Her perusal embarrasses me more than just a little, but I try to play it cool.

As quickly as it started, the moment is over as Heather suddenly switches topics and asks, "I don't suppose you're free next weekend?"

"Aside from watching football and a little NASCAR with Denny, I am. Why?"

"You don't have to work?" she asks tentatively.

"No, I've got training this week. Then I'm working three night shifts in a row. I'll be off until Tuesday. Why? What's on your mind?"

"I don't even know if I should ask you this. I'm not sure if we're even at that point in our relationship. It seems a lot to ask but I am not sure what else to do."

I watch as Heather nervously tears up a straw wrapper in front of her. I reach out to cover her hands with mine as I murmur, "Gidget, I thought we already established the fact you and I are friends. Friends don't have any trouble asking favors from each other. Just last week you brought cookies for my entire station-house, right? If anything, I owe you one. So, spit it out. What do you need?"

"I need you to come to Texas with me. I think I made enough money today to buy your airline ticket. I don't want to face my family and all those memories alone," Heather confesses in one big long breath, her voice breaking with emotion. "Kiera can't come because of her job and Tara has the dance studio. I don't know what else to do. I'm not sure if you want to be involved in all this drama. It will not be fun to hang out with my family. Things can get ugly quickly. I can't even imagine how weird it's going to be without my grandma there to be the peacemaker."

Heather's speech trails off at the end as she runs out of steam. She buries her face in her hands as she awaits my response. Gently, I remove her hands from her face as I look into her eyes. "Heather, all you had to do was ask. If I can, there's no other place I'd rather be."

Heather's eyes narrow. "What do you mean? If you can —"

"It means I have to check with my CO with the National Guard. I might not be cleared to leave the state." I answer cautiously.

"Why? I thought you didn't have drill for two weeks," responds Heather, confusion clear in her eyes.

I scrub my hand over my face and through my short cropped hair and grapple with what I'm at liberty to say. "I might be facing changes in my deployment status soon and no one knows how eminent that change may be."

I wait for a second as the implications sink in. As the news washes over her, she blanches paper-white to the point where she's almost luminescent as she exclaims, "They can't ask you to do it again. You might not make it home this time. Your poor mom! Does she know? How did she take it?"

I squeeze her hands. "Gidget, slow down and take a breath. No, my mom doesn't know. You're the first person I've told because it's not a done deal yet. It's just in the pipeline. I didn't want to get my mom all riled up over nothing. But, chances are — it is something. I want to be upfront with you because I feel like you should know what's going on in case it changes how you feel about me," I respond earnestly, hoping to convey the depth of my emotions in just a few words.

"Why would the actions of the Army change the way I feel about you?" Heather asks incredulously.

"I don't know. I just know what happened before. I know being the partner of someone who's been deployed is no bed of roses. You might want to think twice before you sign up for that tour of duty. You can still bail out of this while it's early. It would be like a no harm, no foul situation."

"Now look who's being mean to themselves?" Heather glares at me. "Come to think of it, you're not being very nice to me either, if you think so little of my character that you think I would be so shallow. I'm made of tougher stuff, Cowboy. Just watch me."

I'm a little stunned by the passion in her voice, because, by traditional standards, you might consider this our first official date. Though, our hanging out activities have developed a very date-like feel to them recently.

I change the subject because the topic of the future of us is just too big to contemplate right now. "Assuming I get permission to go on this little journey with you, what are we expecting to encounter?" I ask.

"I don't know. When my grandpa died, my family decided at thirteen, I was still too young to understand all the grown-up discussions and the mourning process, so they excluded me from the memorial ceremony. It was frustrating because I never got to say goodbye. When I go down to Texas, I always stop and visit his gravesite to pay my respects."

"I thought you said your mom was from North Carolina?" I ask.

"She was, but her daddy was an oilman from Texas."

"I'm sure you've got family legends worthy of a miniseries," I say as I butter the last piece of garlic bread and hand Heather half.

"I expect my brother and sister have also been told to be there. So, you'll have a chance to meet the whole gang. There's going to be a memorial service. My grandma didn't want any graveside service. She specifically put it into her advance directive and will she wanted to be cremated as soon as possible."

"Knowing my dad, he probably has a meeting set up with my grandma's legal counsel to go over her legal papers. It will likely be a very contentious session. My dad might view it as another opportunity to tell me why I should be leading a different life. I don't know if I can deal with that on top of the death of my grandma. Just being in her house with her things is will be hard enough."

"Hopefully, I can be there for you. Your dad will have to get through me. You should have the right to mourn before any of the rest of that stuff comes up. I don't understand how he feels like he has the right to stand in judgment of your career choices."

Heather shrugs. "Let's just say you're not the only person who's done something in your past to let your parents down. The only difference is your parents have allowed you to move past your mistakes. I think mine will haunt me for the rest of my life. Some days, I'm not so sure they shouldn't."

CHAPTER EIGHT

HEATHER

I STILL CAN'T BELIEVE I'm standing on Grandma Lydia's front porch holding Tyler's hand and she didn't even get to meet him. The irony of it all makes me want to cry. We used to spend hours in her kitchen as she taught me how to cook and she would share stories with me about how a big brash oilman swept her off her feet. She told me she and Grandpa often fought like cats and dogs but the sweetest part of it all was making up. I think about how much my grandparents would've liked Ty's straightforward approach to life. He and my grandpa would have gotten along famously.

As we open the door, Ethel, my grandma's bloodhound, a dog descended from animals long raised by my grandfather, greeted us like long-lost friends. "How are you doing, sweetie?" I try to duck to get out of the way of the flying slobber as she shakes enthusiastically at my presence. "Want to meet my friend Tyler?" I reach behind me to pull Tyler forward, but it's too late as Tyler is already on his hands and knees in front of Ethel and has her enveloped in a full-body hug.

"Oh, look at you, you gorgeous thing!" Tyler exclaims. "I bet you miss your mama. But, we'll take care of you now."

"Tyler! Don't make promises we can't keep," I chastise. "I don't know what will happen to the dog. For all I know, my dad might make her go to the pound."

"Over my dead body!" Tyler declares forcefully. I swear my heart just did a somersault.

"We'll have to see if grandma had any plans for her in the will. Knowing my grandma, Ethel will probably retire in better surroundings than most people. She might even have her own maid and butler," I joke.

I grab Tyler's hand and walk silently into the living room. Instead of collecting precious photographs and other artifacts of his childhood, my dad is taking an inventory of all the furniture and knickknacks. He's double checking the value of them on eBay. The whole process makes me sick to my stomach. Before I can even say hello, I have to run to the restroom to throw up.

When I return to the parlor, all the men are sitting in the room. Everyone is glaring at each other and no one is saying anything. When Tyler sees me, he stands up. I smile at him when he does this because it's such a quaint, gentlemanly thing to do. Before I met Tyler, I can't remember the last time a man stood for me just because I entered the room. I give Tyler my hand and he starts to escort me to a chair. I interrupt him to introduce him to my family. "Dad, Carlton and Madison, this is my friend Tyler. Tyler, this is my dad, Carl, my brother Carlton and my sister Madison. My mother, Victoria, is around here somewhere."

Tyler makes a move to tip his hat, obviously he's forgotten that he took it off and left it with his coat in the foyer. He quickly recovers and sticks his hand out for a handshake. "Nice to meet you sir. You have a lovely daughter."

My dad looks at me in shock as if he's seeing me for the first time. "Yes, I suppose she is. It would help if she lost some weight. You can't imagine the amount of money her mother and I wasted on fat camps when she was little. We always tell her it's a matter of will power. It can't just be genes because her mother is slim and so is Madison. So obviously, she's just not trying hard enough."

"With all due respect sir, I paid your daughter a compliment. You should try it sometime. It's a good habit to get into. I think she's gorgeous without losing an ounce. But, even if I didn't, I would never say anything like you just did; because it was uncalled for and downright rude," Tyler challenges, the disgust clear in his voice.

I have little time to relish the praise Tyler has just heaped on me because my father draws himself up to his full height and gets in Tyler's face. "Just what do you know about being a parent?"

"Actually, I know nothing about being a parent other than I would work really hard not to be the type of parent you're being right now. It doesn't take a rocket scientist to figure out you need to act like a civilized human being to everyone including your own children. Personally, I feel like you owe her an apology for those snide remarks. But, that's just me," Ty replies confidently.

"Thank you, Cowboy," I murmur under my breath. "I wish I was brave enough to do that more often."

"You're welcome, Gidget. That's what I'm here for, right?" he whispers. I squeeze his hand in return.

"Where did you find this guy?" my dad asks snidely.

"Interestingly enough, I found him in another place where the guy was a bully. It didn't end very well for that guy either," I respond with a small smile as I remember how Tyler calmly, but assertively dealt with Kevin Buckhold for Kiera.

"The way I remember it, you were holding your own pretty well on that occasion too, Gidget. You were doing a bang up job of helping Jeff's mom hold it together until the police arrived," Ty compliments me.

"What could Heather possibly do? She's a disaster in a crisis," my dad asserts.

"Sir, were you there?" Tyler asks evenly.

"Of course not," my dad spits.

"Then maybe you shouldn't comment on things you know nothin' about," Ty suggests. "Because, as a law enforcement officer I respond to a lot of emergencies and I can tell you that your daughter performed like a rock star. She kept a domestic violence victim calm and helped stop the situation from escalating further. She impressed me so much that day I wanted to keep her in my life."

"Daddy, where's mom?" I ask, eager to change the subject and stop the confrontation between Dad and Tyler.

My dad answers, "She went to go find some decent food in this godforsaken place."

I sigh and roll my eyes. "Really Dad? I could've made something. I've only been cooking in this kitchen since I was about three years old and I've got a degree from one of the top culinary programs in the nation."

My dad crosses his arms over his chest as he shakes his head in disgust. "Don't remind me. You could've gone to one of the top Ivy League schools and gotten a perfectly good solid business education like everyone else in our neighborhood, but you had to 'go find yourself' like some hippie. I hope you're happy. I can't even show you off to my friends because I have to explain to them you sell food out of a truck like some huge tailgating party. When are you going to grow up?" he asks, his voice full of accusations.

I look up at Tyler, my eyes full of silent pleas. I have no idea if he understands. In fact, I'm not even sure what I'm asking. I know I don't want to have this conversation right now. I haven't even had a chance to say goodbye to my grandma. We just got off a plane ride with more turbulence than the newest attraction at Disney World. If I can't relax with my cooking, I want to take a nice long bubble bath and collapse in the bed while reading a nice suspenseful Karen Rose book.

To my relief, it looks like Tyler has received my silent telepathic messages because he doesn't rise to my dad's bait. He merely shrugs. "Gidget, babe, you look tired. Why don't you take a shower while I unpack?"

"You're not sleeping with my daughter!" asserts my dad pointing his finger at Ty.

I shake my head and roll my eyes as I blush, "Geez, tell me something I don't know dad. Did I introduce him as my boyfriend? No, I did not. I introduced him as my friend. He's not even my boyfriend. If you continue with remarks like that, he won't ever be my boyfriend," I state baldly.

Tyler brushes an errant curl out of my face. "Gidget, I've faced down terrorists and insurgents, overprotective dads don't scare me much."

I grin at the expression on my dad's face as he processes Tyler's words. "In that case, by all means let's go. I think I hear a bubble bath calling my name from here."

⸻ ⬩ ⸻

The silence around the conference table at the lawyers' office is deafening. My brother is looking at me with absolute disdain on his face. My little sister looks like someone slapped her. I can't even venture to guess what my expression looks like. I know what I feel like and I wonder if it's reflected on my face. I feel hollow. No amount of money will ever fix that.

"Did you know this was coming?" asks Carlton. "Is that why you brought your muscle with you? There's no way I'm buying the story that he's here because he wants to date you. The last guy you brought around was a total loser; he totally cleaned you out and tried to gain access to all of dad's business holdings, remember? Maybe you brought this guy just to intimidate us. I looked him up online. There's a picture of him floating around with his military buddies. He's holding an AK 15 to the back of a woman's head. So, are you sure about what kind of guy you're letting in your life this time?"

It takes all the discipline I've got not to let my eyes fly to Tyler for an explanation. Clearly, he has one. Otherwise, he wouldn't be allowed to continue to serve in the military. So, I'll have to put my curiosity on hold. I don't want to give Carlton the satisfaction of knowing he might have unnerved me.

"I know exactly what kind of guy I'm letting into my life. He's a decorated combat veteran who still serves in the military to save the lives of others. He's received commendations from the Sheriff's Department for his bravery, and if I say so myself, he's a pretty decent sous chef. To top it all off, animals and kids seem to universally love him."

To my surprise, Tyler flushes under my praise. I'm amazed at his reaction. It would seem to me he would be used to all the hoopla by now. "Thank you Gidget," he murmurs under his breath.

"So, how long have you known Grandma was going to give you this huge piece of her estate?" Carlton probes venomously.

"I swear, I knew nothing about it. I figured it would all go to mom since her sister died from MS. The only thing I knew about was that she planned to give some to the charity that fights Lou Gehrig's disease. But even then, it was just a philosophical discussion. I know nothing about what she put in any paperwork," I clarify.

"Well, it's abundantly clear that you were her favorite. None of the rest of us got $200,000 to do with what we please," Carlton replies sarcastically.

Tyler looks up from the paperwork he is studying. "Actually, that's technically not true. First, there are conditions on the gift to Heather. Second, those four Arabian horses your grandma left for Madison are worth way more than $200,000. Their pedigree is spectacular. The stud fees she can generate could be enormous," Ty explains.

Carlton flushes bright red as he practically screeches, "Oh well, that's just great! She took care of everyone else and forgot about me. Wonderful. Being the oldest child sucks. I should have been cute and adorable like you two."

Tyler interrupts him. "Carlton, man. Pull yourself together. I think you got more than you think you did. You got ownership of all leasing and mineral rights on your land. That means when the government or the gas stations want to pull anything from your land, they have to ask you and you can charge them a fee. It doesn't seem like much, but by the time you multiply it by the number of gallons of oil that could be removed, it adds up very quickly," he explains.

"Oh, it makes much more sense that grandma would give me the business related ventures. The girls don't really need that kind of stuff," Carlton reasons.

"Geez, not you too." Tyler shakes his head. "Do they put it in the Kool-Aid out here? I bet you that your sisters are every bit as competent as you are. But, this isn't the time or place for that conversation."

Madison looks up at Tyler, clearly startled to be included in the conversation. "Umm, I guess I should thank you for that. But, you should also know you're probably never going to change his mind. I've been trying for years to no avail. It's like talking to a brick wall. Thanks for trying though. I appreciate it. Things must be interesting between you and Heather because she's as opinionated as you are," she states with a small, knowing smile.

I wait to see what Tyler says. This could be enlightening.

Tyler grins at Madison. "It's the thunder and lightning that makes a summer storm interesting. Otherwise, it just gets you wet."

Madison winks at Tyler. "You make a valid point."

<hr>

Tyler and I are having coffee at a 24-hour truck stop. It's a habit I developed when I hung out with Kiera and her dad. Denny taught me that there isn't any problem in the world so serious that it can't be solved over a piece of cream pie and a few cups of coffee. Also, it gives me an opportunity to talk to Ty in a place where there is zero chance of running into any of my family.

"Tyler, I don't even know how to process this. I've always wanted to open a place of my own. But I didn't want my grandma to have to die for it to happen. It feels wrong to use the money to open the shop."

Tyler reaches across the table to hold my hands, "Gidget, your grandma knew about your dreams. Otherwise she would have just given you something general from her estate like she did your brother and sister. But, she didn't. She specifically gave you cash and earmarked it as capital for you to invest in your business.

She was even more specific when she said it had to be a food related business. I have a hunch she was trying to make sure your dad couldn't manipulate the way you spend your money. That's just my theory."

I flash him a droll grin, "Given the strained relationship between Grandma and my dad, I wouldn't doubt her motivation at all. She was not a big fan of my dad. She thought he was pompous and selfish and she made no bones about sharing her opinion as widely as possible. I'll never forget the time she wrote it in a blog and emailed my dad the link to it. She claimed she accidentally sent the link to everyone who worked for my dad's company. You'd be amazed how many people bought her story because she was a senior citizen learning how to use email. Most of those people would've been surprised to know she set up her own YouTube channel. She was crafty that way." I smile at the memory. But, my heart clutches at the realization that there will be no more funny blog entries from my grandmother.

"I don't even know what direction I want to go in. This is so far-fetched that the possibilities are endless. I could open up a small little restaurant specializing in retro cooking or I could do something like a bakery, or maybe I'll do catering. I could do something entirely different like make candy for a gift shop where I sell my soaps and shampoos."

A big smile slowly crosses Tyler's face. "Gee, it's too bad you're so talented."

It takes me a moment to register that he's kidding.

"Very funny Ty," I scold. "These are huge decisions. I don't know how I'll make them by myself and my family is no help."

Hearing the distress in my voice, Ty straightens up in his chair and pulls a tablet of sticky notes out of his pocket and hands me a pen.

"Whenever I have a hard decision to make, I make a list of pros and cons. I pretend what would happen if I make the decision and what would happen if I don't. Maybe you should make a decision tree for yourself and we can see where it goes," he says pushing the block of sticky notes in my direction.

"What if I make a mistake? What if I don't make the right decision? What if my dad is right and I'm too stupid to do any of this?" I ask, as a cold sweat breaks out along my spine.

"What if your dad is a total dipwad who likes to hear himself talk? Gidget, you are incredibly talented. I saw you make half my monthly pay in a single afternoon just by making sandwiches and you did it working out of a place that's the size of a postage stamp. Imagine what you could do if you had a real place. I don't think it's a matter of whether you can succeed it's just choosing which of your many skills you'll use to make it happen. You need to choose what makes you the happiest."

"I don't know Tyler. None of this makes me happy. My grandma was supposed to do this with me —"

"Supposed to do what, babe?" Ty interrupts. "Describe the dream. When you guys talked about it, how did you envision it?"

"My grandma said there were not enough old-fashioned bakeries in the world anymore. You know, the kind with glass cases with dozens of varieties of pastries, cookies and cupcakes behind big panes of glass. A place where a bride could order a custom wedding cake and know it would be done correctly and be confident her guests can stand the flavor of her cake. My grandma wanted me to have an old-fashioned soda bar at the bakery as well to add a nostalgic touch," I explain, remembering the long fantasy planning sessions we had when we were baking cakes in my grandma's kitchen when I was younger.

"It sounds like you guys put a lot of thought into this."

"We did. But, after I made Thanksgiving dinner for her one year, she decided maybe I should open a family restaurant instead. She made elaborate plans for me to build all these log cabin themed restaurants. She wanted me to serve rustic comfort food with historical themes. She planned a bunch of themed menus. There was duck a l'orange, pheasants with walnut stuffing, and range fed prime rib with garlic mashed potatoes."

Ty puts up his hands in a gesture of timeout. "Stop! My mouth is watering and I just ate. That sounds phenomenal too. I'm beginning to see your dilemma here. Is there an idea you feel more attached to than the other? What about location? Would you stay in the Willamette Valley or would you come to Texas or would you go back to the Boston area where you're from?"

I sigh as I bury my head in my hands. "Tyler, I think I'm going to need way more than a few sticky notes to do this. I didn't even think about location. How do I even start making a decision like that? I know where I don't want to be. I don't want to be in Boston where my parents can be looking over my shoulder and judging every move I make," I comment wryly.

Tyler chuckles. "See, this isn't so hard. You've already made a decision. One down, about a hundred thousand to go."

I roll my eyes. "Oh goody! I can't wait."

"You know, you can get mentors for this kind of thing."

"I'll definitely check into that because if I screw up again, my family is never going to let me live it down," I reply.

"Personally, I think you worry a little too much about what they think of you. If my family had done to me what yours did to you, I would've written them off a long time ago."

"You're right, I probably should've. But, they're not wrong about me. I was too naïve and trusting. I let Fletcher Heaves get away with everything. I should've known better, but I didn't. So, even though he was the one who committed the crime, it was ultimately my responsibility because I let him into my life," I explain, remembering how horribly betrayed I felt when I discovered the depth of his duplicity.

"Gidget, you can't prevent what you don't know yet. You know now and it's not likely to ever happen to you again. You're much more cautious now than you ever were before, right?"

I nod.

"You learned from the experience and that's all anyone can ask. They keep beating you up over it and it's akin to bullying. It's not fair. You need to tell them to knock it off. They're your family, they're supposed to love you despite your mistakes. I don't understand this hyper-criticalness and it's pissing me off. Why aren't they in your corner supporting you?"

"That's a question I've asked myself far too many times to count. I don't think there's a real answer," I respond. It's been a long time since I've had an outsider's view of my family dynamics. I had forgotten what an odd bunch we can appear to be. "I don't know, maybe it's the best he can do. My mom seems happy with him. My brother doesn't seem to have any issues with my dad and my sister seems to make both my parents happy. Maybe it's just me who doesn't fit in."

"I don't know, I might consider it a blessing if I were you."

I scrunch up my face and stick out my tongue. "You think you're too cute don't you, Tyler Colton?"

"Yes ma'am. Don't you?" he replies as he tips his hat in a gallant manner.

I leisurely ogle him as he sits semi-sprawled in the booth with his foot propped up on the chair next to him. In honor of meeting my family, he's upgraded his wardrobe to 'formal urban cowboy'. Today, he's wearing a black dress shirt with the sleeves folded up to his mid-forearms and some skin-tight black jeans with his black cowboy boots with silver embellishments. He is wearing a black belt with a silver eagle on it superimposed over the image of the twin towers. It's a simple but imposing look when you stick it on a frame as large as his. He gives new meaning to the word sexy.

I wink at him as I tease, "Actually, I do. But, I'm afraid if I tell you too many times. Your ego might just get over-inflated like a big ole' party balloon and pop. I can't run the risk of you injuring yourself like that."

"I could work with that, Gidget, because then you'd have to play nurse which could be all sorts of fun."

The word hits me hard, like a punch to the gut. "Did I tell you my grandma used to be a nurse? She worked on soldiers during the Korean War. That's how she met my grandpa. She was so proud of that. She had a career back in the day when it was unusual for women to work. Apparently, she had to fight her dad to get his approval too. Maybe that's why we were such kindred spirits. She never gave up her nurturing nature. She was forever taking in strays. Stray people, stray animals, or stray causes — it didn't matter. If you needed help, my grandparents were there to give you a hand. It was always remarkable to me."

Tyler kisses the back of my hand as he comments, "Sounds like someone else I know."

"It's funny, you would never have guessed my grandpa was a high-powered oil executive. He wore these beat up flannel shirts and thermal underwear around town with his overalls most of the time. If he had to get all spiffied up to go into town for a business meeting, folks didn't quite know what to do with him. It was pretty funny. If he and my grandma dressed to the nines, they were pretty much unrecognizable." I snicker at a private memory. Tyler squeezes my hand as he waits for me to continue.

"Every once in a while, I think they did it for the

shock value. They took great pleasure in stunning my mom's side of the family who came from old money and were from generations of cultured society in North Carolina. My grandpa knew he could probably buy them many times over, but simply didn't give a rat's butt. He didn't really give them an idea of who he was in the business world because he didn't feel like he needed to show off. After years of being judged harshly for being a backward country hick, the opportunity arose in a business setting for Grandpa to take over my other grandpa's business. My grandpa didn't make a big to-do or fuss, he bought the business and fired all of the executives including my dad's dad. That story became the stuff of family legend. Nobody messed with my grandpa after that."

Tyler chuckles softly at my story. "Wow, I see you get your moxie honestly."

"Oh Tyler, I am going to miss them so much," I say as I wipe tears from my face with the back of my hand.

Ty stands up and removes a handkerchief from his back pocket as he holds out his hand to draw me to a standing position. He dabs at my tears with it. When he finishes, he tucks the handkerchief back into his pocket and holds his arms open wide.

Wordlessly, I walk into them. I'm still baffled by the feeling of home I have when I'm in his arms. This shouldn't feel so right. Not long ago, we didn't even know each other. Now, he feels like the compass that's keeping my world upright.

Tyler folds me into a tight hug and rests his chin on the top of my head. For the longest time, we stand there, like a quiet statue in the middle of the hustle and bustle of the truck stop. In the background I hear the distant clanking of dishes and the vacant chatter of patrons discussing the news of the day and sporting events, yet, the sound echoes the loudest in my mind is the sound of my heart beating in syncopation with Ty's. It's a comforting rhythm soothes my frazzled nerves. I sigh in contentment and settle into a more comfortable position on Ty's shoulder. As he feels me relax, he hugs me a little tighter I can feel him grin against my hair.

"Happy?" I murmur against his chest.

"Anytime I've got you in my arms, I'm downright ecstatic. Of course I'm happy. Why wouldn't I be?"

"It is nice isn't it?" I concede. "I feel like I don't ever want to leave."

"I don't recall asking you to," Ty pulls away and kisses me. This wasn't a nice pleasant peck on the cheek either. This was a deep exploratory kiss, filled with need and passion. When he breaks off the kiss, we are both breathing heavily.

Just then, a trucker sitting at the counter yells out, "Get a room, why don't you?"

Ty looks at me and raises an eyebrow in question. "With the atmosphere you've got going on at your grandma's house it sounds like a spectacular idea. Are you game?"

The question stops me cold. Am I game? I have a reputation for being out there and adventurous, but the truth of the matter is since I've been burned, I'm much more cautious than I once was. This would be a step I don't know we could retreat from. But, then again I don't know we would want to.

"Come on Darlin', we're not creating world peace here, we're just deciding where we're going to spend the night," Ty teases after I've been silent for a while.

"I know. This could be a big deal. It may have ramifications for the rest of our relationship."

Tyler shrugs and runs his hand through his hair. "I think you're over-thinking this Gidget. I have no grand plan of seduction. I'm just trying to make the situation less stressful for you. I'm not trying to pressure you into anything you don't want. If it makes you feel any better, we can get one of those executive suites where there are two rooms," he offers.

I can't help but smile at his assessment of me. "Welcome to 'Over Thinkers Anonymous'. It's part of the reason why I have a hard time making a decision. I want to make sure I've weighed every option carefully. Because, the few times I've just gone with my heart, it's ended in disaster for me. Now, I sometimes find myself paralyzed and unable to make any decision for fear I'll make the wrong one — even when it comes to small things like where I'll spend the night on vacation or where to go out to eat."

"So, what does your brain tell you on this one?" Ty asks, watching me carefully.

"That it's a terrible idea to go back and be in front of a firing squad when they're all really mad at me," I respond before I have a chance to censor my thoughts.

"So, why are we even discussing this? Why aren't we finding a nice hotel with a hot tub somewhere?" Ty asks as he strokes my cheek.

"Well, they'll assume we're doing it like bunnies and I don't really want to face down their knowing looks when I go to grandma's memorial service tomorrow," I answer.

Tyler tilts my chin up so I'm looking at him and plants a gentle kiss on my lips. "Sorry to tell you this, Gidget, but they'll assume that anyway. We've already been gone for several hours, so they've already made the assumption whether we want them to or not. We might as well get ourselves a room and save ourselves all the aggravation."

I flush bright red at his assertion that my family has already made the leap in their minds. But, I know what he's saying is most likely true. My dad has been challenging Tyler as if he's already been designated as the official guy in my life.

"Okay, let me text Madison. I think if anyone will understand, it will probably be her," I acquiesce.

"You're saying yes?" Tyler clarifies. "At least something's going right today. I promise to be a gentleman if that's what you want, Gidget. I want to get you out of that toxic environment. You're going to have enough on your mind tomorrow at the service. You don't need to put up with their remarks tonight."

"I never thanked you for standing up for me earlier today. It means a lot to me." I brush my lips across his in a light kiss of gratitude.

"That's what I'm here for. That man needs to be taken down a couple notches. As we say in Oklahoma, he's just a little too big for his britches." Ty responds.

"Well, I'm not exactly in a position to argue with

you.”

Chapter Nine

Tyler

I glance over at the clock on the nightstand. It's one of those oversized digital numbers you can't miss from a block away. At the moment, it's blinking 04:45 like some deranged heartbeat. At first, I wonder if the power went out. But, I'm able to check the time against my watch and it's consistent. I'm trying not to move because I don't want to disturb Heather. She is currently wrapped around my torso and left thigh like a python.

It has taken many small gifts of trust for her to find herself in this position. At first, I was afraid maybe I had pushed her too far by suggesting we share a room together, but eventually we got here.

After a brisk grilling from her sister, Madison, in which I had to swear on my life not to harm her in any way and give up the name and phone number of my commanding officer, we stopped by a local store and picked up some art supplies. Heather was really confused by this. It was fun to keep her in the dark. She was like a little kid trying to figure out where the Christmas presents were hidden. When we arrived at the hotel, I chose a large executive suite with plenty of room to spread out. While Heather took a bubble bath I set up our little project.

When she came out of the bathroom, all of my good intentions almost became derailed. She looked so adorably sexy in her Betty Boop nightshirt and oversized robe. I know it should have been impossible to look sensual wearing cartoon bunny slippers, but somehow Gidget managed to pull it off. Her curly blonde hair was laying in darker ringlets down her back with her face scrubbed free of makeup. It was a completely different look for her because her look usually consists of artfully placed and composed makeup, but I like this look just as much. It made her appear much more fragile. I wonder if the change is caused by the lack of makeup or if there's more to the transformation. Heather doesn't strike me as the type of person who gets her self-esteem entirely from a bottle, although she's already told me her wild wardrobe choices are sometimes a defense mechanism.

Throughout the night, I used my highly neglected skills as a former architecture major to bring her vision to life using pens and watercolors. Through a series of questions, we ruled out her soap making business. She decided to keep it as a hobby so she could make them only for her closest friends. The decision between opening a bakery and a restaurant was more difficult. The list of pros and cons was significantly longer and more complicated. But, in the end, she decided to start with the bakery and if it went well, to expand from there. To me, this seems like a common sense approach. If her dad gives her any flack over this, he'll have to answer to this ticked off soldier.

After that decision was made, then the fun part came. Heather was able to reach into her memory and pull up word pictures I was able to visually represent on paper. I regretted my drawing and painting skills were so rusty because I would've given anything to be able to capture her vision as perfectly as her words painted it. I did the best I could. By the time we were done, you could really get a sense of how Joy and Tiers would eventually come together. I thought her name for her shop was just perfect. Heather said she chose it because although she would always be happy her grandma gave her the opportunity to live her dream, she would always have a sense of sadness that her grandma would never see the outcome. She loved the play on words because only she would know how it represents a secret sadness.

Although Heather was ecstatic to see Joy and Tiers come to life, the process was draining. Remembering all the stories involving her grandmother was a double-edged sword. In some ways, it was quite cathartic for her. On the other hand, it just underscored all the things she would be missing. Heather seemed to be coping well until it hit her that Lydia wouldn't be with Mindy and Becca to celebrate with them at Christmas time. As the enormity of all the Christmas, birthday and Easter celebrations without her beloved grandma loomed large, Heather fell apart in my arms.

Frankly, I expected this days ago. Gidget has been such a trooper. I don't think I would've coped nearly as well as she has if I had been in her shoes. Despite the constant barrage of criticism from her family, she has remained positive and upbeat. We have been here for two-and-a-half days, and she has helped make all the arrangements with the pastor and the ladies group at the church for the memorial service. She even managed to locate Lydia's gardening and bridge group online and notified them about what was going on. One of them owns a local deli and coffee shop and she offered to let Heather use her commercial kitchen. So, very early yesterday morning before the coffee shop opened, Heather and I baked little pecan tarts and macaroons. As a thank you gift, Heather baked extra for the owner of the shop and was offered a job on the spot. Heather laughed it off as a joke, but I don't think the woman was kidding. They were very good pastries. I don't think Heather truly understands the quality of her work.

I'm not sure how Heather is supposed to have any sense of self-esteem. Every time I turned around, somebody was saying something snarky to her. The way her mother talks to her, you would think she weighs a thousand pounds. The other day, we were sorting through her grandmother's belongings and trying to decide what would be kept and what would be given to charity. It was hard, physical work. Heather and I had sandwiches from the deli. Heather was eating roast chicken on whole wheat bread with tons of vegetables. On the side, she was eating carrots with ranch dressing. She had a small container of homemade sweet tea. Her mom was all over her for excessive eating. I couldn't believe it! If the meal had more than 600 calories, I'd eat my hat. Besides that, Heather is a grown woman if she wants to eat peanut butter, marshmallows and chocolate for lunch it's her own business. I wanted to just let Mrs. LaBianca have it and tell her I would rather have Heather any day of the week rather than a scarecrow like her, but

I held my tongue. I figured I didn't need to be fighting with every single member of Heather's family and her mom probably wasn't going to listen to my opinion anyway. It's still burns me to hear them talk to Heather that way. I can't imagine what it does to her.

Eventually, it all came to a head. We were sitting in the hotel room exchanging stories about our hopes and dreams, when for a moment Heather slipped and said, "Won't this be great? When I get Joy and Tiers all up and running, I'll have to take a video of it so Grandma can post it to her blog."

As soon as she said it, Heather gasped. "Oh my Gosh! I can't believe I just said that. Even worse, I can't believe she's not going to be around to see my bakery when it's all done."

The pain on her face was so raw, I instinctively reacted. I scooped her up and held her to my chest as I strode over to the bed. I toed off my boots, sat us both down in the center of the plush bed, and I just held her as she sobbed. At first, the deep sobs consumed her. I could feel each one travel the whole length of her body. As the time between sobs lengthened, she got the hiccups. At first, she was embarrassed, but then she started giggling every time it happened which made them worse.

She began to apologize for breaking down. I tried to explain to her that there were no apologies necessary. I would be far more concerned if she weren't emotional about the situation.

I started to rub her back to soothe her frazzled mind and body. She was like a kitten that's had a full meal and is taking a nap in the sun. She began to get sleepy and soon she was completely relaxed in my arms. So, I gingerly worked the comforter out from under us and covered us with it after I edged us down in the bed. For propriety sake, I chose to leave my clothes on. We haven't had any conversations about moving our relationship forward and I don't want her to feel like I've taken advantage of the sad circumstance. I've slept in far less comfortable situations, so a pair of dressy Levi's wouldn't kill me.

━━━●●━━━

When I wake up again, my arm is tingling because it fell asleep from the weight of Heather's head. I flex my hand to improve the blood flow. Heather must've felt the movement, because she woke up with a jerking motion and almost broke my nose with her elbow.

"Crap!" she exclaims. "Do you see what time it is? We're supposed to have breakfast with my parents at nine o'clock. If we're late, they'll never let us live it down."

"Gidget, it's only 7:15. Relax. You've got plenty of time," I reassure her, as she's trying to comb her fingers through her hair.

"Argh! You're such a guy," she replies the frustration clear in her voice. "You really don't have any idea how much it takes for us to be presentable, do you?"

"Obviously not," I respond, taking in her wild, rumpled appearance. She looks sleepy, soft, and ready to cuddle. I don't see anything wrong with the way she looks. In fact, this might be my favorite of all of her chameleon-like choices. I know there is no way on God's green earth she would ever agree with my assessment, but that's the way I see it. She looks fresh and comfortable in her own skin. This is the real Heather after you peel all the social armor away. I'm finding as much as I like the bright witty affable public Heather, I prefer the toned down version even better. "I think you look amazing just the way you are."

"Then you need to get into the eye doctor right away because there is something seriously wrong with your vision. I am a mess this morning. My hair needs its own disaster declaration." She grimace as she once again tries to run her fingers through it.

I reach up and gently remove her hands from her hair. "One of these days when we know each other a whole lot better, I'll explain to you why men look at messy hair like yours and see something entirely different, but for now I'll go down and get you some coffee while you take a shower. Sound good?"

"That sounds amazing, thank you," Heather replies with a grateful smile.

When I return to the room after I've located a coffee place, I'm stunned by the transformation. It looks almost as if Heather has put on armor. In a way, I suppose she has. Gone is the soft, natural Heather, and in her place is a cool, sophisticated Jackie O inspired creature. She looks amazing, but different. She's seems unreachable in a way. It's disconcerting. It's almost as if she's two different people.

"Wow," I comment. "You look a bit like you're going to battle."

"That's funny, because that's almost exactly how I

feel. Part of the reason I dressed this way is that it's expected of me. It's part of the uniform of a proper lady. Although, I can tell you my mom is going to hate this outfit because it won't be modern enough for her tastes."

I make a face. "I'm sure you don't want me to say what I'm thinking, otherwise you might hit me and it's a little early in the morning for me to duck. I think you look right pretty and your mom would be crazy not to like your outfit. You look like you could have been Jackie Onassis's best friend. Are you going to want to stay here tonight or do you want to stay at your grandma's place? I need to know so I can check out of the room."

Heather looks up at me in the mirror as she fastens her earring. I watch as a blush overtakes her. But, she quickly gathers herself as she responds, "I don't know, Cowboy. We seem to get along okay. We didn't kill each other last night. Maybe we should try it again and see how it goes. I like the Jacuzzi here."

"I like it too. I like the company even better."

"Alrighty then, I guess we've established that you're not going to pick up any random strangers at the memorial service," Heather answers with a wink. "So, let's come back here and go out to eat. The restaurant here looks phenomenal. I can only eat so many casseroles from the church ladies. I'm starting to adopt your casserole phobia. I need to eat a steak or something."

———◦———

To say breakfast was a strange affair is the understatement of the century. Even after several conversations with Heather's dad and brother, I can't tell whether they respect me more or less because of my military service. It's clear they don't think my service warrants the same amount of respect as their relatives who served in the Civil War, World War I and World War II. They didn't want to talk about Heather's grandmother's service in the Korean War. Her dad went as far as saying it didn't really count as military service because she was only a nurse. Although I strongly disagree with his sentiment, I let the matter go for the purposes of keeping peace. I don't claim my military service is more meritorious than their relatives and I refuse to touch that one with a ten foot pole. Every time her dad challenges me, Heather just sinks further down in her chair. It makes me wish we were like Tara and Aidan and could communicate privately between us in a separate conversation. I try to give her a reassuring smile to let her know none of this BS is really bothering me, but given her expression, I don't think she's getting the message.

It pains me to watch her shed her vivacious personality to try to conform to who her parents want her to be. It hardly seems fair that the men in the family are eating hearty omelets with biscuits and gravy and the women are eating cantaloupe and yogurt. I know from our previous discussions about food yogurt is one of the few foods Heather really dislikes. Yet, she's eating it to meet some unrealistic social expectation.

The longer I think about it, the angrier I become. Finally, I move my coffee cup and scoop some of my omelet and sausage and biscuits together with a generous helping of the hash browns on to the saucer. I place it in front of Heather. "Come on Chef, I bet you can't identify all the spices in these dishes," I challenge.

The look of pure sunshine Heather gives me would've brought a dying plant back to life. I haven't seen her grin that wide in a while. "You do realize this is my field of expertise, right?"

"Yes, I'm aware of that. This is so good that I'd like a formal analysis of it so I can re-create it at home."

"Food is food!" her dad huffs. "I don't see what the big deal is."

"Oh hush Carl," Heather's mother interrupts. "I doubt she'll be successful. I don't think her palette is sophisticated enough to tell the difference. You can tell by looking at her that all she eats is French fries."

I'm trying hard not to buy into their drama, but right now it's taking every bit of discipline ever drilled into me as a soldier not to break into a curse-laden tirade against that vindictive woman. I'm clenching my jaw so tight that my teeth hurt. I look directly at Heather. "Gidget, you were saying?"

"Well, the omelet has several layers of flavor. They've put some spinach and garlic and onions in it, which is standard. What's unusual is the basil pesto and pine nuts. It's a stroke of genius if you ask me. The hash browns are my favorite kind. They make them kind of like they make steak fries and they've added just a touch of balsamic vinegar and tarragon. The biscuits and gravy are your pretty standard fare. The sausage they use is heavily loaded with fennel," Heather explains.

I take a bite of each item as she explains the composition of each one. It's amazing how much more I can taste once I have an idea of what I am looking for. "Wow, that's great. I had no idea everything was so complex," I respond.

"There's no way she can tell all that from just a few bites. She's making up all that crap just to try to impress you," her dad snarls.

"That's it. I'm done trying to be civil," I announce directly to Carl. "Your daughter has tried to make peace since she arrived here and you've done nothing but tear her down. Have you actually ever eaten anything your daughter has cooked for you? If you had, you wouldn't have a single, solitary doubt about her skill level as a chef. As good as this food is, her food leaves this food in the dust. I'm amazed you don't know. Since you apparently don't know or don't care, I think we have better things to do with our time this morning. So, we'll see you this afternoon at the service." I stand up and tip my hat at Madison. "Madison, it was nice to see you, perhaps next time it will be more pleasant, but this isn't your fault." I pull out Heather's chair and help her on with her coat. We walk out of the restaurant in silence, hand-in-hand.

When we get to the rental SUV, I walk her around to the driver's side where she's sheltered from the windows of the restaurant. I notice we are both trembling. I open the back seat of the vehicle and grab my raincoat. I place it around Heather shoulders. As I tried to button the top button, I notice my hands are shaking from adrenaline.

"Oh God Heather, I'm so sorry. I ruined your family breakfast. I shouldn't have lost my temper like that. I can go back in and apologize," I offer as I turn back toward the restaurant.

Heather catches my arm. She captures my face in

her hands. "Tyler Colton, don't you dare apologize, my dear sweet man." She kisses me passionately in the middle of the parking lot. As she pulls away she continues speaking. I have to shake my head to clear it from the endorphins that race through my body at the unexpectedly intimate touch. Her voice fades in, "You said all the things I wish I could say and never think of in the moment because I'm too angry. I could kiss you for that, Cowboy. In fact, I just did," she teases breathlessly as she giggles. "Come on, I know how these breakfasts go. They'll be drinking mimosas until one o'clock in the afternoon. If it's a typical family breakfast, they'll probably have difficulty standing during the prayer service at church."

"Seriously?" I ask.

"As a heart attack. Getting sloshed before church is a family tradition."

"I've heard of a lot of family traditions, but that one's a new one on me."

"Oh, my family's got some doozies," she confesses.

"I can only imagine," I deadpan. "On the bright side, it might explain much of your childhood."

Heather grins at me. "Good point, I never thought of it that way. Come on, I want to show you something. Let's go to the barn."

"Wait! What? You've got a barn, and this is the first time you've mentioned it? How many days have we been here?"

"Well, it's not like we haven't been a little busy."

"You're right. We barely had time to take a breath,

let alone do anything extra. Where is this barn?"

"It's on the back of my grandma and grandpa's property. These are just pet horses, not the fancy horses Grandma gave to Madison."

"How many pet horses are we talking about?" I asked with trepidation, knowing how big the ranch is.

"Well, the last time I was here, there were two. But, one of them was very sick and my grandma was planning to have the old gelding put down. There should be one left. But, don't quote me on that. Because, you never knew with her. She had a huge heart she collected strays like most people collect stamps or commemorative coins."

I sigh heavily. This could go badly, people who have been in the hospital for a long time or those in need of home care can have extremely neglected pets and people with big outdoor animals like horses, cattle and even sheep can be among the worst. I steel myself for a bad outcome, but I have no way of warning Heather without sounding like the world's biggest jerk. As we hike to the back of the field, I am pleasantly surprised. Although the barn looks weathered from the outside, it's actually in good shape. It's clean and well-kept. The tack is organized and not tattered. There's water and fresh feed out for the horses. I breathe a sigh of relief. Just then a beautiful black head pops up from over the stall. Just from her elegant lines, I'm guessing this beauty is the mare in question. She tries to steal my hat with her teeth. "I know you're trying to get my attention, but that's no way to win a cowboy's heart. What's your name, sweetheart?" I ask as I stroke her flank.

Heather giggles at our interaction, which I consider real progress considering where she started. "Her name is Velvet. My grandparents got her for me when I was a little girl. They didn't realize I would be completely terrified of all animals. My grandpa was so disappointed I didn't bond with her like every other little girl who adores horses. I think he wanted me to be like Elizabeth Taylor in the movie. I always felt so sad I couldn't be that kind of grandchild for him. But, with what you taught me the other day, I'd like to try now. She's not included in the horses Grandma gave my sister, so I don't know what will happen to her. I'd hate to see her go to the Humane Society. She's kind of old."

"How old is she?" I gently pull up Velvet's lip to examine her teeth for wear.

"Look at me, I don't even know how long horses live," Heather mutters. "But, I suppose she's about seventeen or so."

"Oh, she's just barely into middle age. Horses usually live to be about twenty-five or thirty. If she's a good riding horse, she'd make a great training horse for Mindy," I suggest.

The look on Heather's face is priceless. It's a cross between horror and hopefulness. "Where do you suppose I would keep her? Tied out behind the food truck?" She snickers as she grins. "That'd be a good one. I could just throw her cake scraps and the left over lettuce from sandwiches. She'd have a bonanza on the days I serve coleslaw. I make an excellent coleslaw which has apples in it. She would grow fat and sassy from all the apple cores."

I grab a currying brush from a hook on the barn wall and start to brush out Velvet's mane. "No, that's precisely why I'm offering to board her for you at my place. My guys could do with a little less feed and Fannie could use a friend."

"Why would you do that? You don't even know this horse and Mindy isn't even your kid."

"Well, you might have noticed I don't like leaving horses at the Humane Society and I'm not real fond of your parents at the moment. Your mom would probably just as soon use Velvet as raw material for a handbag than keep her as a pet. I don't know much about your brother, but to be honest he doesn't strike me as a real horse aficionado, unless he can bet on them."

Heather laughs out loud. "I'm still not sure how you managed to nail my family so well. But, you so have Carlton's number."

"Madison is probably going to have her hands full with the four Arabians she got under the terms of the will. Call me sentimental, but I'd like to see you be able to give this horse to someone who would really benefit from her the way your grandpa intended. I think she'll make a great little riding horse."

Heather sighs and in a shaky voice admits, "That would make Grandpa so happy."

"I know Mindy's not my kid. But, she has had such a rough start in life and I want to do everything in my power to help make all of her dreams come true. So, if I can pitch in and help Jeff and Kiera, that's what I'm going to do. Mindy has been bugging me to teach her how to ride horses ever since the wedding. Apparently, Justice

Gardner told her if she learned how to ride horses, she can ride his horse, Snowball, on the beach next summer when they go back. So, it's been her singular focus. She was highly incensed that she had to ride on her grandpa's lap the last time. She is bound and determined to do it independently the next time."

"Yes, that's true, Mindy is very stubborn when she sets her mind to something," Heather agrees chuckling. "She saw someone making baked Alaska on television a couple of months ago and she's trying to convince me she's ready to try that. She won't take my word for it that it's a pretty advanced technique even for a culinary student. So, we've been working on cookies and yeast breads. But she still has her eye on the prize. It won't be long before she's making that baked Alaska."

"So, what do you say?" I toss Heather a brush. She looks down at her tight fitting A-line dress and her little kitten pumps and gives me a look akin to 'get real'.

I shrug as I walk over to a row of coveralls hanging on the back wall of the barn. I sit down on a stool that's intended for a horse farrier and strip off my jacket and my cowboy boots. I put on the coveralls over my clothes and put the boots back on. Then, I pull a set of women's coveralls out of the pile and hand them to Heather. I raise my eyebrows in challenge.

Heather rolls her eyes at me as she snatches the coveralls from my fingers. "Turn your back please," she orders.

I dutifully turn around and go back to brushing Velvet. I can hear her rustling and muttering under her breath.

"I can't believe the things I do for you. I let you talk me into the craziest things —"

"Are you ready to do one more?"

"What do you mean?" Heather looks at me with narrowed eyes.

"Well, by the looks of that tack, I'd say Velvet here is used to being ridden every day. She's probably pretty lonely right about now. I'd ride her, but I'm too tall and heavy. You're about the size of your grandmother, so you should suit her just fine. Don't worry, I'll lead you around the pasture at a nice slow trot. I'll take great care of you, but this old girl needs companionship or things will be much worse for her. Can we do that for her?"

I watch as Heather's compassionate side far outweighs her fear. Her spine stiffens and her jaw juts out. "Tyler, do you think the sugar cube trick will work for Velvet the way it did for Fannie, Julia, and Jacques?" she asks.

"I'm sure it would, Gidget," I smile warmly. I knew it would only be a matter of time before she would conquer her fear. Everything I have seen from her indicates that she has nerves of steel. "I think I saw some over in this other stall."

I walk over to the other stall and find an old canning jar with sugar cubes sealed inside. I wonder how many times Heather's grandparents came out and fed the horses out of this very jar? I stick a handful of the sweet treats in my pocket and return the old dusty jar to the windowsill. I return to the barn and hold a couple of sugar cubes out to Velvet. At first, it seems like she's going to refuse them from me, but eventually she gently sucks them up. After I've confirmed her temperament, I hand the sugar cubes to Heather. Heather holds the sugar cubes out in the palm of her hand. I didn't have to show her twice how to hold her fingers. She is so still that nothing on her body moves, including her eyelashes. Velvet is understandably curious.

Velvet takes the sugar from Heather and a lifetime of fear seems to start to melt away.

"I should really do this," Heather resolves. "It would be selfish of me not to."

"That's entirely up to you. I'm not going to judge you one way or the other. I want you to be comfortable with your decision. I'll support you either way," I announce as I rub her shoulders.

"You promise to be beside me the whole time?" she probes.

"I promise," I answer solemnly. "I'll be on you like chocolate on a Reese's Peanut Butter Cup. I won't budge an inch."

Heather takes a deep breath. She places her hand in mine she places her other hand on Velvet's neck. "Come on, girl. Let's go take a walk around the corral before I chicken out and change my mind. Mindy was not quite seven when she went on her first horseback ride, I can't have her completely showing me up. As a member of the Girlfriend Posse I've got to at least make an effort to hold my own, don't you think?"

Velvet seems to make a knowing nod as she nickers. I pull a bale of hay out of the spare stall and set it in front of the barn I placed an old saddle blanket on top of it and gestured for Heather to sit on it.

"You might as will make yourself comfortable. It'll take me a bit to saddle Velvet up properly," I comment as I start pulling the appropriate tack off the wall. "There's a few pairs of old boots here if you want to change out of your dress shoes."

Finally, I get Velvet all geared up. When I look over at Heather, she's very pale. She appears to be praying. "Are you all right Gidget?" I ask, with concern in my voice. I don't want to make today any worse for her than it already is.

"Yeah, I'm just talking to my grandma, trying to summon the courage to do this. If she can go to war, I can ride a horse around in a circle. I think she told me to 'get my britches out of a bunch'. I swear I heard her say that. I know you're going to think I'm nuts — and at this point, I probably am — but I'm just going to go with that. Velvet and I are going to go for a ride because my grandma just told us to."

"Babe, you're talking to somebody who has been on the battlefield. You have no idea how many people speak to you when you're in a foxhole. I'm not going to think you're weird. Don't worry about me judging you. That should be the furthest thing from your thoughts."

"Okay, I'll try not to pass out here. Does that sound like a plan?" Heather answers in a shaky voice.

I walk over to her and gather her up in an embrace. It never ceases to amaze me how perfectly she fits in my arms. Usually, when I so much as touch women, I feel like I'm going to break them in half like a toothpick. Yet, holding Heather in my arms feels like she is the key to my lock. It's fascinating. Ever since I was a little kid and I was too large for the desks in kindergarten, I've never felt like I was the right size for anything. The fact that we match together is amazing.

I hold her close for a moment and instruct softly, "Ready? I'm going to lift you up and place you on top of the horse. Just hook your feet in the stirrups and hang on to the straps that are wrapped around the horn of the saddle."

"You mean this part that sticks up? Can I hang on to it?" she asks with panic in her voice.

"Yes," I answer indulgently. "It should fit your hand just about perfectly, but you might find it's in an awkward position to hang onto for long. Most people hang onto the reins."

It isn't the most graceful mount in all the world, but it'll do. Heather is up and on a horse, which is something she never thought would happen a few weeks ago. I attach an external lead rope to the reins so I have control over the bit as well. But from all appearances, Velvet has a very soft mouth and seems to respond to the smallest of corrections almost instantaneously. Velvet seems to sense she is dealing with a real beginner even though Heather is not a child. Velvet is moving with extreme caution. It's almost as if she goes in slow motion. As Velvet lopes around the corral, Heather gradually relaxes into the rhythm and her death grip on my shoulder lessens some. Soon, Heather lets go of me completely and she starts to control the reins by herself. I'm still walking beside her with the lead rope, but Heather has no direct contact with me.

As her confidence grows, so does her smile. Her

back straightens with pride and her eyes light up with joy. "Look! Look what I'm doing! No one would ever believe this. Heather Lydia LaBianca is actually riding a real live horse. I wish my grandparents could have seen this. They would have been totally shocked. What about Tara and Kiera? Their jaws would be on the ground too. I wish they could watch me."

Heather's excitement is contagious. I'm grinning from ear to ear like a kid who just discovered Santa Claus and the Easter Bunny and the tooth fairy are all real. "Heather, I'm so proud of you. You look amazing up there. You look like you've done this your whole life," I compliment as I tie the lead rope off to my belt loop. I pull out my cell phone and start videotaping.

"Hey Gidget, what do you want to tell Mindy about horseback riding now?" I ask as I'm filming.

Heather chortles. "Very funny Cowboy! Okay, so you were right. I should've done this a really long time ago. This is the most fun I've had in a really long time. Mindy, this is a blast. You'll have so much fun with your horseback riding lessons. I can't wait to ride with you. Tyler is a great teacher. Velvet is a wonderful horse." Heather turns to me. "Can you believe I said any horse is a great horse? That's so amazing to me."

"I had no doubt you were going to slay those dragons Heather. I'm so proud of you," I gush as I snap one last picture of her. "Speaking of dragons, you have a few more to conquer today. We should probably get going."

Heather's shoulders slump. "Is it evil of me to think I don't even want to go?" she asks with a sad sigh. "I don't want to have another showdown."

"It's perfectly understandable. This one is for your grandma's friends. The rest of 'em can take a fly'n leap for all I care. This is your chance to say goodbye. Let's not let them ruin that for you," I answer as I lift her off of Velvet.

"Yeah, it's gonna be a heck of a party, right?" Heather replies wiping a tear away.

"Of course it is because you're going to be there and you cooked. In my book, that's all any good party needs," I assure her.

———•———

"Are you sure that Jeff doesn't want us to tell her anything in advance?" Heather asks me from the passenger seat as she looks back at the horse trailer. "Velvet is an awfully huge surprise."

"No, that's the beauty of the whole situation; Jeff plans to keep it from both Kiera and Mindy. So, he'll get double mileage out of it for Christmas. Since I'm leasing to buy my place, I'll add a platform onto the barn so Kiera can get out here with her chair and watch Mindy ride."

"That'll be so much fun. I still can't believe we managed to get out of there with my horse. As mad as my parents are at me, I never thought it would happen."

"Well, it probably wouldn't have if there weren't specific instructions you were supposed to inherit all the pets and then a note specifying that your grandmother considered Velvet to be her favorite pet," I explain. "It was a clever move on her part. She knew your dad would consider all the horses nothing more than property. What a way to brutally bring him to his knees! She took measures to specifically counter that notion in writing. It was a darn stroke of genius if you ask me. I only wish your dad had been completely sober so that the impact would have been more severe."

"True, it was intense when he threw up on Pastor Mike in the middle of the memorial service. It's too bad he was so drunk he won't even remember the embarrassment."

"Somehow, I suspect your dad would believe it was someone else's fault anyway. What did your sister give us?"

"I don't know. She made me promise not to open it until I got here. The suspense is killing me. I know it's long and heavy and in a tube. You have no idea how much restraint I'm showing in respecting my sister's wishes. This is atypical for me because I'm usually very impulsive. You need to know that about me, by the way."

I nod. "Heather, I think I do. You once changed the entire menu on the food truck because you saw on TV it was national donut day."

Heather laughs as she exclaims, "Hey now! That was brilliant marketing, if I do say so myself. Now, it may not have worked so well on National Liverwurst Day."

I groan as I make retching noises. "Please tell me you're kidding."

"I am," she responds with a grin, "but it would've been funny."

"Probably, but not so much for your bottom line

and the neighbors surrounding your food truck probably wouldn't have been so amused."

"Well, there's a party pooper in every crowd, I guess."

Chapter Ten

Heather

"Kiera, this is the craziest roller coaster ride ever," I try to explain as the girls are helping me do laundry and clean up my house after my unscheduled trip to Texas. "One minute, I can't stand him and he's pushing buttons I never even knew I had, and the next minute, it's like he's my greatest cheerleader. Seeing my family through his eyes was a scary sight, but he had my back the whole time. All I know is I would've never survived this trip without him."

"Heather, Tara and I have been trying to tell you about your family for years," Kiera says with a shrug. "At one point, I think even my dad tried to talk some sense into you."

"Yeah, but I thought maybe your opinions of him were skewed because you knew all about our long sordid history. But, Ty was just coming in to all of this as a virtual stranger and he came out of it with the same impression. So, it's been a real eye-opener for me. Who knows, if I hang around Tyler long enough I might just become less tongue tied around my dad and tell them what I really think."

"It would be a refreshing change of pace for you. I wonder what your family would think if they were ever introduced to the Heather that we all know and love?" Tara asks as she looks me over carefully. "Speaking of that, I like this new you. It's less artificial and more real. It's the Heather we all knew was in there under all the makeup and vintage clothes. You're showing glimpses of your true self."

As I process the implications of Tara's statement, I blush a deep shade of red.

Kiera just laughs at me. "Oh, have I ever been there! But, unlike some people, I will not demand you tell me every single detail — unless of course you want to tell us. On the other hand, it might be awkward for me to know since Tyler is Jeff's best friend."

Hmm, I could have some real fun with this. "So… I suppose that means you don't want to hear how we had hot, monkey sex for hours on end while we were away?" I ask, working hard to keep my expression the picture of innocence.

Kiera chokes on her Nantucket Nectar — serves her right for drinking that stuff, why can't she drink a good old-fashioned pop like the rest of us?

"Pardon me?" she asks when she stops wheezing. "I think I've listened to too much of Mindy's One Direction and Justin Bieber and it's beginning to affect my hearing. I don't think I heard you correctly."

I smirk at her. "Nope, you heard me just fine."

Tara interrupts me. "You talk big. Uunfortunately, you're not telling the truth. So, what were you really doing in Texas?"

I should have known Tara is more accurate than any polygraph machine and I wouldn't be able to get away with it. I just laugh and say, "I'm just kidding—although we did have a few epic make out sessions, there was no sex involved. He did help me draw up some plans for the new bakery. Do you want to see them?"

Kiera nods vigorously as she exclaims, "Of course we do, silly woman! This is more exciting than hearing about your alleged sex life."

I pull out the drawings Tyler and I made. The simultaneous gasps from Kiera and Tara confirm my suspicions that we are on the right track.

"I give you Joy and Tiers," I announce with pride. The emotion of saying it out loud is more powerful than I expect and I tear up.

"What's that?" Tara points to the other tube.

"Oh, it's just something I got from Madison. I'm not sure what it is. I think it's something from my grandmother's estate but I'm not really sure," I explain.

"Well, don't keep us in suspense. Open it," Tara directs.

"Okay, hold your horses, I will. But, I don't want to break something. Whatever's in here looks fragile."

As I open it, I'm stunned to see pictures very much like the ones Tyler and I developed. They are much older, of course, and done in pen and ink. Yet they are incredibly similar. Across the top written in my grandma's neat penmanship, it says Heather's Fine Bakery.

Unable to contain myself any longer, I collapse to the floor in a puddle of tears and sob. Tara gets on her knees behind me and wraps her arms around me in a tight hug. She clings to me. Obviously, being around Aidan has really helped her with her comfort level around people. Kiera brings me a glass of water and a warm, wet washrag. I wipe my face and collect myself.

I go back over to the table to examine my grandmother's plans. A date catches my eye. A chill travels up my spine when I realize that I was only nine years old when she had these drafted for me. I carefully lay hers side-by-side with the ones I drew up with Tyler. There are stylistic differences, but the basic concept is strikingly similar.

"So, if these came from your grandma, where did you get these other drawings?" Kiera asks as she studies both sets.

"Would you believe Tyler drew these for me?" I explain with pride in my voice.

"He did?" Tara and Kiera exclaim simultaneously.

"Who knew a heart of an artist beats under all that muscle of your G.I. Joe?" teases Tara.

"I know it shocked me. I had no idea he was this talented. Talk about hiding your light under a bushel. He'd like you to believe all he does is issue tickets for underage drinking and pot smokers while breaking up a few bar fights now and then," I remark.

A look of astonishment crosses Kiera's face as she tentatively remarks, "You guys haven't really honestly talked about what he does on the job, have you?"

"Not really. Every once in a while, he'll make a cryptic remark here and there. But, he doesn't really talk about his job all that much," I confess.

"The confidentiality thing is hard on Jeff too, but don't let Ty fool you. His job is extremely tough and complicated. He's only sharing the tip of the iceberg," Kiera advises. "So, when he does talk, you need to really listen. I've been friends with him a while and I didn't even know he had this talent."

"He said something about being an architecture major when he was in college," I explain.

Tara is studying the drawings carefully, she looks at me with a look of admiration on her face and says absentmindedly, "Huh, I wonder why he quit? This shows more than just technical skill. He could have been absolutely brilliant. So, what are you planning to do with these?" She says as she traces the graceful lines with her fingers.

"I don't know." I answer honestly. "I wasn't expecting to get any money for my grandma's estate and now I have enough to make my wildest dreams come true. Unfortunately, I have to run a business plan through my family as a condition of getting the money. So, I have to find a specific location and develop a marketing plan. I guess I'll probably need to find myself some staff as well. I'm hoping Piper will want to make the move to a physical location with me. I don't know yet whether I'll need to hire more staff or not because I don't know how large my location will be."

"Did you know the candy store next to

Gwendolyn's floral shop is planning to go out of business? They are going to go back to Ohio to take care of their aging parents. I don't know if they would have the ovens you would need for a bakery, but you could always ask Gwendolyn," Kiera suggests.

"That's cool, but how would Gwendolyn know about the ovens? Besides, there's probably a waiting list for that place. The location is the perfect retail space for a little restaurant."

Kiera and Tara look at each other in surprise and laugh as they say in unison, "You haven't heard?"

"Heard what?" I ask, in confusion.

"Gwendolyn bought the whole building with her divorce settlement from Kevin 'The-Jerk-Wad'. When she leased her place, she was smart enough to ask for first purchase rights if the landlord ever wanted to sell and the timing just happened to be perfect. She got it for a song because she'd been such a long term tenant," Kiera explains.

"Do you think she would be interested in renting it to me even though the only experience I have is on a food truck?" I ask, almost afraid to get my hopes up.

"Probably," Kiera answers, nodding her head. "Gwendolyn is an honorary member of the Girlfriend Posse now and one of your biggest fans. She would want to see you succeed. Why wouldn't she rent to you? You've turned your food truck into an amazing success."

"Should I call her, or would it be too presumptuous?" I press, barely able to contain my excitement.

Tara rolls her eyes at me, "Just call already. You know you're not going to do any more laundry after the conversation we've just had. You might as well call your hunk of a boyfriend and let him know about your grandma's plans and show Gwendolyn too. If I know anything about Gwendolyn, I suspect you all will be meeting with her favorite decorator before the end of the week. But, if it were me, I would just use Donda. That girl has some mad skills."

"I know about a certain little girl's bedroom that tells me you've got some pretty mad skills too."

<hr>

"So, they're just planning to leave all this equipment behind?" I ask as I look around at the twenty quart mixers and industrial food processors.

"Yes, they said they have no use for them. They wanted me to try to sell all of it for them. I was going to go on eBay or Craigslist and see what I could get for all of this stuff," Gwendolyn replies.

"Don't you have a new tenant lined up?" I inquire carefully, not wanting to appear overly anxious.

"No, honestly I was hoping that they might change their mind. They've been here for so long I didn't want them to lose their family business," Gwendolyn explains sheepishly. "I was hoping if I didn't do anything, the situation might just resolve itself."

"Well, I don't know if you're willing to take a risk on a new business but I have an idea for you. My grandmother just passed away and left me a substantial pot of money with the caveat that I start a bakery with the proceeds. I think a bakery that specializes in special occasion cakes would complement a florist well. I graduated in the top of my class at culinary school and I specialize in pastries and baked goods. My grandmother has had this dream of me opening a bakery since I was nine years old."

"That sounds lovely, dear." Gwendolyn replies. "I think you'll do a fine job. I was eating at your food truck long before I was introduced to you. Your barbecue brisket slider is one of my favorites and your strawberry cheesecake is heaven on earth. Imagine my surprise when Jeffrey introduced you as Kiera's best friend. I think you should meet with Justice Gardener. I'd have you talk with Jeffrey, but he considers himself my attorney now and I think he can get in trouble if he gives us both advice. So, I think you should talk to William instead. I think we can come up with an agreement that's beneficial to us both. May I see those plans again? These are quite remarkable. Are you sure these were drawn nearly 20 years apart?" Gwendolyn inquires as she studies the plans side-by-side.

"Positive," I confirm as I watch her go over the plans with a fine tooth comb. "I watched Tyler draw these right in front of me."

"He did?" she asks, sounding surprised. "What a clever boy! I knew there's more to him than he lets on. He must like you a lot to put his heart and soul into these sketches."

Her observation makes my heart skip a beat as I consider its veracity. It's true. Despite all of his assertions to the contrary, Tyler has done everything in his power to cement our bonds and make them very permanent. He has shared things with me he doesn't usually share with anyone else. In fact, he's been quite open with me about things from his past. He has done everything in his power to make his feelings known about me — even when it makes me feel uncomfortable to know how he's feeling.

"Gwendolyn, is it okay if I ask you a question?" I ask. "This isn't related to the business. This is personal. I'm not very close to my mom, and I don't know who else to ask."

"Of course dear. I don't mind. But, you might want to take my advice with a grain of salt. As you might have noticed, I'm not the best at relationships."

"Oh, that's okay. I'd rather have that kind of advice. Because it's real world and not just something they can replicate in a lab somewhere because it makes a good research paper," I respond with a quirky smile.

"That's me for sure. Just call me Ms. Real-Life-School-of-Hard-Knocks."

"You've probably guessed by now I kind of have a thing for Tyler," I admit sheepishly. "But, I'm not sure where we stand. He helped me through a difficult time in my life and I'd like to do the same for him but I don't know if I have the right to. To make matters worse, he might not even like what I have to say. It might drive a wedge between us before we even start to get to know each other. I don't want to ruin a good thing."

"Well, if there's anything I learned in the whole debacle of my farce of a marriage, it's that secrets are poisonous. If you guys have any chance at success, you need to be telling the truth to each other right up front." Gwendolyn advises.

"What if the truth has the potential to hurt him, but withholding it has the potential to hurt others?" I ask, deep despair clawing at my gut.

"Do you feel you can trust Tyler? Is he the type of man that would take the truth without striking back and hurting you?" Gwendolyn probes with a look of concern on her face.

"Of course," I confirm without hesitation. But, then I remember his comments about his post-traumatic stress disorder and how it has affected his temperament and emotional well-being and I wonder if I can be so unequivocal in my defense of him. "I worry most about hurting him," I reply honestly.

"Honey, as difficult as this seems, I think you need to have this conversation. Otherwise, you're building your relationship on false pretenses," Gwendolyn responds as she pats my shoulder. "I'm sure you'll find a way to figure it all out because you're a smart girl. I'll have paperwork drawn up for you. I do want you to go see William. I want another set of eyes to understand that our contract is on the up and up. It will be great fun to have a bakery next door although it will be terrible for my diet."

After meeting with Gwendolyn, I'm on cloud nine. I even call Tyler at work. The dispatcher is so confused by my giddiness that she patches me through to his work radio thinking it's a family emergency. I can't resist taking a moment to share my good news even though technically it doesn't fall within the rules of an emergency. Tyler is gracious in dealing with my absolute silliness. He quickly congratulates me and promises we will celebrate when he comes home. My good mood lasts up until I call my family to let them know I found a potential retail space.

My dad takes the opportunity to inform me that if needed, they are planning to contest my grandma's will based on the fact that they thought she was no longer of sound mind because she gave me an opportunity to own a business, even after I allowed my ex-boyfriend to swindle money from me and my family. They threatened to tie up my money in probate court for months and months, unless I agree to postpone my plans to open the restaurant for at least six months, but preferably a year. I could not even muster a reply.

I simply hang up the phone and sob. It was almost like I have to mourn Grandma Lydia all over again because it's akin to the death of a dream. I know that this is more than just a dispute about a particular location or even a simple stalling technique. My family is going to fight me every single step of the way. It doesn't matter if I have the perfect location, in the perfect spot, in the perfect city. They will never, ever support my dream. It's as simple as that.

When I finally stop sobbing, I strip down to my tank top and boy shorts and climb into the shower like a slow-motion radio controlled robot toy that's seen better days. Too exhausted to stand, I sit in the corner of my shower and curl up in a ball, letting the water beat down on me as tears continue to trickle down my cheeks and mix with the tap water. I silently cry until there are no more tears left. I thought I was finished crying yesterday, and the day before and the day before that. However, the tears still continue to come. I don't know when they'll stop. If I can't do this shop in the memory of my grandmother, this may never get better. It's all she ever dreamed of for me since I was nine years old. How can I turn my back on all her hopes? It's not fair.

I can hear the voice of my father mocking me in my head, "The world is not fair, Buttercup. Just get used to it. Of course, it's fair to the beautiful people. Oh wait, you're not one of those either. Yep, you're screwed." His voice is so clear, I self-consciously look around to see if he's in the room with me. Of course, he isn't. I shrink back into myself and put my head down between my crossed arms and let the water beat down on the back of my neck.

I don't know how long I sat there, but the next thing I know, Tyler is lifting me out of the shower and brushing my heavy wet locks of hair out of my eyes.

"My God, Gidget, what happened to you? You're freezing cold. Did you fall down?"

"N-N-No," I stammer as my teeth chatter like a jack hammer on asphalt, "I'm okay. I'm just sad."

"I know you miss your grandma, but she lived a very full life. She'll always be in your heart," Tyler wipes my tears away with his thumb.

"I know," I sigh. "I wish it was that simple. But, I got a call from my dad and he's threatening to put all sorts of roadblocks in the way of the bakery. He's even going to challenge the validity of the will if I don't postpone the opening of my shop. I've already found the perfect location. Gwendolyn is willing to rent to me. I'll never find another space like that. It even comes with commercial baking equipment. But, I can't ask her to hold it for me."

Tyler is quiet for a moment as he holds me close to his chest. "Why don't you put some warm clothes on and I'll make you something hot to drink?"

I nod against his chest, hoping I don't get snot all over his shirt. I hate that he has to see me this way. Although, he doesn't seem to notice anything is out of the ordinary, even though I'm getting his clothes completely soaked.

"Thank you," I whisper, my voice hoarse from hours of crying.

"Do you want tea or hot chocolate?" Tyler asks gently.

"Doesn't matter," I respond as he sets me down on my bed. Much to my mortification, there's a basket of laundry sitting on my bed and several pairs of my underwear are sitting right on top.

Tyler eyes a pair of leopard-print underwear with approval and winks at me. "Nice! I like my women with a sense of adventure."

If I could've fallen through floor right then, I gladly would have. I'm sure I could give Rudolph's nose a run for his money right at this moment.

Tyler takes one look at the expression on my face and laughs as he quips, "Oh relax Gidget, for all you know, I could be wearing something far racier, right this very moment."

I snort. "I bet you just talk big. You're probably wearing tighty-whities. I don't think you have the guts to wear anything racy. I think you're too old school."

Tyler howls with laughter. "Well, it's a good thing

you didn't have anything riding on this one, Gidget; because you would've lost big time," he responds as he pulls down the top of his well-worn jeans to show me his Yosemite Sam cartoon underwear.

I choke back a laugh. "I didn't know they made cartoon undies for big boys."

"Well, they do if you're a dedicated enough fan. These babies are not easy to find. Thank God for the Internet," Tyler responds with a good-natured shrug. "You go get dressed. All this talk about underwear is making me horny. I'll meet you in the kitchen."

As I puzzle over my wardrobe choices, it's astonishing that I'm even considering wearing something this ridiculous in front of Tyler, but it speaks to my level of comfort with him. One year, Kiera, Tara and I all volunteered at the same camp for the Big Brother/Big Sister program. They had a pajama day and the Girlfriend Posse bought gag pajamas for each other. For me, they bought footie pajamas which feature Jessica Rabbit and Roger Rabbit splashed down the front and back. Something tells me Ty is one of few people on the planet who could truly appreciate the beauty of my PJ's.

After I put my hair up in a sloppy bun and try to remove the trails of black waterproof mascara from my face, I put on my favorite Bonnie Bell bubble-gum lip gloss and go out into the kitchen. I know it's not very sophisticated, but clearly, that's not the look I'm going for here. While Tyler has his back to me, I take a moment to study him. Oh Lawdy, the man is hot! His flannel shirt is pulling across his broad shoulders and his waist tapers in, highlighting his incredible abs and obliques. He has this funny habit of scratching his stomach when he's nervous and he thinks no one is watching; I've caught more than one glance at that washboard in the last year. I listen carefully to what he is humming and realize it's Aidan's latest hit. I smile to myself. What an unreal world I live in. My best friend's fiancé is a huge pop star. My other best friend's godfather is an important Former Oregon Supreme Court Justice. As I reflect back on my last conversation with him, it's hard not to feel defeated.

Tyler turns around with two large steaming mugs of hot chocolate. "Darlin', why are your eyes sad again? I thought we chased all that away."

"It's going to take more than just a few giggles about underwear to do that," I sit down at the kitchen table.

"That's too bad, because I'm digging those pajamas," Tyler responds as he slides my hot chocolate in front of me. I notice he's melted marshmallows all over the top of mine.

"I figured you might," I answer with a watery grin. "This is about as sexy as I'm going to get today."

"I don't know how many times I have to tell you that it doesn't really matter what you wear; I'm always going to find you sexy whether you have bunnies on your butt or not," Tyler insists. "But, I have a feeling you're just trying to change the subject. What's really going on?"

"Well, I told you most of it. In a nutshell, my dad doesn't think I'm responsible enough to own a business because of what my ex-boyfriend did to all of us. So, he plans to throw up every obstacle on the planet to stand between me and the money granted to me in the will. He thinks I'm flighty enough if he makes me wait six months or a year, I'll get distracted and forget about owning the bakery," I explain, feeling dejected.

"That's bull!" Tyler exclaims pounding his fist on the table causing the hot chocolate to slosh out of both mugs. "Does he realize that it's not really his money to mess with?"

"My dad isn't really big on boundaries. Whenever I complained about that as a kid, he would counter with, 'Are you ashamed to be Italian or what?' I was never sure what one thing had to do with the other. My grandparents and aunts and uncles were perfectly reasonable people."

"Sometimes you can't explain family. But, yours is really something else. It's not like you're the only person on the planet that's been taken in by a con man. Being in love can make us blind to all sorts of stuff. Don't even get me started," Tyler comments wryly as he shakes his head.

"I know that now. But, I still feel like a stupid fool. I was just so taken in by Fletcher. I thought he accepted me for me and didn't care about how I looked. It felt so good to seem like a normal woman and be out dating. We even went out dancing. He was like a tornado of fun and I was sucked into it. Apparently, so was my common sense."

"Gidget, I've got news for you. You are the one who's normal. All these girls who starve themselves to death and eat twigs and air and bake themselves under florescent light bulbs? In my book, those girls are the strange ones. The guys who are not falling all over you are stupid because you are beautiful."

"I really wasn't fishing for compliments." I blush to a deep shade of red.

"I know. That's what makes it so wonderful." Tyler responds. "So, I've been thinking the best way for me to help you is to give you a bridge loan until your dad gets over all of his craziness."

"What?" I ask dumbfounded by his suggestion. "I can't ask you to do that. We've barely started dating. In fact, I'm not even sure we've actually started officially dating."

"I know," Tyler responds nodding his head. "That's one of the reasons I offered. You are always giving to other people and never asking for anything for yourself. I've got money from my military service socked away in CDs. It's not doing anything terribly productive anyway with interest rates the way they are. Come on Gidget, let me help you. Don't let your dad have that much power over your life."

"But, what if my business is a huge failure?" I ask, still amazed he would even consider doing such a risky thing.

"That's a risk I'm willing to take. I know you're brilliant. I've seen you cook, I know what your customer service skills are. I know how you thrive under pressure, you're going to be amazing. I don't have any doubts your business is going to skyrocket to the moon. Everyone you know — especially your close friends, like me, will do everything in our power to make it so."

"Tyler, I have to think about your offer. If I did this, it would change everything in our relationship. We would be more than just boyfriend and girlfriend, we would now be business partners. Are you ready for that?" I inquire.

Tyler pulls me into an embrace and nuzzles my neck as he answers in a rumbly voice, "I've got no problems multitasking, do you?"

CHAPTER ELEVEN

TYLER

"I can't believe we've kept this under wraps. Mindy will have a conniption fit when she sees her," I say, as I brush Velvet's coat one last time.

Heather grins and continues to tie red and green ribbons into Velvet's mane. "You should be even more amazed I was able to keep it a secret. Usually, I can't keep my mouth shut to save my life. You should have wagered money."

"Speaking of bets, you still haven't collected on the multitude of wagers you have won against me. I'm not sure I like all this outstanding debt."

"Don't we have a date next week to take care of one of these debts?"

"Yes, ma'am, we do. Dress warm and wear your tennis shoes or boots. Don't let Lucky get near them this time."

Heather sticks her tongue out at me. "Did you forget that I actually made the wager and I know what we have planned? I know better than to wear stilettos to the gun range."

"I know Darlin', but I also know you're planning to spend Christmas with Jeff and Kiera. Lucky has a thing for your shoes."

Heather snickers at me. "Mine and everyone else's. It's a wonder everyone in that household doesn't run around barefoot. Are you coming over for Christmas Dinner?"

"I don't know. It depends on my work schedule. I may work and give the family guys some time with their kids. Will you save me some leftovers?"

"For a guy who's doing something as sweet as that? Absolutely."

"Don't be too impressed, Gidget. I'm low on the totem pole. Chances are, I would've drawn the short straw and had to work anyway."

"Come on, Ty. I'm sure your willingness to step up counts for something."

I shrug noncommittally. "What about your other markers? I still owe you dinner, but you also beat me fair and square at lawn bowling and video games."

Heather peers around Velvet's neck. "I did, didn't I? But, you're forgetting one."

"What am I forgetting?" I ask, puzzled.

"That I'm the undisputed movie trivia champ of the Northwest." Heather teases with a wink.

"You're right. I don't know how that total shellacking could've slipped my mind," I sigh. "Just add it to my pile of indebtedness." I don a sad pose for effect.

"You poor baby! I'm feeling bad for you now. In all fairness, though, I told you not to bet against me when we played video games, but you wouldn't listen."

"As I told you before, I tend to be way too stubborn for my own good. I can only hope I've learned my lesson now.

Heather sets the ribbons down and walks around Velvet. She stops mere inches from me, removes her gloves and runs her index finger down the bridge of my nose, across my lips and down my chin. "In an uncharacteristic move, I'm going to hand the reins of my wager over to you. I still expect you to cook me a meal someday. With that understood, however, I trust you to choose the remaining rewards — or is it punishments? — as you see fit." After her stunning pronouncement, Heather gently closes my suddenly slack jaw and seals the deal with a surprisingly hot kiss.

My body and brain immediately go to war. A bolt of white hot heat goes through me, energizing every nerve fiber, as I briefly envision a few very carnal ways those markers might be paid off. Those images are so vivid, I have to bite back a harsh groan. I open my eyes to find Heather regarding me with a curious smirk.

"Are you all right, Cowboy?"

I nod tightly. "I'm good, why?"

Heather shakes her head as she chides, "I'm not the only one who should avoid the poker table. You can't lie worth beans, Tyler."

Pulling down a bale of hay, I sit down and maneuver her until she is practically sitting on my lap. "Okay, fine," I admit with a sigh. "For the first time, I wish my best friend and his adorable family lived in an entirely different state and would not be here in twenty minutes. Right now, you and my feather bed are all I can think about."

Heather's eyes widen and she gives a small startled gasp. "Just to clarify, are you considering this a reward or punishment?" She quickly hops up and becomes preoccupied with picking bits of hay out of her sweater and off of her shapely backside.

Trying not to lose my train of thought in light of the fine distraction. "Unquestionably, a reward for both of us." I guide her so she's standing between my thighs.

She blushes even deeper. "You've never seen me naked, or you might rethink that."

Clearly words are not enough, since we've had this conversation several times already. I fish my cell phone from my pocket and hit redial.

"Hey Jeff, I'm glad I caught you. Do you mind if we rearrange the schedule? Can you take the kids to lunch, swing by Denny's, and make us your last stop? I agree, it makes more sense this way because the kids will probably get dirty anyway. Great. We'll see you in about four hours. Bye."

I tuck the phone in my pocket and turn to Heather. She's watching me in shocked silence. Finally she quietly asks, "Why did you do that?"

I reach out and take her hands in mine. I notice they're trembling. I'm fairly certain her proximity to Velvet is not the cause. Over the last few months, she has become quite the horse aficionado. She comes over several times a week to ride and groom both Fannie and

Velvet. "I've tried for nearly two years to get across to you that I think you are stunning, sexy, breathtaking, amazing, and a million other adjectives. Somehow, you don't seem to think I'm talking about you. So, I'm done talking. I'll show you."

Heather draws in a sharp breath and her eyes mist over with tears. "You might be disappointed," she whispers.

I squeeze her hands. "Gidget I could never be disappointed in you. That fear goes both ways, you know. I left parts of my body tangled up in an IED. There are chunks of my skin missin' that will never grow back. You might find me downright repulsive."

Heather pulls my head down and rests her forehead against mine. "I guess we're both being stupid."

"I guess the only question is whether I have to call in a marker or whether you just want to go have a hot make-out session?"

Heather scrunches up her face as if deep in thought. "Well, I guess I'm a winner either way, so I'm going to let you hold on to that marker and find another creative use for it."

On the way up the stairs, I turn off the lights and close the Dutch door behind me, so Ethel and Annie don't follow us, I take a moment to consider how much of what I told Heather was mere reassurance and how much of it cuts way too close to home. I haven't had a serious relationship since before I was injured. As much as I'm ashamed to admit it, the caliber of women I was with immediately following my recovery really didn't care one way or the other. They probably weren't sober enough to notice I'd been injured, and I was too drunk to tell them. Fortunately, that coping mechanism didn't last long, and I didn't permanently revert to the idiotic college student I once was.

I suspect this will be as nerve-racking for me as it is for Heather. I struggle to place my casual, fun-loving guy mask back in place. Heather is nervous enough. She doesn't need to have nerves for two of us.

When I catch up to Heather outside my bedroom door, she looks like she's about to face a firing squad. I brush my fingertips lightly across her shoulder and she almost jumps out of her skin. "Relax, Gidget, you seem to be forgettin' the agenda for this afternoon is reward," I murmur in her ear.

"So you say," Heather replies with a shaky smile. "If that's so true, why do I feel like I am suddenly five years old and you're fixin' to make me eat my mushy canned peas?"

I make a dramatic gesture as if she's stabbed me in the heart, "Oh, I'm wounded. Not only did you cast me in a parental role, you paired me with terrible food. From you, isn't that like the kiss of death? Should I just throw in my cards, now?"

My antics earn me a halfhearted giggle from Heather. "I don't know, I guess it depends on how persuasive you are," she answers me with an arched eyebrow.

Never able to let a challenge go unanswered, I scoop her up Rhett Butler style and walk her into the center of my room. Looking around the room, I try to envision it from her point of view. I'm relieved everything looks neat and tidy and there isn't anything overtly embarrassing hanging around.

I stand next to the bed and let Heather's body slide slowly down mine. Even totally clothed, it's a sensual experience. I look down at Heather's upturned face as her eyes flutter shut. It's a look of vulnerability she rarely lets me see. I'm so used to seeing her tough facade that this completely open, expectant expression is at once a complete turn on and scary as hell. It shows just how far we've come that she trusts me this much.

Threading my fingers through her hair, I work the bandanna loose she was using to constrain her curls while working with the horses. As her curls tumble over my forearms, I catch the light scent of lemons. I smile to myself. Few women could spend the morning working in the barn and still smell good, but somehow Heather has managed to beat the odds. "Mmm, I might skip dessert and just have you," I comment as I bury my nose in the hair at her temple.

A quick, satisfied smile crosses her lips. "Good, I'm glad you like it. I made a whole line in lemon meringue just for you, because you said it's your favorite. I made soap, shampoo and lotion."

"No toothpaste?" I ask, tongue firmly in cheek.

Her brows draw together in thought. "No, but what a great idea. Why didn't I think of that?"

"Oh, I don't know, maybe it's because you're spectacularly good at a hundred other things, and you've been a little too busy for product development."

I lean down to leisurely kiss her. My hands tighten reflexively in her hair as desire rockets through my body.

In my haste to get closer, I reach down to scoop Heather up and plop her in the middle of the bed with much less grace than intended.

"Geez Cowboy! I may look like a sack of potatoes, but it doesn't mean you have to treat me like one," Heather remarks as she takes an ungainly bounce in the middle of the bed.

I have to take a deep breath and count to ten, because I don't want this to come out wrong and upset her.

"Heather, remember when you were a kid and you went over to someone else's house to play? You always had to play by their rules? Well, the rules in this room are, you're not allowed to put yourself down. You can only say positive things about yourself. I don't even want you to say cutting remarks about yourself in the form of a joke."

"Tyler, I was just kidding. It's no big deal," Heather insists.

"It is to me. No one should use words to hurt you. Especially you. So, I want you to go out of your way to find things you like about yourself, okay?"

Swallowing hard, Heather nods. "Do you mind if I freshen up?"

I can see she's struggling to sort through her emotions. I knew before I said anything, I was walking a thin line. She doesn't like to be bossed around, and I'm taking a huge risk of ruining any intimate mood between us. But I figure, if I'm going to lay my cards on the table, they all should be there.

"No, go right ahead. The door is on the left. There's a cupboard under the sink with fresh towels."

"Thanks, I'll be right back."

While Heather is in the restroom, I run downstairs to get a couple of glasses of iced tea and some candles from my emergency kit. Jeff's mom brought over a poinsettia the other day, and I grab it too. I haphazardly throw it all on a TV tray and run back upstairs. I quickly unload everything onto the bedside table and stash the TV tray in the closet. Fortunately, I keep a lighter in the bedside table to melt the shoe polish I use to shine my boots for guard duty. I light the candles, recline on the bed and casually pick up a hunting magazine as if I haven't had a little mini-workout in the last three minutes.

When Heather comes through the doorway and spots what I've done to the room, we stare at each other for a moment. The corner of her mouth hitches up as she exclaims with the very southern drawl, "Why, Tyler Joseph Colton, you are just the sweetest thing ever!" Her accent is so exaggerated, I'm not sure she actually means it as a complement.

I'm going to err on the side of caution and decide that she means it. "Thank you Darlin', I try. You look absolutely ravishing."

Heather looks down at her purple eyelet corset and skirt and says, "This old thing—"

I raise my eyebrow and she quickly corrects herself.

"Thank you. I love this color. I think it makes my eyes look especially blue."

I smile as I get off the bed and walk over to her. I

brush her hair back from her face and tenderly kiss her luscious lips. As I pull away, I murmur, "See, that wasn't so hard." I take her by the hand and lead her to the bed. This time, I gently pick her up and place her in the center of the bed.

She looks unnerved for a second, then collects herself and quips, "Oh my gosh, Tyler. If this were my bed. I don't think I would ever want to get out. This is the softest bed I've ever been in."

I grin like a kid in a candy store. "Isn't it great? It was one of my big splurges after I came back stateside. I was tired of sleeping on government issued mattress equivalents. So, I got the biggest, baddest, most blinged out mattress I could find. You're welcome to sleep over anytime."

Heather turns bright red. "Well, I don't know if I'm ready for that quite yet, but I might sneak up here for a nap."

"How about we play it by ear?" I suggest as I pull her hair to the side and kiss her neck. She arches to give me better access. As I place a line of kisses down her jaw line, she nods.

When I feather my fingertips over her collarbones, her breath catches. I trace the top of her feminine corset with the pads of my thumbs. I know my fingers are calloused from all the woodworking and odd jobs I do around here, but next to her delicate skin, I'm afraid they must feel like sand paper. As she takes a deep breath, my fingers brush the soft swell of her breast. Her eyes lose their focus and her cheeks grow pink as she whispers hoarsely, "I need more."

Heather's stark admission stokes my desire like a five alarm fire. I fight my inner instincts to react like a freshman on his first date. "Happy to oblige Darlin'," I murmur.

When I search her face, I see tears gathering on her long lashes. I immediately remove my hands.

"Gidget?" I probe as I wipe away the tears. "Talk to me."

Heather squeezes her eyes shut. Finally she opens them and takes a steadying breath. "I'm not like other women you've been with."

"Well, thank God for small favors!" I mutter under my breath.

Heather punches me in the shoulder. "No, you dumbass! I'm trying to make a point here. I'm a lot squishier than those women. I've probably got more cellulite in my left calf than they'll ever have in their whole body. I'll never be perky."

"Heather, look at me. I'm making a point too," I say, as I point to my long frame. "As you've observed many times, I've got an awful lot in common with the Jolly Green Giant. Small and delicate is not my speed. I've discovered I like my women to be hot girls from the East coast who are transplants to Oregon and happen to be of Italian decent. By the way, you broke the house rule, you have to name a positive thing."

Heather looks befuddled for a moment, then confesses, "I've never had to stuff my bra."

"Trust me, as a guy who was repeatedly let down during my explorations in junior high, that was probably a really good thing."

"Tyler Joseph! If you had your hands down a girl's shirt in junior high, you deserved to be let down. Does your mother know you were such a precocious young man?"

I chuckle. "Oh, I think she had a pretty good idea. I suspect my mama has calloused knees from all the time spent praying for me. Truth be told, she still probably spends a fair amount of time praying for me, just to be on the safe side."

"It sounds like she might have had good reason."

"Heather, I've grown up a good bit since then, but I still know what I want and I know that I want you. Despite what you might think, you've had my attention for a long time. If I wanted somebody that looks like an anorexic Victoria's Secret model, they are a dime a dozen. I want someone with a heart, a soul, and a brain. Of course, it doesn't hurt that I find you sexy as all get out. I have since the first time I laid eyes on you in Jeff's kitchen, when you threatened to decapitate me with his spatula if I messed up your grill marks."

Heather is now propped up against a pile of pillows.

"Heather, you call the shots here. Anytime you want me to stop, I will. But, keep in mind this will be out of both of our comfort zones."

"See, I knew my size was going to be a problem—" Heather interjects.

"Before you jump to conclusions, you may want to wait to hear the rest of what I was going to say."

Heather blushes as she mumbles, "By all means proceed, Cowboy. Although, I'm not even sure you can talk your way out of this one."

"You might be surprised when you hear my answer. The reason this is so uncomfortable for me has nothing to do with how you look or what size jeans you wear. It has everything in the world to do with who you are. That's because, for the first time since in a month of forevers, the outcome of this really matters. You matter to me. It's been an embarrassingly long time since I've let anybody get close. Now that I've let you in, I don't want to completely blow it."

Stunned into silence for a moment, Heather blinks slowly as she lets out a breath. "I think that's the most words I've ever heard you string together in the two years I've known you. I don't really know what to say to that — other than just wow. You know me, I'm rarely at a loss for words."

"I think we were doing just fine a minute ago without any words, don't you?" I bring her fingers to my lips and softly kiss her finger tips and then the back of her hand. When I kiss the tender spot on her inner wrist, I can feel the galloping beat of her pulse. I suspect it matches mine.

"Ty, not to criticize your technique or anything," Heather gasps as I kiss the inside of her elbow, causing her to flinch and jerk it back reflexively. "But, I was having way more fun when you were covering other territory, if you know what I mean."

Chuckling softly, I murmur, "Darlin', that sounds kinda like a challenge to me, don't you think?"

Heather's eyes dilate and widen as she mutely shakes her head.

"You know me … I can't pass up an opportunity like that. I guess I'll have to step up the pace."

I'm the first to admit I am an aficionado of women. I like everything about them. I like the way they look … the way they smell … the way they feel. Unfortunately, I've never been able to put all the puzzle pieces together to successfully be someone's partner.

Nothing in my past has prepared me for the connection I have with Heather. Maybe this time will be different. I struggle to stay in control as she moans softly. Suddenly, this is no longer about light-hearted flirting or teaching lessons about self-esteem—it's so much more. I've been focused on her for so long, I'm hyper-aware of her reactions and I'm ready to combust.

Heather purrs a sigh of contentment as her eyes drift open. She tilts her head a bit as our eyes meet. "I thought you said we were both getting rewards, Cowboy. I see you handing them out, but I don't see you getting many."

"See, there's where you're wrong, Gidget. The look of pleasure on your face can't be measured. It's a reward all on its own."

Heather's luscious lips form a frown as she argues, "Maybe so, but I think you're just trying to welch on your end of the deal."

There are certainly disadvantages to dating a woman as bright as Heather. One of them is that she doesn't miss a single, solitary thing.

Heather smiles coyly at me as she reaches up and slides her slim fingers under the collar of my shirt. "Well, I'm an even better friend than I am a lady, and friends always take turns," she murmurs in a low sexy drawl.

As her cool fingers touch, hot, destructed scars, my vision dims around the edges as my mind drifts back to the chaotic days at Landstuhl Air Force Base. I can still remember the awful stench of burning flesh and antiseptic. Suddenly no one would look me in the eye and I couldn't get any straight answers when I asked about my men. People were either eerily silent or irritatingly cheerful. Hours and hours of physical therapy and skin grafts have taken care of most of the external damage. I don't know if there is enough medical care on the planet to erase the memories of holding my friend and colleague after he was blown to pieces.

I look down at my hands and notice they are shaking. I glance around the room in a frantic bid to find something to distract Heather from my discomfort. Yet, it's clear from her expression it's far too late for that tactic to work.

Heather gathers my hands between hers. "Tyler, look at me. I'll be gentle I promise."

With excruciating slowness, Heather unbuttons my shirt, brushing her lips across the spot her fingers just left. I can feel every nerve ending as my pulse races like I've run sprints with all my gear on. I squeeze my eyes shut as I try to regain focus.

Heather gently brushes her thumbs over my closed eyes as she gently massages the muscles in my face. "Relax Cowboy, I'm not going to hurt you. Pleasure is the name of the game, remember?"

Her low husky voice is almost enough to send me over the edge. We've been playing these flirting games for months. The anticipation is killing me, but I'm trying to do the "right" thing. But, between us, who the hell knows what that is. Nothing about our relationship has followed any rules. We've been dancing around each other for months like fencing opponents squaring off in a match before we ever went out, but I felt the chemistry way back then. So, this moment has been a long time coming.

Without warning, Heather captures my lips in a deep wet, hot kiss. I leave my eyes shut as I focus on the myriad of sensations flooding my body. Heather looks up at me through her thick lashes as she murmurs, "I guess there's something to be said for collecting rewards." She pushes me back on the bed and pushes my shirt over my shoulders briefly trapping my arms at my side. When she sees the labyrinth of scar tissue and surgical incisions she grimaces. The pity in her eyes is almost too much for me to take and I start to pull away.

Heather stops my movement with a heart stopping, scorching kiss directly on my ugliest, angriest most painful scar. With excruciating slowness, she kisses each and every scar on my torso, neck and face. I guess she has been paying more attention to me than I thought because she even kisses the one I keep hidden under my cowboy hat. Finally, I can wait no longer to see her reaction. I use my fingertip to tilt her chin so I can see her eyes. My eyes seek out the answers my words are afraid to ask.

CHAPTER TWELVE

HEATHER

IN THE TWO YEARS I've known Tyler, I've seen many facets of him. I've seen him be gregarious and fun with Denny and Mindy, I've seen him be serious and businesslike with Jeff and Justice Gardner and I've seen him be furious and downright lethal with Kevin Buckhold and my parents. Until this moment I don't believe I've ever seen Tyler Colton be scared. The fear and pain in his eyes is enough to shatter my heart. This is Ty at his most raw. Tears gather on my lashes as I try to express in words what has been forming in my heart over the last few months. I kiss him gently on the lips and pull away. "Don't you realize that these are part of what makes you so beautiful? The fact that you are willing to lay your life down to save someone else's make these imperfections meaningless."

I feel a shudder go through Tyler's body as he gathers me into a tight embrace.

"What if all my so-called sacrifice just messed up the lives of a bunch of innocent people and didn't save anything? It's not so noble then, right?"

I stare directly into Ty's eyes. "And what if things would have been exponentially worse without you there? You couldn't have known what would happen that day. You didn't cause your men to be hurt, the terrorists did. The fact that you run toward danger when others run away speaks volumes about your character. You forget I've seen you in more than one dangerous situation. If I were a soldier, I would always want you in my foxhole or guarding my six as they say. In fact, I'm not a soldier and I still want you guarding my six."

Despite the serious nature of our conversation, Tyler can't resist acknowledging the mention of my backside, the corner of his mouth hitches up as he quips, "Gidg, it would be an honor to guard your buns any day of the week. Just tell me when and where."

Suddenly, the tension in the room is broken when I see his shorts peeking over the waistband of his jeans. I can't help myself as I laugh out loud. "Now, those are some sexy drawers, Tyler."

He spins me around so I'm sitting in his lap. "What? You don't like Daffy Duck?" he asks, as the tips of his ears turn red.

"I like him just fine, I didn't expect to find him on your underwear. In case no one has reminded you recently, you're a grown up."

"Says the person who has Jessica Rabbit pajamas and bunny slippers," Tyler parries.

"Touché." I respond, winking. "They're just not the usual seduction-wear I encounter on dates."

Ty's jaw tightens as he asks, "Is this usual dating behavior for you?"

I stiffen my spine. "I'm not sure I should have to answer that unless you do, but to answer your question, not recently. I'm a little more selective than I was in my younger days since I've been burned. I haven't dated a whole bunch in my life because I don't look like Madison and her friends. I'm more like the wing woman. But, I have played a little backseat baseball to try to become popular. So, in college I saw a few pairs of men's underwear and what goes into them. Not to be crass or anything but once you've seen a few guys' junk, they're pretty much interchangeable regardless of what all you guys think."

Tyler runs his hand down his face as he closes his eyes briefly and shakes his head to clear it. "Gidget, I'm sorry. You're right. I'm in no position to judge anybody. Just some ghosts from my past trying to haunt me. So, have I completely ruined everything?"

I study his face carefully and see nothing but honest regret and pain. I sigh as I run my fingertips over his brow trying to relieve the tension. "For two people who like each other as much as we do — and Tyler Joseph Colton, I really do like you. In fact if I'm truly honest with myself I'm probably more than just a little in love with you — we have a remarkable gift of saying exactly the wrong things to each other at exactly the wrong times."

Tyler's eyes widen a bit at my unexpected confession. I don't exactly blame him. I didn't expect those words to come flying out of my mouth either. If you would've told me even a few months ago that I would say such a thing to this giant, contrary, smart-mouthed cowboy who on the surface doesn't seem to have a care in the world, I would've told you that you were certifiably insane. But I've come to know him as a man of great heart and integrity who has my back like none other. With him at my side, I feel beautiful and invincible.

I'm not even consciously aware I'm holding my breath until Tyler run fingers over my collarbone, "Breathe, Heather. How can you not think that's the best news I've heard in forever? In my book, those are exactly the right words at exactly the right time."

"Really?" I ask skeptically, "You don't think I'm jumping the gun? We haven't even really been officially dating all that long. I have a list of annoying habits so long you might hate me by the time you get to the end of it. We still argue like cats and dogs in the middle of a hurricane. At the end of the day, you're this big strong soldier tough guy and I'm going to make cupcakes for a living."

Ty stuns me into silence by kissing me. But, this is unlike any kiss we've had before. He starts out tenderly kissing away the traces of tears from earlier. Before he gently claims my mouth, he reverently brushes his lips over mine, slowly savoring each pass.

Tyler rests his forehead against mine as he gulps for air. "Heather, I wish I could promise you forever, but I can't. You know what I do for a living. I could get shot tomorrow on a routine traffic stop or they may make me go play in the sandbox in some godforsaken country somewhere and I might never come back to you. But, if you're willing to take that risk, we could be great together.

Our differences just make things interesting. Just look how much we've learned about each other since we've been together. You've pretty much overhauled the way I eat. Heck, I'm practically a food snob now my own mama won't recognize me. You would make any rodeo queen jealous, you're so comfortable being on the farm. For the first time since I was practically a kid, I want to make this work."

Tyler's words are some of the scariest I've ever heard. Of course, I know what he does for a living. But, somehow his affable, happy-go-lucky attitude seems to disguise the level of danger. He so rarely ever talks about the raw, ugly side of his duties I sometimes forget that he is in peril every day. If he shares stories from his day, they are often about chasing down a wayward wildlife or a five-year-old that got caught shoplifting. I know he purposefully hides the more serious anecdotes from me.

"Tyler, I know there are going to be some things you cannot share with me because of the nature of your job, but you can't protect me from everything. I'm a big girl and I'm not going to run from you because you're not the star athlete and not perfect. If I was going to do that, I would've done it a long time ago. Because, quite frankly the hot and cold number you pulled on me in the beginning of our friendship drove me absolutely crazy. So, as long as we can be honest with each other and we're in this together — whatever this turns out to be — I'm in. Cowboy, you've had my heart for a while now. Just try not to break it, okay?"

"That goes both ways, Gidget. Understood?"

A sense of calm contentment settles over me as I

process his gruffly murmured words. For a few moments, I simply lay my head on his chest and listen to the comforting cadence of his heart beat as it gradually slows down. Tyler is stroking my back and shoulders while he runs his fingers through my goofy, random corkscrew curls. "Your hair is so much fun. It's like a toy box full of Slinkys."

I look up at him and smirk, "I'm sure there's a compliment in there somewhere."

He chuckles, "There is! I swear. I love everything about you. You're stunning."

I push Tyler back against the pillows and kneel between his legs.

Tyler lifts me off of him abruptly and pins me with a serious gaze. "Heather, when you said all in, I'm really hoping this is included. If not, we need to stop now because, at this moment, I can still be a gentleman. If we cross that line and go any further, it will be much harder for me to keep my hands off of you."

With much more boldness than I actually feel, I murmur, "Remember what you asked me on one of our first outings? You wondered if you looked like a person who didn't know what they wanted. Well, I'll ask you the same question now. Have I at any time today seemed indecisive about wanting you?"

Ty mutely shakes his head and relaxes his arms at his side.

"I guess you could say that this mission is a go, Soldier."

Tyler lets out a whoop of celebration that's so loud

it causes Annie to bark downstairs. A moment later, he grasps my hands in his. "Really?"

I nod. "Whatever floats your boat."

"Oh Gidget, you float my dinghy, my jet ski, my paddle boat, platoon, my battleship… are you catching my drift here?"

Embarrassed, I look away and then sneak a peek at Tyler's expression. I'm taken aback by the look of total adoration and concentration on his face as he reaches out to stroke my cheek. His other hand is tangled in my hair as if he's afraid I might disappear if he let's go. "Oh Gidget, you don't fight fair." Ty grits through his teeth.

"Who says we're at war? I'm on your side remember? This is your reward. Just let go. I'll keep you safe."

Chapter Thirteen

Tyler

THE INCESSANT BEEPING OF my annoyingly high-tech watch wakes me from the best sleep I've had in forever. As I struggle to turn the stupid thing off, a whiff of lemon scent catches my nose as a lock of Heather's hair falls across my face. When I finally succeed in silencing the offensive gadget, I stroke her hair back from her face. She smiles in her sleep and snuggles close to my chest. It's probably a good thing I set the alarm, because given a choice, I would rather stay right here. However, I know Heather has been looking forward to giving Velvet to Mindy for months and I don't want to step on that joy.

As the light reflects off of my military surplus watch, the weight of the decisions I've just made start to spin around in my head at a dizzying pace. In the blink of an eye, I see that watch-face covered in blood as I tried to use it to keep track of a teammate's fading heart rate. How can I ask her to make that kind of sacrifice for me when I don't know how many days like today we'll have? I curse at myself under my breath. For a sliver of time I was blissfully happy. Why can't I leave my brain in that headspace? Why do my thoughts have to fall back into all the dark crevices of despair and anger at the most random times? I try to use some of the breathing and visualization techniques I was taught in the VA hospital to bring back some balance.

Heather must sense my distress in her sleep because she slides her arm up my body and cups the side of my face with her hand before she settles into my chest with a soft sigh. I watch her sleep for a couple of minutes as I acknowledge that she's the best thing that's happened in my life in years. I don't know how I'll make this choice. Today we have other things on the agenda and little girls waiting for Christmas presents get impatient.

I kiss the top of her head to wake her up. Gradually, she stirs and looks up at me with a puzzled expression, "What are you doing with my hair now? Your fascination with it borders on the downright odd."

"Although I admit I love your hair, this time I plead innocent. Nothing terribly kinky this go around. I'm just trying to wake you up. Jeff and Kiera will be here in about a half an hour and we probably shouldn't answer the door naked."

"Tyler Joseph Colton! I'm feeling a bit less warm and fuzzy about you right now. I know we've had this discussion before. I cannot turn this mess into a hint of fabulousness in an instant. It takes me a little time. Kiera is going to know exactly what happened here just by looking at me. This is beyond embarrassing!"

I try hard to keep my expression neutral but she's just too cute when she is all wound up. I suppose I should feel bad; she does have a point. I did push the timeline a little close. I raise my hands in surrender as I sit up and apologize, as I help her out of the deep featherbed, "I'm sorry Darlin' I was havin' way too much fun with you one-on-one and wasn't thinking about how it might look to everyone else. But, I would venture to guess they probably wonder why this hasn't happened a long time ago and they'll love you regardless of how you look. So, it's up to you. The jeans and sweatshirt you wore the other week are out in the laundry room. I washed them up for you. Or, you can get all 'spiffified'. You know me, I think you're gorgeous regardless of what you wear."

Heather rolls her eyes at me. "You're such a guy!" She sticks her tongue out at me as she turns and runs toward the bathroom.

"Well, I'm not going to argue with that. That would be extremely counter-productive, don't you think?"

Holy smokes, I did cut it a little close. I barely got myself showered and dressed and the bedroom back into some semblance of order before the doorbell rang. Mindy is an exceptionally curious child and considers my mini-ranch her personal Fisher-Price Little Red Barn come to life. I don't want her stumbling across anything which would embarrass Heather.

When I open the door, Mindy launches herself into my arms and opens her mouth as wide as she can. At first she tries to talk with her mouth open, but then thinks better of it. "Look, Uncle Ty! See! I'm going to get braces just like Gabriel did. He says all the cool kids get braces.

Did you get braces? Uncle Aidan had braces when he was a kid."

As I gently set her down, I shake my head. "Nope, I didn't have braces, but I was jealous of everyone else who did. Everybody got to change their rubber bands to cool colors and I didn't. Why don't we move out of the doorway and let your mom and dad in the house? Where's Becca?"

"Dad's carrying her. She runs really fast now. She's getting so big it's hard for me to hold her. It's a good thing I don't have to save her from my Nana now; I don't think I could run very far."

Her casual mention of what was a horrific time in her past is a startling reminder of how much has changed for all of us in two years. I don't think I will live long enough to forget seeing the graphic crime photos of Mindy's hand after her grandmother held it in a pot of boiling water because Mindy interrupted her soap operas. Nor will I ever forget the horrifically infected pressure sores and diaper rash Becca had as an infant because the adults in her life were too consumed with drugs and alcohol to pay attention to their children. Finally, Becca's condition had gotten so dire that as a six-year-old, Mindy, attempted to take the bus to run away with Becca. It was a miraculous escape. Kiera was the social worker on the case and fell instantly in love with both girls. Since Jeff was already head over heels in love with Kiera, the girls were just a bonus.

I'm a little stunned when I see Becca. She's often down for a nap or already in bed when I go over to see Jeff, so it's been a while since I've seen her. She has lost her baby-like appearance and is very much an independent toddler as she fishes out goldfish crackers from a baggie in Jeff's hand and silently stuffs them in her mouth. While it's clear she and Mindy are sisters, her hair has taken on a more amber tone like Kiera's and her eyes have turned more green than blue. She is also much more reserved than Mindy. However, it's not a big surprise. Most people on the planet are more reserved than Mindy. I'm not sure Mindy has ever met someone she doesn't instantly consider a friend as long as they pass whatever internal radar Mindy possesses. Mindy and Tara seem to share some spooky ability to take the measure of somebody's character just by watching them. Their skills would be handy in my line of work.

"Where's Heather? I thought I saw her car outside," Kiera asks, looking around.

"Oh, you know her she's probably whipping us up something to eat," I answer vaguely. "Do you guys have presents you need me to bring in?"

Much to my surprise, Becca nods vigorously and takes her fingers out of her mouth before exclaiming, "Uh-huh lotsa Santa pwesnts."

I hold my arms out to her. "Do you want to show me where they are, Princess Peanut?"

She looks a little dubious at first, but I guess the lure of presents is enough to overcome her shyness with me. I guess she doesn't remember all the days I spent rocking her in a rocking chair when she had colic.

From behind me I hear snickering. I see Heather has come downstairs wearing her jeans and one of my T-shirts with the sleeves rolled up. It's all I can do not to puff out my chest with approval. At the moment, Heather and Mindy have their heads together and they are dissolved in a private moment of whispers and laughter. "All right, you two … what's so funny?" I ask, clueless about what I've done.

"We think it's funny you called Becca, Princess Peanut. Because she's not little anymore. Did you forget?" Mindy responds with a giggle.

"I noticed that she is growing like a tumbleweed. But, if I can't call her by her nickname, does it mean I can't call you Mindy Mouse?"

Mindy's eyebrows draw together in concentration as she considers my point. "But — I like my nickname. I suppose you can still call her Peanut since she's still smaller than me. But, someday we're going to have to come up with a different name."

Heather pulls Mindy up and walks to the front door. "Did somebody say something about presents? That's my favorite part of Christmas."

At that point, Mindy, Kiera, Jeff and I respond in unison, "No, it's not!"

Heather spins around and places her hands on her hips. "What do I like better?"

"Baking Christmas cookies!" Mindy exclaims. "I can't wait! Did you save the ones I helped you make?"

"I sure did. Maybe Tyler can help us carry them in from my car."

I shoot her my grumpiest look. "You had those in your car all day and didn't tell me about them? How mean are you?"

"Tyler, I know you a little too well, and you're not big on sharing dessert. These are my friends and I cherish them. If you had gotten to the cookies first, there probably wouldn't be any left and my friends would be sad. I didn't want sad friends on Christmas. That's why the cookies got left in the car. Never fear though, I made an extra-large cookie just for you."

I walk over and give her a kiss on the forehead since I'm still holding Becca. "You're so sweet, Gidget. Can I eat it now?" I plead with big puppy dog eyes.

Mindy eyes me suspiciously. "Have you had dinner, Uncle Ty? Everyone knows you can only have cookies after dinner."

Heather stands on her tip toes and kisses me softly. "Oops, the Voice of Authority has spoken. I guess you have to wait."

By the looks of astonishment on the faces of Kiera and Jeff, I'm not the only one taken off guard by Heather's openly affectionate gesture. In the past, she's always teased me about being a handsome cowboy, but she's never been physically demonstrative with me in public.

Heather looks around self-consciously at the curious expressions and my look of total befuddlement. "Really people? After the song and dance this lovable oaf and I have been through for literally years, is anybody going to pretend to be surprised I finally caved?" she asks shaking her head. She takes her finger and gently closes my slack jaw. "You should be the least surprised of anybody. Was I supposed to keep it a secret?"

I struggle to find the right words. I'm not even sure

what I want to say. I guess in my head, I've been a couple with her for much longer than we've actually been dating. I really haven't been pursuing anyone else since I met her. I kept up the friendship ruse for months just for an opportunity to be close to her. After I met her family, it became clear our relationship had deepened a great deal but I've never been entirely sure until today where I stand with her. I have two warring factions in my head. There's a large part of me that wants to brag to the world about this wonderful treasure I've found and tell everyone how special she is to me. But, an opposing force wants to keep what we found private, secret and untouched by the world around us. Intellectually, I know it's going to be impossible to do and is probably completely unnecessary. But, the last time I thought I had a great relationship, the real world intruded and smashed it to smithereens.

Heather still has her finger on my chin and she's looking at me expectantly. I lift her hand and kiss her fingertip. "Of course I don't want you to keep us a secret from your friends, I thought we would break the news with a bit of subtle handholding, a Facebook status update or something."

Jeff lets out a hoot of laughter. "In case it has escaped your notice, Ty, your girlfriend rarely does subtle. In fact, get used to it. None of the Girlfriend Posse members do quiet and unassuming well."

"Hey, it's not exactly like Mr. Cowboy/Soldier/Cop does subtle very well either. Have you seen that monster truck he drives? What about those jeans he wears?" Heather argues, rolling her eyes.

"I think you're pretty well matched. Although I am

surprised it took this long for you guys to get your timing right," remarks Kiera.

"It's so cool that Aunt Heather has a boyfriend now. Heather and Ty K-I-S-S-I-N-G in a tree," Mindy sing-songs.

Heather blushes to an impressive shade of red. She tweaks Mindy's ponytail as she playfully threatens, "I'd be careful if I were you. Your teenage years are right around the corner."

Jeff dramatically clutches his chest as he asks, "Did you really have to go there?"

I take a little pity on my best friend. "Breathe buddy. You have years. It's not tomorrow. She's only nine." I turn to Heather and whisper in her ear, "The sooner you finish causing a ruckus here, the sooner we can all eat Christmas cookies and send everyone home."

Kiera glimpses Heather's reaction to my comment and just shakes her head as she mutters, "You know what? There are just some things I'm better off not knowing —"

I wink at her. "Probably. But, now you know what it was like the whole time you and Prince Charming over here were dating. It was impressive and nauseating all at the same time." I can't hide my smile as Kiera blushes as much as Heather.

As Jeff and I are unloading the car, Jeff's father-in-law Denny pulls up. I shoot Jeff a questioning glance, he shrugs in response. When he sees his mom climb out of the passenger's side of Denny's old truck he just about drops the tray of cookies in his hands. "Oh man, we're going to be busted for sure. Mindy's too smart for this,"

Jeff mutters under his breath. When Gwendolyn approaches he says, "Mom, I thought we talked about this. You're going to blow the surprise."

Denny looks chagrined. "Sorry, son. I tried to talk her out of it. She insisted Mindy needs a new saddle made just for her."

Jeff looks slightly pained but pats his mom on the shoulder and responds, "Okay, new game plan. You and I will go distract them with all your fancy food and Ty and Denny will take care of what needs to be done out here."

As we're putting the new saddle on Velvet, Denny takes note of the festive state of her mane. "That's not something I usually expect from you," he observes as he slides a slipping bow back into place.

"Yeah, it's definitely a little fancy for my blood. But, let's say my horizons have been expanded lately. Heather has been like a stylist to the stars for that mare. In fact, none of my horses have ever looked better."

"You need to be careful with that one. She acts tough and brash, but her heart is tender. She's been surrounded by a lot of jerks in her life. Don't be another one, okay? Look, I know she's not really my daughter, but I think of her as my own. I haven't known you for as long as some of Kiera's friends but you strike me as a good guy. Don't prove me wrong on this one."

"I appreciate your endorsement sir. It's been difficult being stationed so far from my parents. It's been a privilege to share Jeff's friends and family. I can tell you without hesitation that Heather is the most important person in my life and I will do everything in my power to make sure she feels loved, cared for and safe. Jeff knows better than anybody the one thing I can't promise her is that I'll be here forever. I had to hold a team member in my arms until he drew his last breath. The last thing he asked me to do was to beg his wife's forgiveness that he didn't make it home for the birth of his child."

I haven't shared that part of the story with anyone except my commanding officer before. It's still makes me weak in the knees. I fumble around for a place to sit down. Denny pulls a bale of hay down from the loft and pushes me down until I'm sitting. He takes off the backpack he's wearing and fishes out a couple of cans of root beer. He scoots over a nearby stool and removes the tackle that's sitting on the top. He sits down and nods for me to continue. I'm grateful he doesn't say anything because if he would have, I might not have the courage to continue.

I try to concentrate on gathering my thoughts and I continue in frustrated bursts of speech. "I'll be honest with you. That's the part of this equation I haven't yet figured out. I don't know how I can live my life without Heather in it, yet I don't know how I can ask her to look at the kind of future she might be facing if she marries me. Either way, it isn't fair to either of us. I can't ask her to face the possibility of that black car pulling into our driveway with the uniforms coming out. You've met her family. They would destroy her."

Denny leans forward and puts his hands on my shoulders causing me to look up at him. "Tyler, you need to listen to me here. Life isn't fair to anyone, soldier or not. I'm not sure how much of my back story you know, but I lost my first love to a cancerous brain tumor that almost cost my daughter's life too. My wife was accused of intentionally trying to kill my daughter. It was incredibly hard to stand by both and not be angry at the world. I can't say I was successful every single day, but dandelions if I didn't try. My wife did not deserve to die and Kiera did not deserve to be paralyzed because of her mother's brain cancer — still that's what life did to them. You can't wait for life to be fair before you find love. It just isn't ever going to be. If you find love, you have to capture the moments and treasure them while you can. You can't worry about what might be, because you can't change the might-be's. The only day you can live is today. Not yesterday, not tomorrow — just today."

I'm not a huge hugger by nature, years of being alert has pretty much trained that out of me. But, I feel compelled to hug this man. I think he just saved me from making a huge mistake. "Thank you sir, I'll take your advice to heart."

Denny pats me on the back as he disengages from my hug, "Now, I'll tell you the same thing I told my son-in-law. Stop calling me sir. My name is Denny. If you call me sir, I'll start looking around for my dad," he teases.

"I'll tell you the same thing my best friend told you, 'I'll try my best, but my training runs deep.' I suppose we had better get back inside before all the food is gone."

Denny smirks. "Get real. Between your girlfriend and mine? The possibility that they might run out of food is between slim and none."

My eyes widen a little as I ask, "So, it's like that, huh? What do Jeff and Kiera think of their parents dating?"

"I don't know. I'm not even sure Gwendolyn

realizes I'm courting her yet. I'm trying to give her time to get over whatever garbage that ant-turd of an ex left behind. She is becoming stronger by the day. I consider it remarkably good news she still wants me to be around. So, I'll stay, until she tells me to go. I consider her to be my second shot at happiness."

"What about your advice to live today for today and seize as much love as possible?"

"Who says I'm not? It looks a little different at my age. I'm happier than I've been in years. Until I need to rock the boat, I won't."

When we reach the house, I realize what I thought was going to be an informal get-together of my best friends has turned into a bona fide Christmas party. It makes me miss my family even more. I wish I could take Heather to meet my parents. They would absolutely adore her.

The entire kitchen island is covered in food. Jeff's mom made a thick beef stew and some crusty French bread. Kiera and Mindy made fancy salads and of course there's the smorgasbord of cookies created by my girlfriend. They are almost too pretty to eat —almost.

My mom would have been in seventh heaven during the dinner conversation. Everyone is chattering about kitchen cutlery and knife techniques. Mindy is turning out to be quite the culinary student and was eagerly displaying all the work she had done on the complex salads. When we finished dinner, Mindy was shocked when her Papa suggested that she open her biggest present first, but we wanted to unveil Velvet while there was still plenty of daylight left.

Heather took one of her bandannas and blindfolded Mindy and carried her out to the barn. Jeff wasn't quite as dramatic with Kiera but asked her to close her eyes. We didn't tell Kiera about the improvements to the barn, but I built a wraparound ramp to the corral so she could get into the barn and see over the fence to watch Mindy ride in the corral. I'm not sure how much Jeff shared with Kiera, so I don't even know if she knows about the horse. This may be as big a surprise to her as it is to Mindy. I reach out and squeeze Heather's hand as I open the barn.

We warned Becca and Mindy in advance that we are going to use sign language instead of our voices so we don't wake up any sleeping elves. We've all gotten pretty efficient in sign language thanks to the tutelage of Tara and Aidan. Tara, a sign language interpreter, started a creative arts studio where she teaches dance and arts and crafts. I've gone there to help teach some woodworking courses and picked up some rudimentary sign language skills along the way. I've also helped her fiancé, Aidan, take some of the kids out rock climbing. Since Aidan is deaf, I've had the opportunity to pick up a much more colorful sign language vocabulary from him as he explained what signs the kids were using.

Heather removes Mindy's blindfold and we all sign Merry Christmas and wave our hands in the deaf equivalence of applause. I realize as I catch Kiera filming the whole thing with an iPad she's on Face Time with Aidan and Tara live. So, the sign language is actually both keeping the horses calm and allowing Aidan to fully participate even though he's backstage at a very noisy concert.

Despite her best efforts, Mindy can't help but shriek, "Look Mom, it's a horse just like I asked for."

Kiera narrows her eyes at Jeff. "Imagine that! What a surprise … for everyone." She has a smile on her face, but she's glaring at Jeff with disappointment and resentment in her eyes.

Heather and I look at each other in dismay. This is not going well at all.

Heather tries to intercede, "I don't think you understand Kiera. This is like a big group gift. Velvet was my pet horse when I was a little girl, but as you all know, before I met Ty, I was far too scared to ride her. She was kept at my grandma's house until she passed away. Velvet was so impossibly lonely after my grandma was gone that I knew I had to find her the perfect owner. Fannie was really needing a new companion too, so Tyler offered to keep her here. Since he's leasing to own the place, we wanted to make this a place where you could enjoy horseback riding alongside Mindy. So, Jeff decided to surprise you too. It was all done with the very best intentions. I promise."

Mindy scrambles off of the stall railing where Heather had perched her for the big reveal and throws her arm around Kiera's shoulder. "Please Mom, don't be mad. I promise I'll do all my homework and pay special attention to Uncle Ty's lessons. Justice Gardner already taught me how to brush the horses, remember?"

"Oh sweetie, I'm not really all that mad." Kiera reassures her. "I guess I should be used to your Dad's big surprises by now. It's just that it would've been fun to be in on this one."

"It's okay, Mom. One of these days, we're gonna have a big secret from him that he'll never be able to figure out and then he'll know what it feels like, right?"

"I suppose that's possible. But, it will have to be a mighty big surprise to compete with a surprise wedding and a horse. That's going to take some planning."

Mindy thinks about it for a minute. "Well, it's a really good thing you guys decided to get married forever."

Chapter Fourteen

Heather

"Tara and Donda, I can't thank you enough for helping me paint this place. Can you believe it's only a month before Valentine's Day?"

"It is a bit wild. Are you ready to be an up-and-coming entrepreneur?" Donda asks as she folds up a tarp.

"As Ty would say, 'Does the military love camo?' After the asinine court fight my parents put me through to keep me from getting this place, I'm more determined than ever to make it a success. I can't believe they were arrogant enough to think they would win. It's so awesome that your brother is a lawyer and practically the adopted godson of a former Supreme Court Justice in Oregon. It made finding someone to take my case so much easier."

Tara shakes her head at me. "I don't think that was the deciding factor in your case as much as the letters and drawings you and your grandmother exchanged back and forth over the years, discussing potential strategies if you were to ever open a store. The box of handwritten recipes she had collected for you and named with commercial sounding titles and the blueprints she drew out for you when you were still a child were pretty much irrefutable proof she had been planning to open a business for you for decades. This was not a decision she made last-minute under the influence of blood pressure medicine or whatever bogus medical diagnosis they made up. I talked to your grandma on a regular basis. She was sharp as a tack. She knew dance moves she learned when she was twelve and she remembered what college courses I was taking in any given term."

Donda pipes in, "You know what the funniest thing was? I thought it was hysterical they accused you of being selfish and greedy, but in the end those are exactly the terms that the judge used when describing them when he ordered them to pay all the court costs and your attorney fees because they abused the judicial system with a frivolous lawsuit."

"I don't know if I told you this, but their attorney told them they didn't have a case. So, they fired that attorney and tried to hire two more and when that didn't work they acted as their own. I guess my dad thought being a CPA and an attorney were pretty much interchangeable."

"How has this affected your relationship with your family? Is anything salvageable?" Tara asks.

"I don't really know yet," I sigh. "As you know, there wasn't much to salvage with my parents after I made the break and decided not to follow my dad into the family business. After I saw the way they treated me through Ty's eyes, I knew I wasn't ever going to accept that from them again. I think they knew I had reached the end of my rope and they could not bully me into believing less of myself. I can't believe it took me so long to summon the courage to find my voice. It makes me really angry at myself."

Tara pulls me into a tight embrace. As she lets go she says, "Sometimes it takes your true soulmate to show you where you have to heal before you can truly find love."

Donda gives Tara a double-take and shudders. "Girl, you give me goosebumps every time I'm around you."

Tara shrugs nonchalantly. "I'm not really making any profound statements here, and I'm just telling you what I've seen happen in my life and the lives of the people I love. I understand it even better now that it's happening to me. It took Aidan loving me despite my frailties and flaws for me to see where I needed to get stronger to be able to accept the gift of love he was giving me. It was like I couldn't see all of me without the full light of his love. I would either focus only on my strength or only on my weaknesses and without addressing everything that was going on in my life, there wasn't ever going to be balance."

Donda studies Tara carefully. "I still can't believe you found a guy who doesn't care that you've been raped."

I have a reputation for being blunt, but Donda usually has me beat by a mile. Yet, this is extreme, even for her. I can't disguise my gasp of surprise.

Tara places her hand on Donda's forearm as she looks into Donda's eyes. "No, I think you've misunderstood what I said. Aidan cares very deeply that

I was raped. In many ways, I think he still feels like he should have been there to prevent it even though he was dealing with his own crisis at the time. The thing I had to learn to accept is that I am still worthy of Aidan's love. That's part of the healing I was telling Heather about. Not everyone has as many wounds as I did, but everyone's got something. The person who loves you can help you heal those wounds."

Donda blinks away a tear and whispers, "What if I never find that person?"

Tara takes the tarp from her hands and sets it down on the floor. She clasps Donda's hands between hers and pledges, "Then, we as your friends and family will do our best to be that light for you until you find your own. Don't forget, you've been inducted into the Girlfriend Posse. We do not take our duties lightly. We watch each other's backs. So, if you need us, we're all a phone call away."

I give Donda a crooked grin. "Just a word of warning, you don't even always have to call Tara. Sometimes she just knows you're in deep trouble. So, don't be freaked out by that; it's perfectly normal."

Donda lets out a snort of laughter. "Okay, I'll consider myself forewarned."

⬤

"Hey, I didn't say you could take that off!" I scold as I catch Tyler trying to take off the bandanna I placed over his eyes before I had him fully seated.

"This looks a lot sexier in the movies," he whines. "I feel like a kid playing pin the tail on the donkey."

"Tyler Joseph Colton, please just sit down. You're making this far too complicated. The blindfold isn't there as a sex toy; it really is just a blindfold. I'm trying to surprise you, you big dork."

Tyler flashes me a big cheesy grin. "Yeah, but I'm your dork."

"Yes, yes you are. That's the only reason I'm not leaving you tied to the chair with the balloon hat on your head."

"I don't know, that kinda sounds like fun."

"I think you've been on maneuvers for too long," I quip as I sneak a kiss to his ear lobe.

"Sitting in a classroom learning classified stuff I can't tell you about for a whole month is not my idea of a vacation, even if it was at the request of Uncle Sam."

I run my hands through his close cropped hair as I untie the bandanna. "I hope you expect me to treat you a little better, otherwise, we'll have to work on your expectations. I thought you might be a little hungry after eating military rations for so long, so I fixed a few of your favorites."

Tyler opens his eyes and looks around. I wish I'd planned ahead and recorded his reaction to seeing my shop for the first time because it was everything I hoped it would be. I guess if I were to describe the decor, I would say it's a cross between a faded photograph and a watercolor painting. My grandmother wanted this place to feel like it had been here for decades and had been passed down from generation to generation. So, I used checkerboard tiling on the floor reminiscent of old soda shops but instead of doing them in black and white, they are in sepia tones. Gwendolyn went a little crazy with the renovation budget when she found water damage during one of the inspections. She was incredibly generous in compensating me. This allowed me to add some cool aesthetic touches like copper backsplashes and a brick wood oven for baking artisan bread.

Donda and Tara painted huge murals that look like large advertisements from the 1900s. They show families enjoying cookies and cupcakes. I can tell the moment Ty sees my favorite painting. It's on the back wall of the shop in a cozy back corner where I plan to hold all of my wedding cake consults. It shows a couple playfully feeding each other wedding cake. But, to anyone familiar with Tara and Aidan, it's their love story portrayed generations before, right down to the ballet shoes on the bride and the piano in the background. Even their fingertips are linked in the familiar handhold that's second nature to the couple. "Wow!" Tyler murmurs, "Tara really outdid herself on that one."

I shake my head as I correct him, "Would you believe Tara doesn't even know about it? Donda painted it as a surprise wedding gift."

Ty walks over to take a closer look at the painting. "This is just incredible. I knew she was talented because of what she did in Becca's room, but this is amazing. This cake looks edible. Did you make her a model cake?"

"No, that's the cool thing. She seems to have really become part of our group and nailed our personalities. As far as I know, Tara hasn't had a free second to talk about wedding cake with anybody. Heck, she is such a health-nut, she may not even have a wedding cake."

Ty chokes back a guffaw of laughter. "Gidget, you've met Aidan and his band, right? Darlin, you're going to be making so many sweets, dentists will name a holiday in your honor. Get prepared. Joy & Tiers will be the home of the chi-chi treats that brought America's favorite couple together."

"Just the thought of that is daunting. I wonder how long they're going to wait until they get married. I hope they're not my first order or anything. As much as I would like a little positive publicity, I'm not sure I'm ready for my shop to be overrun by paparazzi." I look around the shop anxiously. "Ty, this is a lot more than my little food truck. What if I'm not ready for all of this?"

Tyler gathers me in a warm embrace and kisses me tenderly. "Heather, I work with generals routinely and they've got nothing on you. It's only been about five weeks since I've seen this place and I hardly recognize it. When I left, workers were hanging sheet rock. What you've done here is nothing short of a miracle. Especially when you consider your original timeframe was messed up by the bull crap your dad pulled. By the way, when I offered to help you, I meant it as more than just a character reference."

"I know you did. But, it was important for me to do it on my own. I didn't want you to feel like I was just using you or your status to reach my dreams. Besides, I want to be able to prove once and for all that if you have talent and a dream, it's possible to be successful regardless of what field you choose."

"Gidget, I would've never given it a second thought. If I had any doubts, I wouldn't have offered. I would've been honored to help make this dream come true because I know it'll be spectacular. Just look at this place. I thought I knew what it might be like when we were drawing it up, but this just completely blows my mind. It's beyond perfect. I can't wait until you open."

"You're such a great cheerleader. I feel like I should get you some pom-poms or something."

"Did you forget I'm a big macho dude? I don't do pom-poms. Tight Levi's to attract customers, maybe; but pom-poms are a line I won't cross," Tyler teases. "Didn't I hear you mention food?"

"Why, yes I did. But, somebody I know got up from the table. Can I show you to your table, sir?"

When I walk Ty back to the table, his expression is priceless. His jaw drops to the floor as he sees the overwhelming variety of food I've prepared for him.

"Gidget, I love you for doing this, but I don't know if I can eat all this. Pardon the pun, but you could feed an army with this amount of food."

I shrug. "Well, I figured you'd be hungry. I didn't know exactly what you'd want. I'm really good with leftovers. So, just eat what you want and I'll figure out the rest. I wanted to bring some happiness back into your life. I could tell from our phone calls and texts that this was hard on you and I only got to send you one care package. Consider this one big care package, okay?"

Tyler swallows hard. "I'm not sure I say this enough to you. But I can't thank you enough for the hundreds of small ways you take care of me. I want you to know I don't really expect you to, but I appreciate the heck out of it. Stuff like this astounds me. I don't know many people who would go through all the hassle to make homemade dog food for my dog because she's got allergies or develop special conditioner for my horses' manes so they don't tangle. I notice you even take the time to iron my uniforms for me on top of everything else you've got going with your business and the fight with your dad. How do you do it all? Why do you do it all?"

"First of all, sit down and eat before this all gets cold and we'll talk okay?" The expression on his face when I mentioned the word 'talk' was like a thundercloud. "Wow, I didn't mean to scare you. Talking can mean good things too. I'm not planning to ambush you with bad news."

Tyler loosens the grip on his fork slightly as he admits, "Sorry for jumping to conclusions, but I don't have the best experiences with conversations that start out with 'We have to talk…'

I can't help but snort. "Come to think of it, neither do I. So, I won't keep you in suspense and I'll answer your question right now."

Tyler nods stiffly as if he's bracing for devastating news. "I guess now is as good a time as any."

I'm completely confused by Tyler's reaction to our conversation, but I figure the only way to move forward is to be honest. "I'm not sure what you're expecting me to say, so I'm just going to go with my heart here and answer your questions. I hope it's what you are looking for. I guess the reason I do all the things I do for you is the same reason you were willing to loan me money without having an idea of whether you'd ever get it back.

I believe in you. I believe in us. It's really as simple as that. I want to do things to make your life easier. I can't make your job safer, or bullets less painful. I can't kill the terrorists or make the war go away and sadly, I can't erase the memories of what happened or heal your scars. But, I can use my skills to make your life as happy and joyful as possible despite whatever chaos is going on in your life."

Tyler pales at my words as he slowly sets down his fork and slumps down in his chair. He flicks tears from the corners of his eyes and scrubs his hand over his face. As I watch his reaction, my heart sinks. For the first time in months, I wonder if I've completely misunderstood everything about our relationship. My heart pounds and I mentally calculate whether I can make it to the bathroom before I collapse into tears.

As I'm having that mental debate with myself, Tyler reaches out and pulls me onto his knee. "I don't know what I ever did to deserve you. But, I swear I'm never giving you back. I was so afraid that you would decide you had had enough of the uncertainty of military life. What we just went through is just a taste of what might be coming and although I can't imagine my life without you, I'm afraid to ask you to be part of this life. My nightmares and scars are small casualties compared to what could happen and part of me wonders if I'm just being selfish by asking you to stay."

This time, it's my turn to melt in relief. "Tyler, I'm sorry to tell you this, but it's too late. I fell in love with you a long time ago. This has been my life for months. I pray every day whether you're scheduled to work on a shift or not because I know that even if you're not on the work schedule, those are your colleagues in danger and if one of them were hurt, it would be as if it happened to you. I watch breaking news with fear and trepidation and I know a frightening amount about weapons systems I never thought I'd need to know. I follow political debates and military spouse message boards so I know how to support you. I've already made the decision and I'm not un-making it."

Tyler looks as if I've kicked him in the solar plexus with one of Tara's fancy martial arts moves. "That's a lot," Tyler declares bleakly. "I had no idea. At the risk of sounding completely cotton-headed, I have to ask why would you put yourself through that? I don't do nearly that much for you."

I'm sure the look I give him is worthy of a cartoon double take. "If I hadn't been with you all day, I'd be asking you what you'd been drinking. I'm going to spell this out as clearly as I can. Tyler Joseph Colton, I love you. Get that? If I have to name the reasons why — we could be here all night. Let's start with the fact that you were one of the first people that actually saw the real me. You didn't see Heather, the joke cracking, fashion-smart dress-up doll. You saw who I was at the core and still fell in love with me. Not only that, you gave me the courage to love myself. I hadn't had the courage to do that for a really long time."

Tyler swallows hard, like he's fighting the urge to stop me. But, I hold up my hand to halt him because I am not done. He asked, So, I want him to hear all of it. For all of his complaints about me not being able to take a compliment, they don't go down much easier for him.

"When I could finally love myself, I could forgive myself for mistakes I made in the past." I continue in a steady confident voice. "You gave me freedom. Freedom to be who I really am, freedom from the past, and freedom to be whoever I want to be in the future. That's huge. You stood beside me and fought for me in a way no one else did before. You make me feel beautiful and cherished. You believe in my dreams and you don't tell me they're stupid. You make me feel empowered and smart. Is that a long enough list for you or would you like me to go on?"

Tyler clears his throat and swallows hard. "No, that's a pretty impressive list. I'm not sure I can claim credit for all that. I can't pinpoint the second I fell in love with you. It might have been when you tricked me into eating eight kinds of pasta or the first time you trusted me enough to get on the back of a horse or it may have even been when you yelled at me about not being immune from bullets. All I know is that from the moment you entered my life, it's never been the same."

Tyler helps me to a standing position and then kneels on one knee in front of me. My heart literally stops. This is so not like I planned this moment in my head. I'm wearing jeans and an "I heart my soldier" T-shirt—not some elegant evening gown and stilettos. Ty fishes something out of his pocket as I blink away tears. "Heather, this is probably not what you think it is because I stupidly wasn't prepared for us to have a 'moment' like this tonight. But, I want to give this to you so you understand that I understand where we're at."

I glance down at his hand and notice in antique looking coin. When he notices my puzzled expression, he hurries to explain. "This is my Saint Michael's medal. It's the soldier's saint. According to family folklore, it was personally blessed by a Pope. My parents gave it to me to remind me they were always thinking of me. It was the thing I kept closest to me until I met you. Until I can get you a more suitable ring, will you allow this to be a stand-in?"

I am completely speechless for just a moment. "Ty, just so this isn't open to any misinterpretation, are you asking me what I think you're asking me?" I ask breathlessly.

"Sorry Gidget, sometimes my heart gets ahead of my brain. Heather Lydia LaBianca, will you do me the honor of being my wife? A man I respect a great deal, gave me some wonderful advice. He reminded me I can't relive yesterday and I can't shape tomorrow. Today is the only day I can live and today I choose to live and accept the love you've given me and I hope you accept the love I give you for as many days as we have left together."

"Tyler Joseph Colton, I would love to be your wife. I knew from the moment I laid eyes on you, falling for you was going to be a dangerous endeavor. But, we can be brave together. I would much rather take the risk of loving you and losing you than face the choice of never having you in my life at all." I pull Tyler to his feet and practically launch myself into his arms as I rain kisses all over his face.

Suddenly, a funny thought occurs to me. "You weren't planning to ask my dad's permission were you?"

A dark look crosses Ty's face. "Under ordinary circumstances, I might extend the man the courtesy, just for tradition's sake. In this case, I refuse to give him one more reason to even almost view you like his property. He doesn't even deserve the right to breathe the same air as you as far as I'm concerned."

I smother a giggle. "Oh good! I thought maybe you were going to try to talk some sense into him or something. I'd much rather have Denny walk me down the aisle anyway. The only ones I don't know about are my brother and sister. I think I'm still cool with Madison but I really don't know about Carlton. He could fall either way on the family divide."

"You know who else will think this is pretty hysterical?" Ty asks smirking at me. "I probably shouldn't have given Jeff so much lip about his 'almost' engagement to Kiera since we did exactly the same thing. Jeff's probably going to hatch a plan with Denny to beat their previous wedding planning record as soon as they hear about us. How fast do you want to get married?"

That question stops me in my tracks. I've always envisioned having months and months to plan every last detail of my wedding from the bridal shower to the reception with painstaking detail. But, then again I never envisioned a wedding without my grandma there and I always figured my parents would eventually figure me out. My eyes travel back to my wedding consulting corner. There is so much to consider. How many people should we have at the wedding? I haven't even met my future in-laws yet. As I try to consider the possibilities, the mural catches my eye. "Oh my gosh! Tyler, we can't get married before Tara and Aidan. It was their turn first, it would be rude to steal their thunder. This may be complicated."

Tyler wiggles his eyebrows suggestively at me, "Do you want to run away to Vegas?"

I gasp in disbelief. "Take a good look around, Cowboy! How many wedding cakes do you see in here?"

Tyler spins around in a slow circle. "Oh, I guess I see about eight."

I nod. "Guess who made each one of those cakes? How could you possibly think I haven't been planning my wedding cake since I pulled my first pan of cake-like-substance out of a cute little Easy Bake Oven when I was about four? You do realize that I make the majority of my income from the wedding industry? What message would it send if I skipped my own wedding?"

"Okay, point taken. Big opulent wedding it is. I'll even wear my dress uniform for you or you could choose a monkey suit if you prefer. I don't care if your brother and sister are involved. I thought your sister was cool and your brother might have potential. I'm going to fly my parents out here as soon as possible. I'm sure my mom would love to help with your grand opening."

Tyler's stomach suddenly lets out a huge growl of hunger. "Sorry, there wasn't much food on the plane."

"You should have listened to me. I told you I didn't have bad news. Go ahead and eat the wontons and I'll warm up the other stuff. I wouldn't want you to expire from hunger. We have a lot to celebrate tonight."

Chapter Fifteen

Tyler

ON THE WAY BACK home from the bakery, we stop by the grocery store because my refrigerator was almost bare after such a long absence. I had a young college student who was studying veterinary science take care of the animals while I was gone. Judging by the boxes in the trash, he eats like I used to eat before I met Heather. Clearly, I've become spoiled.

As I'm carrying groceries in from the car, I get a text from Aidan.

"Hey Heather, if Aidan is trying to hunt down William, why wouldn't he call Jeff? Why is he asking me what the weather is like on the coast in February? You guys are the locals. I grew up in Oklahoma. He said something about needing a few days of privacy so fate can take its course." I ask as I stash the produce in the fridge.

Heather practically trips over Ethel and Annie in an effort to look over my shoulder. "What did you say?"

"I got this really weird text from Aidan and I'm

trying to figure out why he didn't simply ask Kiera or Jeff for that info. I barely know the judge."

"Oh Geez! Tara is just too spooky for words! Don't you see? Aidan is trying to tell you Tara knows what's going on. He's trying to protect our privacy in case we have told no one yet. If he called Kiera and Jeff, they would know something was up."

"How in the world did you figure all that out from a strange text message asking about William's phone number, the weather forecast on the coast in February, a request for privacy and musings about fate?" I ask, incredulous at her leap of logic.

"First, I've learned to never underestimate Tara's ability to predict weird stuff. I personally have never seen her be wrong. Secondly, Aidan is a big romantic, mushy guy at heart. Valentine's Day is right around the corner. He might not be quite the big gesture guy that Jeff is, but he's darn close. If the two of them team up, there's no telling what could happen. Something tells me I'll be trying to find fresh strawberries in February."

"Why do you sound discouraged? Isn't this a good development for us? Doesn't that mean we don't have to wait so long to get married?"

"Yes, that's the upside. But, the downside is that if they do it right away, Piper and I will still be working our way through the kinks in the new shop and something might go wrong. It could be a million and one strange things like the refrigeration not working or the ovens running too hot. I don't want those nightmares to play out in front of the worldwide press."

"Gidget, Piper's mom is in the hospital, right?"

Heather pauses as I interrupt her. She nods, her expression reflecting her befuddlement. "Yes, she had gall bladder surgery."

"Heather, you cooked the whole gourmet meal for me all by yourself on all of your new equipment and picked me up at the airport today without breaking a sweat. Your shop is beautiful. You chose things well. Whether you do Tara's wedding two weeks before you open, two weeks after you open, or two years from now, it's going to be phenomenal. She is your best friend. You won't allow it to be anything less than spectacular. Remember what you were able to do at Kiera's wedding when all you had was the food truck? There is no way this will not be a million times better because now it will be a signature Joy & Tiers cake."

"Geez Ty, maybe your talents are wasted at the Sheriff's Department. Someone should pay you to write ad copy. You should be writing press releases for me. I can just have you walk around as my arm candy and you can be my public spokesperson."

"That would be fun wouldn't it? I wish I had the luxury to do that. I'd be happy as a clam if my job was to brag about you all day to anyone who would listen."

"You are so funny. You would be so bored that you'd soon start carving on the furniture in the hotel rooms at the wedding venues."

"Well, that would be an interesting side business. I could make your party favors. Seriously, Heather, you will slay this." I put the groceries down and walk Heather over to the couch and tuck her in next to me. Ethel, her grandmother's bloodhound insists on being part of the conversation and places her head on Heather's lap. "We probably need to have a strategy. If you're right, our news isn't going to be private much longer. As much as I wanted to savor this private time between us, we might need to work on a plan for telling folks in a reasonable manner. Our plan for winging it at Christmas didn't work so well."

Heather smirks at the memory. "Yeah, we should probably be a little more strategic unless we want Mindy to be serenading us with the K-I-S-S-I-N-G song all the way up the aisle during our wedding procession. So, it looks like we could start with three choices, your family, my family or the Girlfriend Posse."

"It's up to you. Do you want to tackle the unknown, the hard or the fun first?" I tease.

"Do I have to choose?" she asks, swallowing hard.

"I suppose we could play rock, paper, scissors if you really want to."

Heather scowls at me. "Next, I suppose you'll suggest that we should play spin the bottle or something?"

"That's even better than anything I had planned. I love how creative you are."

She rolls her eyes and blows a wayward curl out of her face in exasperation. "Come on Ty. I guess I'll do the hard thing first and call my family. Please don't tell me you were thinking that your family will be the hard choice."

"Do you think I should talk to Carlton man-to-man first?" I ask as she walks over to the kitchen island to get her cell phone from her purse.

"Honestly, Tyler I don't know if there's going to be a right way to do it with my family. So, you have to play your gut on this one." Heather hands me her cell phone. "The only advice I'm going to give you is you might as well skip my parents. I think they're pretty much a lost cause and I don't want to waste our happy mood on them."

I take a moment to think about all of my years of service both in the military and on the force and a trait that seems to run universally through families of every background is guys are protective of their little sisters even if they don't seem to get along. It seems worth the risk to make the call. But, just in case it gets ugly, I prefer to do it outside of Heather's earshot.

Heather must be able to read the indecision on my face, because she abruptly kisses me on the cheek and says, "I've been cooking in the kitchen all day and I'm a sweaty mess. Why don't you go check on the horses while I take a quick shower? Do you think it will be too late to Skype your parents when you get back?"

"No, my parents are huge fans of the Tonight Show and they always stay up to watch it. I'll send them a text message and let them know we'll be Skype-ing later. My mom will be thrilled. I bet she's waiting for me to call anyway. I think she knows I was due back from training today."

"Geez Ty, we should've called her from the airport. She's probably worried sick. Let me put on some makeup and we'll Skype your parents first. That way, they won't have to wait."

"Gidget, you don't have to do your make up routine for my mom. My mom will think you're totally gorgeous just because you love her baby."

Heather tucks a wayward ringlet under her bandanna and wipes her hands on the backside of her jeans as she walks over to my cluttered desk. "Come on Cowboy, let's do this before I come to my senses. I swear you can sweet-talk me into anything."

I pull up a big, battered leather executive chair and pull her down on my knee as I aim the Webcam so we are framed in the center and I dial up my mom.

As soon as my mom picks up the Skype call, I can tell that she's got the tablet in the kitchen. "Hi Mom!" I greet. "What are you making?"

My mom just shakes her head. "Well, it's a recipe for pâte à choux, but I think I might be accidentally making joint compound for sheet rocking instead. I don't think I'm doing it right. It looks so simple on TV."

"That's okay Mrs. Colton," Heather reassures her. "My first few batches were unrecognizable, I promise. It's definitely an art."

My mom looks up with a startled expression. "Oh dear, I'm sorry. I was so focused on doing my own sweet thing, I almost overlooked you. Being a chef, you must think this is a dreadful mess."

"Oh, no ma'am! I think your kitchen is beautiful. I would love to have those classic appliances. You should see what my work area looks like at the end of a busy day. You wouldn't even know I'm a professional. I look like a five-year-old who's been making mud pies in the backyard. You and I are going to have so much fun."

"Mom, where's Dad? I want to properly introduce Heather before you guys start exchanging recipes."

"Oh, you know him. He's probably scouring the paper for yard sales." My mom steps out of frame and I hear her yell down the hall, "Harold, get in here. Your son wants to talk to you." I hear my dad mumbling as he sits down at the kitchen counter.

"Did they break your dialing finger at that fancy military college?" he asks pointedly.

Heather raises an eyebrow at me, but mercifully doesn't say anything. "You're right, Dad. Heather told me I should have called sooner. I sometimes forget you guys still worry about me."

My dad looks over at Heather. "It's clear she's not only beautiful, but exceptionally smart."

Heather blushes prettily. "I can see why Tyler is such a natural born charmer. He obviously had a very good teacher."

I watch with some amusement as my dad's ears turn red. He makes a motion to loosen his collar even though he's wearing a T-shirt with overalls.

"Harold Oran Colton, stop flirting with your son's girl. You're so scandalous!" my mom admonishes with a laugh.

My dad reaches out and grabs my mom's hand and kisses the back of it, "Sally Ann, I'm not going to stop flirting with beautiful women until the day I die and you're the most beautiful woman I know."

Heather can't help herself from sighing a soft, "Aww" under her breath. She whispers in my ear, "That's just about the most romantic thing I've ever seen."

I wink at her and say, "Hold that thought —"

Heather scrunches her nose at me. "Wha —?"

"Sally and Harold Colton, I'd like you to meet my fiancée Heather LaBianca."

My mom's face goes slack with shock. Her eyes immediately travel to Heather's bare ring finger.

"Tyler Joseph Colton! Did you not even bother to get the poor girl a ring? For as long as you've been in love with her, there is just no excuse for that! You even got that fame-seeking floozy a ring!" My mom slaps her hand over her mouth when she realizes what she's inadvertently disclosed. "I'm so sorry Tyler, I didn't mean to speak out of turn."

"It's all right Mrs. Colton, Tyler and I have already talked about Stacia. Although I'm sorry she trampled on his feelings like an old cow in a barn, I can't say I'm not grateful it didn't work out. I think your son is amazing. If she was too stupid to see that, it's her own fault. As far as the lack of ring, you can blame that on me. Apparently, I'm the queen of ill-timed conversations. He wasn't quite prepared for my confession of undying love." Heather graciously tries to soothe my mom.

My dad scoffs. "Since when are you not prepared for something? She must really have you turned upside down and inside out, son," my dad grins as he teases me. "That's exactly how I was with your mother. I fell so head over heels in love with her, I darn near forgot my own name."

Heather winks at my mom as she responds to my

dad, "I know I just met you, but it seems to me, not much has changed in all these years. I hope Ty is equally forgetful in forty years when we're talking to our kids about their new loves."

My mom's eyes mist over. "Tyler, where did you find this jewel? You better have the good sense to keep her."

"Mom, you probably don't want me to be totally honest and tell you I first laid eyes on her in the middle of a crime in progress," I answer jokingly.

Heather playfully smacks me on the bicep. "Tyler Joseph Colton are you trying to give your mother a heart attack? Although technically your son is correct, the long answer is that his best friend is married to my best friend. We have spent the last couple of years getting to know each other. He finally wore me down with his charm and good looks."

A look of amusement crosses my mom's face. "Oh honey… are you under the impression that you are somehow a surprise to us? The only surprising thing about you is how long it took our son to get you to come around. He's been in love with you forever and a day. I have to say he didn't do you justice when he told us how pretty you were. I would love to have your complexion."

Heather looks completely befuddled as she asks, "Really? I could've sworn he hated me. Sometimes, he acted like he could barely stand to be in the same room with me. We've only officially been dating for the last few months." She turns to me and asks, "Why didn't you say something to me earlier if you felt that way?"

"We've already established I have a habit of being

stupid and stubborn. In the beginning, I was suspicious of everything and by the time I figured out I could trust you and my emotions, I'd already ticked you off and I didn't know how to get my footing back, so it was easier just to pretend to be your friend."

Heather just shakes her head at me. "You're so lucky I love you, because you're a big ole' dork. It makes me sad to think about all those months we could have been together supporting each other when we were pretending to be mortal enemies. How dumb were we?"

"Well, it seems like you've worked it out now. So, that's all that matters, right?" my dad asks.

Heather and I nod. "Yes, sir we have. We'd like you to come meet the family we've built in Oregon. I'm opening my cake shop and I'd be honored if you came to the grand opening," Heather offers.

My mom just beams. "We wouldn't miss it for the world."

After the screen turns black, I turn to Heather and I say, "See, that wasn't so hard."

She smirks at me. "I think you're forgetting that we skipped the hardest call. We still have to call my family."

"I bet it will be easier now, because admit it, you're in a great mood now. It's impossible to be in a bad mood after you've talked to my parents."

Heather grins at me. "Yeah, they have the whole June and Ward Cleaver thing down pat. It's like salt-of-the-earth Midwestern charm. I totally love your parents already. Can we just pretend that they're my family too?"

I cuff her chin softly, "I know you too well, Gidget.

You would never forgive yourself if you left Madison out of this and even if you don't want to admit it, the same is probably true of Carlton. So, let me man up and give Carlton the obligatory man-to-man call. Then you can have a girly, giggly call with your sister, okay?"

Heather snorts with laughter. "Tyler, you remember meeting my sister — you know the hard-hitting, nosy news reporter? I don't think girly and giggly are in her vocabulary anymore. But, you can keep that fantasy in your head if you want to."

"I don't know, she seemed to be on your side when we went to your grandma's funeral. I can imagine that as kids you were once co-conspirators."

A smile washes over Heather's face as she reminisces, "Yeah, we did pull some good ones when we were younger. Some days poor Carlton didn't know whether he was coming or going having to keep up with the two of us."

"I'm going to go out to check on the horses in case your brother is less than happy with your choice of suitor. I might have to be a little more persuasive than I feel comfortable being in front of you. So, I'll be back in a few minutes." I give her a brief kiss as I shrug into my jacket and leather gloves.

Heather walks over to my kitchen cupboard and pulls out a baggie of sugar cubes and sticks them in my pocket. "Take care of the babies while you're out there, please. They missed you. Please don't threaten to kill my brother. He can't help the way he was raised."

I can't disguise my surprised expression. The last thing I expected her to do was defend the brother who constantly harasses her. "Okay, I promise to play nice for the sake of family unity and all. But, if he's a jerk, I will defend you. He doesn't get to treat you like garbage."

"Cowboy, I know you wouldn't stand for that and if he doesn't know you well enough by now, then he's a bigger idiot than I give him credit for being and he doesn't need protection from me. I'm just asking you to be nice — not to change who you are."

"Great, just so were on the same page." I scoop her up into a tight embrace and kiss her. As she grasps my hands tightly, I still marvel she has agreed to become my wife. I call Annie and head out to the barn.

I stop and sit on the porch where we set up a viewing area in front of the corral and I take out my cell phone. Earlier in the evening, Heather and I combined contact information for both families on our phones. The symbolism of that was huge to me. Somehow, I don't think merging our families in real life will be as painless as combining our phone and contact lists via the Internet. But, I promised Heather that I would give it my best shot, and I'm a man of my word. With more trepidation than I care to admit, I dial Carlton's number.

"'Lo," answers a sleepy voice on the other end of the line.

I glance down at my watch and notice it's 7:30 PM our time. "Oh Crap! I'm sorry Carlton. I completely forgot about the three hour time difference. Do you want me to call you back tomorrow?"

"Nah, it's too late to worry about that now. I'm up. Who is this?"

"Oh, sorry. This is Tyler Colton."

"Heather's Muscle? Oh man … what did she do now. Before you call the police, let's see if we can work through this. I swear I always pegged her to be smarter than this —"

"Carlton, do yourself a favor, dude. Shut up." I advise as my frustration level rises exponentially with each word he utters.

"What? What are you talking about?" Carlton asks, clearly confused.

"I'm just suggesting before you badmouth your sister, you should actually know what's going on."

"Okay, since you called me, why don't you explain why you called?" Carlton challenges.

"Again, I apologize for calling so late. But, I called to let you know I'd like to marry your little sister."

"Are you sure you don't have the wrong number? Shouldn't you be talking to my dad about this?"

"If you were me, would you bother with your dad?" I counter.

Carlton chuckles wryly. "No, I suppose not, but that doesn't really answer the question why you bothered with me. Most people assume I'm just a chip off the old block. What makes you think my opinion will be any different?"

"Well, to be honest I don't have any guarantees it'll be. But, I gave you fair and truthful advice about the water and mineral rights and I'm a straight shooter. I figure you either respect me or you don't. I know your little sister loves you something fierce and it would break her heart if I let my stupid ego get in the way of making her happy. So, I'm here to tell you I love your sister more than I have loved anybody my whole life and I will move heaven and earth to make her happy. I'd like you to be part of our happiness if you can make that happen."

The phone line becomes eerily quiet and I wonder if he's hung up the phone. Finally, I hear him clear his throat. "Man, I've got to respect you. I've never seen anybody stand up to my parents. You need to realize this puts me in a hell of a spot. I'm not quite as free of the parental units as my dear little sis. Mom and Dad have their fingers in my mortgage, my business, my car loans, heck — they even co-own the time-share."

"Understood. You've got to decide what's important to you. But, here's a thought, you might respect yourself more if you can let go of some of those ties."

"You sound like my soon-to-be ex-wife," Carlton admits sadly.

"I'm sorry to hear that," I declare sympathetically.

"No, if I had taken some cues from a guy like you and protected her instead spending so much time running around chasing money, I might still have Whitney in my life."

"Maybe it's not too late for you to get your priorities in order," I suggest. "I'll start by making sure you get to give your sister away."

"Are you sure it means that much to her?" Carlton asks. "She's always been a little weird when it comes to me."

"I wouldn't bother askin' if it didn't. Seriously, we both want you there."

"Then I'll be there. Just make sure she doesn't make

me wear pink or something."

"I can put in a request, but I make no guarantees. My aim in life is to make Heather happy. If pink makes her happy, what can I say?"

Chapter Sixteen

Heather

"So, do you think you'll be totally disinherited if you talk to me, Maddie?"

"I was likely disinherited long ago. Probably around the first time I took a job at the student newspaper and supported recycling. Having your own opinion is not a popular sport in this family — in case you haven't noticed. By the way, great win in court against Mom and Dad."

"Are you being sarcastic, or do you really mean it?" I ask with trepidation. With Madison, it's often hard to tell whether she's kidding — especially when you're on the phone with her and you can't see her facial expressions.

She snorts back a laugh. "Of course it's a compliment. I think you're an absolute rock star. I know I'm a few years younger than you are, but I remember you and Grandma talking for hours about opening a restaurant or a bakery. Every time we went on vacation to a new city somewhere, you guys would go on

271

undercover missions to all the new cool places in town and talk about how your business would run. I think it's so bogus Mom and Dad pretended they didn't know Grandma intended for you to have a bakery all along. That's a total lie and they know it. I'm so glad you won your court case. The tantrum that they're throwing is completely epic and embarrassing. They're even turning off long-term clients. Several of those clients know you and like you. They think Mom and Dad's attitude is totally disgusting."

"Wow! That's interesting. The way Mom and Dad make it sound, I don't have any friends left in town. They said I destroyed everything when I left town to go to culinary school."

Madison makes a sound of dismissal. "Are you kidding? People around here think you're downright heroic for breaking the mold of the Stepford wife and striking out on your own to do your own thing. Hey, why are you just now calling me? The lawsuit was over a couple months ago."

"Well, I have pretty big news —"

"Are you pregnant?" my sister shrieks through the phone.

"What? No! A man can want me without me being pregnant," I argue indignantly.

"I didn't say nobody wants you," Madison insists. "It's just when somebody starts a sentence like that, it's usually followed by news of a positive pregnancy test."

"Well, not this time! I called to see if you wanted to be my maid of honor when Tyler and I get married."

"You and Ty are getting married?" Madison repeats slowly.

"Yes, we're getting married! Is the phone connection bad?"

"No, I can hear you just fine. I'm just worried — that's all. Are you sure you know what you're getting into? Being a military spouse is hard. It'll be a lot harder than what you went through with that Heaves dude. If he caused you to run all the way to Oregon, what is it going to be like for you to be married to a soldier?"

"First of all, Fletcher didn't make me move to Oregon, he was just a kick in the pants that made me brave enough to finally do it. I would've done it anyway eventually. Fletcher just gave me a big push. Second, I only thought I loved Fletcher. I wanted to be in love so badly, I thought he was it for me. But, Fletcher only cared for himself. Now, I know the meaning of true love. Tyler is the real thing. He respects and trusts me. He believes in my dreams and allows me to pursue them. Ty makes me feel like a whole person. I realize that he has a duty to his country and it comes first. I won't lie to you and tell you that it doesn't scare the heck out of me. But, it's as much a part of him as being an artist is part of me. So, I have to let him go save lives every day so he can come back to me and be at peace. It's the scariest thing I've ever done in my whole life."

"Okay, I wanted to make sure you understand that the lifestyle you're choosing isn't for lightweights."

"No, Sis, I think I got it. I practically pass out every time I hear his scanner go off and I have to practice newfangled meditation techniques to get through the nightly news these days. Trust me, I have a whole new understanding of the dangers of the world now that I'm dating a first responder."

"Great! Now I can tell you why I think Tyler's the most awesomely perfect man ever for you. Speaking of that, what do Mom, Dad and Carlton think?"

"Obviously, I figured I wouldn't waste my breath bothering to tell Mom and Dad or seek their approval. So, I really don't know. I'd like to say I don't care, but I guess there's always going to be a piece of me that seeks out their approval. So, there's a teeny tiny small part of me that's sad that they won't be involved in this. I guess there's a larger portion that's relieved I won't have to mess with their criticism. Because, I know nothing I will ever do with Tyler, this marriage, or anything in my career will ever make them happy."

"I'm sorry it has to be that way. I'm afraid you're right. Dad is way too stubborn to admit that he might have been wrong and until he does that, Mom is stuck in the middle. I don't have any problems siding with you. I think they were wrong. I don't care if they know I think that they made a mistake. If that pisses them off, I'm sorry, but you're my big sister and I'm going to be your maid of honor. If they don't like it, that's just too bad. What does Carlton say?"

"I don't know. Ty's on the phone with him right now. They've been on the phone for a really long time. I'm not sure what that means. That could go either way."

"We should cut him some slack. He's been having trouble with Whitney. I think they could do okay if Mom and Dad would stay out of it. But, Mom and Dad are so worried about looking perfect, they don't give people a chance to live life and figure out how to work out their differences — to just live and breathe. It's stifling. I don't blame them for splitting up."

"Oh no! Is it official now? I feel terrible asking them to be part of my wedding if they're on the outs. There is nothing more awful than being around a happy couple if you're not."

"No, I think it's great. Maybe it will make Carlton reevaluate what's important to him. If he has to look true happiness in the face, maybe he'll realize what a farce he's been living and pull his act together."

"Maybe, but it still seems mean —"

"So, when are these big nuptials taking place and can we dress Carlton in pink, pretty please?"

"Well, the timing is a little tricky because my best friend Tara got engaged first, so it would be rude to cut in line. I am sure that Carlton will have an opinion on what he wears and his first choice definately won't be pink."

"Oh, that's right. Tara is marrying that gorgeous pop star. Aidan O'Brien, isn't she? Are you planning to make the wedding cake for that?"

"Well, you know anything can happen with the Girlfriend Posse so who knows whether they're even going to have a wedding cake," I respond mysteriously.

My sister snorts. "Oh, I see. You've already signed the confidentiality agreements and can't say anything."

"You are just too nosy for your own good. But, you're barking up the wrong tree. In this case, I really know nothing. We haven't talked wedding cake at all, I swear."

Madison laughs. "Uh huh, you always talk wedding cake. So, you'll pardon me if I don't believe you. Send me a text when you've got a more plausible cover story in place and a solid date set and I'll clear my schedule. Congratulations Sis. This one's a keeper."

I'm still smiling when I hang up the phone. It's funny that even though I'm totally telling the truth, no one believes me. Maybe that's why Tara hasn't said one word about the wedding to me. She already knows I'm terrible at keeping secrets. What I don't know, I can't accidentally spill.

I hear the back door open, so I run to meet Ty. As I look him over, he doesn't look any worse for the wear. I breathe a sigh of relief as I take in his relaxed demeanor. "You don't look like you're ready to skin my brother alive," I observe.

"It actually went really well, Gidget. He's coming to walk you down the aisle as soon as you give him the word."

"Really? Just as simple as that? In case you haven't noticed, Carlton isn't really my biggest fan. What did you do to coerce him?"

"Nothing. Once he knew how important it was to you for him to be there, he was totally on board. Of course, he's a little nervous about how your dad will retaliate, but he's willing to take that risk."

"I wonder why he's suddenly willing to stick his neck out for me. Usually, he is the one picking on me."

"Maybe he's finally fed up. Maybe he's decided that it's time he makes his own decisions for a change," Ty suggests, shrugging. "I support his decision to be his own man. More power to him."

"Me too. Unfortunately, he doesn't have great friends like ours," I remark wistfully.

"Not yet, but it doesn't mean he couldn't. Justice Gardner has lots of friends in many states—"

"You're so funny. Dropping names left and right. Next thing you know, you're going to be suggesting Aidan call his BFF, Billy Joel, to play at our wedding or something."

"Nah, as far as I know, Aidan hasn't met Billy Joel yet. But, did he tell you he met one of the members of Big and Rich when he covered their song on an award show last year? He said it was pretty cool. They thanked him for bringing awareness to their song. They were cool about the cover. Speaking of your friends, are you ready to tell them? This should be the fun part. Who do you want to start with and should we do it over the phone or video call?"

"We should definitely do this via video and I think we should start with Tara and Aidan because that'll hopefully settle some answers for us."

"The artistic lovebirds, it is." Tyler says as he walks me over to the computer and pulls me down into his lap.

As Aidan's head pops up on the other side of the computer, I see a look of relief on his face, "Blimey! It took you guys long enough. It was not easy to keep this one from crawling through the computer screen to try to figure out what was going on. Can you confirm what she already knows so she can relax? She is like a cat standing on tinfoil right now."

Tara practically pushes Aidan out of the way as she addresses me. "It was romantic, right? But, totally not what you expected. About as far from typical as you could get, am I right?"

I shake my head in silent shock. Her skills are so impressive. I don't believe Tyler could have telegraphed his intent to ask me to marry him because I don't think he decided to ask me until the actual moment it happened. If he had planned it in advance, he would have done a far more advanced, romantic over the top, epic never forget it in a million years type of event. As much as the superficial, clothes-horse fashionista side of me might have wished for an exotic marriage proposal with all the bells and whistles. The real, down-to-earth-hot-chocolate-sipping-Netflix-movie-watchin'-hair-in-a-ponytail side of me, really appreciates the sweet sentiment of the simple heartfelt proposal.

"It was perfect," I murmur. "He's rather perfect for me. I know I'll never hear the end of it. You guys told me this was coming months and months ago."

Tara just sagely shrugs and sighs. "The heart is ready when it's ready. There isn't much you can do to speed it up or slow it down."

I think about the simple wisdom of her words. I suppose she's right. Tyler and I could have settled into a quick and easy relationship that both of us were comfortable with and kept it superficial. But, because of the odd nature of our relationship, I was forced to look beyond the affable good guy persona Tyler puts up and find the haunted hero with the fragile heart underneath. I discovered as much as I have fun with gregarious Ty, I love the more vulnerable sides of him just as much. "Tara, why didn't you tell me about him? Maybe I would have been a better friend," I ask, somberly.

Tara casts her eyes down and a look of sadness crosses her face. "Some stories just aren't mine to share and sometimes it's the telling of the story that brings the most healing. Still other times, my knowledge won't change the outcome."

"I suppose you will be as tightlipped as usual and not give me any clues about what you mean. I was never any good at solving riddles."

Tara raises an empirical eyebrow at me, "Well, considering you are beaming out more happiness rays than the sun, I would venture to guess things are going okay between you and Ty. So, I doubt you have much to worry about on the relationship front," she observes dryly.

"No, you're right about that. I know you all already 'know', but I thought I should officially tell you that Tyler and I have gotten engaged. Well, I guess we technically have followed in Jeff and Kiera's footsteps and done the 'sort of' engagement thing."

Tara's eyes widen in surprise. "I'm amazed Ty was caught flat-footed. The way he talked to Aidan, I thought he would have been prepared for this moment months ago."

"What do you mean, prepared? Prepared for what?" I ask incredulously. "If you go back too many months, Tyler and I were barely speaking."

"I guess I just don't look at your conflict the same way. You two may not have been talking in the traditional sense of the word. But, you two were speaking volumes to each other. For two people who spent a great deal of time professing enormous dislike for each other, you two got along like two peas in a pod."

"Tara! Are you blind? We fought all the time. We couldn't even agree if the sky was blue or whether we should drink Coke or Pepsi. The man is insufferably bossy and competitive. Forget personal space or boundaries; He simply doesn't have any. From the moment we met, he was always pushing me and goading me," my speech trails off as I run out of steam and throw my hands up in disgust.

Tara nods sympathetically. "Oh, I won't disagree. Tyler is one hundred percent overwhelming, especially when his attention is focused on you, but isn't that the beauty of it? His attention and adoration is totally focused on you. I've never seen him do or say anything that isn't completely supportive of you. Even the quirky pet name he chose for you is based on the fact that he thinks you're classy and cute. So, I've come to the conclusion that Tyler's been in love with you for much longer than either of you are probably willing to admit. That's the reason I'm surprised he wasn't carrying around an engagement ring with him."

"So, it's not like it was with Kiera and Jeff? You didn't have an instant vision of us together for life?" I ask with trepidation, not exactly sure I want to know her answer.

"Heather, you know I don't ever answer questions

about my visions unless it's a matter of life and death. It messes with fate. Besides, you and Ty have been doing just fine on your own," Tara says with a small sigh.

When I see the expression on Tara's face, I feel instantly guilty. I've been friends with her long enough to know her special insight can be a mixed blessing at best and a terrible burden at worst. "Well, this is a tad awkward. Now, I don't know if you don't want to tell me because it's bad news or if it's just your standard I-have-spooky-powers-policy. The only reason I ask is because Tyler is so scared about the future. It almost seems like he feels like he has one foot in the grave already."

Tara smirks. "I've never denied I'm spooky and I've never truly thanked you enough for being my friend in spite of that. Would it make you feel any better if I told you that it's pretty much my blanket disclaimer? As far as Ty goes, if you could see what goes on in that man's head and understand the stresses he faces in either line of work, I think you would better understand his fatalistic attitude."

"That's just it Tara, I can't understand what he doesn't tell me," I lament with frustration.

"I think there are a couple of factors at work here. Ty's bound by a sense of confidentiality. He isn't really the artistic sensitive type like Aidan. He's going to be more reticent to share. He's used to being the strong silent type that doesn't need anyone. Relying on someone else for emotional support is a brand-new experience for him. If I were to guess, you are probably the first woman he's ever fully trusted. It's going to take a while for him to develop a new communication style with you, so you need to be patient. You may need to listen to the things he doesn't say as much as the things he does."

"Well, hello 'Dear Abby' — how did you get so smart about relationships? I thought you were the shy one," I tease.

Tara giggles. "There's something to be said about the love of a good man to give you added perspective about life."

CHAPTER SEVENTEEN

TYLER

"TYLER, I DON'T KNOW why you think any of us would be shocked. We all saw the writing on the wall months ago. You two have been throwing off more sparks than a firework factory since the moment you met. Congratulations, Buddy! I have to ask though, where is her ring?" Jeff asks as he crosses his arms.

"It's funny you should ask … the engagement sort of snuck up on me. I meant to be better prepared."

Jeff practically falls off of his chair because he's laughing so hard. When he finishes, he says, "Let me get this straight — you've been in love with her practically since you laid eyes on her, and you're the guy who plans military missions and undercover operations for a living — but you forgot to plan for your own engagement? That's just too funny — she's not pregnant is she?"

"No! Remember how insulted you were when people assumed that about you and Kiera? Well, ditto."

Jeff looks slightly chagrined, but still snickers, "Sorry. I shouldn't assume anything. But, I'm still trying to figure out how this went down, especially after you flicked me so much crap about Kiera. I would've expected you to propose with a horse-drawn carriage and a whole eighteen piece orchestra."

I rake my hand through my hair. "I hear you. That's the kind of proposal she deserves. In fact, I think that's what she was expecting, but we were having this intense conversation and it seemed right to improvise. So, that's what I did. Never in a million years did I expect to do this backwards. Thank goodness she seemed okay with it."

Just then Heather walks back in to the room followed by Kiera, Tara and Mindy. It's clear from the expressions on their faces that they've been sharing secrets. Mindy hops up on a bar stool and pops a blueberry in her mouth. "Uncle Ty, are you getting married at the same time as Uncle Aidan?"

I concentrate on not dropping the pancake I'm flipping as I answer, "No, they got engaged first, so it's their turn."

"Aunt Heather caught the wedding bouquet at Mom's and Dad's wedding, remember, same as Uncle Aidan. It was a tie. So everybody has to get married at the same time," she argues.

I chuckle at her logic. "I'm not sure that the superstition is quite that precise Mindy Mouse. I think it's enough that I plan to marry her. We'll let Tara and Aidan have their own special day, okay?"

Mindy frowns and looks back and forth between Heather and I with a serious expression on her face. "You should really listen to me. I don't think that's the plan."

I flip the pancake out onto a plate and put it in front

of her. "Mindy, I promise I won't change my mind. I love Heather. She's next. Look on the bright side, this means you'll get to be in three weddings instead of two."

Mindy just rolls her eyes. "Maybe someday I'll be old enough that people will pay attention to what I say."

Just then my pager beeps shrilly, disturbing the impromptu early morning engagement celebration. I'm on call today. Crap. Blueberry pancakes are my favorite too.

I kiss Heather quickly as I run out the door. "I love you, Gidget. I'll see you whenever this wraps up. Will you make me some pancakes when I get home?"

Heather jogs beside me as I hop in the department SUV. I roll down the window. She passionately kisses me one last time and whispers, "I'll cook you whatever you want to eat, just be safe Cowboy. I love you too. Go rid the world of crime and all that jazz."

I check the computer in the console. Unfortunately, I recognize the description of the vehicle all too well. I've been on far too many DUIs and domestic violence calls involving this guy. It's like a revolving door. I flip on my lights and head out toward his predictable hangouts. On the way there, I see his car weaving in and out of traffic. *Shoot. Here we go again.* I radio in my location and pull a sharp U-turn.

As I walk-up beside the car, I see a head of dark curls. My adrenaline kicks up another notch. This call just escalated to deadly serious. You've got to be kidding me. I've met this kiddo before. His name is Nathaniel and I don't think he's quite two yet. He's sitting so low in the car, I know that he can't even be sitting in a booster seat let alone a proper car seat for a child his age.

As soon as Allan Divers sees it's me, I see him utter a string of profanities and try to shift his car back into gear. I throw open his car door and grab his keys from his ignition. Suddenly, he grapples with me. My first responsibility is to protect my weapon. I'm able to toss his keys under the car as I drag us both out of the vehicle. I order him to let go and put his arms in the air. It's no surprise that he's not responding to commands because the guy smells like a brewery. His son is screaming in abject terror from the car but that doesn't seem to faze Allan at all. I duck as a meaty fist comes flying toward my face.

"Come on, Allan, man — you don't want to do this. Think of your family. You start messing with an officer and your charges go way up."

"I got nothing else to lose. They're gonna take my boy. I won't let them do that. You'll have to kill me first."

Faster than I can blink, a six inch switchblade appears in the hand I wasn't focused on and he has it pressed to my side.

"Allan, look over there. Your boy is watching everything you're doing. He thinks you're Superman. Do you really want him to see this?" I ask trying to keep my voice even. Mentally, I'm trying to calculate how long it might take for backup to get here. I didn't really escalate the call when I asked for backup because I foolishly thought it would be routine. I forgot the basic rule of policing. There is no such thing as routine.

"It don't matter. He's too little to remember anyway. He'll be better off without me. My old lady is right. I'm only good to him dead."

"Allan, that's just not true. My best friend lost his dad when he was not much older than your son and he blamed himself most of his life for his death. Do you want Nathaniel to go through his life with this on his shoulders? It would be so much worse for your son because my friend wasn't even present for his dad's death. Don't make me shoot you in front of your son."

"How am I supposed to live without him? He's gonna know his dad is a total loser. The judge said I can't even visit him without somebody being there with me."

"If you're honest with yourself, did the judge have a reason to rule that way? Was he keeping your boy safe?"

"Yeah. You've seen me. I spend more time in a bottle than I do sober and I got no job. My stupid old lady won't shut up about it. She's always yappin' in my face I gotta take more responsibility. Well, I showed her who was boss and then she called the cops over a couple little bruises. I don't get it. My dad used to beat the crap out of my mom and she never said a word. I barely laid a hand on Debbie and she goes and turns me in. It's all her fault little Natey got taken away. Now, I don't know what to do!" Abruptly, he puts his hand down by his side and paces. "You got a light? I need to smoke."

I shake my head as I step behind him to cuff him, "Sorry Allan, I don't smoke. I gave it up when I was a teenager. Couldn't be a jock and smoke at the same time. But, what if I could get you some help with the other stuff? You know the best friend I was telling you about? Well, he married himself a phenomenal woman who happens to be a brilliant social worker. She knows tons of people in the field. She could probably help you find a great treatment program to help you pull your life together. It's not too late to turn your life around. Isn't your son worth it?"

Allan looks up at me from the back seat of the SUV with skepticism written on his face. "Why are you being so nice? I tried to kill you."

"Let's say I've seen stress make people do a lot of crazy things. There is enough death and destruction in this world. If I can prevent one more family from being torn apart, I'd like to. Consider this a second chance. Use it wisely. Not everyone gets one."

"Dude, you are the weirdest cop I've ever seen."

"Thank you, I'll take it as a compliment."

After hours and hours of paperwork and endless phone calls to get Allan situated in a detox program with treatment to follow, Nathaniel processed through Child Protective Services and reunited with his mom, I finally pull up in my driveway. As I watch Heather's silhouette dance in the kitchen window as she's back lit by the bright lights of my kitchen island, the adrenaline dump hits. That was a close call. I never know what I'm going to roll up on. What the hell am I going to tell Heather? Do I tell her I was a fraction of an inch from not coming home today? What purpose would it serve? Am I lying to her if I don't tell her?

Fatigue overwhelms me and I rest my head on the steering wheel as I try to gather my thoughts. I don't know how long I've been there with my eyes closed, listening to the rain, when I hear the vehicle door open and feel Heather's cool hand on my forehead.

"Come on, Cowboy. Let's get you inside. You look exhausted. It's a little late for pancakes, but I made you chili and cornbread."

At the mere mention of food, my stomach emits a loud growl. I smile weakly. "As you can hear, I've got no complaints." I unfold my long frame from the utility vehicle, scoop Heather up in my arms and make a run for the front porch. When I set her down, I gather her up into a tight embrace and just wordlessly hold her for several minutes.

"I love you too," she murmurs in my ear. Heather pulls away from me and slides her arm around my waist as she walks me into the house. "I understand you had a tough day," Heather comments as she pours me a cup of coffee in my favorite mug.

I try to school my features to cover my surprise. "I've had better days. Why? What have you heard?"

Heather looks a little defensive. "Relax Cowboy, I'm not going to ask you to divulge any state secrets. I just know something big happened because Kiera went into super-secret confidential work mode not too long after you went on your call. I put two and two together. I know you guys can't talk about this stuff. I wouldn't ask you to reveal anything which would jeopardize your job."

Sighing heavily, I kiss the top of her head. This is really hard. I've never had anybody I've been responsible to and before now, I've never wanted to. Now that I want to share the whole story, I'm not sure how appropriate it is. "Sometimes, I forget you're entirely too smart for your own good. I'm not sure how much of this I can share. But, I had a closer call than I was comfortable with today and it scared the living crap out of me. Part of me doesn't want to tell you anything because I don't want you to be scared and the other part of me wants to tell you everything because I want you to know what you're signing up for when you marry me. I don't know if it all makes me certifiably insane or what?"

The throbbing ache at the base of my skull becomes a full-blown headache and I rub my eyes in an effort to erase it. Heather pushes a huge bowl of chili in my direction and places a basket of steaming cornbread beside it. "Did you even eat any lunch today?" she demands.

I shrug. "Does a pack of M & Ms count?"

Heather rolls her eyes. "Have I taught you nothing? Of course not! No wonder you have a headache. Eat."

I take a big bite. My tension melts away as the warm food hits my stomach. I used to think I had the worst luck in the world, but now I'm considering myself blessed. I not only walked away from a dicey call this afternoon, but so did everyone else. Better yet, a guy who's been messed up for years may actually finally get the help he needs. I'll call it a win. The best thing of all, is at the end of the day, I have someone to come home to now. Not just anyone, my perfect balance. Someone who sees my cracks and became my glue, saw my weaknesses and became my strength, saw my sorrow and became my joy.

Heather is watching me like a hawk as I demolish every bite of food on the table and drink my coffee with absolute relish. "How are you, really?" she asks, concern creasing her brow. "Tell me how you really are, not what you think is the prettied up answer for public consumption. This is a conversation between us — the one safe place on the planet for you to be yourself. If you're not safe here, you're not safe anywhere."

I rake my hand over my face in a gesture of frustration. "Shaky. Okay? There. Are you happy? I admit it. I feel as weak as a kitten. As that lowlife was holding a knife on me, all I could think about was everything we have built together could be gone in an instant and I didn't even tell you goodbye. You would've been just like so many others except you would've been so much worse off because I haven't even set you up to be taken care of after I'm gone. It was the worst feeling in the world. I kept playing our relationship over in my head wondering why I had waited so long to make my move. We wasted so much precious time together. All I knew was that I had to get out of there alive so I could tell you I love you every day for the rest of our lives."

Heather blinks back tears at my unexpectedly emotional confession. "I can't believe you even had a minute to think about me with all that was going on. Honestly, I don't know how to process what you said. Am I supposed to know how? Is there some innate knowledge the other spouses or partners know I don't know yet helps them cope? I'm so relieved you're safe but I'm glad I didn't know about the knife. Even with what little I knew, I was completely freaking out. It was so hard not knowing. I can't pretend otherwise."

I watch as a tear slides slowly down her cheek. The salty trail it leaves behind mirrors the cracks of pain in my heart. As unprepared as I was for the sheer joy, contentment and sometimes outright silliness of being in a relationship with Heather, I was equally unprepared for the pain and abject fear as my wall crumbles. Before she came into my life, I was perfectly comfortable being the good-time guy floating along in life pretending like I didn't give a care attitude cost me a shot at college and my athletic career. It was only by the grace of God and through the quick thinking of an Army recruiter I ended up turning my life around instead of becoming a lost soul. I had the attitude, risk factors and the recklessness. Thank God for people like my parents and Jeff who never gave up on me even when I tried to push them out of my life. Now, I've got one more anchor keeping me grounded if I can manage not to scare her away. If only.

I stand up and pull her into my arms. "I'm sorry, Gidg. I wish I had a magic wand to make all the evil in the world go away, but I don't. Before I met you, I had a healthy respect for the dangers involved in my job, but to be honest, I really didn't give it much thought. It never really mattered. Don't get me wrong, it's not like I had a death wish or anything. It's just no one on the planet — outside of my parents —really cared whether I won the Nobel Peace Prize or turned into caterpillar poop."

Heather scoffs at me and clicks her tongue at me like a schoolmarm. "That's a lie right there. Your friends would care a great deal. I bet the men in your unit would too. You always sell yourself short. Many people would be devastated if something happened to you."

"I don't know about that. I guess I'll have to take your word for it. But what I know is for the first time in a really long time I feel like I would miss out on something if I weren't around. It's a great feeling to be checked back into my life, but it's also terrifying. Because as I was so rudely reminded today things can go sideways in a hurry. My mind kept thinking about all the times I could've told you I love you and I didn't. I'm so sorry I wasted so much time living in my own head."

"Tyler, quit being so hard on yourself. A relationship takes two people. I wasn't exactly making it easy. I had my own fears and insecurities to overcome. I learned a valuable lesson today too. I learned if you get deployed, it's going to be exponentially harder than I ever expected it to be. Based on the time we spent apart during your class, I figured it was going to royally suck; but when you add the danger factor, it takes it to a level beyond what I could understand. I thought I understood what it would be like because I have been hanging out on the military support boards and hanging out down at the station. I realize now, I really had no idea what those families are enduring on a daily basis until now. I guess all I can do is cherish every moment we have together until you're gone and treasure those moments until you come back."

"What if I don't come back? I almost didn't today. Is it fair of me ask that of you?" I ask in an anguished voice as I crush her to me in a tight embrace.

"I can't un-love you. It doesn't work that way. You didn't ask me to love you. I just did. So, you can't ask me to fall out of love with you. Besides, love never deals in the realm of fair or not fair. If it did, parents would never have to bury their kids, pets would never die and spouses would never have to say goodbye. If the unthinkable happens and you die, I pray I would remember the amazing joy you brought to my life and somehow gather the strength to move on because I know that's what you would want me to do."

"I would want you to move on," I answer in a harsh whisper, against her temple.

"Of course you would, because that's the kind of person you are. You're the one who taught me how to fall in love with myself. Because of that, I'm able to freely love you. I know you're waiting for the other shoe to fall. After all you've been through, I don't know how you couldn't live that way. But, you have to know that for my sanity, I can't live that way. There's still a really big part of me that believes in happily ever after, Disney Princess fairytale endings. I want the kind of love story my grandparents had. When I envision a future with you, I want to think about whatever version of Skype-ing with the grandkids will happen in fifty years as we're managing a sprawling ranch somewhere. I don't know, maybe we may even own some famous bed-and-breakfast by then — who knows? But the point is, whenever I think about the future, I never, ever see facing it without you in it."

I kiss her tenderly. "Oh Gidget. If only it was that easy, from your lips to God's ears —"

"I wish it was that easy too. But, is it really going to help anything to focus on all the scenarios that could go wrong? Let's just dream about how wonderful our life is going to be when we finally get married, okay?"

Chapter Eighteen

Heather

"I sorta figured we'd have red dresses since Aunt Tara's wedding is on Valentine's Day," Mindy twirls around in her peach taffeta dress.

"Red would have been a good choice too. I like these though. They are understated and elegant like Tara. Besides, they match the flowers on her cake."

"Does Aunt Tara know I helped make the leaves on her cake?"

"I don't know, but I will tell her you are the master of gum paste leaves, okay? Can you wash your hands and help me set out chocolate dipped strawberries?"

As I turn to pick up a tray of fruit and place it on the counter of the exclusive country club Justice Gardner has procured my purse plays the Army fight song. My heart plummets to my stomach as I recognize the special ring tone that Tyler has assigned to his commanding officer. Ty must have left his phone in my purse when he, Aidan and Jeff went to go shoot hoops in the gym facility this morning. I rush past Mindy as I grab my purse.

"Which direction did the guys go?"

When she points to the back patio area, I take off at a dead sprint. Fortunately, I'm still wearing my bunny slippers as I round the corner of the building and almost run straight into Tyler's chest. He steadies me as I almost topple over. "Whoa Gidget! You didn't set the kitchen on fire, did you?" he teasingly asks. His expression instantly sobers as he hears the strident cadence of his ringtone. His complexion pales and he sways slightly. "You have to be kidding me! Today of all days, really? I swear, they do this just to mess with my head." As I fish the phone out of my purse, he grabs it from my hand and answers tersely, "Colton."

He turns away from me so I can't hear the other side of the conversation. Reading his tense body language, I catch Aidan's eye and make a request in sign language, "Take care of him please. I'll be in the kitchen when he's ready to talk. He probably needs you guys more than me right now."

Walking away is excruciatingly difficult. I can tell from the expression on Tyler's face he is having a difficult time keeping it together and the last thing he needs from me is for me to be a clingy-uncertain emotional parasite. It's not the most flattering description, but that's what I'm feeling right now. My first instinct is to get into his face and shout, "You've done your duty. You've gone far above whatever is expected of you. Let someone else go in your place because you've already made enough sacrifices for your country." I know that that's not what he needs to hear from me right now. I need to get some distance and perspective, so I can collect myself and find the right words to say to be the supportive fiancé that I need to be.

I wipe the tears from my face as I walk back into the kitchen to face Mindy and finish putting the dessert plates together for my best friend's wedding. *I hope Donda used waterproof makeup.*

Mindy looks at me with empathy in her eyes. "It's bad isn't it? I just knew it."

"Honestly, Mindy Mouse, I don't know yet. If I had to guess, I suspect you're probably right. But, I won't really know what's up until Tyler tells me."

"But, Uncle Tyler knows you love him, right?" Mindy pushes.

I chuckle lightly. "Yes, Little Miss Romance, he knows I love him. I'm wearing an engagement ring." I flash my shiny ring in front of her so she can study the beautifully designed diamond surrounded by sapphires and aquamarine stones.

"Ooh your new ring is pretty. I heard Dad tell Mom that he got his other girlfriend a ring too and she still didn't marry him. Are you sure a ring is enough?"

I gasp softly. I always forget how insightful and mature Mindy can be. "I hope so. What else am I supposed to do? It's Tara and Aidan's wedding day. This isn't Vegas or anything."

Mindy just shakes her head and rolls her eyes at me. "I wish that people would listen to me. I tried to tell you about this earlier. It's kinda important."

"You did. So, I'm listening now. What do you suggest?" I wish I was still in my casual clothes because I suddenly feel like tearing my hair out by the roots. I walk around the kitchen island and peek out the window. Tyler is still on the phone. This cannot be a good sign.

As I turn around to face Mindy, she is regarding me thoughtfully and doodling on a piece of paper. "You know he has to concentrate to make the bad guys go away?"

I nod, feeling thoroughly confused. "Of course. He's a soldier — that's what he does, Mindy."

"I don't think you understand. If he doesn't think you believe in forever, he can't concentrate and the bad guys will get him."

"Mindy, we are getting married. We have engagement rings and everything."

"I know," Mindy replies with a frown, "but I still have that funny feeling in my stomach. Something tells me Uncle Ty is still really worried. I think you should do something to make him not so worried before he faces the bad guys. These people make him have super bad nightmares."

"Oh Sweetie, I'd do anything I could to take Ty's nightmares away. I'd marry Tyler today if it would make his life easier."

"Why don't you? The Judge-man is gonna be here. Aren't you already friends? I bet you if you told them it was an emergency, he would do one of those Sybil ceremonies."

"That's a spectacular idea and I'm sure Justice Gardner would do his best to help us. Still, I'm not sure he could do much about the paperwork. There are certain legal technicalities like the marriage license that need to be taken care of first before we have a ceremony — even a civil one."

Mindy crosses her arms in front of her and blows her bangs out of her face. "Are you going to try to be helpful or just throw obstacles in the way of success?"

The exasperated expression on Mindy's face makes me laugh out loud. Biologically, she may not be Kiera's daughter, but she can do a dead-on impression of her sayings, complete with attitude.

I blush a little as I'm taken to task by the preteen. "All right, give me my phone. I'll text him to see what I can do. But don't get your hopes up. This gives a whole new meaning to the word last-minute — even for this gang."

⎯⎯⎯ ◆ ⎯⎯⎯

I thought Kiera's wedding was the most romantic wedding I had ever been to. But, Aidan and Tara were giving Jeff and Kiera a run for their money. Instead of the traditional wedding march, Aidan and his band serenaded Tara with a song he had written specifically for the wedding. Aidan's parents and his brother were in the front row along with the family that took him in when he was a teenager. Dolores had been especially sweet to Tara — stepping up to be her surrogate mother figure after she learned that Tara was feeling sad because her mom had passed away when she was a teenager and she had no one to help with any of the traditional bridal rituals.

As I watch Becca run up the aisle and launch herself into Jeff's arms in a giggling heap of apricot colored taffeta and-lace petticoats, I marvel over how much has changed in a little over two years.

Tyler holds his elbow out gallantly and I'm reminded of the last time we walked up a church aisle together. He made what I thought at the time was a wisecrack about wanting to walk me up an aisle like this. At the time, I dismissed it as outrageous flirting. Now, I'm not so sure. Perhaps, he was serious about me even way back then. I guess, I'll never really know when exactly it was that we began to fall deeply, madly in love.

I study the expression on Tyler's face. The effervescent, ever present joy that's usually on his face is barely detectable. He looks like he's aged twenty years in the space of three hours. He looks like the mythological character Atlas holding the weight of the world on his shoulders. Things have been so absolutely insane that I haven't really had a chance to talk to him other than to find out he has been given only two days' notice before he has to report to his commander at his base. I can't believe how emotional I am. I mean, it's not like we haven't been preparing for this for months. He's been on high alert status since before we became serious. I knew this day was coming. Ty has done his best to prepare me. We've sifted through reams of paperwork and done tons of advance planning. I know more about his life than any fiancée should. Yet, somehow this day has still managed to sneak up on me.

As I feel the heat of his solid bicep through his suit as he escorts me up the aisle and catch a whiff of his cologne, a wave of preemptive longing goes through my body. In a matter of hours, I won't be able to even touch him. Interestingly, Tara does not separate the members of the bridal party into bridesmaids and groomsmen. She allows us to stand together as couples. I am profoundly relieved to feel Tyler's solid presence behind me throughout the ceremony.

I am especially grateful not to be standing alone when Tara becomes emotional. It's such an unusual reaction from her that it catches me by surprise. When Justice Gardner asks the audience, "Who gives this woman to marry this man?" It takes us all off guard. We hadn't had a chance to run through the ceremony because there was bad weather and Tara and Aidan's flight was delayed. Spontaneously, all of Tara's friends in the audience — and there are many — answer with a resounding, "We do!" It was traditions like this that Tara was most dreading because she lost both of her parents as a child, but it may turn out to be one of the most uniquely touching parts of her wedding. Tara is usually completely unfazed by emotional chaos, so it's disconcerting to see big fat tears roll down her face.

Just then Mindy sits down her junior bridesmaid bouquet and runs over and gives Tara a hug as she advises in a loud stage whisper, "It's okay. Your Mom and Dad are watching from heaven. They're sitting right next to Mom's Mommy and Aunt Heather's Grandma and Grandpa. They're probably having a better time than us because they don't have to wear itchy clothes and tight shoes."

Tara hands me her bouquet and gathers Mindy into a tight hug. "Mouse, you know what? I bet you're right. They're probably having a grand time. They would be really upset if they thought I was sad today. Daddy always wanted me to find somebody just like Aidan. He would've liked him so much."

"Don't forget, your mom would have been so proud of your dance studio and craft school too," Mindy adds.

Tara gives a little sigh and hiccup of emotion as she responds quietly, "Yes, she would be and she would've loved the fact that I found true love. It's the kind of love story that she and Daddy would've had if he hadn't been killed."

Mindy hugs Tara one last time and goes back to her place.

Kiera wheels forward and hands Tara some Kleenex. She squeezes her hand and says, "Go claim your piece of perfect. You deserve it."

Tara nods mutely and walks up to stand in front of Justice Gardner.

Justice Gardner clears his throat, "Well, after all that, I'm not sure if we need formal vows." He winks at Aidan.

Aidan looks at him with comical alarm and checks his cochlear implants to insure he heard correctly. "Oh no you don't! Do you know how hard I worked on these?"

"Just teasing, son. People tend to get sleepy when I talk, so I am just checking to see if you all are paying attention," he says with a totally straight face. All those years on the bench certainly served him well. If I didn't have dinner with him twice a week, I'd never know he was kidding.

"Hanging on every word, sir." Aidan stands straighter.

"Who wants to go first?" Justice Gardner asks looking between them.

Tara points to Aidan. "I'll let the professional wordsmith go first. That way people won't be dying of curiosity the whole time they're listening to mine. They'll have more realistic expectations."

Aidan shrugs. "Whatever makes you happy Gracie."

Justice Gardner turns to the audience. "Ladies and gentlemen, Aidan and Tara have written their own vows today. In an interesting twist, I have not seen them, so this will be as big a surprise to me as it is to you. But, what isn't a surprise is the depth of love they have for each other. Even if their love story only started the moment they met at Jeff and Kiera's wedding, it would be extraordinary. But, their story has many deeper layers. Painful layers and triumphant layers, but like the layers of straw that make a basket stronger, they work together intricately. Aidan, I'll let you start."

Aidan pulls a piece of paper out of his pocket, looks at it briefly then seemingly changes his mind and puts it back. "I'm fooling myself if I think my thoughts about you could ever be organized into something coherent. From the moment I met you, you blew every logical thought out of my head. When most kids are in kindergarten, they worry about sharing their toys, I was worried about having to share you. Even then, you were the best thing that ever happened to me. No matter what I tried, you were my biggest fan. You willingly subjected yourself to endless knock-knock jokes, magician's tricks gone horribly wrong, and my epically failed ventriloquism career. Never in all that time, did you tell me I couldn't or shouldn't do something I dreamed of, regardless of how silly the endeavor. When I watched you fall so stereotypically in love with my much more dashing, athletic big brother — my heart was broken in every sense of the word. Yet, you respected our friendship enough to match me up with all of your friends, never once suggesting that I go from musical mentor to boyfriend material."

I watch as Tara flushes under her elegant birdcage veil. "Oh my gosh. I can't believe you remember that. Worse yet, I can't believe I did that. I didn't really want you to date anyone else, but I didn't want you to be sad either. You must've thought I was so terrible." Tara clasps Aidan's hands.

"Never in my life have I thought you were terrible. Beautiful, ethereal, perfect, stunning, brave, funny, witty, strong, tough, graceful, smart, amazing… Those are the things I think of when I think of you. Never, ever did the word terrible cross my mind. You once asked me why I call you Gracie. Sure, some of it's an obvious play on your middle name but it's mostly because I feel so outclassed by you—much like George Burns explained about how he felt about his partner Gracie. I've always felt like your presence in my life makes me a better person — that my star shines brighter because you're beside me."

At this point, Tyler knows me well enough to know I've completely lost it and he pulls out a handkerchief from his jacket pocket and silently hands it to me so I can wipe my tears. But, as I look around the elegant meeting room we've turned into a makeshift chapel, it's clear I'm not the only person who's having difficulty containing my emotion.

After everyone — including Tara — collects themselves, Aidan continues, "When you disappeared from my life, I felt like part of me was missing. I tried to fill the void with adventure, travel, women, more travel and work — lots and lots of work. But, I could never find that elusive piece of happiness and joy no matter how hard I searched. Then one day, I decided to take a last-minute gig for a wedding which was crammed in between other gigs. I wasn't even sure I wanted to take it because it required quite a bit of driving and was quite frankly in the middle of nowhere. But, something told me I shouldn't miss the wedding of Jeff and Kiera Whitaker. I am forever grateful I listened to my gut feeling."

Many members of the crowd titter with laughter as he starts to recount the story because they were there when it happened.

"I'll never forget my total shock as I watched you come down the aisle carrying Becca on your hip. You were like the personification of my daydreams and fantasies — yet so far beyond. It was like you were a walking, talking miracle materializing in front of me. That's what it's been like since you came back into my life."

A collective, "Aww," filters up from the audience.

Tara turns back and looks at everyone. "See, he's irresistible. I didn't stand a chance."

Aidan grins. "I seem to recall telling you that a time or two along the way."

Tara narrows her eyes. "Come to think of it, you always were a really big flirt."

"Well, I promise to never stop flirting with you. As

your husband, I promise to love and cherish you the way you've always deserved to be. I promise to be the man your dad always wanted you to have. I promise to bring music to your soul and dance to your heart and always look at you like you hang the moon. Tara Grace Windsong Isamu, I've loved you for as long as I can remember and I will love you until we dance at the gates of heaven. It is my honor to join with you in this dance called marriage today."

Tears are streaming down Tara's face. I don't blame her. I'm sure my makeup is a mess. Aidan isn't even my guy and I'm a blubbering mess over his emotional words. Tyler slides his arms around my waist and squeezes me from behind.

Tara delicately wipes her face as she answers in a voice rough with emotion, "Throughout our relationship, you have always been the one to push me to be brave and bold. If I thought something was outside of my comfort zone, you were always right there to help me expand my boundaries just a little more. You always believed I could do anything. When we were kids, you were always my biggest cheerleader and champion. If there was a dance or lift that was too difficult for me to do, you were the one who made sure I had enough practice and coaching to get it done. You were my number one coach and confidence builder. When I was lonely and scared, you were there for me in a way no one else was. Quite simply you were my best friend. When you disappeared from my life without explanation, I assumed the worst and never bothered to correct my assumptions. I will bear the responsibility of that forever. I should have been there for you and I'm sorry that I wasn't."

Aidan wipes away tears.

"Even when we reconnected, and you heard the whole story, you never held my shallowness against me. Instead, you reprised your role as best friend, chief cheerleader and confidence builder. You gave me the strength to face down my rapist and stop giving him power over my life. You brought music and dance back to me in a more powerful way than I ever thought possible. I feel whole because you enabled me to bring parts of my life together I kept separate before."

Aidan is trying hard not to cry. We all are. Tara does not say much as a rule, so when she does, her words tend to be profound as they are at this moment.

"Before you came back into my life, I had come to believe that love was never going to be in the cards for me. It was the unreachable, untouchable goal that had been stripped from me — first by the death of my parents and the fairytale that they embodied and then again by the violent attack which destroyed all of my faith in humanity. But, just as you did when you were a small child, you rebuilt my trust and faith one drop at a time until suddenly I didn't just have a small cup, I had an ocean full of love, trust and faith. You told me once if I was patient and had a little trust and faith, you would help me find my inner music so that my heart could dance. It turns out you were not just full of malarkey. You did help me find all that and so much more. So, Aidan Jarith O'Brien, as your wife, I promise to follow you wherever the music in your soul takes you. I am your partner in good times and in bad. I promise to be your biggest fan and your most honest critic. I promise to love you for who you are and not who you show to the world. If your fame ever goes to your head, I'll be sure to remind you that you were the guy who climbed on the desks at school in the third grade and nearly fainted when the hamster escaped from his cage and made it all the way up onto the chair."

The crowd roars with laughter and Aidan turns bright red as he quips, "Now who's got a memory like a vault?"

"Aidan Jarith O'Brien, my parents would've been thrilled if they had gotten a chance to know you. My dad would have been pleased as punch to know I love you the way that he loved my mom. I would be honored to have this dance for the rest of my life. I think we've wasted enough years trying to find each other again, please make me your wife."

Justice Gardner coughs discreetly. "Technically I think that's my job."

Tara steps back. "Sorry, you're right, William. Please proceed."

Justice Gardner beams at Tara. "See now? This one understands how it's done. I like it when you all treat me like a kindly old grandfather," he says as he chuckles. "Okay, I may be less than comfortable with the old part, but the rest of it's fine."

He turns to the gathered audience. "Ladies and gentlemen—excluding those of you who are paparazzi — we are gathered here to celebrate the love story of Aidan O'Brien and Tara Grace Windsong Isamu. They have one of the most extraordinary love stories I've ever seen. I've only been witness to the second half of their love story but based on what I've seen, the first half must have been phenomenal. Not very many people get the chance to fall in love twice, but it's exactly what happened with these two best friends. To hear Aidan tell the story, he fell in love with a shy heartbroken little girl who just lost her hero before Aidan even knew how to tie his shoes."

The audience laughs as Justice Gardner pauses briefly and looks down at Aidan's untied shoe. Tara rolls her eyes and hands her bouquet to Kiera. She gracefully swoops in to tie his shoe almost before we can blink. I hear Mrs. O'Brien comment from the front row, "Isn't that so sweet? She used to do that as a kid too. It's a wonder my baby ever learned to tie." Aidan and Tara both flush a dusky shade of red.

Justice Gardner clears his throat softly. "But, this isn't just a story of unrequited love. That timid little girl blossomed and became his confidant and his best friend until tragic life circumstances tore them apart. When they found each other again, Tara became his lifeline and helped him overcome his limitations and fears allowing him to become more successful than he'd ever dreamed. Throughout this process, they discovered that through the years they had not only been the best of friends but truly in love with each other."

Aidan and Tara raise their linked fingers and smile at each other. They are clearly at peace with their choice of each other. It's the happiest I've ever seen Tara.

"Separately and together Aidan and Tara have been through some incredible challenges, but they have learned to pull together as a team, so it is my pleasure as a member of the judiciary in the State of Oregon to marry them."

Justice Gardner turns to Tyler and holds out his hand for the rings. At first, Tyler pretends not to be able to find them.

Aidan raises an eyebrow at him. "Are you sure you want to do that? Your wedding is right around the corner and paybacks suck."

Tyler gives an exaggerated wink to the audience as he comments, "Geez, put the epic practical joker in the monkey suit and suddenly he gets all serious. What's up with that?"

Aidan shrugs. "Just wait. You'll see. The pressure for it to go perfectly is more than you might think."

Justice Gardner chuckles. "Anyway, as I was saying; You, Aidan and you, Tara, have come to me signifying your desire to be formally united in marriage. If there are no legal, moral, or religious barriers that hinder this proper union, please join your hands and carefully consider these questions."

Aidan and Tara position themselves so they are linked by their right index fingers. The smile that Aidan gives Tara is heartbreakingly tender. She reaches up and tucks a lock of his long wild rock-star hair behind his ear.

I'm startled when Tyler leans forward and whispers into my ear "I can't wait until this is us."

I have to fight to keep my expression neutral. This is not the place for me to spill my beans. "I know, me either." I try hard to focus on the rest of the ceremony, but, I am acutely aware of Tyler's presence behind me.

Aidan and Tara are holding hands they are standing

so close to each other, it's almost as if their foreheads are touching. "Aidan, I love you so much." Tara signs discreetly. Aidan makes the sign for the same.

Justice Gardner clears his throat softly because it's obvious that he's interrupting a private conversation even though it's perfectly silent. Tara and Aidan look embarrassed to be caught in such an intimate moment. But, all of us that have spent any time around them at all are quite used to this experience and a light laugh travels throughout the audience.

The judge gives Aidan a good-natured pat on the shoulder and remarks, "That's all right son, I understand. My wife still affects me the same way. Shall we continue?"

Aidan nods. "Yes, sir — I mean William."

"Very well. Aidan, in taking the woman whom you hold by the right hand to be your lawful and wedded wife, do you promise to love and cherish her, to honor and sustain her, in sickness as in health, in poverty as in wealth, and to be true to her in all things until death parts you?"

Justice Gardner looks solemnly at Aidan.

"Is this your promise?"

Aidan answers by both speaking and signing, "Yes, I promise."

Tara wipes a tear from her eye before turning back toward Justice Gardner. He smiles gently at her before continuing.

"Tara, in taking the man whom you hold by the right hand to be your lawful and wedded husband, do you promise to love and cherish him, to honor and sustain him, in sickness as in health, in poverty as in wealth, and to be true to him in all things until death parts you?"

I can see that Tara has a death grip on Aidan's hands as Justice Gardner presents the vow. "Is this your promise?"

"Yes, I gladly promise," she answers in a steady voice as she simultaneously signs.

"Tara and Aidan have elected to exchange rings today and have written their own sentiments they will share with you."

Justice Gardner holds out the ring to Aidan. For the first time, I noticed that his hands are shaking as he starts to speak in a clear, deep voice.

"Tara, I give you this ring as a symbol of my love. As it encircles your finger, may it remind you always that you are surrounded by my enduring love and cloaked in my strength."

As Tara looks down at the ring he's placing on her finger, her eyes widen with shock. "You added to it!", she exclaims as she studies the white gold band engraved with music notes that match the stylized notes in Aidan's tattoo.

The corner of Aidan's mouth hitches up in amusement. "Yeah, I get to do fun stuff like that now because someone I love helped make me a hugely successful pop star. It's funny how that works." Despite his unsteady hands, Aidan slides the ring on Tara's finger with ease.

Justice Gardner just shakes his head as he remarks, "You kids have some of the most unusual ceremonies

I've ever been involved in."

Tara looks chastised as she snaps back to attention and recites her portion of the rings ceremony.

"I will wear it gladly. Whenever I look at it, I will remember this blessed day and the vows we've made."

Tara takes Aidan's ring from Justice Gardner and places it on Aidan's finger as she repeats the vow. "Aidan, I give you this ring as a symbol of my love. As it encircles your finger, may it remind you always that you are surrounded by my enduring love and cloaked in my strength."

Aidan examines it closely. "Looks like I'm not the only person who had a few surprises up my sleeve," he signs.

At this point, Justice Gardener starts impatiently tapping his toe for comedic effect.

Aidan looks around as if shocked. "Oh, that's right. I'm not quite done yet."

Mindy just rolls her eyes. "Grown-ups are weird."

Tara just laughs. "I won't argue with that. But, we'll be serious now. Aidan, hurry up and finish so we can get to the good part."

Aidan looks at Tara with feigned innocence. "You mean the kiss? I've been looking forward to that part all day too."

Tara grins as she shakes her head. "No, I was actually referring to the cake Heather made. I'm absolutely starving."

The entire audience erupts with laughter as Justice Gardner gives an epic eye roll. "Perhaps I should've been clearer about my role as officiant." He turns to Aidan. "Are you planning to finish those vows sometime today before your wife passes out from hunger?"

Aidan looks down at Tara and tucks a stray lock of hair behind her ear. "Tara, I will wear this ring gladly. Whenever I look at it, I will remember this blessed day and the vows we've made."

Justice Gardner gently turns them around so they are facing the crowd and announces, "Ladies and gentlemen, by the power vested in me by the state of Oregon, I happily pronounce that Aidan O'Brien and Tara Isamu are now husband and wife. I am pleased to present to you — finally — Mr. and Mrs. O'Brien. Aidan, you may now kiss your lovely bride."

Aidan very gently lifts the veil from Tara's face and kisses her tenderly as if he's been waiting a lifetime for that moment. I suppose in a way, he probably has been. Knowing all that both of them have overcome to get to this moment, it is a profound moment to watch. I am completely caught up in the emotion of it all. I barely even notice when Ty gently wipes away the tears that are freely falling down my face. "It's okay Gidget," he soothes. "It won't be long until we have our own fairytale ending." He tucks my hand around his forearm as he carefully escorts me out of the ceremony.

Chapter Nineteen

Tyler

"They're not planning to ditch us already, are they?" I ask as I watch Aidan and Tara get into a limousine right after they walked down the aisle.

"No, they're just going to go have a private tea ceremony to honor Tara's parents before we take pictures and the reception starts to rock. They figured that if they took off right after the ceremony, it would fool the paparazzi. No one would expect them to cut out of their own reception. Besides, one of Tara's dance students is playing her double right now. I thought that was clever. Hopefully, the press will stay in the dark. Tara tried to tell me how crazy their life has gotten, but I had absolutely no idea what she meant until we tried to do something as simple as go bra shopping the other day. It was insane."

"I have to admit, I'm a little jealous of them right now though. During the whole ceremony, I couldn't help but wish it was us standing there. I know that sounds bizarre, especially considering my mindset when we first met. But, I feel like I'm running out of time with you," I confess as I thread my arm around her waist.

Heather walks me back to the pantry area in the kitchen. I smile at her choice of locations. Somehow, this doesn't surprise me. Although Heather can be social when she wants to be, this is where she feels most at home. She spots a couple of metal stools stacked in the corner and pulls them down. I think she's forgotten that she's wearing stilettos and an elegant bridesmaid's dress. I help her up onto the stool and try not to be distracted as she crosses her shapely legs.

When she looks at me, her composed expression is completely absent and her eyes are filled with fear. "I'm sorry Tyler, I know you probably don't want to talk about this here, but I can't wait any longer. What did your commander say?"

I scrub my hand over my face and untie my bowtie. I've broken this news to people I've loved before, but it's never been this hard. I swallow and take a deep breath. I'm ninety-nine-point-nine-percent sure history is not going to repeat itself. This time, Heather already has a ring on her finger and she seems like she loves me for the person I am rather than the status I can bring her, but being a military spouse is not an easy road to take. She may decide I'm not worth it once all the cards are on the table.

As I pause to gather my thoughts, I notice she's become even paler. She trembles slightly. "Oh my Gosh, it's so bad you can't even tell me, right?"

"Crap, I didn't mean to totally freak you out. It's just that I love you so much. This is harder than I expected." I lean over and kiss her forehead.

"Are you breaking up with me?" she asks, panic edging her voice.

"No! Oh heck no! I'm just trying to tell you they are sending me back to Iraq."

"When?" she whispers harshly.

"I have to report to base in two days."

"For how long?"

"Gidget, I can't tell you that. It's classified," I reply sadly.

"Are you going to be fighting on the front lines? Could you be kidnapped by ISIS?" Worry creases her brow.

"Heather, I can't tell you any of that. I'm sorry. I probably shouldn't have even told you which sandbox we were going to go play in. It's for your safety as well as mine. I have such a high level of security clearance because I'm responsible for mission planning. If you knew what was happening, people could use you to get to me. Family members in my unit need to be totally kept in the dark. That's part of what makes what I do so hard. It's very isolating."

Heather is very quiet for about two minutes. I feel like my heart is about ready to beat out of my chest by the time she speaks again. "Tyler, pay attention for a moment. On a scale of 1 to 10, when you said you wished that it was you and I who were getting married today, how serious were you about that?"

The sense of relief I feel wash over me is palpable. It's an odd question, but one I can easily answer. "I'll answer you like I used to answer my mom when I was a kid. Eleven-dy-fifty-five-thousand-billion. Is that high enough for you?"

"Yes, I suppose it is," she answers with a big smile. "So, what if I told you we can get married today?"

I'm sure that my eyes spring wide like a mechanical toy at her surprise announcement. "How? Oregon has a waiting period and I know we haven't gone down to go get our marriage license yet."

"Well, it turns out we have some friends that are well-versed in the law who know all about the exceptions and waivers. It seems that we have good cause for a waiver of the waiting period. The clerk of the county happens to be a guest at today's wedding and has agreed to issue us both a marriage certificate and a waiver given our unique circumstances. So, Tyler Joseph Colton — I have one question for you: Would you like to marry me today?"

I expected many things to happen today, but this was not one of them. Then again, my time with Heather has taught me to expect the unexpected. I stand up and walk over to her. I leisurely kiss her and then reply, "Heather Lydia LaBianca I would be thrilled to marry you today or any other day. This is perfect."

Heather slumps a little on the stool. "Oh, thank goodness. I thought you might be upset with me for being too pushy."

I chuckle. "You should know me better than that by now. One of my favorite things about you is your ability to know your own mind and to get things done. This is a perfect example of why you'll make a perfect military wife. While I hemmed and hawed about the logistics of it all and worried myself stupid about how I was going to shelter you while I was gone, you definitively figured out how to solve the problem. I already know who's gonna be the brains in this operation — and it's not going to be me most of the time."

A strange expression crosses Heather's face as she admits, "I really wish I could take credit for this one. But, you can chalk this one up to the brilliance of Mindy Mouse. That girl is scary bright. She can give Tara a run for her money in the spooky department."

"Well, whoever came up with the idea, I'm extremely grateful. It takes a load off my mind and I'll be able to focus on the mission now. In the end it will make it safer for everyone."

Heather shakes her head in disbelief. "Wow! I don't know how Mindy was able to understand how you would feel, but she told me almost word for word that's what you were going to say."

"I don't claim to understand that little girl. I just know I'm blessed to know her. I'd like her to be part of our ceremony even if she's not old enough to be one of the witnesses, okay?"

Heather places her arms around my waist and rests her cheek on my chest and nods. "I'm totally on board with that plan because we wouldn't be here without her help," she mumbles as she hugs me.

"What do we do now, my bride? Do you have special clothes we need to change into or something?"

She giggles. "Would you believe I don't? Me, 'The Queen of Fashion' does not have a backup outfit for this occasion. So, we'll collect your parents and Jeff, Kiera and

Mindy and go meet Justice Gardner in the pool room. We're going to go try to get married before I have to serve hors d'oeuvres and cake."

"That sounds like a plan. So, does this mean I don't get to marry you in my dress uniform?" I tease.

"Cowboy, you know me better than that. Do I look like I'm gonna let you off the hook quite that easily? I don't think so. When you get back from wherever the heck you're going, we're going to throw the biggest party you've ever seen. There'll be so much lace and tulle you won't even recognize me. It'll look like a scene from Gone with the Wind. If you think there is a lot of food at this wedding, it'll be nothing compared to ours."

"Gidget, that sounds wonderful. I'll paint pictures in my head of how you look in your gown and the many creative ways I'll get you out of it. Those visions will help sustain my morale when I'm over in the hellhole. If you're feeling generous, you can send me pictures of your gorgeous body to drool over."

I watch with fascination as color travels over the tops of her breasts through her face to the roots of her hair. "I don't know if I am the boudoir photo gallery kind of gal, Cowboy."

"I've seen your delectable body, remember? I can say without hesitation you are definitely pinup material. In fact, I think pictures of you would be the perfect wedding gift."

Heather's bottom lip slides out in a perfect little pout, "Really? I was thinking more along the lines of some cool kitchen gear."

I snicker. "Wow! You and my mom really are two

peas in a pod. That's an answer my mom would have given in a heartbeat. Speaking of my parents, do they have any idea I'm getting married today?"

Heather shakes her head and grins. "Nope! No one except you, me, Justice Gardner and the clerk know. Well, I guess that's not technically true. Mindy knows. But, then again Mindy knew about this plan weeks ago when she tried to tell us we were going to get married on the same day that Tara and Aidan got hitched. Remember that conversation? We were silly enough to argue with her. I'm not sure why I even bother to second-guess either one of them. I should know better by now. It's like having my own paranormal team at my beck and call."

"Do you ever get used to it? Isn't it strange having people in your life that know what's going to happen before it really does?" I ask, genuinely curious and a little creeped out.

"It's a little weird. I'm used to it by now. Tara is careful about what she shares with me so it doesn't become overwhelming. She is not obnoxious about it. She hates it when people ask her to use her abilities like it's a party trick. We don't talk about her abilities all that much. Most of the time I completely forget about them until something strange or scary happens. The depth of Mindy's abilities has come as a really big surprise though."

"I wonder how my parents will react to all of this." I ponder.

"I think your mom will be cool with it. She seems open-minded. If Mindy and Tara can provide any information that would help keep you safe, your dad would be all over that in a New York minute, so I think he'll be fine with it too. I'm not so sure how they'll feel about you getting married today. If I was your mom, I think I'd feel a little panicked. I think most moms want more time to prepare for this kind of stuff."

"My mom thinks you're the bees' knees. She's gonna be okay with the fact that you will be my wife. My dad already thinks I'm a blooming idiot for taking so long to ask you out, so I think he'll be fine with us heading to the altar. He probably thinks if I wait around too long you'll come to your senses and run away. He doesn't have much faith in my ability to hold onto a woman on my own."

"I think we should probably go tell everyone," she suggests as she grabs my hand. She does a funny little skip and hop. "I can't believe I'm actually going to get married today!"

I stop dead in my tracks as a sobering thought occurs to me.

"What's wrong?" Heather asks, alarmed.

"Are Tara and Aidan gonna be okay with this? Aren't we going to be stealing a bit of their thunder?"

Heather blows a raspberry with her lips. "Trust me. They've had enough of the limelight in the last few months to last a lifetime. They want nothing more than a quiet little gathering with a bunch of their friends. In fact, they would be thrilled if people thought this was our wedding instead of theirs. It might even help with the paparazzi situation. It's too bad Tara and I aren't even remotely the same size. That would've been handy for the dress situation."

"Gidget, you look phenomenal. I think the peachyorangey color looks stunning on you. So, if you think that I would prefer you in something else, you're just wrong. We are going to be lucky enough to have two wedding days. For this wedding, that dress is perfect. You can surprise me with something else later, okay?"

Heather's eyes cloud with tears. "I don't know how you do it, Cowboy. But, you always know the perfect thing to say. Come on, let's go shock the heck out of people. This will be more fun than announcing our engagement."

Heather finds my parents first, so I let her collect them while I find Jeff, Kiera and Mindy. We shepherd them all into the pool room where Justice Gardner is waiting for us, still wearing his official robes. Mindy eyes them suspiciously. "Am I getting adopted again?" she asks abruptly.

Heather laughs out loud. "No, Mouse. I think you know why you're here." Heather pauses dramatically.

Mindy is quiet for a moment as she thinks about what Heather said. Suddenly, her eyes widen. "No way!"

Heather giggles at Mindy's reaction. She nods and confirms, "Yes, way."

Mindy starts jumping up and down. "I told you he would say yes!"

Sally and Harold look back and forth between us and Sally declares, "I'm sorry, but I'm still lost."

"The Judge-man is going to marry Uncle Ty and Aunt Heather right now. But that's okay because they're not really my aunt and uncle. They are just pretend family because they're best friends, so we just call them family.

Sometimes, your friends are better than real family. It's kind of like being adopted, but not really, right Judge-man?"

Judge Gardner smiles at Mindy. "You're absolutely right, young lady. I've always considered your mom to be like my daughter even though we're not really family. But, her family has always been really good friends with mine."

I look over at my mom and it's clear that she's still processing what Mindy said. I can tell when she fully unscrambles all the words because she shakes her head as if to reorder the words and try again. "Wait! You're getting married! Today? As in right now? You're not going to invite any other family members or people from town? I'm so confused. Is somebody sick or dying?"

The look of panic on my mom's face breaks my heart. I didn't expect her to take the news in a negative light.

"No Mom, it's nothing like that." I hasten to reassure her. "Heather and I always planned to get married as quickly as we could. Uncle Sam just decided to move up our timetable more quickly than we had anticipated."

"What do you mean?" my dad interrupts sharply. "What's happened now?" he asks with a narrowed glare. "Don't even think about sugarcoating it. I watch the news and I know all about ISIS."

My shoulders slump a little in defeat. I wanted to avoid talking about this as long as possible. The more I talk about it, the more I run the risk of saying something I should not disclose. I sigh. "Yes, there will be an operation underway; but as usual, I cannot disclose anything about it. Heather is aware that I'm going but is also in the dark about the details. She sensed my unease about the uncertainty of being able to protect her if I was shipped out of the country. So, she made arrangements for Justice Gardener to do a small civil ceremony until I can get back and we can have a large wedding for the family to attend. So, for today it's just us."

"But, what about Heather's family?" my mom asks.

"Mrs. Colton I understand your concern but my sister could not make it today because she's on assignment with her job and my brother had to work today as well. I was not able to give them advance notice of the wedding. But, they'll be at the next one. As far as my parents go, I doubt that they would care enough about my life to even bother attending my wedding. But, even if they were interested, after the way they treated Tyler and I, I'm not sure that they would be invited."

"That's too bad. You strike me as a lovely young woman. I suppose that's their loss. Please promise me you'll take care of Tyler. He seems to think he doesn't deserve to be taken care of. You and I both know that's not true. Can you try to convince him he's worth saving?"

Heather's eyes fill with instant empathy. She instantly leaves my side and runs over to hug my mom. "Of course I will. Your son is everything to me. He taught me how to love and respect myself, so the very least I can do is return the favor. With all that he does for me and everyone around him, it's beyond me how he doesn't see himself as heroic. Perhaps one day he'll understand that none of what happened was his fault. But, you can be sure I will spend a lifetime trying to convince him of that fact. Your son is hands-down the finest human being I know — both inside and out."

Harold slaps Ty on the back. "Son, I don't know how you lucked out and found this one, but she's absolutely perfect. Hurry up and marry her before she gets away."

Everyone in the room chuckles at his sentiment. "Don't worry about it, Dad. I plan on it," I reply.

"On that note, shall I begin?" Judge Gardner asks.

Heather and I nod eagerly in unison.

Judge Gardner meets my parent's eyes at the side of the room. "Aren't they just too cute for words?"

My parents nod eagerly and snap a couple pictures with their cell phones.

"Do you have anything specific you'd like me to use?"

Much to my surprise, Heather nods. "These are the ones that my grandparents used. Can you use them? I hope our marriage lasts as long as theirs did."

"That shouldn't be a problem. I'll just have you read the vows instead of repeating after me. I think it sounds more natural that way. Would you like to go first Heather?"

"Yes please," she answers softly clearing her throat and unfolding a piece of paper she had cupped in her hand.

"I, Heather Lydia LaBianca take you Tyler Joseph Colton to be my husband, my partner in life and my one true love. I will cherish our union and love you more each day than I did the day before. I will trust you and respect you, laugh with you and cry with you, loving you faithfully through good times and bad, regardless of the obstacles we may face together. I give you my hand, my heart, and my love, from this day forward for as long as we both shall live."

All of my teasing words are coming back to haunt me right now. When my friends got married, I openly teased them about becoming emotional wrecks at what was essentially a walking, talking advertisement for Hallmark cards. I really didn't understand what makes this day different from any other time a woman dresses up and makes herself presentable. But, now that I'm looking down at the woman who will be my wife in mere minutes, I totally get the feeling of being able to move heaven and earth and all the planets between to make her happy. My eyes mist over at the emotions contained in the simple words passed from generation to generation.

Heather squeezes my hand as she passes me the vows. I have to swallow a lump in my throat when I recognize the handwriting as that of her grandmother from all the paperwork I helped her sort through when we went to Texas. I felt that I had gotten to know the feisty woman that Heather adored so much through reading her love letters and diaries when we were trying to prove her intent in court. I can only imagine what this means to Heather to bring this moment full circle.

I grasp Heather's hands in my own and get a little lost in her blue eyes as she blinks away tears. I carefully repeat the words on the page, my voice full of emotion. "I, Tyler Joseph Colton take you Heather Lydia LaBianca, to be my wife, my partner in life and my one true love. I will cherish our union and love you more each day than I did the day before. I will trust you and respect you, laugh with you and cry with you, loving you faithfully through good times and bad, regardless of the obstacles we may face together. I give you my hand, my heart, and my love, from this day forward for as long as we both shall live."

I make the mistake of glancing over at my parents. My dad is wiping away tears with the back of his hand. The sight of that is almost enough to make me lose it right there. I've only seen my dad cry on a handful of occasions. The last time I remember him truly breaking down was at my bedside in Germany. But, the smile on his face makes it clear that these are happy tears. It feels incredible to make my parents proud for a change. I know that they have long ago forgiven me for the bad choices I made when I was younger, but I still feel terrible for letting them down. I would do anything I could to erase the pain I caused them. Yet, had I not made those choices, I wouldn't be standing where I am right now.

Justice Gardner looks at Heather. "Do you have rings to exchange?"

"Yes, we do, your Honor," she answers.

He rolls his eyes. "How many times do I have to explain this? Unless you're standing in front of my bench, my name is William."

Heather giggles. "Whatever you say, sir."

Justice Gardner just shakes his head. "You guys are a lost cause."

"What can I say? I was raised with good Southern manners, sir," she teases.

I look at Heather with sheer panic on my face.

"Gidget, I hate to tell you this but you've caught me without a ring again."

Heather winks at me. "Don't worry, Cowboy. I've got you covered. I'm not the middle child for nothing. I'm always prepared for every contingency."

Heather fishes a little silk pouch out of her bosom area. She whispers in a not so quiet stage whisper, "Sometimes my body type has its own advantages."

My mom who has also struggled with an ample pear-shaped figure her whole life just laughs. "Amen to that."

Mindy just shakes her head. "Are all wedding ceremonies this weird?"

Justice Gardener laughs. "This group likes to add its own little flair, that's for sure," he remarks as he hands the rings to Jeff. He turns to Heather and hands her the other ring. "Heather, please repeat after me."

I give you this ring

as a reminder

that I will love, honor, and cherish you,

in all times,

in all places,

and in all ways, forever.

I have to catch my breath as she slides the hard metal ring on my finger. I've never heard more beautiful words in my life, she could not have chosen a more perfect vow. They are everything I feared I would never hear. As the ring settles in place it's almost as if I can feel a hole in my heart physically heal over. For the first time in years I feel like I can take a full breath. The weight on my chest is gone. I don't even realize that I'm crying until Heather wipes away a tear with the pad of her thumb.

"It's all right, Cowboy. I know you're really a marshmallow. You don't have to pretend with me," she teases.

"I know. You've had my number for a while now."

Jeff hands me two rings. I realize one is Heather's engagement ring, and the other is her grandmother's wedding band. I didn't realize it until now how well they complement each other. Maybe that's why Heather was so drawn to her engagement ring. It took her about two-and-a-half seconds to choose her ring when we went shopping. I offered her a much more expensive ring, but she couldn't be talked out of the one she chose.

"Tyler, as you place the ring on Heather's finger, please repeat after me," Justice Gardner instructs.

I give you this ring

as a reminder

that I will love, honor, and cherish you,

in all times,

in all places,

and in all ways, forever.

As I repeat the simple vows, I can barely keep my voice from cracking with emotion as I repeat them. My hands are shaking so violently as I place the rings on her fingers you'd never guess I sometimes help the bomb disposal unit in the field. Usually, I have ice in my veins when the pressure is on. But, it seems all bets are off today. It's like I'm starring in my own sappy Hallmark special.

As I'm lost in my thoughts, I almost miss the fact that Justice Garner is rapidly moving forward with the ceremony.

"Now, by the power vested in me by the State of Oregon, I hereby pronounce that Tyler Colton and Heather LaBianca are now husband and wife. Officer Colton, you may now kiss your bride. After all, she practically made miracles happen to pull this off."

I flash the judge a wide grin as I respond, "I know! Isn't my wife amazing?"

I pull Heather close to me and give her a long, deep thorough kiss. Eventually my dad pipes up from the corner of the room and says, "Son, I know you just got married and all, but you have to remember there are children present in this room."

"Oh, I'm used to it. All the grown-ups around me are always kissing. It's like watching the soap operas at Grummy's house. I think it's gross but, whatever." Mindy shrugs.

My mom just laughs. "Just give yourself a few years honey, you won't think it's so gross then."

"Let's hope it's more than just a few years," Jeff mutters under his breath. He turns to me and louder he says, "Well, it's true what they say. Couple-hood is contagious. We've managed to marry everybody off in our little group. I wonder who's next?"

Justice Gardner looks a little startled by Jeff's question. He opens his mouth to speak then closes it and starts again as he looks back and forth between Jeff and Kiera.

Jeff and Kiera look at him quizzically. "What?" they ask curiously.

"Well," he begins cautiously, "if I were a betting man, I might lay odds on Denny and Gwendolyn."

Jeff looks a little shell-shocked, Kiera much less so. "Really? My mom swears they're just friends," he argues.

Justice Gardner nods sagely. "In my experience, there's a thin line between friendship and love. I'm just saying I'm not sure which side of the line Denny's on. It's been a long time since Karen died. I haven't seen him this happy in a long time and I think Gwendolyn is responsible for that."

"I have to say, I think I agree with you. At first, I was a little weirded out by our parents dating, but I've gotten used to it now and I actually think it's kind of cute. They've both been through so much. They deserve to find love again. If they make each other happy, I'm all for it," Kiera responds with a shrug.

Justice Gardner spreads some paperwork out on a nearby pool table and pulls a fancy gold-plated pen out of his pocket. "I have one formality I need you, as Tyler and Heather's friends and family, to take care of before this is all official. As witnesses to this union, I need you to sign this paperwork."

"Can I sign too?" asks Mindy.

"Unfortunately, the official witnesses have to be

grown-ups, but there is a small space on the certificate where I can draw in a line so you can sign your name," Justice Gardner explains.

"Awesome!" Mindy responds. "I know how to write my name in cursive too."

My mom smiles as she gives Heather a side hug. "Great, let's get this over with. I can't wait to cut into that cake. I've heard great things about my daughter-in-law's cooking and I'm looking forward to it."

CHAPTER TWENTY

HEATHER

"WHERE IN THE WORLD have you been?" Tara asks as I run into the kitchen. "I figured you'd be back here obsessing over every little detail."

I loop an apron over my head and carefully give Tara a side hug so I don't mess up her impeccable hair and makeup. I whisper in her ear, "Would you believe I just got married?"

Initially, she looks shocked but then a thoughtful expression crosses her face. "Huh… I guess Mouse called this one a while back, didn't she?"

I nod. "That she did. I don't know how, but she did."

Tara smiles. "I'm starting to understand how people feel when they encounter me. It's odd being on the other side of things. So, how do you feel about the change of plans?"

Her question surprises me. I haven't even taken a moment to stop to think about it. "It all happened so fast, it seems like a blur. I'm excited, scared, elated, amazed — I'm not sure. I guess I feel a lot of everything. It's hard to feel truly blissful about getting married when I know in a few short hours I'll have to say goodbye. If I let myself think about it too much, I get really scared because I don't even know if it's our last goodbye."

"So, it's official then? Tyler got the call?"

I nod tearfully. For the first time all day, the full weight of it sinks in. "Tara, I've got less than forty-eight hours to be his wife, then I have to send him off to fight the stupid terrorists. This isn't one of my video games. They're frickin' beheading people now! What if he never comes back?"

Tara gathers me into a hug.

"I'm going to get makeup on your beautiful dress," I mumble as I grab a napkin and wipe my eyes. "Your wedding pictures will be ruined."

Tara raises an eyebrow at me. "Do I look like I care? Honestly, I don't care if no one ever takes another picture of me for as long as I live."

"I know you feel that way now, but someday you'll want to show your grandkids your wedding pictures and you don't want my mascara blob in the middle of them."

"Well, you'll always be more important to me than any dumb pictures. Seriously, you can't think that way. You're going to be Tyler's wife for decades to come. His deployment is only a temporary thing. Joy and Tiers will keep you incredibly busy. Hopefully time will pass in the blink of an eye. The Girlfriend Posse will do our best to keep you distracted, I promise. Besides, you have the wedding of the century to plan for, right? Because I know you well enough to know you won't pass up another opportunity to cram me into a froufrou dress, especially since I've started wearing dresses now."

"You bet your bippy! You're so much more fun now that you can actually distinguish colors and styles. Consider yourself forewarned, we'll be hitting the bridal salons as soon as the wheels go up on Tyler's plane. I've been planning my wedding since before I started elementary school, so this could take a while."

Tara groans. "I should've known mine and Kiera's wedding were only warm-up acts for the really big show."

I stick my tongue out at her. "Well, yeah — I had to practice on somebody."

Tara surveys the cake and the dessert bar I created as well as the plethora of hors d'oeuvres. "If this is just practice, the 'real thing' is going to be spectacular."

"Oh Hush!" I chide. "As if I would ever give my best friend anything but the absolute best. It might've been a rushed, super-secret order, but you still got the Joy and Tiers super deluxe, customized treatment. I even put real twenty-four karat edible gold leaf on your monogram topper."

"I know. It's amazing. It's like you crawled into my head and pulled out the design I always dreamed of, but didn't know I wanted. I love that you included a dream catcher filled with musical notes on the groom's cake. I shouldn't tell you this, but Aidan teared up a little when he saw that."

"Doesn't it make your heart do a little somersault when our big tough guys get all emotional? Wait until you see the video of our ceremony. I think Jeff caught most of it. You would never guess that my husband is a big strong, kick-butt Sheriff. It was the sweetest thing ever. I wish my Grandparents could have seen it. Tyler is a lot like my grandpa. He's all tough as nails on the outside but at heart he's a total teddy bear."

"Aidan doesn't give the appearance of being tough but his spirit is tenacious. It's funny being in the business that he's in now. He's almost too innocent to be in that world."

I must have given Tara a strange look because she quickly clarifies her statement. "No, I guess I didn't put that exactly right. Aidan isn't hard and jaded like me. He never expects the worst of people. The music business is cutthroat and being in the public eye is brutal. He wasn't prepared for the nasty side of things."

"I can see how that could be hard for a guy like Aidan. He's pretty optimistic."

"You have no idea, Heather. It's absolutely crazy. The other day I had to fly back early from one of his concerts because I had to go to a dress fitting and sign paperwork dealing with the dance school. First, the paparazzi ambushed me in the airport bathroom wanting to know if we had broken off our engagement because we were traveling separately. Then, when he flew back, he was flying next to a lady whose husband is stationed overseas. The poor woman had three children under the age of six and was traveling by herself. Aidan offered to hold one of her kids while she got the other two situated in their seats. One of her children happened to have green eyes, so some junk tabloid ran a story claiming Aidan has a mystery family. It was insane! They followed this woman home. Aidan had to hire a bodyguard for a perfect stranger to keep her safe from the vultures because he was nice to a random mother on a plane."

"That's terrible!" I exclaim. I knew it was awful, but I had no idea it had gone to those extremes.

"As much as I love Aidan, I don't love this crazy lifestyle that comes with his success. But, I accept it because his music career is part of who he is. I don't think Aidan would be able to breathe if he didn't have music. So, I've just had to make peace with the parts of this I absolutely hate. I suspect Tyler is much the same way about being a savior whether that comes in the form of being a soldier or a law enforcement officer."

I shudder and sigh. "I don't know if I'll ever be able to truly make peace with the fact that my husband puts his life on the line every day. I live in fear every time he walks out the front door. I do my best to hide my internal struggle from him because I know he has unfinished business with the terrorists who killed his team. So, I guess you could say I've reached an uneasy truce with Uncle Sam."

"Oh Heather, you're being far too hard on yourself. If you were totally Zen with your husband facing off with crazed radical terrorists after they already injured him once, I'd be marching you into Kiera's office for a mental health evaluation. I think as supportive spouses, it's our job to worry about the men in our lives. But, it's also natural to downplay our level of stress about it. As much is Aidan likes to talk about stuff — and Geez! Can I tell you? The man can talk a subject to death! — I don't always tell him how much the fame stuff freaks me out.

I save that to share with the Girlfriend Posse. It's not because I don't trust him with it, it's just that he doesn't need one more thing to stress over."

"I would've never guessed our guys worry about us as much as they do," I muse.

Tara grins. "Crazy, isn't it? I know Aidan worries about how I'll react to the over-the-top fans who throw their underwear onstage or send him naked selfies. But, I trust him to not be tempted by all the garbage. I can't let that stuff bother me. The thing I find the most intrusive is the paparazzi who follow us everywhere. I found one guy digging in our trash the other day. I hope he was thrilled with what he found because we made homemade sushi. There was some pretty disgusting stuff in the garbage can."

The mental picture she plants in my head causes me to laugh out loud. "Well, serves the jerk right for poking around where he shouldn't be. I don't feel sorry for him at all."

Tara giggles. "Me either; I hope he lost his lunch in his car on the way home."

"I don't tell Tyler everything either," I continue. "He's got a deep-seated fear that I'm not going to be able to handle all of this. I'm afraid if I tell him that I'm frightened for his well-being, he might misinterpret my fears. I am scared every single day, but it doesn't mean I don't want to be his wife. It just means that there's a pit in my stomach every time he leaves and it stays there until I can put my arms around him again. I don't know how I'll cope with him being gone. It will be the hardest thing I've ever done."

Tara studies me carefully. "Remember a while back you and I had a conversation where you referred to me as a Warrior Chick?"

I chuckle. "Yes, I remember. As I recall, I didn't just refer to you as a Warrior Chick. I said you were the toughest Warrior Chick I knew, and that you could probably kick my butt about fifteen different ways."

"True enough. But, I also see you as a pretty tough Warrior Chick. When life knocked you down, you didn't just stay down. You chose to get back up and mold yourself into the person you wanted to be despite huge family pressures to be somebody you weren't. That takes an amazing amount of courage. You turned down the opportunity to live on easy street and take the path of least resistance so you could live your own dream. I think you underestimate the strength of character it takes to do that."

I can feel my face grow hot as I blush. "You make it sound like I have overcome horrendous odds like you or Kiera. I basically have a rude family who doesn't know the meaning of personal boundaries; that hardly compares to surviving child abuse and life in a wheelchair or triumphing over date rape."

"Actually, I don't see it that way. In many ways I see what you overcame as being more difficult than what happened to me. Once people understand what happened to me, it is clear I was a victim. But, your victimization was much more subtle. You were bullied bit by bit over time so gradually no one saw that your self-esteem had completely crumbled and fallen away until you had nothing left. Even Kiera and I didn't know how bad it was until Tyler came into your life and could see the real you. You had gotten so good at putting on a fake front that you had even your best friends fooled."

I know that she doesn't mean to be hurtful, but her words feel like a slap in the face. "I didn't feel fake. I wasn't trying to be deceptive," I argue defensively.

Tara holds her hands up in a placating manner. "You didn't let me finish. After you began to see yourself through Ty's eyes and saw your true worth, you started to shine. All of those protective facades you had been carrying around for years began to fall away. The fact that you were courageous enough to drop them is amazing. Many people, including me, hold onto the hurt far longer than they need to because it's like a comfortable old blanket. But, you were a Warrior Chick and boldly let go of the past and explored a brand-new future. I'm so proud of you."

It takes me a moment to gather my words. Rarely am I ever stunned into silence. But, it's one of the longest speeches I've ever heard Tara give. She's usually so quiet and spends her time merely observing. That she has so many positive things to say about me has me completely befuddled. "Wow! I don't know what to say. I guess we should go celebrate that we're brides today. I think we've forgotten it's a party. We've got two very handsome husbands waiting for us."

Tara picks up two glasses of champagne and hands me one. I clink our glasses together. "Here's to a long happily ever after. Now, enough of the heavy stuff. Let's go dance. I promised my husband an extra sultry rumba."

"Hear, hear!" I reply. "But, I am not sure Tyler has

a sexy rumba in him. Dancing isn't really his thing. Getting him up on the dance floor at Kiera's wedding was a minor miracle. I'm not sure I'll be able to pull it off twice."

"Have you looked in the mirror? You're scorching hot. That man's eyes haven't left your backside since you put your fancy little dress on. He's going to take any excuse he can get to put his hands on you, I guarantee it."

I clink my glass against hers again and offer my own toast. "Here's to hot women and the hunks who love them."

Tara grins. "I'll drink to that."

"Speaking of that, where are Kiera and Jeff? Did they sneak off to go have a roll in the hay?" I ask, smirking.

Tara looks exasperated. "No, she only wishes it was that glamorous! Becca was playing with the bridal favors and stuck a bubble wand too far down her throat. She gagged and threw up all over herself and Kiera. So, they're back at the hotel getting changed. Kiera is worried she's going to mess up all the pictures because now her dress won't match. I told her not to worry about it because we'd solve the problem by sitting on her lap."

"Funny! We should do that. It would make a great picture. A Girlfriend Posse Pyramid —"

"Don't worry, I plan to. You know what? Let me text Aidan. The guys should sit on Jeff's lap too; that would be hysterical. If we have to sit through the darn things, they might as well be fun."

"Gee, why don't you tell how me you really feel,

Tar?" I tease. "It still baffles me how someone as pretty as you could hate to have their picture taken. By all rights, you should be on the cover of Vogue."

"You could stand right beside me Mrs. Colton," Tara responds.

My mouth drops open and my eyes widen as I shriek, "Ho-lee-cow!"

"What?" asks Tara looking around, suddenly on the alert for danger.

"Nothing! It's just that when I woke up this morning, I was single and now I'm married. It's really weird to be called by a different name. I thought I would have months and months, if not a couple years to plan for this and it's all happened in an afternoon. My life is so crazy. I knew that man would be trouble the second I laid eyes on him."

Tara smirks at me, "Yeah, but isn't he the best kind of trouble?"

Something about the gleam in her eyes tells me there's more to that comment. Sure enough, at that moment, Tyler steps behind me and kisses me on the neck. "I heard you guys were talking about trouble. So, I naturally assumed you must've been summoning me."

"You're such a great mind reader. Tara and I decided that we need two handsome dance partners and the handy thing about it is we happened to marry two handsome ones today. Do you see them around anywhere?" I wink at him.

"You're a funny girl for someone who wants me to dance. You might want to be a little nicer to me. You know, I'm a sensitive guy. My ego could be easily bruised. I might have to sit on the sidelines and nurse my hurt feelings."

"Oh, I'm so sorry. I wouldn't want that to happen. I might just have to kiss you to make you feel better."

"You've got a deal. I'll trade you a two-step for a kiss any day of the week," he answers.

I link my arm with Tyler's as he escorts me back toward the room where we're holding the reception. I can't believe the transformation in just a few short minutes. I guess that's one of the perks of having two songs at the top of the Billboard charts. They can afford the extra help now. Even though I supervised all the catering and did the cake with the help of Piper — with a boost from Mindy, I had a lot of help with the catering this go around. The logistics were just too complicated to make it a do-it-yourself affair like we had with Kiera.

Tyler looks around and whistles softly through his teeth. "Clearly, my buddy is movin' up in the world. You say our shindig is going to put this one to shame? I better start saving now. I might be able to afford it when our kids hit high school."

"Yeah, about that … I may have overstated my ability just a tad. I can cook really well, but there is no way I can match this level of grandeur."

"Gidget, I don't care. As long as you, our friends and family are there — all the rest of this is window dressing. All I want or need is you. Coming home safe to you is my only priority."

"You mean to tell me you won't miss your menagerie of animals even a little?" I ask, tongue in cheek.

"Of course I will. I always do, but it will pale in comparison to how much I will miss you. I have become so accustomed to having you in my life I don't know if I remember how to function without you in it."

"Me either, Cowboy. It's as if I've completely forgotten my life before you busted into my personal space and forgot to leave. I decided you make a rather comfy teddy-bear."

"Teddy bear!" he scoffs as he swoops in for a naughty kiss. "I patrol the mean streets and rid the streets of crime, remember?"

"Yes, sir! Whatever you say, Officer Hotness," I reply as I pinch him playfully on the butt.

"Wait — what did you call me? Shouldn't I feel all objectified or something?" He sticks his lower lip out.

If I didn't know him better, I might almost be convinced. "Oh please! Don't tell me you don't know the little Criminal Justice interns from the Community College call you that. You probably even hung the hash tag suggestions on the bulletin board in the break room."

Tyler flushes. "Hey! It's not like I didn't have accomplices —"

I roll my eyes and look over at Tara as I mouth, "Help! I married a twelve-year-old. What do I do now?"

Tara smirks and giggles. "Don't look at me! Mine still practices with his buddies in the garage while munching on potato chips and drinking copious amounts of pop. I think it's a guy thing."

Kiera whips her chair around the corner at breakneck speed, "What did I miss? What's a guy thing?"

Tyler raises his hands defensively as he answers, "I don't know what they're talking about. Seems like normal stuff to me."

Tara raises an eyebrow at him as she answers Kiera, "You didn't miss much. We were just talking about how much Heather is going to miss her overgrown man-child here when he has to go off to save the world from bad guys."

Tyler pins me with a lethally sexy glare and replies, "Darn straight. Told you I was a kick-butt soldier, not some wimpy teddy bear."

I pull the ends of his bowtie down so his mouth is level with mine and I kiss him very thoroughly before I respond, "Oh, trust me — being my teddy bear is not such a bad thing. You didn't ask who I sleep with every night."

By the time I'm finished, Tyler is breathing heavily. "If that's my reward for losing an argument, I'll lose every day."

Kiera shields her eyes and scoffs, "Geez guys, go get a room."

"Oh hush your mouth! He is my husband now! It's not like I didn't walk in on you and Jeff making out like teenagers at the breakfast table this morning. Besides, we've got plenty of time for that. We've got a dance floor to conquer," I quip. But, my heart sinks as I remember we don't really have a lot of time for anything. All those years when I imagined my wedding and honeymoon, I never thought I'd have to condense time into warp speed.

Falling into patterns and rhythms I've always used to soothe myself when I'm upset, I start compulsively cleaning the kitchen and putting away food. As I'm covering the third tray with Saran wrap, Tyler comes over and wraps his arms around my waist. "Heather, stop. They have people to do this today. You don't have to shoulder it all. Today is our wedding day too. We can't ignore the moments we have together just because we might not have more in the future. You know I don't dance, but today, I'd like to dance with my bride."

I feel a tear slide from my eye. "How can I be so happy but be so heartbroken at the same time? It's like my heart already misses you and you're standing right in front of me."

Ty strokes his hands down the sides of my face as he wipes away my tears with the pads of his thumbs. "I know, the timing sucks. But, I've got to hold these guys accountable for what they did to my team. Even if I can't find the same bastards, maybe I can make this system stronger so it doesn't happen again. Every time I look at you I'm memorizing something about you so I can recall it later when I'm alone over in the sandbox. So, let's go make some memories, okay?"

"Okay. But just don't get killed. I'd hate to have to hear from my dad how I should've married his partner's nephew who's a nice safe golf pro."

Tyler pulls me into a close embrace, enveloping me in his warm woodsy scent. I can feel his heart pound against my cheek as his arms tighten around me. He forgot that we're in a room full of people as he stands there and holds me for several minutes. We just breathe in sync. It seems like such a simple act, but it feels profound. It feels as if our hearts are beating as one and it occurs to me that's really what's happened to us over time. We've become so interwoven it's hard to determine where one of us starts and the other one ends. Don't get me wrong, we still have our differences, but it's as if we've become interlocking parts of an engine. We're largely dysfunctional and useless alone, but powerful together. I can't really pinpoint how or when the transition happened. Yet, I'm so glad it did.

Gradually, Tyler loosens his grip and murmurs in my ear, "Heather, I'm going to do my best to come back to you in one piece, because we've got a lifetime of living to do. Now, I know Aidan is waitin' to show me up on the dance floor because of all the lip I was throwing him earlier."

I grab his hand and pull him out to the center of the dance floor. "I don't know about that, I seem to remember you have a few moves of your own, Cowboy. I think you're just pretending that you don't like to dance."

Ty holds up his hands in protest as he argues, "Seriously I really don't like to dance. But, you seem to make me break all my rules."

From behind Tyler Aidan says, "Hey! Thanks for reminding me how much I love that song." He abruptly runs on stage and grabs the microphone from the band leader and says, "You don't mind do you?"

The guy looks a little awestruck as he answers, "No dude, go right ahead."

Aidan looks out into the audience and asks, "Where

are my mates?"

From the side of the stage, a loud voice calls out, "Right here. We were wondering what took you so long. We figured you'd be hogging the stage long before now."

Aidan's band swamps the stage as the other musicians step aside handing over their instruments with great aplomb.

He strides over and whispers to his band leader and everyone nods while they look at us knowingly.

I nudge Tyler whose attention has momentarily been drawn away by Becca who is tripping over her dress. He helps steady her and Becca scampers off to dance with Mindy. Tyler leans down so he can hear me over the decidedly country music sounds coming from the band. I cup my hand and shout into Tyler's ear. "What do you think we're in for now? Aidan looks like he's got something up his sleeve."

Tyler shrugs. "I reckon we're gonna find out right quick. Brace yourself."

Aidan steps up to the microphone and announces, "Over the last couple of years, I've had the really good fortune to meet a whole new group of friends thanks to my lovely new wife. One of the coolest has been a guy named Tyler. I've always thought Ty and I had lots of stuff in common. Today, we've got even more in common. The man did me a solid and snuck in a wedding today too. A lot of guys would be pissed off about having to share the limelight. But man, you've just let me off the hook big time. So, I owe you a huge thank you."

A smile of genuine affection crosses over Tyler's face as he laughs at Aidan's antics. "I know I'm going to regret asking this, but why is that?" Ty shouts up to the stage from the dance floor.

"Well buddy, I hate to break it to you, but you and your beautiful wife now have the dubious honor of having the first dance at the wedding of a professional dancer. So, once again, I have to say, 'Thank you so much for taking the pressure off.' Knock yourselves out, kids. Can I have a large round of applause for Tyler and Mrs. Heather Colton as they have their first dance together as a married couple?"

Since we are never in the business of backing down from a challenge, Tyler escorts me to the middle of the dance floor with a flourish. He bows deeply as I curtsy as if we had choreographed this for months in advance. We're bluffing pretty well together until Tyler recognizes the opening strains of Lee Brice's song aptly titled, *I Don't Dance.*

He looks up at Aidan and grins. "Very clever. But also appropriate for the situation. I don't dance for anybody except Heather. She has changed my outlook on so many things."

"I thought you might like that. It's one of my favorite songs too. Now, go dance with your wife," answers Aidan as he masterfully sings the touching lyrics.

Tyler pulls me close for the slow country ballad. For a guy who claims he doesn't dance, it's incredibly sentimental. I feel like the star of every romantic comedy I've ever watched. The clichés are true. By the time the song ends, I could've sworn that everyone else in the entire world melted away leaving only Tyler and I standing there. Tyler kisses me with all the tenderness and urgency of a love song translated in a single gesture. We have so much to say to each other with so little time to say it.

Abruptly, the world around us starts to intrude as some of our friends start to chant, "Speech, speech … speech."

Tyler is such a natural born ham it's rare to catch him being reticent. However, he flushes a dusky shade of red as he responds, "You all know me. I'm not much for big fancy words like my best friend, Jeff, and I'm definitely not a poet like Aidan. But, I want you all to know I love Heather more than I've ever loved anyone." Tyler looks over at his parents as he adds. "Sorry guys, but she's become my first priority now."

Tyler's dad laughs. "Son, I'd be concerned if it was any other way."

"So, I haven't had a chance to tell most of you yet, but I've been called up again. As usual, I don't know exactly where I'm going or how long I'll be there. Now, I've got the best reason in the world to come home safely. So, I'm asking all of you, please take care of the person who holds my heart in her hands while I'm gone."

There isn't a dry eye in the room as one by one and in small groups his friends and mine come up to greet us and say goodbye. Tyler seems a little overwhelmed by the show of support. I ask him about it when he starts to feel uncomfortable. "I guess I didn't realize this many people care about my deployment."

"What was the reaction the last time you were deployed?"

"I don't know, I didn't really tell anybody except for

my supervisor at work," Tyler explains, shrugging.

"Well, I think there are a couple things happening. If people don't know what you're going through, they can't support you and your friendship circle has grown exponentially since Jeff and Kiera got married. There are simply more of us to care about your stubborn self."

Tyler threads my fingers through his as he admires our wedding rings. "I think you're right. But, it looks like I don't have to worry about them watching out for you while I'm gone. In fact, it looks like it might drive you a little crazy. It looks like they might sign up to do it in shifts."

"Yes, thanks for that, you overprotective oaf," I tease. "I'm not going to be able to sneeze without somebody offering me a Kleenex from half a state away. Your parents sound like they want to move from Oklahoma to help me with the bakery."

Tyler looks mildly surprised, "Really? I never thought my dad would give up the hardware store."

"Oh, I don't think it's a done deal. But I think your mom is trying to talk him into it."

"How do you feel about that?" Ty asks, concern evident in his voice.

"Relax, Cowboy. I think your parents are cool. It's sweet they are more willing to be involved in my life's work than my own parents. Don't worry about it, we'll figure it out."

Tyler heaves a heavy sigh. "We have so much to figure out. Crazy war!"

"Well, for now what we need to figure out is how

to get the other newlyweds up on the dance floor."

Tyler slides his arm around my waist and swings me around the perimeter of the dance floor. "Come on, I have an idea."

CHAPTER TWENTY-ONE

TYLER

Can you believe how shocked Aidan was to learn that I know how to play the guitar?" I ask with a smug grin.

"He wasn't the only one. I had no idea you could play. How long have you been playing? If I had known, I would have been asking for private concerts a long time ago."

As I steer my truck back to our hotel room in a blinding rainstorm, I realize how much about each other we don't really know yet, despite hanging out for the last couple of years. "It wasn't something I really planned to pick up. I was the quintessential jock in high school and we didn't really hang out with the so-called band geeks. But, after I got deployed, I found myself with more free time than I knew what to do with. After Stacia dumped me, my buddies were so tired of seeing me mope around, they taught me how to play three basic chords so I could play in their 'band'. Soon, three chords became five and so on. I'm so competitive, if somebody learned a new piece of music, I had to learn how to play it too."

"I still can't believe you didn't tell me you're so good. You could give Aidan's guitar player a run for his money."

"Okay, now you're just being a loyal wife. I'm not even in that guy's league. I mess around a little. After the IED blew away part of my shoulder, I wondered if I'd ever be able to play again. It turns out playing guitar is great rehab because you have to work on all the fine motor skills in your fingers. I'm not as nimble as I once was, but I've got most of my dexterity back."

"Still, the look on Aidan and Tara's faces when we got up and sang their first dance song was priceless. I still can't believe you talked me into that with only one glass of champagne. Usually, it takes more than that to talk me into simple karaoke. It's a good thing I love Lee Ann Womack. *I Hope You Dance* is one of my favorite songs."

"I can't believe how much all of our lives have changed since Aidan first played that song for Tara at Kiera's wedding. You could get whiplash thinking about it all."

Heather grins. "I wonder if Jeff and Kiera knew how much they would change the world just by falling in love."

I think about that for a moment. "You're right. Many people's lives would be completely different. There's you and I, Aidan and Tara, Denny and Gwendolyn and who knows who else. Wow! Do you think someday our love story will impact somebody else's life like that?"

"I don't know, but that would be phenomenal. I'd like to think there is an ongoing chain of love linking one love story to another throughout time. That's an amazing concept. It would mean time really isn't relevant. Right now, I would give anything for time not to matter so much." Heather takes a deep shuddering breath.

"Gidget, I didn't mean to make you sad. I want the time we have left together to be as happy as we can make it. There'll be time for tears later. But right now, I want to store these memories in my memory bank as the most spectacular times I've ever had in my life. It won't be hard, trust me; because I'm with you and you are my definition of happy."

"Ty, it's not really that I'm sad. I'm just suddenly aware that each and every moment we spend together is precious. I feel stupid for not being more cognizant of that earlier. I've known all along that every day could be the day you may be dispatched on a call you don't come back from or that any time you could be called up with no notice, but I guess I stuck that reality in the back of my head and chose not to deal with it. Now, I'm kicking myself because we could have been storing phenomenal memories away for much longer if I had been paying attention."

I place my hand over hers as soon as we stop at a stop light. "Gidget, it's not like you made those decisions in a vacuum. I was an active partner. I spent a fair amount of that time playing mind games with myself about my past and whether I could trust in the future. So, like Denny is fond of reminding me. The only time that we can live for is today. So, for today let's celebrate the incredible fact that we got married. Yesterday is done and we'll let tomorrow take care of itself, okay?"

"Okay, dear husband. Oh my gosh! Does that sound as odd to you as it does to me? I always imagined what my wedding day would be like and today was nothing like what I always pictured in my head. But, in so many ways, it was more perfect than what I'd always pictured. Except for my brother and sister — and of course my grandparents — everyone that I wanted to be there was."

We pull up at the hotel and I park the truck. I walk around to her side and help her out as she continues her explanation, "Since, it wasn't officially my wedding, I didn't even have to sweat all the small details. I wish I would've gotten to wear a traditional white gown with all the trimmings though."

"I think you've forgotten this was just the warm up act. Did you forget that I've promised you a world-class shindig when I get back from the sandbox? I mean it, Gidget. Throw yourself the party of the century. I don't really care. You can dress me in a red white and blue sequined spandex tuxedo if that's what floats your boat. I'm down for whatever makes you happy. I'll be there with bells on."

Heather shudders as she responds, "Gee, thanks a lot. I'm having a hard time getting the visual of you looking like a ringmaster in the Barnum & Bailey Circus on our wedding day out of my head. I think I'll skip that one."

I wink at her as I reply, "Hey, don't knock it till you've tried it. It could be really hot."

"It turns out I like alpha-military type guys in their swanky uniforms. The thought of running away to the circus was fun when I was a kid. But, I came out with a much better guy when I decided to pay attention to your pestering," Heather replies.

"Pestering?" I ask with mock outrage. "I'll have you know, that was a highly orchestrated, sophisticated seduction effort."

Heather raises an eyebrow at me. "If you say so, Cowboy. It felt an awful lot like pestering."

"Whatever!" I scoff, as I roll my eyes. "It seems like we have some revisionist history going on here since the results are in the pudding, my dear wife."

Heather giggles. "Okay, point taken, you big ole' egomaniac. I might've liked the pestering a little more than I let on."

We walk hand-in-hand through the doors of the hotel. When we left this morning, never in a million years did I think we would be returning tonight as a married couple. I can't imagine the red tape Heather had to cut through to make it happen. It's even more phenomenal when you consider she was also in charge of making Tara and Aidan's wedding cake under the glare of the media. Her assistant, Piper caught reporters sifting through the garbage tasting cake scraps to determine what flavor of cake our friends were having at their wedding. In the midst of all that, 'their' wedding had somehow also become *our* wedding and it was truly spectacular.

I stick the key in the locking mechanism and pick up a very stunned Heather. After I finish kissing her soundly, she laughs as she says, "What are you doing, you silly man? It's all legal now, I'm not running away. There's no need to go all macho-GI Joe on me. I'll come very willingly."

I roll my eyes at her. "I can't believe I'm the one who has to explain this to you, Little Miss-I've-Been-Planning-My-Wedding-Since-Before-Kindergarten, but this here is called carrying you over the threshold."

She gives me a coy look. "Oh I see. I figured you were just trying to get closer to my zipper."

"I'm not sayin' there aren't perks to the tradition," I admit as I set her down on the bed with the tasteful blue, tan and ivory comforter. I look around the well-appointed room, including the sunken Jacuzzi tub in the corner. "It's not the feather-bed, but it'll do. Mrs. Colton welcome to your new household with me. May God always bless those who cross our threshold and may only love reside here for generations to come."

Heather reaches up to wipe away tears as she reverently kisses my cheek. "You never stop surprising me. Just when I expect something silly and crass to come flying out of your mouth, you come up with a sentimental gem like that. You melt my heart at the most random times. I love you so much Mr. Colton and I can't wait to build our household together."

"Really?" I ask, wiggling my eyebrows suggestively. "Can we start tonight? I always thought it'd be cool to have three kids. I'd like two boys and a girl so she can have built-in protection from creeps."

The look of astonishment on Heather's face is almost comical as she sputters, "Wow! I guess you've chosen to completely blow off the toning down conversation. Eventually I want kids although I'm not sure I'm sold on three. But, the timing sucks right now.

I'm just starting a brand-new business and you're going to be gone for who knows how long. We have to think about all of that before we rush headlong into parenting."

She's right, of course. There are a lot of complicating factors. But, I can't help but wish we could set those aside and just start our lives. "I'm sorry, Gidget. It's hard not to get ahead of myself. I see you with Mindy and know you'll make an amazing mother."

"Tyler, it'll happen. We just need to be patient. You've got some unfinished business with some insurgents to take care of first. When you get back, we'll see what we can do about putting a family on the to-do list."

"Maybe it's selfish of me, but for tonight can we pretend I'm not leaving in a few hours?" I brush a stray lock of hair out of her face and try to memorize the flakes of color in her eyes.

Chapter Twenty-Two

Heather

THE LOOK OF SADNESS on Tyler's face is so profound it makes my heart ache. Paying my poufy dress no mind, I scramble onto Tyler's lap and draw a line of kisses down his sensitive jawline. "It's a deal, Cowboy. As far as I'm concerned, tonight Uncle Sam doesn't exist. He's been disinherited. It's technically our honeymoon and I will not share it with anyone because our goodbyes are going to come far too soon."

Tyler groans and scrubs his hand over his face. "I don't even want to think about goodbyes."

I become bolder as I continue to kiss him and remove his tuxedo shirt. "Then don't. Tonight, we're just a regular couple on a sexy honeymoon in a swanky hotel."

Tyler kisses my earlobe and murmurs, "Sounds like a plan to me." A white hot lick of desire travels to my center. It seems like such an innocuous kiss, but I find it unbelievably sensual. I shift my body to respond to the sensation.

Tyler takes a harsh breath in my ear as he confesses,

"Darlin', there's nothing I want more in the world than to continue, but for my own safety, I need to shed this monkey suit."

Not for the first time today, I take a moment to admire his large athletic frame highlighted by the lines of the dark tuxedo. "As much as I approve of this look for you, I wouldn't want you to hurt yourself. By all means, make yourself comfortable."

"I will, if you will," he quips with an anticipatory expression on his face.

"I'll take you up on that offer." I declare as I reach behind me to unzip my dress.

"Let me," Tyler commands softly. "This is the stuff of fantasy. Stand up Heather."

Deciding to go for broke and play up the moment, I walk over to the built-in fire-place and turn it on. I stand in front of the mantle and slowly pull the pins from my hair, I shake my curls free.

There is something deeply satisfying about the way Tyler watches me, transfixed with an expression of unadulterated passion on his face. It's oddly empowering. I silently walk over to him and turn my back. He kisses the base of my neck and my knees practically buckle as a fresh bolt of heat travels through my body. He pulls the zipper of my dress down. The dress drops to my feet in a pool of rich taffeta and lace. I step out of it, using Ty's arm for balance.

His eyes glitter with passion as he studies me. "Are you telling me I spent two hours dancing with you, when you were wearin' nothing but this the whole time?"

I give him a smoldering smirk. "Is it my fault you were less than observant?"

"How was I supposed to know what you were hiding when you were wrapped up so pretty?" he asks, as he nips lightly at my collarbone.

"Well, for as much as you've had your hands on my butt all night, you should have figured that I was wearing a thong. A woman just should not have visible panty-lines."

Ty chuckles softly. "I definitely underestimated the perks of dancing all these years."

I raise an eyebrow at him, "If you danced with other women like we were dancing tonight, you might have gotten a drink or two thrown in your face. As your wife, I felt free to give you a few liberties."

"If I had known this little white scrap of lace and those 'come-get-me' shoes were all you were wearing, we would've skipped the dancing altogether."

"No way! Some traditions are important. You already didn't get to have a bachelor party and I'm sure that's one of the things you were looking forward to."

"I know you don't believe this, Gidget. But, my wild, single days are behind me. They have been pretty much from the moment I met you. You are so far above anything I had before, it doesn't even compare."

I fan my face with my hand. "There you go with those panty-melting compliments again. What are we going to do about that?"

Tyler moves behind me and points out our reflection in the mirror. Watching him touch me brings a whole new level of heat. "You should make it your mission to make your husband a very happy man."

"Yes sir, Officer Colton. I look up at the mirror and quip, "I guess I have become a little more receptive to your orders since we first met. Just don't take advantage of that, okay?"

"If it makes you feel any better, I'm pretty open to orders from you right about now. There isn't much I wouldn't do for you," he responds.

I tap my chin as if I'm concentrating hard. "Wow, Cowboy! I would think you'd have learned before now not to present me such a wide open offer, I might just get creative. You've lost a few challenges before."

"See, that's where you're wrong. Even if this was some kind of competition, I can't see any scenario under which I come out the loser. It's the beauty of being all in. As your husband, I get to sit back and watch you work your magic."

I shake my head. "Not so fast, Cowboy. If we're going to be issuing orders, they need to be a two-way street.

Suddenly, a case of nerves overtakes me. I feel ridiculous since Ty and I have long ago passed this point in our relationship. But, tonight it feels somehow different — like all my protective barriers are gone and I am left feeling vulnerable and scared. It's just us now. For the first time since I can remember, I can let go of the fairytale. I no longer have to rely on vague promises of someday finding my Prince charming who will vanquish all my fears and make me feel safe. I don't have to worry about whether I'll someday find some mythological story creature. I'm married to Tyler Colton with all of his strengths and weaknesses, fears and triumphs through the good and bad.

Letting go of someday is going to be a challenge for me. It's a constant refrain in my life. Someday I'll meet someone who understands the real me — the one I take great pains to hide. Someday my family will understand wanting to be an individual doesn't make you evil, it just makes you different. Someday I'll be brave enough to open the store my grandma and I always planned. Someday I'll be the type of wife and mother I've always admired but never thought I'd actually have the opportunity to become. Today is the start of putting all those somedays behind me and living in the present. I realize how much I have grown over the last couple of years. Being secure in Tyler's love has had a lot to do with my ability to move forward.

Tyler catches me staring off into space and says, "Gidget, I know it's not the same as being at home in the featherbed, but we'll make it beautiful, I promise."

"It's not it, Ty. I was just having a moment of gratitude and reflecting about how much I've changed over the last couple of years. You were a big part of that and I don't know how to say thanks."

He pulls me closer to him so we are laying face to face. "It's not just you, Heather. Before you came into my life, I was an angry guy who was just pretending to be the life of the party. You have helped me put a crappy past into perspective and move on. By fighting your battles with such grace and overcoming your fears, you gave me permission to start dealing with the mess that happened with my team. Meeting with the support group has been the healthiest thing I've done in years. It took having you take care of me first before I realized that I had stopped caring for myself. The guys on my team would have gone crazy if they had been around to see what I was doing to myself. It was a terrible way to honor their memories, so the way I figure it, we rescued each other from a life of total BS. We are so much stronger together. I can't wait to see where life takes us."

I lay quietly for a moment just absorbing his words. I tend to think of my contributions to our relationship as pretty benign and a lot traditional. I've always felt a little out of place among my modern peers. It's more than just my fashion choices and my car. Sometimes, I feel like I was born at the wrong time. Although I am proud of my accomplishments as a chef and an entrepreneur, there is a part of me that gets a bigger thrill out of making sure Ty has a nutritious lunch and a hot dinner on the table. When I dated before, I always felt like I had to choose between being a career woman and revealing my domestic side. Tyler makes it effortless for me to do both, so it's a little stunning for me to hear how much he values what just comes naturally to me.

Tyler pokes me in my right breast. "Hey Sleepyhead, did I bore you to sleep. I have to admit, I kinda had bigger plans for tonight."

"No, I'm not bored. I'm just processing the day," I admit. I shake my head slightly in an effort to clear out my maudlin thoughts. "But, I think I've done enough serious thinking for the day. I can think of more exciting ways to entertain ourselves."

"Is that so?" he challenges with a smirk. "Care to share your nefarious plan?"

I reach down to unbuckle my stilettos and send them flying across the room. I sigh with relief as I flex my arches.

Tyler's bottom lip slides out in a mock-pout. "I have to say, I'm a little sad to see those go; they would have dressed up my fantasy nicely."

I snicker. "I'm not sure if that's sexy or a tad on the weird side. It's clear you've never worn those stupid things. Because, if you had, you would never equate them with pleasure."

"Why do you wear them then?" Ty asks, his brows drawn together in confusion.

"We wear them so big tough guys like you nearly swallow your tongue when we walk by. Some days it's even worth the effort when men like you fall under our wiles," I tease.

Tyler snorts with laughter. "Oh is that what happened? I could have sworn you fell for my overwhelming charm."

"It was overwhelming something, that's for sure," I mutter under my breath.

Ty grabs me from behind, rolls me over on the bed and starts to tickle my ribs. "I'll show you a whole lotta something, if you don't stop sassin'."

"Okay, Okay," I plead with tears of laughter streaming down my face. "Will you stop if I promise to use my feminine wiles on you?"

Immediately throwing his hands in the air, Ty

declares, "Hey, I know a good deal when I hear it. Wile away."

Taking him by surprise, I push him onto his back and straddle him. "Are you sure you're up to all this?" I ask as I drop a line of scorching kisses down his chest. "It's been a long day."

"Gidget, no day is that long. Do your best," he half moans.

⸻ ◆ ⸻

We were able to hide in our cocoon of lust and desire for nine hours before the real world starts bleeding into our bliss. As corny as this sounds, my wedding night was everything I hoped it would be, even though it was spontaneous. Sometimes, Tyler's intense focus can be a really, really good thing. Quite simply, the man knows how to pay attention to small details. So, it took a great deal of restraint for me not to conveniently misplace Tyler's phone when I heard the ringtone he associates with all the numbers tied to his military service.

I knew from the look on his face our reprieve was over. I try not to resent the fact that I'm on the world's shortest honeymoon as I'm throwing our belongings into suitcases.

Tyler yells at me from the bathroom as a pair of shoes makes a decidedly loud bump when it hits the bottom of the suitcase. "Are you okay in there Gidget?"

"Yeah, I'm just packing. I hope you're not picky, I'm not as anal-retentive about this stuff as Tara is."

Tyler comes out of the bathroom with his toothbrush in his hand. "You know what's cool?"

I shake my head as I reply sardonically, "I can't imagine anything being cool at this time of morning."

"Don't you have to get up this early to work at your shop?"

"That's just the point. This is my day off. If a girl can't sleep in on the day after her wedding, I don't know when she can. But, no, I don't know what's cool," I reply with a fair amount of snark.

"Wow, you weren't kidding about the coffee thing, were you?" he quips. "I'm sorry you're tired. I had planned far more creative ways to wake you up. Anyway, I was just sayin' that it's cool we can pack joint suitcases now."

I groan and cover my head with the pillow. "Don't remind me. I still have to figure out what I'm going to do with my place."

"Yes, but you don't have to do it today. That was my CO returning my call. Today, we have to get all of your ID changed to Mrs. Colton because the military has reserved its own tree worth of paperwork to sign before I go. After all, in the eyes of Uncle Sam, we're not married until we've signed everything in triplicate."

"Does your CO know you're on your honeymoon?" I ask, unable to keep the whiny undertone at bay.

Tyler smiles wryly. "He's aware, Gidget — and on a personal level he's extremely sorry about that. But, officially, the Army doesn't give a rat's butt about our marital bliss."

"I really wish they did. It might get you home sooner."

"I'll do my best, but I'm not really in charge of scheduling the war."

The look of frustration on Ty's face makes me immediately regret my words. I feel like such a shrew. "I'm sorry. This is harder than I thought it would be. I was thinking that I would be able to think about your deployment like one big long undercover assignment. But, my mind and heart know better. So, I'm having a mini-meltdown. I understand that you have to go, I just wish you didn't have to."

"As much as I've been waiting to even the score, it's much harder for me to leave this time. You have become as important as the air I breathe and I'm not looking forward to figuring out how to function again without you by my side."

"Ditto, Cowboy. Ditto."

⸺ •◦• ⸺

Our last hours together flew by as if they were seconds on a stopwatch. I wanted to yell at the universe to simply stop time. It seemed like we were putting out one fire after another. Some of them were literal fires. One of the vents at the shop kitchen developed a short and started a small fire. Piper apologized profusely, but felt she needed to get me involved when the police asked her questions about the business she couldn't answer. The rest of the stuff we dealt with was much more mundane but frightening nonetheless. None of this was new to Tyler because he's been deployed several times. But, signing the paperwork naming me as beneficiary in the event he's not able to come home really brought things into focus. This was not the way I had hoped to spend my honeymoon, but sometimes, life happens.

We were mentally and physically exhausted by the time we climbed into his giant featherbed. I don't even know if I can describe last night. It was a celebration of all we've become but an acknowledgment of what we'll be missing. It's difficult to feel so cherished and completely bereft at the same time.

As soon as I wake up, I realize something is not right as the sun hits my face. Tyler was supposed to set the alarm to some ungodly early hour. Yet, the house is completely silent except for Ethel's snoring. I reach out to pet her and encounter something attached to her collar.

Fighting the sinking feeling in my stomach and blinking back tears, I open the card. I have to catch my breath when I read the front of the card. It's a Bugs Bunny card that says, "Miss you already."

I spring off the bed and run downstairs as I frantically look for Tyler. No! It's simply not possible. He would not have done this to me. Could not. Should not. Yet, even as I fight the bile in the back of my throat, I can't escape the conclusion that he did.

White hot anger courses through my body as I try to understand what's happening. Why did he make all those promises if he planned to leave me high and dry? This is my worst nightmare. I sob gut-wrenching sobs. Ethel and Annie come rushing in to check on me. As I see the empty envelope hanging from Esther's collar, I remember the card I left lying on the bed. In seeming slow motion, I creep back up the stairs and crawl in bed.

As I pick up the card, I'm having a huge debate with myself about whether I want to know what's inside of the kitschy little card. I feel paralyzed with indecision. The minutes tick by as I sit in the middle of the bed waiting for my dreams to shatter.

The sound of my cell phone pierces through my private pity party. If it was anybody else, I would've just ignored it. But, it's Tara. Knowing she's on the road with the crazy paparazzi and reporters following her every move, I know I have to answer the call.

"Hello," I say through tears and blow my nose on a paper towel.

"So, now you know," Tara states without basic pleasantries. "You know my policy and I hope this makes sense to you, because without context, I have no idea what this means."

I can tell Tara is reluctant to divulge more. Finally, after a bit she continues, "I guess I wouldn't be interfering with fate if I told you to look right in front of you before you make any big decisions."

"Wait! What does that even mean?" I demand.

Tara sighs as she wearily responds, "I'm sorry Heather, I've done all I can. You have to determine that on your own."

"Can I just say, sometimes your so-called gift sucks?"

Tara chuckles wryly. "Tell me about it. You're preaching to the choir. Someday you'll thank me, I promise."

"It's a good thing you're my best friend because I

could really hate you right now," I threaten.

"I know." Tara concedes. "But, lucky for me, I already know you won't stay mad forever. Call me when you have this sorted out, okay?"

"We'll see," I answer with a glower in my voice.

After I hang up a new wave of tears hits. It'll be impossible to be around my friends now. Everyone is so flippin' in love. Why can't it ever work for me? I flop back on the bed and my hand brushes the card from Tyler. Could it really be that simple? It is right in front of me.

Cautiously, I open the card, steeling myself against the heartbreak I know is coming. My mind is working a million miles an hour as I try to square what I'm reading with my expectations.

My Gidget (It seems like I've been waiting forever to call you mine):

Please don't hate me. I had to do it this way. Remember when I told you I was building memories for my deployment? Well, this weekend has been so perfect it's exactly how I want to picture my memories of you. I couldn't bear to see your stunning blue eyes be sad. Please know I will do all I can to come back to you in one piece. But, if I don't, you have made me the happiest man on the planet. I love you.

Love,

Your-Stubborn-Cowboy-Husband

PS: I'll check in when I hit the sandbox. But, it can take a bit to set things up so don't panic.

Holy Cow! I'm not sure whether I want to laugh or cry at my stupidity. When am I ever going to learn that Tyler Joseph Colton is almost always going to do the very last thing I expect?

A glint from the nightstand catches my eye. I notice that Tyler's St. Michael's medal is missing from its usual spot in my ring holder. In its place is a delicate silver necklace with its own St. Michael's medal. There is another small gift tag in Tyler's writing.

It's not blessed by the Pope, but I hope it helps keep you safe and protected while I'm gone. I love you. —Tyler.

EPILOGUE

TYLER

TREVOR AND MATT ARE trying to grab the package from my hand after mail call. "Back off! Don't make me issue orders. These are not cookies," I warn, trying to keep a straight face.

"Oh come on, man!" Matt complains, "You get better mail than all the rest of us combined. Share the wealth a little."

"He's right. It's time for a cookie shipment. You holding out on us?" Trevor peeks over my shoulder. He claps me on the back when he catches sight of the boudoir photographs Heather has tucked into her latest flowery letter. "He's holding out all right. But, if she were my wife, I'd be doing the same. I still can't figure out how the likes of you landed such a looker."

"I'd never guess you guys are highly trained soldiers. You're acting like a bunch of hormonal teenagers hanging out in the locker room. Back off for a minute while I read this."

Matt nudges Trevor. "I bet he wants to do more

than just read it, should we give him some alone time?"

Trevor grins, "Dude. No joke. I've seen the pictures. If I got those in the mail, I'd want some alone time. I know Colton said his wife was pretty but, he didn't tell us she was centerfold pretty."

The pictures take my breath away. They are stunning. I've been married for several months, but I still have to pinch myself. She is absolutely magnificent. She is the stuff of fantasies. I can't believe she was brave enough to take these pictures, let alone send them. I remember when we talked about the idea. She seemed reluctant at best. I'm honored she shared them with me. It's the ultimate exercise in trust because I know how shy she is about her appearance even though I think she's gorgeous. She could totally give vintage pinup girls a run for their money.

I turn around and nail Trevor with a withering glance. "I know I have to cut you some slack because you helped save my butt and all that jazz, but my patience is running a little thin."

"Hey, now! Where's your gratitude? I threw myself on a bomb for you! Shouldn't my gimpy-ness be worth something every now and again?"

"Technically, you threw yourself on the bomb for Uncle Sam — I happened to be in the way. Don't you feel the least bit guilty trying to use your amputee status to view naked pictures of my wife?"

Trevor looks around as if I'm talking to some other amputee who spent years trying to get back into the military after losing a limb. He looks at me with a self-deprecating grin. "You're right. Using my prosthetic to get cookies is perfectly acceptable but using it to lust after your wife crosses all sorts of ethical boundaries, my bad," he teases.

Matt groans. "Some guys have all the luck. She sends you homemade food and sexy pictures. How in the world did you find the perfect woman?"

I shrug as I respond, "I stopped letting the world decide the definition of what was perfect for me and listened to my heart. It turned out she was in front of my nose the whole time."

"Does she have a sister?" Trevor asks thoughtfully.

"As a matter of fact, she does," I concede. "But, Madison and Heather might as well have been raised on two different planets, because they are nothing alike."

Trevor picks up a picture of Heather — dressed in baby doll pajamas cuddled with Ethel and Annie — reading a book. "I understand, I'll be out of your hair as soon as we hit stateside."

"Don't be stupid. That's not what I meant. I'm just overwhelmed by this show of support. I'm not used to having people encourage me from the sidelines. It's cool. I don't want to get too used to it because I'm afraid that it might not last. You all have every right to hate me based on the SNAFU the last time we were deployed as a team. I mean, give me a break. You lost half of your leg because I trusted the wrong people. We lost one of the best pilots around because I thought someone could be trusted to keep their word. So, you have no reason to trust my word for crap now."

Trevor just shakes his head at me. "With all due respect, Lieutenant, I know I had my leg amputated —

when exactly did you have your brain amputated?"

"I beg your pardon?" I sputter. Aside from the men who were killed, Trevor is among the men who lost the most in the field that day. I figured he'd still be the angriest. His attitude confuses me.

"Look, they spell out the risks pretty clearly when we sign up. We all know we're not selling Girl Scout cookies over here. You weren't the one who made the operation go sideways. As I recall, I wasn't the only one who tried to throw myself on an IED that day. I just happened to have better aim. If you hadn't gotten up and around to tie tourniquets on people and call in backup help, there would've been fewer of us around to tell the tales."

I reach up to rub my aching shoulder as I shrug off the compliment. "I was just doing my job as a soldier. But, I can't get the thought out of my brain that I should have figured out sooner that the Iraqi soldier was playing both sides."

Trevor narrows his eyes at me as he asks, "Why? What makes you so special? He fooled people with way more brass than you. He hood-winked people whose job it was to give him high level security clearance. Was that part of your job?"

I hang my head in frustration. "No, my job was logistics and mapping."

"So, was the accident a failure of logistics and mapping?"

"No … not really. We were where we were supposed to be according to our stated objectives. Although, I tried to tell our superior officers I didn't want our unit to be stranded in the middle of such an indefensible area without high ground to retreat to. Unfortunately, my concerns fell on deaf ears."

Trevor nods sagely, "Sounds like typical bureaucracy to me. You did what you could do. Am I pissed that my leg is gone? Some days — yes. Other days, it doesn't bother me as much. But, if you're asking me if I blame you personally, no. This crap happens all the time in war. As cliché as it sounds, it's the price I paid for defending my country. Now, if we run across that little piss-ant while we're 'retraining' the Iraqis on proper techniques I can't guarantee you how 'proper' my training will actually be."

Relief tumbles out of my body as I let loose with a low laugh. "It's amazing how much sand gets in my eyes over here. I miss an awful lot of random stuff."

Matt gives me a small salute. "Roger that, Sir."

<hr>

"You realize that every soldier in my command wants you to be their commanding officer now instead of me, right?" I tease good-naturedly.

I can see her blush even through the pixilated screen of the Skype call. The technology isn't perfect, but it's a far cry above stale letters or even above the tape recordings I used to send my parents at Christmas time.

"It was just a few cookies. It's Christmastime. Everybody needs cookies this time of year."

"You must've made a thousand cookies, Gidget; you sent everybody in the unit a box."

"Well, Piper and your mom helped too. In case you didn't notice I own a bakery. So it is a little easier for me. I'm not baking them on the food truck anymore."

"Speaking of success, how did your TV appearance go?"

"I don't know. It seemed to go well. I picked up a couple of wedding bookings from it, but it's not something I want to do full-time. I'd rather just bake. I'll let Aidan do the show business thing. I'll just keep everybody fed."

"Well, you can feed me any day of the week. I love your food and so does everybody here. I love you so much. I can't wait until I get home."

"Why are we always talking about me and never about you? How are you? Are you safe? Do you need anything?" Heather asks in an urgent tone.

I rub the back of my neck. I hate that I can't divulge anything. The secrecy is killing me. I want to tell her everything. At the same time, I want to tell her nothing. She doesn't need to know about the horrific smells that singe your nose hairs and never leave. She doesn't need to know about the vacant stares of starving children who are willing to blow themselves up for a militant cause they're too young to understand. We're here to somehow help fix all that. Somehow I doubt we're making a whole hill of beans worth of difference here, but I'm only here to follow orders not question them. Questioning them can get you killed in a hurry. "I'm sorry, Gidg, you know I can't tell you all that. I wish I could. The CO's are telling us we need to wrap up our phone calls. I wanted to talk to you face-to-face because we're getting ready to do a mission that I can't talk about. So, I wanted to let you know how much I love you and how much I'm gonna miss you. I won't be able to be in touch for a while. But, you'll be in my thoughts every single day."

A look of dread crosses Heather's face before she carefully schools her expression, "I love you, Cowboy. Come home safe Tyler."

A tear slides down Heather's face but our communication is cut off before I'm able to say another word...

(Ty and Heather's story will continue in Love Naturally)

Dear Reader:

Thank you so much for reading *Joy and Tiers*. I hope you found it entertaining.

The series continues with Heather's sister Madison in Love Naturally.

Madison never figured she'd have to run away from home.

Yet, when she receives multiple threats at her job as a reporter, that's precisely what she does.

Her sister's wedding is the perfect cover.

Will Heather be the only perfect thing she finds in Oregon?

You'll love the twists and turns in Love Naturally, a contemporary romance novel which will have reading until the very end.

Thank you so much,

~Mary

Because love matters, differences don't.

ACKNOWLEDGMENTS

I would like to thank all my friends in the Cake Community for their loyalty, advice and help. Huge kudos to my beta readers for taking the time to painstakingly read what sometimes must've seemed like chicken scratches and giving me honest, helpful feedback.

For my mom who has been patiently waiting to be acknowledged in a book, this one is for you. I appreciate the fact that you taught me to cook from scratch and save recipes from disaster. I always feel like I should deeply apologize that I don't sew better than I do since you and dad have worked so hard to build the fabric store to its greatness. Unfortunately, I'm just not that coordinated. (It's a good thing Shawna has become such a sewing star.) But, I did learn to love cooking from you and pass that love of cooking to my sons. Because you shared your gift with me, I was able to make Brandon's wedding cake with him. I will be forever grateful for that. I love you Mom.

I became an author so I can change the world of fiction and change the way we perceive what an acceptable leading character is. In this novel, Tyler Colton is a fictional character who has had multiple tours of duty and has post-traumatic stress disorder. Unfortunately, post-traumatic stress disorder is all too real among returning veterans.

Joy and Tiers

In this book, family plays a big role in the lives of the characters. Heather is influenced strongly by her grandparents. I was lucky enough to have grandparents who believed I could do anything or be anything that I ever dreamed of being. It's a powerful force to know someone is always in your corner. Sadly, all of my grandparents are gone now. Yet, their influences in my life remain.

Granddad and Grandpa, thanks for showing me what real compassionate macho guys looks like. Yes, Grandma H. I am taking my vitamins… and Grammy, they're making bubble wrap that doesn't pop now, what fun is that? I miss you all every day.

~Mary

About the Author

I have been lucky enough to live my own version of a romance novel. I married the guy who kissed me at summer camp. He told me on the night we met that he was going to marry me and be the father of my children.

Eventually, I stopped giggling when he said it, and we've been married for more than thirty years. We have two children. The oldest is a Doctor of Osteopathy. He is across the United States completing his residency, but when he's done, he is going to come back to Oregon and practice Family Medicine. Our youngest son is now tackling high school, where he is an honor student. He is interested in becoming an EMT.

I write full time now. I have published more than thirty books and have several more underway. I volunteer my time to a variety of causes. I have worked as a Civil Rights Attorney and diversity advocate. I spent several years working for various social service agencies before becoming an attorney.

In my spare time, I love to cook, decorate cakes and, of course, I obsessively, compulsively read.

I would be honored if you would take a few moments out of your busy day to check out my website,

MaryCrawfordAuthor.com. While you're there, you can sign up for my newsletter and get a free book. I will be announcing my upcoming books and giving sneak peeks as well as sponsoring giveaways and giving you information about other interesting events.

If you have questions or comments, please E-mail me at Mary@MaryCrawfordAuthor.com or find me on the following social networks:

Facebook: www.facebook.com/authormarycrawford

Website: MaryCrawfordAuthor.com

Twitter: www.twitter.com/MaryCrawfordAut